SWEAT at TIFFANIE'S

Pernille Hughes has had many words printed in the *Sunday Times*, most proudly the word "boobs". Seduced by the promise of freebies she took her first job in advertising, but left when Status Quo tickets was as good as it got. After a brief spell marketing Natural History films, she switched to working in Children's television which for a time meant living in actual Teletubbyland, sharing a photocopier with Laa-Laa. Now, she lives in actual Buckinghamshire, sharing a photocopier with her husband and their four spawn. While the kids are at school she scoffs cake and writes in order to maintain a shred of sanity.

🐦 @pernillehughes
📘 www.facebook.com/pernillehughesauthor

Pernille Hughes

SWEATPANTS at TIFFANIE'S

hi

A division of HarperCollins*Publishers*
www.harpercollins.co.uk

Harper*Impulse*
an imprint of HarperCollins*Publishers*
The News Building
1 London Bridge Street
London SE1 9GF

www.harpercollins.co.uk

This paperback edition 2018

First published in Great Britain in ebook format by
HarperCollins*Publishers* 2018

A catalogue record for this book
is available from the British Library

ISBN: 9780008307707

This novel is entirely a work of fiction.
The names, characters and incidents portrayed in it are
the work of the author's imagination. Any resemblance to
actual persons, living or dead, events or localities is
entirely coincidental.

Typeset in Birka by Palimpsest Book Production Ltd,
Falkirk, Stirlingshire

Printed and bound in Great Britain by
CPI Group (UK) Ltd, Croydon CR0 4YY

MIX
Paper from
responsible sources
FSC
www.fsc.org   FSC C007454

To Ian, my love, as always.

Chapter 1

It took balls to dump someone on your anniversary, but that was one of the things Tiffanie had always admired about Gavin: his single-mindedness and determination (not his balls as such, because he'd recently developed a thing for all-over waxing and she'd never been quite sure).

'So today felt like the right day to draw it to a conclusion, Tiff,' he said, scoping his eyes over his plate, the steak still steaming from the skillet. Usually she liked the smell of steak, tonight it made her want to hurl. 'Closure, you know? Neat and tidy. So when you look back on it you'll know it was ten years exactly.' Tiff couldn't quite work out why that would be relevant, but it seemed logical to Gavin.

'What about when *you* look back on it?' she asked, totally dazed and not a little confused. She'd been delighted when he told her they were going to *Lorenzo's*; their usual table booked in the bay window. She'd bought herself a new dress to mark the occasion. Ten years. Many marriages didn't last that long.

Marriage. That was where Tiff thought the night might head, as she'd given him a handmade card that morning and a new watch. He'd simply thanked her, kissed her forehead and deposited the box on the bedside table. She figured he'd wear it later to the restaurant where he'd give her Forever in return. That's what she'd thought.

'Me?' he asked surprised, as if the notion of recalling their relationship after tonight hadn't occurred to him. 'I'll think we had a decent innings. A neat ten-year package.' He popped a chunk of steak into his mouth, and she watched as his delight at the taste crossed his face.

'But why?' she asked, at a loss. Gavin was her Everything. 'Why does it need to be a package? Why can't we carry on?' While he saw some neat package, all she could see was her world unravelling and changing. In Tiff's experience, change was rarely a good thing.

Gavin sighed deeply. He took his time chewing the meat. Gavin had always been a keen masticator.

'We've been over this, Tiff.' He'd been talking for some time, calmly and persuasively, but she'd zoned out approximately when, instead of saying 'I love you and will you do me the stupendous honour of being my wife?', he'd pronounced the words, 'Tiff sweetheart, we've had a good run, I think we should call it a day.' Everything thereafter was a foggy haze.

'We're going different places, Tiff. You're happy where you are, but I've got ambitions I need to realise, and it'd be unfair to drag you through all the stress I'm going to face. You'll be happier without all of that.'

'You're dumping me, so I can be happier?' This did not make any sense. Despite a disrupted education, Tiff had always thought herself quite a bright, logical thinker and this sounded bonkers.

'Not *dumping*, Tiff,' he insisted, throwing an eye-roll in for her apparent crassness. 'More like *setting free*.'

'You're setting me free like some orphaned animal?' She pinched herself, in case it was a hallucination. Nope. Maybe if she stabbed her thigh with her fork...

'Hmm, okay, no,' Gavin conceded, 'maybe more like protecting you from pain to come.' He seemed happier with that analogy and took another mouthful of the steak. Tiff looked down at her lasagne. Never had comfort food looked so unappealing.

'But Gav, I'm willing to support you through any stress. That's what being a couple is about. Supporting each other, right?' She needed to understand how he saw this as sensible, before she could suggest how nonsensical it truly was. Breaking this down to basics seemed the logical way to go. She wasn't used to this, the disagreeing with Gavin. He was a born leader and she'd always considered it a blessed part of their relationship. She didn't know where she'd be now – in *life* that is, not this bizarre conversation – if it hadn't been for that.

''Course it is, and we've done that, haven't we? I've supported you through all the stuff with your parents, but I couldn't put you through more. I need to do this alone, for your sake.'

Honestly, Tiff couldn't make head nor tail of it. She was fighting an awful lump in her throat and her eyes were rather stingy.

'For *my* sake?'

'Definitely,' he nodded and attacked his food again.

She didn't want hers anymore. Lorenzo's lasagne was epic and she always chose it, even though she'd known it wasn't the smartest idea. The dress she'd splashed out on was a snug fit. Shops had obviously started changing their sizing again.

'After ten years together, Gav,' she asked carefully, keen not to offend, 'are you really choosing tonight and here, where we had our first date, to tell me you want to end it?' Putting it as plainly as that, surely he'd see how ridiculous it was? And if not ridiculous, then at least appalling. Tiff was confused; he'd never been either of those two things before. In Tiff's world Gavin was simply the best thing since sliced bread.

'Start on our new paths,' he corrected, underlining it with a gesticulation of his knife. Tiff watched the splat of horseradish sauce land on her wine glass.

'New paths,' Tiff repeated, 'which are in opposite directions.'

'Well, more like mine is moving forward,' Gav said, giving it due consideration, 'and you've already reached where you want it to be, I think. That's probably quite lucky, you know. Reaching your point of equilibrium. I'm still searching. I may never find it, Tiff, all I know is I need to try.' Tiff had never gone looking for her equilibrium before, least of all assessed its status. She looked down at her lap, where she'd twisted her napkin to the point of fully wrung-out. It matched the feeling in her chest. Lorenzo's choice of melancholy violin music wasn't helping.

'Have you been watching those life coaching DVDs again, Gav?' She didn't know why he was so addicted to them. He'd brought more home this week, with some cap-toothed tosser in a sharp suit evangelising about 'finding your path, pursuing it with tenacity and fortitude and casting off the deadwood from your life'. Not for a second had Tiffanie considered that *she* might be the deadwood.

Gavin abruptly stopped chewing. 'They talk a lot of sense, Tiffanie,' he said, affronted and treating her to a rare view of his semi-chewed food, 'They teach you to focus. If I want to attain a state of contentment like you, then I need to focus, and not get distracted.'

'You ... you think I'm a distraction now?' How had she gone from partner to distraction in the matter of fifteen minutes? At this rate she'd be rendered a fleeting acquaintance by dessert. The sense of her life evaporating before her made her sway.

'Sweetheart,' he smirked, 'you have always been a distraction...' Momentarily, Tiff's heart fluttered. If he still desired her then ... 'But I need to be stronger now. For both of us.' He punctuated the sentence by wolfing his last morsel. Breaking up clearly wasn't affecting his appetite.

'What makes you think I've reached the end of *my* path?' she suddenly asked. 'What makes you think mine isn't the same as yours?'

'It isn't,' he stated as if it was the most obvious thing in the history of obvious things.

'It might be,' she said, hoping he'd reconsider. 'How would you know?'

'You've settled, Tiff,' he said, looking at her intently. He came across, she had to admit, as utterly *sure*. 'You're comfortable, and you've stopped striving. And that's great for you. It really is. I'm delighted for you.' His benevolent smile supported every word he said. 'But I need to go on. I haven't found my place yet.'

'You're leaving?' she whispered. Was this really what

he was saying? *Really* really? 'You don't mean we have a break while you follow this path?' Even the thought of a break left a wrecking ball-shaped dent in her lungs, but she was scrabbling around in damage-limitation mode. Everything was coming apart at the seams.

'No, sweetheart. Never go backwards. You know that. *I walk slowly but I never walk backwards,* Tiff. Abe Lincoln.' He took the moment to refill his wine glass. Tiff had hardly touched hers, but was suddenly overcome by the need to neck the entire glass in one. It still left her mouth feeling dry. 'And,' he added gently, 'technically the flat is mine, so...' It was enough to make her choke.

'You want me to leave?' she heard herself squeak. Her head was swimming now. Tiffanie felt she was a reasonable woman. She'd generally been realistic about life since she'd moved out of her mum's at seventeen. All things considered, she could easily have gone off the rails. But she hadn't; she'd found herself maths-tutoring jobs to fund herself through college, she'd got her book-keeping qualifications, and she'd managed to build up her tiny but loyal roster of clients. That said, she'd only ever lived at home and then with Gavin. GQ-handsome estate agent Gavin, who had been her knight-in-shining-armour and saved her. He, their flat and work were her life. With such a focused world, how exactly had she missed it going pear-shaped?

'I knew you'd understand,' he nodded, mopping his plate with a tear of bread. 'But look, I'm on that residential thing next week, so you've got time to find somewhere new or Shelby'll have you, I'm sure.'

'But Gavin,' Tiff started, now utterly desperate, 'I love you. Yes, I'm happy, because I'm where I want to be – with you.'

Gavin nodded gently along. 'Sure.'

'Sure what?'

'Sure, that's the place where you're at. Contentment. That's what I've been saying.'

'But then what's to change, Gav? Isn't that what people strive for? Happiness. Contentment. Being with the person they love?'

'Yes.'

And then it hit her like a frying pan in the face.

'Oh. So what you're saying is, you don't love me. All this stuff about setting me free, is you saying you don't love me and you want me gone.' Her voice had gone up a couple of decibels and octaves, as the full horror set in. If he didn't want her, then where did that leave her? It wasn't just the rug he was pulling out from under her, but the entire planet. Everything she now was, was down to him.

She was aware other diners were beginning to discuss them, their furtive looks not nearly as subtle as they thought. *Lorenzo's* was one of those quiet intimate restaurants, all subdued lighting and discretion. Not the appropriate venue for a heart-wrenching meltdown.

'Of course not, Tiffanie. Calm down. I've loved you for a long time – still do – and that's why I can see we need to end. I haven't fulfilled myself yet and I need to. I can't take you on this journey.'

'You can't mean that, Gav,' she gulped down with a sniffle, the tears now threatening to get the better of her. 'That can't be right.'

'That's the truth, Tiffanie, and being honest, I'm rather disappointed you aren't wanting me to be happy and content like you.'

'I've always wanted the best for you, Gav,' she said, as one fat tear broke over the rim of her eye, rolling morosely down her cheek and into her Béchamel sauce.

He laid his hand on hers and gave it a brisk squeeze. 'Then I know you'll agree to do this calmly and rationally. We shouldn't fight about this, we're above that, aren't we?' It was true, they didn't fight. Never had. She'd always followed his lead, confident he knew best. Which had her so conflicted now, on top of the abject misery and disappointment.

In the end, what depleted any resistance she might have had was the recognition that when you stripped it all down, he didn't want to be with her, and given his presence of mind, he'd known this for some time.

Essentially, Gavin had been clearing his path for a while, and she'd missed all the signs.

'Is there someone else?'

'No, there's no one else, Tiff,' he sighed wearily.

'You simply don't want me.' Her shoulders wanted to let her head hang, but fear of being an embarrassment forced her to hold her chin up.

'I simply know our journey has come to an end.'

Looking at him now across the table, she knew he was decided. After precisely ten years, everything she had depended on, gained security from, was over. And while he thought he was offering her closure, in fact she felt only loss, exposure and pain underlined by one key question; what would she do – what *could* she do – without Gavin?

The flat felt odd as soon as she walked in. Nothing tangible was different and yet everything had changed. It was no longer *their* home. Everything would be divvied up as either his or hers. While she currently moved like a shell-shocked automaton, soon they'd be tiptoeing around each other, being cordial. Only it wouldn't even be that, seeing as he wouldn't be there. His course started in the morning.

Smoothly sliding off his jacket, Gavin headed straight for the bedroom. Tiffanie stood in the lounge unsure what to do. She urgently needed to bury herself under her duvet, armadillo into a ball and sob her heart out. She figured she'd wait while he got his pillow from their bed. There was a chenille throw over the sofa-arm he could use; surely, as the injured party she got first dibs on the duvet?

'Look, we're both grown-ups, we'll share the bed tonight, won't we?' Gavin called from the bedroom. 'I'm up early tomorrow, so I'll need the sleep and the sofa won't cut it.' He stuck his head back around the door. 'Unless you want the sofa tonight? The bed's all yours for the rest of the week.'

Tiffanie eyed the sofa. It was Gavin's pride and joy; a long black leather monstrosity, all cubey and no comfort. He believed it made the space look like a loft, but it was the pits for curling up and watching telly. Even *Newsnight* wasn't meant to be watched sitting bolt upright.

'One night,' Tiff told herself. 'You can do this.' One night next to the man she loved who apparently didn't want her anymore. One night holding back the sobs racking around inside her body. She could manage that, she reckoned. Silently she walked into the bedroom, grabbed her PJs and changed in the bathroom.

Normally they'd lie sprawled loosely around each other. She liked it best when he had an arm or a leg thrown over her. It made her feel safe; anchored in life. Until now he'd been her point of stability. Tonight Gavin

11

lay on his back, arms draped easily across his chest, having fallen asleep with insulting ease.

Tiff itched to have some contact with him, but felt she couldn't when his mind was so made up. She could see the silhouette of his suitcase. He'd obviously packed it knowing when he left the following morning, he'd be walking away from their shared life.

Mind churning in the dark, she suspected she hadn't put up much of a fight. She'd instinctively recognised his persuasive *It's a done deal* frame of mind. She'd seen it so many times; furniture, restaurants, brands, and essentially, if it was important to him, then it was important to her. After all he'd done for her, she valued his happiness above all else, so what did one swanky venue matter over another? One snazzy chair was probably as good as the next. (Except for the sofa. That bloody thing had always been a mistake.) The conclusion she came to, as she lay staring at the ceiling at 02.42, was she hadn't sufficiently defended their relationship.

Show him what he'll be missing, she thought, knowing he wouldn't be budged by any argument. *Show him how good we are together.*

Slowly, veeery slowly, she began to wiggle her PJ bottoms off. Getting the long-sleeved T over her head wasn't hard, given how stretched out of shape it was. She froze as Gavin emitted a low snore, but used the next one to cover her rustling as she shimmied down the bed to his feet.

She kissed the ball of his ankle. Feeling emotionally frail already, his toes felt beyond her capabilities tonight. There were limits.

Gavin didn't flinch as she continued with fairy kisses around his ankle, then up his calf to his knee, where she noted his skin, if not his mind, was beginning to sense something was afoot. Emboldened by this, she continued in an enthusiastic upward projection.

Sex had never been one of the areas in which Tiff felt particularly proficient. She'd met Gavin having only had one partner, which had primarily been teenage fumblings culminating in a highly-orchestrated and disproportionately-brief losing of virginities. At the time, she'd thought this one-off event was a sound base on which to build what could become an epic repertoire. Circumstances had altered that course.

Gavin, in contrast, was experienced; he knew what to do and what he liked. Feeling she wasn't in any position to critique, Tiff had embraced the positive opinion that by following his lead she'd side-step a lot of awkward experimenting and possible faux pas. Over the last decade, their moves had been firmly cemented. Surely that was a good thing, knowing what worked? 'Dull routine,' Shelby called it, but then her best friend had dated, bedded and graded most of Kingsley.

Tonight though, Tiff was going to have to give Gavin something to think about while he was away. She was going to give him the proverbial ride of his life.

God, she wished she'd had more to drink.

She woke to the front door shutting. Nothing dramatic, but hardly closed with any worry of disturbance. A note lay on the other pillow. She smiled dozily. He wasn't sliding out without a goodbye. Her efforts hadn't been in vain. The smirk stretched across her face as she recalled snippets of the night; how she'd reached his groin to find that clearly the idea of sex with her was still a point of interest on his supposed path. When she'd felt his fingers threading through her hair encouraging her on, something in her had flipped, sending her into overdrive, as she employed every move she could remember him ever requesting.

On other occasions she'd woken up feeling self-conscious, but not this morning. Emotional rollercoaster as the previous evening had been, with the sun now streaming in through the window onto the mussed bed, Tiffanie felt brave and vindicated, slightly slutty and bloody good about herself.

'You were a vixen, Tiff, a sex minx,' she told herself. She'd fought her corner, she'd shown her man what he'd seriously considered passing up. She'd excelled herself. She didn't quite know where it'd come from, but more importantly, though the whole event had happened without a single word, Tiff knew they'd understood one another implicitly.

Intrigued, she slid her hand up to snag the note with her fingertips. Obviously he wouldn't be apologising, that wasn't his style at all – *shows weakness, Tiff, weakness gives others opportunity*. He'd most likely gloss gracefully over the whole thing, tell her when he'd be home, and she could return to life before dinner last night. Flopping over onto her back, she unfolded it.

> *Didn't we go out with a bang?!*
> *That was the perfect closure.*
> *Thanks and all the best.*
> *Gavin.*

Chapter 2

'He's an arsehat, Tiff,' Shelby stormed down the phone when Tiff, through snot-bubbling tears, explained why she wasn't heading to work. They usually chatted on their respective ways in, insisting it was multi-tasking. But chatting had been dropped this morning, in lieu of Tiff's keening account of what had occurred at *Lorenzo's*, followed by Shelby's barked orders to get up, get dressed and get moving. Tiff and Shelby were ardent advocates of tough-love. Judging people on reality TV had taught them that. Which was fine when each of them was comfortable in their own lives. Right now though, huddled under the duvet, phone clutched limply in hand, Tiff wasn't feeling the benefits.

'I ... I can't,' Tiff sobbed, proper ugly-crying. She felt like an empty shell. An empty shell covered in lashings of humiliation.

'You can and you will, babes,' Shelby insisted, and hung up. Next thing Tiff knew, there was an insistent banging on the front door, which revealed a mission-set Shelby, work-ready in her beautician's uniform. Brooking no argument, Shelby frog-marched her through the dressing process until Tiff was vaguely presentable and moving along the street. 'No man, especially that one, is going to bring your life to a halt. It's a principle thing.'

Shelby had always thought Gavin was a tosser. She had, in fact, been very concise and consistent about this since Tiff had first introduced them. Tiff put it down to an extreme personality clash. Shelby, with her magenta hair, had a fairly extreme personality.

'I hate to say I told you so, babes...' Shelby started, as she pulled Tiff along.

'Then don't. You'd be one of those mean, small-minded people.'

'Fair enough,' Shelby agreed. 'Some things don't need actual saying.'

'That's just as bad, Shelb,' she sniffed. Perhaps telling Shelby had been a mistake. Not talking about it at all – bottling it up to fester inside her and make her bitter and twisted until years of expensive therapy finally released it – suddenly held more appeal. 'Best mates do sympathy.'

'You don't need sympathy, Tiff. You can't see it yet, but this is the best thing that's happened to you in ages. Since you met me, probably. You need support. That's what I'm here for.'

'Gavin was my support,' Tiff moaned, the tears starting again. 'He's been my rock.'

'Still an arsehat,' Shelby stated. 'I don't know why you can't see it, Tiff. It's like you have a blind spot where he's concerned.'

'No, Shelby. You just don't like him. You never have and you refused to try. You see him through mean hole-picky glasses. He loved me. He sorted my life out, made it stable,' Tiff insisted. 'He *saved* me, Shelbs.'

'Pff, he fancied you and you were a trophy.'

Had she had any spirit left in her, and had they not already been swimming in salty tears, Tiff would have rolled her eyes at that. It was years since she'd felt like any kind of trophy. The local lads had been interested in her looks in Year Eleven, but she'd been devoted to her sixth-former boyfriend at that point, so they didn't stand a chance. Then, that summer, everything had turned to crap and she'd gone from queen bee to hitting rock bottom. Miraculously, Gavin had swept her off her feet, helped her escape, shaped and nurtured her and the rest was history. Right until now when, as it turned out, it was Tiff who was history.

She couldn't cope with this. The tough-love was proving too much. 'Shelby. Shelby, *please*. Be nice.' It was a truly pathetic, but heartfelt plea, which nature chose to dramatise by turning on the rain.

That was typical weather for the town though.

Kingsley was one of those forgotten towns, wedged between hills, bypassed by newer roads and shielded from the buzz and prosperity of bigger neighbours. Although within visual range of the coast on a fair day, it lay beyond the thrill of the seaside; too far to smell the salty air, but close enough for seagulls to come a-crapping when the sea got choppy. Looking in either direction there was an air of 'Look what you could have had' for the residents.

Shelby stopped in her tracks.

'Oh babes. I'm sorry.' She enveloped Tiff in a hug. 'I really am. It kills me to see you like this.' Tiff realised how in need of a hug she was. Could they spend the whole day like this? 'You're like some ghostly, wraithy shadow of your true self.' That was *exactly* how she felt. *Wraithy*. Shelby stepped back but held onto Tiff's arms to look at her. 'And now, having totally repressed you, Gavin drops this bullshit on you, to top it off. It sucks. But I promise we'll get you through it and bring back the real Tiff.'

'Enough Shelby!' Tiff snapped, pulling away to start walking again. Why couldn't Shelby see Gavin had been good for her? Ten years of good.

'You can stay at mine, obvs,' Shelb offered, catching her. Tiff pulled her hood over her head so Shelb couldn't see her almost break down anew. Shelby's studio flat was the size of a stamp and the thought of living away from Gavin threatened to bring her to her knees.

'Thanks Shelbs,' she said, trying to control her emotions and look less deranged to passers-by, 'but I can't share a bed with you. You talk dirty in your sleep.' She wasn't joking. Humour was way beyond her.

'The futon?' Shelby suggested, neither insulted, nor denying it.

'Yes, if I can't find somewhere before he's back.' Tiff knew that futon. It was a back breaker. Maybe with copious wine to numb her senses...

'Why didn't you come straight over last night? Arsehat. Him. Not you. Obvs.'

'It was late. I thought perhaps I could convince him.' Tiff cringed at the memory.

'So long as it was just talking,' Shelby said. 'Remember my cousin Simon? Ditches his girlfriend on a regular basis cos he reckons she ups her game in bed to claw him back. Works every time. She's such a sap.' Tiff knew cousin Simon, the guy was a douche.

Turning out of Grange Road she saw her destination with relief. If she wasn't allowed to nurse her devastation in bed, then at least she might be able to hide in her numbers. Numbers were stable. You knew where you stood with them. That's why she loved her work, which was a good thing, as currently it was all she had.

'Laters Shelbs.' Feeling every inch the sap, Tiff kissed

her goodbye before Shelby could say more about cousin Simon. She had put it all out there for Gavin and he'd put it firmly back in its box. Argh, thinking about it made her want to curl up and die. She was going to look up 'humiliated' and 'mortified', to see which best applied. What must he think now? Sweat bloomed at the thought; on her league table of fears, ridicule was securely in the medal spots.

Blackie's Gym was Tiffanie's favourite client, by virtue of being her first client and because of Blackie himself. Knocking eighty now, he'd been a friend of her late grandparents. He'd given her a break when she needed one, and she'd always be grateful for that. Plus, they genuinely got on well for the three days a week where she did his books in the office above the gym.

Blackie's wasn't your modern kind of gym, with treadmills and MTV on monitors. *Blackie's* was a vintage-throwback boxing gymnasium, out on the Eastcote Road. Firmly in the rougher edge of town, the gym sat on a small commercial estate, most of which was rundown and scheduled for development. Not *Blackie's* though. Local nostalgic sentiment, underpinned by Blackie's obstinance, meant the place was as good as listed. The three-storey building, which could only be described as an ugly black block, had been getting scallies off the streets and into the sport for generations. Blackie's view was if lads were going to fight they might as well do it with rules and dignity. There wasn't a grandad or dad in town who hadn't set foot in Blackie's ring at least once in their youth.

'Morning B,' she sighed as she passed his desk, pausing only to drop him a kiss on his bald pate. Crying exhausted her. This marathon of tears had her depleted.

'Morning love,' he answered in his rasping voice, the result of shouting at errant youths since his thirties. 'What's making you sigh this morning? Weather?'

'Hardly,' she mumbled. 'Takes more than a little rain to get to me.' She'd hoped she could deflect him, but he was having none of it.

'That man of yours?' Blackie wasn't a fan of Gavin; another one who wasn't, but then no-one else knew him like she did, knew what he'd done for her. Loyalty aside, she couldn't help but let her shoulders sag. Her entire body wanted to follow suit.

'He's not my man anymore, Blackie. He ended it last night. Said we had different paths in life.'

Blackie fixed her across the small office with a long stare, assessing the situation. 'What a prat,' he finally pronounced.

Tiff turned away, busying herself at her desk, thankful it faced the wall. Blackie wouldn't see the wave of panic as she felt the need to weep again.

'How long's that been?'

'Ten years. Exactly.' She plumped into her seat and with shaky fingertips touched all her things on the desk, checking them, owning them, showing herself some things at least, were constant. Soon this would be the only space she belonged to.

'Jesus,' he muttered. 'That's longer than my marriages.'

The first Mrs Black had been a decent woman, though a force to be reckoned with. She'd given Blackie the kick up the backside to establish the gym in the first place. Had a bus not felled her, she would have defied any illness life threw at her. His marriage to the second Mrs Black wasn't a resounding success, but knowing the gym to be a lucrative business, she'd done her utmost to cling on.

'Still, you're young,' he went on, 'and you've no bairns, Tiff. You can move on, find someone who'll appreciate you. Like I do,' he added, with a chortle, which became a wheezing fit.

On auto-pilot, Tiff fired up the computer. While it churned itself on, she stared at the screen trying to contain the impending wail in her throat. It was way too early for the 'plenty more fish in the sea' speeches. It was also too soon to hear how everyone always considered Gavin a prat, though she'd been unable to prevent that too. For once it made her stand up for herself.

'Gavin is a brilliant guy, Blackie,' she said, without

turning around. She couldn't do this face to face. 'He's driven, hardworking and focused. He looked after me, gave me a home, loved me, and sorted my life when I needed it. I could depend on him. He helped me grow as a person, he was always suggesting ways I could improve myself. And while he might not believe in flowers, cards or Valentine's Day,' Tiff paused only to gain her breath, but it was long enough to catch Blackie's audible gasp behind her, 'he's always remembered my birthday, which was more than Mum's done for the last decade. So please Blackie, just for this week, could you not say anything about moving on or about how I can do better?'

The room was filled with silence and Tiff knew he'd taken her words on board. She could feel the contriteness behind her. Blackie didn't offer an apology, but then she loved him and she didn't require one. She felt better for having said her piece. He might not judge her so harshly for being with Gavin. After all she had Shelby for that.

They spent the next hours in silence, as Tiff stared at the subscription fees, trying to reconcile the figures and sort the tax, but failing in all of it. Nothing seemed to go in and the cogs had ground to a halt. Normally this was child's play to her. Blackie was a stickler for his tax, insistent he'd pay his dues to the Queen, and never owe a penny. Tiff regularly wished others closer to her had shared the same principles. How different her life might have been...

At eleven o'clock she gave up. She figured the silence between them had gone on for long enough, and it was time for a truce.

'Cuppa tea, Blackie?' she asked, turning in her chair.

Blackie was staring at her, but there was no recognition in his eyes.

She was across the room in seconds. Holding his already cold hand as she knelt by his chair, she tried not to think about how long he'd been sat there, lifeless, behind her.

*

'D'you think sunshine is technically possible at funerals?' Tiff asked, distracting herself from Shelby's outfit. It was more of a Friday night clubbing dress, but at least it was black.

'Dunno. It's always been this lame drizzle at the ones I've been to. How hard can it be to commit one way or the other?' The dove-grey sky over the church perfectly complemented Tiff's inner status: 'bleak with a risk of downpour'.

Kingsley being a small town, Tiff knew the majority of the congregation. Shelby knew at least half of them intimately and enthusiastically greeted them all, even snapping selfies with a few. Everyone, it seemed, had wanted to give Blackie a good send off. Considering he had no blood relatives, Tiff felt Blackie would've been chuffed to bits with the turnout, although he wouldn't have been convinced by Shelby's Instagram and Twitter coverage.

Despite being barely inclined to pull a brush through her hair that week, Tiff had managed most of the arrangements herself. He'd left clear instructions with his solicitor and oldest mate Eric Leonards, who stood with them at the graveside. Blackie had pre-paid for everything, including the after-do at the *Pig & Whistle* down the street from the gym.

'Well, he knew what he wanted and he got it, I think,' said Leonards. They'd all sat together in the left-hand front pew. The second Mrs Black and her scowling son had taken residence in the front right. To all intents and purposes she'd acted as if there'd never been any divorce, let alone a screaming train-wreck such as theirs.

'She looks like a mafia widow,' Shelby had whispered for at least four rows to hear.

'I doubt those tears are real,' Tiff said more discretely out the side of her mouth. Personally, she wasn't sure she herself had any left, such was the near-constant outpouring in the recent days. If she wasn't weeping as she sorted Blackie's arrangements, she was sobbing over Gavin. It was tear tag. Fake tears would've been handy.

'Not a chance. Pure crocodile – to match her shoes.' Tiff sneaked a glance. They looked expensive and spikey. Much like their owner.

Tiff had met her before when she appeared in the office demanding advances on her spousal allowance. Tiff failed to see what Blackie had been thinking getting involved with her, but then as Shelby had noted, he probably wasn't thinking, at least not with his head. She was, whilst being bereft of any virtuous qualities, in possession of a mind-boggling set of boobs. Well, thought Tiff benevolently, Blackie was only human.

'You've done a sterling job, Miss Trent. He'd have been over the moon with all the people who've come,' Leonards now said to Tiff, rubbing the remnants of grave soil off his hands.

'Well, by his age he'd met enough,' Shelby pointed out, 'He'd had a decent innings.' Tiff hated that phrase this week; Gavin's words echoed constantly in her ears. 'Right, who's for the pub?' Shelby said, clapping her hands together. 'I am gagging for a drink.' She headed towards the cars.

'God, I hope there's enough money behind the bar,' she muttered. Leonards chuckled behind her.

'It's all taken care of. The landlord will pass on the bill if there's a shortfall.' He paused, then said gently, 'You should relax now, Miss Trent. It's been a difficult few days.'

Tiff nodded. It had indeed, on the grand scale of pants, been a steaming pile of a week. Aside from grieving for Blackie, lamenting Gavin, forcing herself to visit her two remaining clients and overseeing the funeral at super-fast speed under Blackie's instruction of 'get me sorted quick as billy-oh', she'd been trying, unsuccessfully, to find somewhere to live.

All the rental properties she'd had details for looked shocking. Maybe she wasn't desperate enough yet. A week on Shelby's futon would sort that no doubt, but for now she allowed herself to procrastinate; crawling into her own bed for the final few nights and blubbing uncontrollably. She'd think about the future tomorrow.

Leonards squeezed her shoulder as they passed through the gate. 'I need to see you, Miss Trent, regarding the will. Is Monday morning 9 a.m. convenient?'

'Me?' Tiff asked, surprised, but then she supposed it made sense; there'd be the financial records to hand over to whoever inherited the gym. Would it be very bad form to offer her continued services to the new owners? What was the etiquette on touting for business at will readings?

'Miss Trent?' Leonards interrupted her thinking, making her feel guilty. What sort of a person thought about scoring work out of their dead friend? A bad one, she answered herself. An imminently skint and home-less one, she countered herself back.

'Yes, of course. I'll be there,' she said and tried not to groan. Pulling the paperwork together would easily consume the hours she'd allowed for flat-hunting. But handing over a decent report was the least she could do on Blackie's behalf, and who knew, they might ask her to stay. She chided herself again for the profligate thoughts. This wasn't who she was. She hoped she could attribute it to the lack of sleep; she was so tired she could hardly walk straight.

'Yes,' Leonards continued, 'Blackie recognised the support you've given him. It shouldn't be a surprise he's left some words for you. Just look,' he gestured at the dispersing crowd, 'you did that. For him.'

Tiff's eyes followed his hand. She'd only done what anyone would have done for an old man who didn't have any family to speak of. Well, maybe not the second Mrs Black, but anyone else. For all her posturing in the church, she'd briskly detached herself from any organising when Tiff had called her, asking only to be informed of where and when. It sent a chill down Tiff's spine how someone could behave like that. Pulling her jacket closer, her eyes came to rest on a figure standing to the side of the church porch.

Tall and broad-shouldered, the man stood with his hands clasped reverently in front of him. Next to him, on the most gravity-defying heels Tiff had ever seen, stood a younger blonde woman with her hair hanging loose, almost down to the hem of her skirt, which ended just under the curve of her bottom. It was safe to say Blackie was no longer the focus of the crowd's attention.

But Tiff's eyes were on the guy. The way his head was cocked slightly to one side, looking at her, appeared deliberate. At first, she hoped he'd remove his sunglasses to give her a better look at his face, work out why he was gazing so intently at her, but as she focused on his features; his shaved dark hair, his tawny brown skin, she realised he wasn't in fact wearing any. He was simply sporting two shockingly-fresh black eyes. A couple of the other boxers wore a bruise or two from recent bouts, but nothing as severe as this. The way he stood, totally still, made an already exhausted Tiff anxious. It'd been a tough day already and now this.

Realising she was staring, Tiff dropped her gaze and started making her way beside Leonards.

'Tiff! I'm dying here,' Shelby shouted from the car, oblivious to the disapproval from other mourners. 'My mouth's as dry as a corpse.'

Much as she would've preferred to look away and disown Shelby at that precise moment, the alternative was to look back at the man. Something about him was bothering her, but the punched eyes convinced her she didn't want to know what that was. Local economy being what it was, Kingsley wasn't without a criminal element and *Blackie's Gym* hadn't always turned out the most upstanding characters. Some had, Blackie was sad to say, been beyond reformation and gone onto careers in less salubrious or legitimate fields. What with everything else, Tiff felt she had enough on her plate and scuttled on.

Chapter 3

'Drink, Tiff?' The shout from the bar was a welcome one, as the *Pig & Whistle* was rammed. There was no way she'd get through, at least not without kicking some shins. Now was exactly the time she needed Shelby's foghorn mouth and industrious elbows by her side, but she'd been shanghaied on the way from the funeral. The evil Lorraine, Shelby's generally absent boss, had unexpectedly appeared at the beautician's salon and had subsequently phoned to shout about Shelby's scrawled *Closed due to bereavement* sign on the door.

'Tiff! Drink?!' Ron, Blackie's assistant coach, had noticed her chronic lack of bar-presence and come to her aid. Tiff was briefly stunned by Ron's offer – he was generally an abrasive man who kept himself to himself, but then funerals often made people behave out of character.

'Gin and Tonic with a packet of scampi fries, please.'

There were times in life when only scampi fries would do. They had seen Tiff through the woes of her teen life and she needed a pack now. 'I'll be over there,' she shouted across the din, pointing to the far corner where there appeared to be a pocket of air available.

Safely tucked into the corner, Tiff surveyed the room. The packed pub was bouncing: the sadness of the day was being sloughed off, as anecdotes about Blackie were bandied back and forth; about his coaching methods, his encyclopaedic knowledge of the sport and from the older set, tales of his own boxing achievements back in the day. By all accounts Blackie could have been something, if not for a leg injury. Instead he'd dedicated himself to furthering the careers of others.

There was something pleasing about watching people reminisce. The sad eyes of earlier were now lit up as they drew on memories of Blackie, shared their experiences and celebrated him.

'Where's your mate?' Ron asked gruffly, setting their drinks on the table.

'Shelby? Currently spitting bricks having been unceremoniously summonsed back to work. I pity anyone being waxed this afternoon.' Ron looked uncomfortable. Tiff suspected it was more at the mention of women's grooming than in sympathy.

'He'd have enjoyed this.' For a second Tiff saw a hint of a smile on Ron's face. It was a rare occurrence.

He normally nurtured a persona of miserable old git.

'He'd be totally narked to be missing it,' she said, letting her own smile unfold for the first time in days.

Ron sat down on the nearest stool, legs spread wide in that way blokes had, as if their tackle was simply too huge to be accommodated between closed knees. Tiff took a long slug of her drink, closed her eyes and leaning back into the banquet seat, took her first moment to relax.

'Know what's happening to the gym?' Ron asked. Ah, that explained the friendliness.

'Nope. You?'

'He never said. Just that it'd be left in good hands. He was a vague bugger when it suited him.'

'Ha!' she said with a short mirthless laugh, remembering numerous occasions when Blackie's hearing got selective and his answers non-committal. 'But on the other hand, he could be as forthright as they came.'

'He didn't suffer fools,' Ron said with a nod, clearly concurring with Blackie's policy.

Oh, how she missed him, and it'd only been five days. Ron apparently felt the same, Tiff thought, as they sat in silence. The lack of conversation suited her; she was still slightly freaked by having spoken more words to Ron in the last five minutes than in the last eight years. Ron had joined as assistant coach the year before she started.

Tiff sensed the change of atmosphere in the bar almost immediately. A whisper flew through the room followed by a hubbub of greetings by the doors. The mass of boxers, visibly gravitated to someone on the far side. Neither Ron nor Tiff could see who it was, until the crowd parted in a Moses fashion and two people gained instant access to the bar.

'There's bar presence for you,' Ron noted, but Tiff was busy staring. The guy at the bar was the guy at the church, still flanked by the woman in heels. From Tiff's current position, it was apparent his face was not only bruised, but also very swollen. And under the swelling, his nose bore a strong resemblance to a banana. Whoever he was, he'd recently taken a fair old beating.

Ron let out a slow long whistle. 'Well well well, Blackie would have been flattered, not that you'd recognise him easily.'

Tiff looked from the guy to Ron and back.

'You know him?' Tiff knew many of the boxers' names, but not faces.

'You *must* know him. From the telly?'

'I don't watch much telly.'

'But you watch the boxing, don't you?'

'Nope. Never,' she stated, tight-lipped. In spite of working a large part of her week around boxing, she'd always made a point to have nothing to do with the sport after hours. She didn't watch it, she didn't read

35

about it. In fact, outside of what was happening inside Blackie's walls, she refused to listen to news from the boxing world. She had a terrible feeling she might, right now, be looking at the reason for that.

'He's a world champion,' Ron explained, incredulous at her ignorance. 'Career like a firework; more wins, more titles than anyone else in the shortest time. Fights like he's angry at the world. Absolutely stellar. But fireworks burn out, don't they? On the brink of retirement, and given those bruises, I'd say it's due any minute.' Ron shook his head. 'How's Blackie got on his radar?'

The deep feeling of dread had twisted a knot in Tiff's belly, but she managed to ask weakly 'What's his name, Ron?'

'Mike Fellner. Mike "The Assassin" Fellner.'

'Right.' Tiff's heart sank another rung down the misery ladder. 'Gotcha.' No wonder he'd been looking at her. Seriously? As if this week hadn't been dire enough. Life had pummelled her twice already and here was a brisk jab to the guts.

'See, I said you'd know him. Household name, even for philistines like you.' Ron gave her an unimpressed snort, but her focus was on the bar, where 'The Assassin' was still greeting fans. Then he was looking for a space to sit or maybe for *someone*. There were only two empty chairs in the room. Tiff retracted to blend in with the flocked wallpaper. An encounter was not something she could deal with. Not today, not this week.

'I suppose he must have met Blackie,' Ron said with a grunt.

'Blackie was his first trainer,' she supplied, tersely. She braced herself as she saw him approach the table, feeling in all senses backed into a corner. His date moved away towards the toilets and Tiff briefly considered joining her, then fleeing via a window.

'You sure?' Ron asked, unconvinced. 'He never told me that. Why wouldn't he have told me that? That's a great claim to fame.' Ron's curiosity had turned to disgruntlement at having been kept out of the loop. 'How would you know, anyway? You don't follow the sport.'

Tiff didn't answer, she'd zoned out, trying to prepare for the imminent arrival.

'Tiffanie Trent.' He said it as a statement. His voice was deep and low, but carried as far as it needed to, in spite of the babble of the room. She felt foolish for not having recognised him immediately. But the bruising, the nose, the growing up – ten years did things to faces and bodies. Plus he was the last person she wanted to see.

'Mikey Fellner.' She didn't know what to say, or what to do, so she settled for matching his opener, although she was moved to fidget and pull at her clothes, in an attempt to escape feeling appraised. Fail. Epic fail. Everything about that moment made her want to crawl under the bench. As if she didn't feel rubbish enough already, seeing him in front of her dredged up every bad thought she'd ever had about herself.

He sat without being invited, knees spread wide, trousers taut against monster-muscled thighs. Tiff sensed Ron instinctively retract his own legs fractionally in what she assumed was some weird macho knob deference. Respects paid, Ron introduced himself with uncharacteristic gusto. Tiff experienced a faint sensation of nausea, as Ron gushed on, not put off by the fact Mike's attention was rock solidly on her.

'So,' Ron finally concluded, 'how do you know each other?'

Mike arched one eyebrow, but he didn't comment. Instead a silence ensued as they all waited for one of them to fill Ron in. Eventually Tiff caved out of sheer choking discomfort.

'Mikey and I went to school together, Ron.' She knew this wasn't enough of the truth, judging by the way the other eyebrow now met its wingman, but she couldn't bear to venture deeper into it. Opening it all up, peering at what it had been, examining what it had done to her, would twist the knife in an already debilitating wound.

She waited to see if he'd offer more.

He did.

'Ron, mate,' he started, genuinely as if he'd known Ron forever, 'this was the first and last girl to break my heart.' He didn't say it with any sense of wistful nostalgia; in fact, it felt as if Mike bore a grudge.

He had a bloody nerve! He had a bloody nerve even showing up here in his fancy suit with his fancy girl-friend and coming up to her like this. Something shifted in her, something akin to anger that overrode the hurt.

'Um, want me to leave you to it? Catch up, like?' Ron was torn; he was sat with a boxing legend, but it was all feeling a bit ... squirmy.

'Stay put, Ron. I'm leaving after this drink,' she said pointedly, refusing to be intimidated by a man who had no right to try to make her feel bad about the past. He was the one doing the heart-breaking, not her. Tiff tilted her chin at him. 'It's been a long week and I've got a killer headache.' This was a whopping lie. She had packing to do, but nobody needed to know that.

'You look different, Tiff,' Mike said, ignoring her headache.

'It's been ten years, Mikey,' she snapped, conscious that after the last week, she did not look her best. Sod's law they'd meet when she was looking rough. 'You're hardly the fresh-faced teen.'

'You should see the other guy, Angel,' he countered. *Angel.* No-one had called her that in years. His tone was curt, and whereas 'Angel' had once made her feel special, it now sounded vaguely like a put-down. 'And don't let the bruises fool you. Every bruise I ever got brought experience, a lesson to protect myself better next time.' Tiff knew he was making a point, but she wasn't having any of it. *He* had let *her* down. She held his gaze, trying not to rise to the bait, but the simmering fury kept building.

'I didn't recognise you at the church. Maybe it was the blinding ego.' He *was* different. He wasn't that lanky lad anymore, whose body was growing in spurts his self-image couldn't keep up with. He'd obviously got the muscles from the boxing, but they now balanced his limbs in a way they hadn't when they were teens. They weren't the arms she'd stroked and clearly not the chicken's legs she'd once entwined with her own. She flushed at the thought, then looked away, hoping he wouldn't notice the bloodrush.

'Looking a smidge red there, Tiff. Maybe you aren't used to seeing me with another woman,' he said, ignoring her swipe. 'I only had eyes for you back then.'

Well, she definitely wasn't rising to *that*. She didn't give a stuff who he was with. That said, she couldn't help but think about what his eyes must see now. Last he saw her, she was sixteen, confident – cocky even – the daughter of the local bank manager. Physically she still looked similar. She'd gained some weight, but who didn't do that when they settled down with someone? That was happiness, right? And her hair could probably do with sorting, but Tiff had learned a long time ago to avoid hairdressers and the insatiable gossiping. But this was a funeral, so she was entitled to look weary and wan, if not slightly dishevelled. He could put it down to grief, rather than her life being a total shitstorm.

Not that she cared what he thought either. Why would she care about his opinion? They'd known each other a long time ago, she reminded herself, for an intense but short time, and in the end, they'd crashed and burned. So why should it bother her, when she was deeply in the throes of losing Gavin, what Mikey bloody Fellner saw when he looked at her? After today she doubted they'd meet again, so, pulling herself up in her seat, Tiff decided she'd look him straight in the eye and not be cowed.

'I'm not used to seeing you *at all*, Mike. It's been ten years since you went. *Ten years*. And you're long forgotten.'

He made a show of looking around the room, where right on cue all the boxers who'd greeted him earlier looked over. Bastards.

'Clearly not *that* forgotten.'

'Oh, get a grip, Mike.' She was finding it hard resisting the urge to punch him in the face. 'They don't *remember* you; they didn't know you. They're just celebrity gogglers. World champion or performing seal, same/same to them.'

That garnered her another arched eyebrow. She'd once spent an hour trying to do the eyebrow thing, to no avail. She'd looked like she was experiencing some form of facial seizure. But his reaction now brought her back to the task in hand. She knocked back the remainder of her drink and pulled on her coat.

'Been keeping an eye on my career, have you?' he asked, with a particularly smug smile. He was patently enjoying winding her up. Infuriating tosser.

'Hardly,' she sneered. 'Ron just insisted on updating me.' Ron looked at her, appalled. He hadn't seen this side of her before, and he definitely didn't want to be complicit in disrespecting a legend.

'Really?' Mike drawled. Not just a git but an *arrogant* git.

'*Really*,' she shot back. 'Not remotely interested; not in sport, not in you.' She stood up, almost shaking from keeping the rage in. 'And the nickname? Seriously? My best friend's got a vibrator called "The Assassin".' She grabbed her bag and the packet of scampi fries before he could respond. 'Thanks for dropping by. Blackie would have been touched you bothered.' See? She could be composed and calm-*ish* – in spite of the way he'd behaved back then. She also managed 'brave' and 'stoic' as she stifled an agonised yelp having hit her shin leaving the table. Dammit.

She left, trying not to hobble, aware of his eyes drilling into her back and that he hadn't said goodbye.

Well, she should be used to that.

Chapter 4

Packing was a bitter affair. Tiff's playlist of Adele's most heart-wrenching songs was enhanced by a litany of swearwords and pieces of mind she'd like to have sent Mike Fellner's smug way. His appearing had been a gobsmacking blow, the cherry on this crappy cake of a week. If it hadn't been happening to her she would've applauded the universe on its ingenuity.

Pulling the zip across the last bag gave Tiff a feeling of finality that punched her in the solar plexus and slapped her around the chops for good measure. This was really it. The End. The realisation came close to demolishing her. Sitting on the edge of her bed with her face in her hands was the only thing she could do. She'd invested everything in this relationship, this flat, this life with Gavin and it was evaporating in front of her. All she saw before her now was a huge gaping void, which she hadn't the first clue how to navigate.

The trill of her phone didn't raise her spirits; she didn't believe this week was capable of good news. Morosely surveying the flat, she picked up. She hadn't taken the piss in selecting what was hers, though she'd stifled numerous sobs as her fingers brushed over his things.

'Babes.'

'Shelbs.'

'Small change of plan,' Shelby began, and Tiffanie's heart flattened a bit, having long since hit rock bottom. Conversations regularly started like that. Shelby was a demon for springing surprises; some crucial detail she'd forgotten to mention, or some impromptu something she'd committed them to.

'I've got a date tonight. I know it's your first night out of your flat, but we'd probably end up watching something shite on the box and that's boring. You'd only spend the night wallowing, so I figured we should all go out.'

'What, like tag along on your date?' Only Shelby could imagine this was a good idea. Being in close proximity to couples was unbearable. Everything reminded her of Gavin.

'Precisely. It's that undertaker. From Blackie's? The short one. Black hair, shiny teeth. So you already know him.'

'I don't think so, Shelb. You go. Have your date. It's

fine.' Was this her future now; home alone or gooseberry?

'Oh. Okay.' As expected, she didn't take much persuading, because Shelby was rarely one to turn down a shag. The shiny-toothed undertaker was already on a promise. 'You get the flat in peace then, and I'll see you in the morning. I'll introduce him properly then. This one's a total H-O-Teeee.' All of Shelby's men were 'total hotties', though some days Shelby had stronger filters than others.

Suddenly the thought of sleeping at Shelby's or not sleeping rather, (because Shelby was wall-defyingly LOUD) was more than Tiff could handle.

'Actually, Shelb, I was about to call. About tonight.'

''S'up?'

'Well, Gav won't be home tonight after all.' Tiff felt awful lying to her best friend, honestly she did, but there were times in life where you had to poo on your moral compass.

'I thought he was on a course.'

'He is. It got extended.'

'So how does a course get extended?'

'Hmm, I guess they have a bonus day for the brilliant ones,' Tiff supplied. 'So, I'll stay here tonight,' she moved the conversation on, 'you know, pack the last things.' Tiff looked at her bags and boxes lined up by the door. A full week's laundry sat damp from a last-second wash-cycle in an Ikea bag. Her instinct for clean knickers was the only functioning survival skill she still had faith in.

'You can spend the evening sowing cress in cock shapes on the carpet and selling his stuff on eBay for 99p,' Shelby suggested. Tiff looked at the sofa and was tempted.

'He hasn't cheated on me, Shelbs. I don't need revenge for anything. It just petered out. We wanted different things...'

'Give me strength,' Shelby muttered at the other end. 'Don't make out like this was some well-considered mutual decision. He decided to ditch you after ten years, on your anniversary, Tiff. His Facebook status was Single by the next day. He doesn't need anyone else lined up, he's still the supernova of all arseholes. What's worse is he doesn't even think he's behaved badly, or else he'd never have dared leave you alone in the flat.'

'See, Shelb, that's where you've failed to appreciate the relationship we had,' Tiff said tightly, needing to claw a modicum of dignity, deliberately expunging the Facebook thing from her brain, lest it break her completely. She wasn't a Facebooker; social media had never been her friend. 'Gav and I can come out of this as two adults, peacefully, respectfully and without my cutting the crotches out of his suits.' Shelby had once peed on a guy's doorstep every Friday night for a full three months, for not calling her. She was sensitive like that. Conversely, it was important to Tiff to vacate the flat in a dignified manner, despite wanting to fling herself wailing across the floor and chain herself to some furniture. Gavin had to think highly of her if she wanted any chance of getting him back. Gavin valued decorum. 'Look, I'll call you tomorrow for the lowdown on the hottie,' Tiff diverted. 'Night Shelbs.'

'Night babes.'

Hanging up, Tiff experienced simultaneous relief and panic. Not staying at Shelby's had felt vital, but it left her in a quandary of where to go. Gavin was due home at ten and she had to be gone by then. He'd made his position clear, she didn't want to appear needy nor, for that matter, squatting. As her middle-of-the-night sex offensive – *oh god, the shame* – had failed so miserably, the only way she'd win Gavin back would be to show him what he was missing in different ways. Who knew, maybe simply not having her around might do it? That could happen, right? He hadn't called her during the week, and no texts had appeared; obviously he was busy, so coming back to an empty flat, tired without her to fetch him a cold beer and a sandwich might bring home how entwined their paths actually were.

Her keys lay on the table by the door. It wasn't a big bunch; there was the key to the flat, which she'd have to leave; Shelby's key and the keys to the gym and her car. She could sleep in the car she supposed, although once her bags, boxes and double duvet were in it, she'd be driving with her knees up around her ears. There was only so much you could get into a Tiffany-blue Mini, four doors or not. That's what happened when your buying criteria was 'adorable'.

Out of sleeping options and time, Tiff decided she'd try the Premier Lodge around the corner from the gym for a couple of nights. In the meantime, she'd reconsider the rental availabilities. Tiff saw her status had shifted from chooser to beggar.

She started loading the car with all her earthly belongings. There was no way she'd be able to truck all of this into a hotel room. Shelby's place was too small for anything more than a spare pair of knickers and her toiletries bag. Jangling the keyring in her hand the answer came to her; storing it all at the gym was the only solution. Thankfully Leonards hadn't seen fit to take her key back. So surely, until the new owners decided what to do with the place, and repossessed the keys, it was – technically speaking – business as usual. It was purely a matter of temporary storage; it wasn't like she was moving in or anything. It'd all be out of the way in the back storeroom and gone by Monday night. No harm done. The plan was set. Tiff functioned best when she had a plan.

With only ten minutes to spare, a sweating Tiff had successfully vacated the flat, although the final locking of the door had broken her dam of sobs and a wet-patch on the paintwork was testament to her face being propped against it for a while. She was officially homeless. But Gavin was a stickler for time keeping –'*Time is everything,* Tiff. *Five minutes make the difference between victory and defeat,* Horatio Nelson' – so she'd forced herself off. The last bags were heaved, rammed, then frenziedly kicked into the car, before she was off down the road, keenly aware of her new fall from grace as the streets became increasingly more shabby as she went.

The gym was closed out of respect. Walking in with the first bags, being met by a wall of darkness and silence, Tiff freaked on a minor scale. She was used to the squeaking sounds of trainers on the varnished floor, the *oof* of men being punched in the belt and the grunts as they tried to plant a revenge throw to the face. And, generally, Blackie had been in the building. It would never be the same; no more 'Morning love,' no more 'Ta love' for the tea.

The building wasn't particularly cold, but it gave her a shiver. With it came a wave of exhaustion so depleting she was tempted to drop and curl up on the spot. Her plan to neatly stash all her things upstairs was back-burnered as she slung them haphazardly inside the door. The gym opened the next morning at 8 a.m. for the Earlybirds, or 'Clinically Insane' as Tiff referred to them. She just had to make sure she was up before then to cover her tracks.

Tiff should have known this wasn't a week where plans had meaning or jurisdiction. Firstly the rain upped its game from drizzle to hoying-down. The sprint to the car wasn't a dry one. Tiff held onto the dream of a steaming bath at the hotel. She'd grab a brandy from the bar on the way up too. Surely it would count as medicinal, all things considered? Only she hadn't accounted for the Friday wedding in the Bothroyd suite which had guests staying in all the rooms. Every last one.

Which was how Tiff found herself back at the gym, curled up on the ancient office sofa, knickers and greying bras drying on the radiator. Heating and toilet access had won the Car versus Gym debate. She'd kept Blackie's desk light on, moved his chair away from her line of sight then wept over every rubbish thing that had happened in the last five days.

Chapter 5

Lying there, wrapped so tightly in the duvet it was tantamount to a defensive shield, Tiff remembered the first night she'd stayed at Gavin's flat. It hadn't been a whirlwind couldn't-keep-their-hands-off-each-other night, but one where she'd cried and he'd held her, as she grieved for the family she'd lost. He'd been the perfect gentleman. Whenever Shelby dissed him, those were the memories Tiff replayed.

That night had been very different from this. Then, she'd slipped from one home to the next, now, she lay in limbo. She was sensitive to every creak from the old building, she twitched at cars racing past and doors slamming out on the street. But sleep must have come eventually as she was woken with a start, by a crashing sound from downstairs.

There was no alarm. Blackie had never bothered, said it wasn't worth the cost. Not that he was a stingy man, frugal as necessitated by the divorce perhaps, but on this he insisted he couldn't see the point. There wasn't really much to steal, unless someone was in the market for an ancient ring and old-school PE equipment. Blackie had stubbornly not succumbed to Tiff's teasing suggestion of filling the building with state of the art kit, and *heaven forbid* make it something which at least gave a nod towards a modern facility. God (and Tiff) knew the space was there, the place just needed an enormous overhaul and the business would have a new lease of life.

I'm far too old to handle all those shenanigans, was his persistent final word on *that* conversation. The alarm came under the same heading. And besides, he'd pointed out, who'd be daft enough to break into a club frequented by half a town's worth of fighters? Even kids looking for larks would steer clear.

And yet, tonight, it appeared someone was exactly that daft.

'Crap,' she whimpered. The sounds hadn't stopped at the initial crash; there was further stumbling and some pretty ripe swearing.

'Choices?' she asked herself, scrabbling for a plan. She could stay there, cocooned in the bedding, hoping not to be spotted, but the lamp was on, drying knickers were on display and the duvet cover was scarlet. Hiding behind the sofa was out too, it being backed against the wall and heavier than a heavy thing.

She was contemplating crawling under it, when there was an almighty thump from downstairs followed by eerie silence. What if the intruder had been hurt? Didn't she have a moral obligation to help someone in need? No, she reasoned, not if they were breaking in and about to harm her, though she'd read about homeowners being sued by injured burglars. But what if it was a kid? Scally or not, if they were hurt, she couldn't lie there doing nothing. *Yes, your Honour, I appreciate the teenager slowly bled out one floor below me, but weighing up the options, I thought it best practice to go back to sleep...*

Peeling herself from her duvetpod, Tiff assumed her night-wee ninja guise as she slid across the floor in her bed-socked feet, pausing only to grab her electric tooth-brush. True, she'd have preferred a crowbar, but the Oral-B without the toothbrush head on its spike would have to do. Holding it like a dagger boosted her courage. Something was stirring with a groan as she stepped carefully down each of the stairs, trying not to think how this scene – *her murder* – would be reconstructed on *Crimewatch*. Hopefully they'd dress the actress in better pyjamas.

Reaching the bottom she could make out a human shape heaped on the floor. Should she launch herself at them while they were down, or should she hang back and watch their next move? Which would the wise

Crimewatch viewers judge as the most foolhardy – beyond having ventured down the stairs in the first place? Given the clear size difference, Tiff decided against the launching. On the spur of the moment, she flipped the light-switch.

'You!' she accused, with an angry hiss. Pulling himself up to his knees, surrounded by the disarray of her bags was a dazed Mike Fellner. By the looks of it, he'd been felled by a Quavers box of Mills & Boon.

'You!' he accused right back.

'How did you get in here?' She looked around for any damage, but found none.

'I used the key,' he hissed, indignantly.

'What key?' Only she and Ron had keys. Leonards had Blackie's.

'The hidden key.'

'What hidden key?' she said in an insistent whisper.

'Why are we whispering and hissing?'

'What hidden key!?' she screeched. The adrenaline was mixing with relief now. Recognising him made her feel better, but owning countless true crime books she was well aware seventy per cent of murder victims knew their assailant. That was printed fact. Ink on paper.

Mike sat back and looked at her.

'The key Blackie obviously had hidden in the same place for the last fifteen years, but chose never to tell you about.' To illustrate his point, he held up a key.

'Where?'

A grin spread across his face. Now, for the first time, she recognised him properly. That grin had bewitched her once. It gave her exactly the same thought then as it did now. *Cocky beggar.* Only this time she wasn't charmed.

'Not telling,' he said, blithely. 'I can't betray Blackie's trust.' His tone was rich with mock piety, as he shook his head regretfully.

'Blackie is dead,' Tiff hissed.

'He is,' Mike nodded solemnly, 'and he took his secret from you to the grave, so who am I to cross him? By the way, you're hissing again.'

Tiff remembered the teasing. He'd loved teasing her, and apparently he hadn't grown up at all. Once she'd have laughed, but right now, in the middle of the night, after a crappy day in a crappy week, having been scared witless, her appetite for being teased was scant. And *then* she remembered how angry she was with him, how deeply furious she was that he'd brought his face into her eye line again.

'Fine. Keep your secret,' she snapped. 'What are you doing here?'

'I could ask you the same thing,' he countered, and stared at her PJs. They involved flannel and baby unicorns. Tiff sat in a predicament; she could admit she was trespassing too, or she could bluff this. Standing

56

as proudly as baby unicorns would allow, she told him primly the first thing that came to mind.

'I'm holding a vigil.'

'A vigil,' he repeated, pulling himself up to his feet. He wasn't sounding convinced.

'A vigil,' Tiff confirmed as slickly as possible. 'Following the wake, I've decided to stay the night to make sure he's moved on.' Mike did that thing again with the eyebrow. Nope, definitely not convinced. 'He died here, you know,' she persisted. 'Upstairs in the office. I was there. I want to know his soul has passed over.'

Mike ducked his head at this, digging his hands in his pockets in a gesture of reverence to the dearly departed. He walked to lean against the wall before looking up at her calmly.

'So, in spite of your killer headache you've decided to put yourself, alone, in what might be a haunted office for the night, for Blackie.' Tiff nodded vigorously.

'For Blackie,' she reiterated firmly. The sides of his lips began to rise, but he reined it in.

'And what, out of interest, will you do if Blackie's spirit is knocking about?'

'Well, obviously I'll have a chat and encourage him to pass over.' She was out on a limb here and decided to curb the subject. 'But I'm not the one breaking in. What do you want?'

'I'm not breaking in if I have a key, am I?'

'What if there'd been an alarm?' Tiff asked indignantly. Mike rolled his eyes with a *pff*. Tiff cocked her head, set her jaw and gave him her best 'I'm waiting' stare. He scratched the back of his neck considering his answer, as if he hadn't actually been sure of it until now.

'I just wanted to come back and have a look.' A simple little reason, but one which hurt her more than she'd expected. After ten years, of silence, having walked out on her, he just fancied a nosy? At a building? *Really?* That couldn't be right.

'In the middle of the night?' She watched police shows. The facts didn't stack up. Maybe she could push him into a confession of why he'd left her. She wasn't going to ask him outright – how desperate would that be? She couldn't afford to lose any more dignity this week. She wasn't sure she had any left.

'Without other people being here,' he corrected. 'I thought I'd have a little nostalgia tour without being bothered by anyone. Remember how things were. How they began. Who I was then.' Something in that riled her further, that he could have forgotten. And still no mention of her. He seemed wistful, then he remembered himself, snapping back into teasing mode. 'Obviously I hadn't counted on Ghostbusters being here. Nor all the baggage it apparently requires.' Tiff looked around at her baggage a.k.a *her life*, but Mike did not. He was gazing at her. Perhaps she hadn't fooled him at all. 'You were never a very good liar, Tiff,' he said, quietly.

'And you never knew when to shut your gob,' it exploded out of her. Who the hell was he to throw her lie in her face? That was it. The bleeding limit. She had reached the precipice of her self-control after days of utter awfulness and this, from *him*, was the final straw that flicked her deftly over the edge. The anger she felt in the pub had merely been a warm up compared to the rage now surging through her. She gripped the banister both for support and to tether her down.

'How nice for you to be able to swan in here and ponder how life used to be, to cast your eye over us poor underlings who never escaped, who never got their chance at international stardom. How very nice that must be. Did you give your *heat* magazine dolly-bird a tour of the stepping stones to your global success?' As the words seared off her tongue, Tiff didn't want to think about all the hours they'd lain on her bed, daydreaming a future, together and far away from Kingsley. The travelling, the mansion, the yacht. They hadn't got down to the small details – like how they were going to fund it all – but they'd been firmly agreed on the plans. God, she really hoped he didn't have a yacht. 'How gracious of you to think of it, to bestow a visit on the old place, to peruse your humble beginnings. How blessed we surely are. And what do you see

Mike, anything good? No. It's still a shithole. You could have Googled it, saved yourself the effort.'

Mike was looking at her like she was totally off on one. She wished her left leg would stop shaking with the raging; it undermined her poise.

'Calm down a minute—'

'No! No, *you* calm down,' she cut him off, faintly aware he was perfectly calm, which wound her up even more. She was beyond stopping. Without the pub crowd to witness her making a fool of herself, she had nothing left to lose. And much as she would've chosen root canal treatment over seeing Mike again, he was the perfect target upon which to unleash the ten years of bile roiling around in her gut. Boy, it felt good.

'What the hell are you really back for, Mike? I can only think it's to take the piss out of me. You got the hell out of this place without a backward glance, you're living the dream – *our* dream – and now you feel the need to return and rub it in my face. Well, I tell you what, you can shove it. You're the one who's a poor liar. You can bite me with your nostalgia; I know gloating when I see it, and that makes *you* the bad person. I do not need your pity, I don't want you to give me one single thought. Ever.'

'I wasn't—' His forehead was furrowed and for the first time Tiff saw him look anything other than confident.

'I don't want to hear it. Not one word. Nothing to come out of your mouth is worth the breath you spent on it. Do whatever lording it was you came here for, but don't expect me to watch. Then you can let yourself the hell out, and if it's not too much to ask of your lordship, I'd appreciate it if I never saw your smug battered mug ever again.'

Tiff and the baby unicorns stomped back up the stairs, pretty sure he understood the dismissal. That'd be the last she saw of him.

Job done.

Chapter 6

E.J. Leonards Solicitors was a proper old-school firm spanning five generations. Now on the brink of retirement himself, Leonards had conducted many will readings, yet still approached each with trepidation. On one hand, not unlike when watching *Antiques Roadshow*, there were joyful moments when he'd surprise the unsuspecting, announcing a windfall they'd never dreamed of. Those were his Fairy Godfather moments – he hoped the deceased wouldn't mind. There were the cases which baffled him, where fortunes were left to cats, while the relatives gained an ornament bordering on the grotesque. He always suggested *Antiques Roadshow* in those cases. And then there were the wills he immediately sensed would be contentious. With Blackie's he had a niggling feeling it might be a mix of all three, and Leonards always trusted his niggling feelings.

Whilst few people had been invited to the reading,

the room felt quite full. The second Mrs Black sat with her son Aaron, Leonards felt he'd be reluctant to meet him in a dark alley. He'd seen enough of human nature in this job to not judge a book by its cover, but in this case the package, dirty tracksuit and all, appeared to match the attitude. They sat whispering about the will contents. Leonards' hearing aid was always turned fully up on these occasions.

Leonards looked steadily at the young man. Mid-twenties with a prison record. He'd been jailed for beating up a girlfriend. Clear-cut case of vicious domestic abuse. Blackie had wanted to clout the boy black and blue, but Leonards had talked him down, convincing him to let the court mete out the justice. That lad had got everything he deserved. Nasty piece of work, that one. Leonards wanted the chair wiped clean once this reading was over.

Then there was Tiffanie Trent of course. She fidgeted at the side, attempting to smooth out the multiple creases in her skirt. A pile of accounts folders sat at her feet.

'They're all here and up to date, Leonards,' she'd assured him on arrival.

'Oh, I don't need those, my dear,' Leonards said cheerily, but seeing her face fall, added 'however it's lovely to have them.'

He liked Tiffanie, she was an unassuming girl of

whom Blackie had been very fond. Leonards enjoyed the fact she felt her presence was simply to account for the book-keeping. For all her family's problems, she wasn't one of life's spongers, unlike some he could think of. Shrewd as he was, he noted Tiffanie was deliberately ignoring the side of the room where Mike Fellner sat. Her appalled scowl when the boxer had appeared was unmissable and a fair clue of some history there. Old people were often dismissed as unperceptive. Not so Leonards, who recognised that the last week had been difficult for Tiffanie, not just regarding Blackie. While unaware of the details, the solicitor knew a troubled soul when he saw one.

Mr Fellner was accompanied by a much younger woman, introduced as his girlfriend, Verity. Leonards' hearing aid had disclosed that while she was curious to hear why he'd been invited, she was keen for it not to last long; she was having her eyelashes extended at lunchtime.

'We're all here, so we should start. I'm sure you're all busy people with jobs to do.' At huge personal effort he managed not to fix Aaron with his beady eye. He had it on Blackie's authority the lad suffered from chronic laziness, complicated by an acute case of entitlement.

'Blackie was not without means, in spite of his past divorce, where his funds were significantly diminished.'

Leonards did not look up, although having watched
Blackie being fleeced, he would've relished the opportunity to have his say on *that*. His professionalism won
out. 'He was, as we all know, a hard worker and fought
to regain his wealth, living frugally, whilst showing a
generosity to the youth of this town that I believe is
well recognised and appreciated.' Both Tiff and Mike
were nodding their heads. Mrs Black sneaked a sly look
at her watch, while Verity drummed her perfectly-mani-
cured fingers on Mike's thigh.

'As it turned out, Blackie has a sizeable estate to leave
– primarily the boxing club with its buildings, contents
and profits – and so you have been asked here today,
as beneficiaries.' He was tickled to see Tiff look confused
and Mike surprised, which was more than he could say
for Mrs Black and her son, who were sporting a keen
shade of smug.

Leonards then began the preamble that Frank Black,
being of sound mind, did leave the following:

'Firstly, to my stepson Aaron,' Leonards read, pausing
to appreciate Aaron's triumphant smirk at being first
on Blackie's mind, 'who I've not seen since the day his
mother asked me to move out, but who has trusted me
enough to telephone whenever he wanted financial aid,
I leave all the inspirational posters from the walls of
the club. You need guidance lad, and as I'm no longer
around to offer it, I leave you the pictures which have

inspired and guided many of the young men who've passed through the gym.'

Aaron's face was no longer beaming. In fact, it looked as if it had been smacked with a flat implement. Something cricket bat-like, Leonards mused.

'Moving on,' he said briskly, knowing from experience it was best to pass swiftly through the lesser-well-received bequests, 'To my ex-wife Bernice, I leave my heartfelt thanks. I thank you for our first two years, which were frenetic and flattering for a man my age, and for the following years which taught me age does not equal wisdom and that a man my age can still be a fool. I paid heavily for that knowledge, for which I also thank you, Bernice. In hindsight it was money well spent, and I'm sure you've spent my money well. Your almost bankrupting me served to remind me that under the paunch I was still a fighter at heart, and without that I wouldn't have pulled myself up and worked as hard for my remaining years. I bequeath you my gratitude and the knowledge your avaricious ways did me a favour.' His hearing aid hurt at the screech and the entire room managed a unified shuffle of awkwardness.

'To Michael Fellner, I leave a couple of things. I pushed you on early my boy and didn't you do well? You've done yourself proud. You've done me proud, as I always knew you would.'

Mike shifted in his seat, discomfited. Leonards ploughed on.

'Your moving from my club was always a point of sadness, but I knew you needed more. At the time this was hard for you to understand; you felt I was rejecting you and cutting you off. But it was for your own good. I believed that then, and believe it still, although it pains me that our friendship was lost in the process. Michael, I said some harsh things back then and I apologise for that. I said what I said not because I meant it, but because I believed without doing so, you would never have left. If you hadn't gone, if you hadn't been able to focus on your talent, you would never have achieved your potential.'

Mike hung his head. Here Leonards wasn't altogether sure of the story, but Blackie's words clearly had poignancy for Mr Fellner. Neither were they lost on Tiffanie, who was suddenly watching the bruised boxer intently, though rather confused.

'You're a wealthy man now, Michael,' the will continued, 'and so I leave you something I wish you'd had at your disposal all these years; the ring. You may sell it of course, but should you have the space, and I suspect you might, then perhaps you'd find it in your heart to use it, and forgive an old man who said some things he regrets in the pursuit of a goal he does not.' Leonards was used to the deceased being cryptic in their wills. They liked the drama. The relevant people usually understood.

'Excuse me.'

The solicitor was surprised to hear Verity's voice. As was Mike.

'Yes, my dear?'

'What sort of ring exactly?' Leonards noticed the young woman's fingers twitch, as well as a pointed glance she shot Blackie's ex-wife who appeared on the verge of a conniption. 'Are we talking about a woman's ring or a man's? Just to be clear. And any carats?' Mike closed his eyes, dismayed.

'There's no jewellery listed in the effects I'm afraid, my dear. Blackie wasn't a man for such items. In fact, I believe he even sold his watch when he needed some capital after the divorce.' Mrs Black studied something through the window at this. 'The ring in question is the *boxing* ring at the gym, an antique if I'm not mistaken, and quite a rarity too.' Leonards spoke as if educating her, but her expression told him it was information she neither wanted nor appreciated.

'Miss Trent,' Leonards turned away from Verity, shuffling the paperwork. Tiffanie sat up straight.

'Tiffanie, you've been through some tough times and yet you've persevered. I've always respected that. We both know, given kinder circumstances, your future could have been very different, and yet you've made a life and business for yourself. You've been a priceless support to me these last years, managing the office, the books and my tea intake, for which I thank you from the bottom of my heart. Sharing an office with you has been a pleasure, even though I lectured you about your boyfriend never appreciating you.' Mike's eyebrow arched and Tiff's face flushed, no doubt wishing Blackie could have afforded her some discretion. Leonards thought them both foolish if they were surprised at Blackie's directness even at this late date.

He continued '...but, in turn, you regaled me about the future of the club. So I leave it to you Tiffanie: the building, the land, and the remaining contents, so you can put your money – in fact my money, as you get that too – where your mouth is and make your dreams come true.'

Leonards discreetly turned his hearing aid down so Mrs Black's response didn't do him an injury.

Chapter 7

Tiff wasn't certain how she got from Leonards' to *Viv's Café* but somehow, when the daze cleared, she found herself sat with a latte and a blueberry muffin at the well-worn Formica table. She must have simply pointed dumbly at any cake, as she didn't particularly like muffins. Not since Gavin had once pointed out her own muffin top.

Blackie had left her the club. Bloody hell. No matter how many times she asked Leonards to verify it, to show her where it said so on the page, she still couldn't understand it. The death stares Bernice Black sent her however, supported his insistence this was really happening.

'You had no idea?' Leonards had asked when they were alone.

'Not a clue. He never said.' Tiff knew she sounded spaced, but *really*. A business. A boxing club. Not in her wildest dreams. Perhaps – and this was awful – perhaps not in her dreams *at all*...

'Well, he liked surprises, did Blackie,' Leonards had nodded, filing the will. 'But he liked his gym more, and he wouldn't hand it over to anyone he didn't trust or think capable.' Then he'd handed her the keys and pointed to her files. 'I believe the accounts are all up to date and in perfect order.' That had tickled him immensely.

The caffeine started doing its job. Yes, she'd teased Blackie about dragging the club into this century, but as he'd pointed out, his was one of the few remaining boxing gyms turning a good profit and it was what he knew how to do.

'What's the point?' he'd asked. 'It'd be like starting again. I'm a boxing coach; I teach people to duck, dive and punch. I don't know my arse from my elbow when it comes to rowing machines and I don't hold with those conveyor belt things. If you want a good walk, get out in the fresh air.' Blackie had still been able to ride a bike, leading a swarm of running boxers around the town twice a week. 'Why sit on a machine in a room when you can use the outdoors for free? Bloody stupid if you ask me.'

'You'll be sorry when some swanky fitness centre sets up nearby and all your clients scarper when their girl-friends suggest a partner membership.' She'd really only said it to wind him up.

71

She could see his point; the club had a decent financial turnover, the clients were loyal and brought their kids along to join, so why at his age would he change it? But she'd always assumed he'd sell it, at which point it'd either be modernised or demolished by developers. She'd never in a million years thought he'd leave it to her. He might have mentioned it, she thought, it would have come as less of a shock.

Her first instinct was to call Gavin. To ask him what she should do. However, Monday mornings were the weekly planning meeting and she knew better than to interrupt it. Besides, she didn't know if he'd welcome a call from her at all. She tried thinking *What Would Gavin Do?*, but came up blank. Her mind didn't work in the same way his did, she supposed despondently. She'd need to fathom this out by herself. Every day brought a new way to miss him.

Tiff laid a steadying hand on the pile of accounts files next to her. Her numbers. *Her* accounts now. Pulling them together hadn't taken Tiff as long as she'd dreaded. However, catching up this last week's-worth of subs had kept her at the desk during the weekend instead of flat hunting. She'd ended up staying on the ancient sofa for the last two nights too, having yielded to the nag of spring-cleaning the office before the handover. She hoped the Premier Lodge would have space for her that night, or else she'd have to bite the bullet and face Shelby's futon.

'I blooming thought it was you!' The boom snapped her out of her ruminating. 'Sitting here like some lady of leisure. Haven't you got work to do? Adding or something?' Tiff didn't need to look up.

'Sit down Shelby and help me sort something out.' Shelby sat with a wince and a groan. 'What's the matter with you?'

'RSI,' Shelby grumbled, getting comfortable.

'Repetitive Strain Injury? From waxing and plucking?'

'Repetitive Sex Injury. From dating and f—'

'Stop. I do not need to know,' Tiff cut in. There were things Shelby had told her over the years that made her want to bleach her ears. 'Back to the helping me, please.'

'Seriously Tiff, what's to sort out? He ditched you, he's a tool, you're better off without him but you can't see it yet. Yada yada yada. Can't we skip to the bit two months from now when you acknowledge I'm right and you've wasted weeks pining over someone who wasn't worth it? Do a sky-dive, a bungee jump, get so wasted you wake up in the gutter with your knickers flapping off a lamppost. Whatever. Embrace your new life however you want, but can we just fast-track to it?'

'Have you considered counselling as a career, Shelbs? Your compassion and empathy is truly a gift,' Tiff said, pushing the muffin over to Shelby, who was eyeing it with intent. Unleashed, she made short shrift of it and Tiff made the most of her mouth being occupied.

'Actually, that's not what I need help with. Blackie left me the club.'

The next few moments were spent sorting Shelby out as she first pebble-dashed Tiff with muffin crumbs in the initial exclamation of 'No. Fucking. Way' and then gasped the remainder back into her throat and started choking when Tiff neatly added 'and all his money.'

Tiff waited patiently while Shelby composed herself, brushing the last crumbs off her uniform. It was quite a novelty seeing Shelby stunned for once. Lord knew that didn't happen often.

'Bloody hell,' she finally managed.

'I know, right?'

'OMG, that's like, amaaazing. You are so bloody doing this, Tiff. You're going to rock that place.' Shelby's enthusiasm was instant. Her confidence in her friend was absolute and it made Tiff feel touched but also self-conscious.

'I think Blackie just didn't want his bloodsucking ex to get it.'

'Stop it. He knew you could sort it out. He knew you have good ideas for it. And maybe, he thought it'd be the kick you needed.'

Tiff's mouth pulled up to the side. Given Blackie trusted her with the figures and the admin, would it be so unreasonable to believe he trusted her to adopt his life's work and develop it?

'But I was just spouting off about the things he should change. I wasn't saying *I* was the one to do it. I've got zero experience in that sort of thing.'

'Stop over-thinking this, Tiff. You set up your own business before and you didn't have experience of that either. You know all this, you just don't dare flatter yourself. You're convinced life'll bite you in the bum if you big yourself up.'

Was that what she did? She knew how it felt to take things for granted, to think she was the bee's knees, only to have it slapped back in her face. It wasn't something she particularly wanted to experience again. *Pride comes before a fall,* Tiff – The Bible.

'You can do this Tiff.' Shelby put her hand on Tiff's arm. 'You'll kick butt. Blackie thought so too.'

'But he gave it to me like it was my dream. And it really isn't.' Tiff had to whisper as she felt so ungrateful. Shelby sat back, considering this.

'It's a business, Tiff. Might be a different flavour than you're used to, but it's still a business. You get the chance to make something bigger and hopefully better. You can further yourself as a business woman.'

'But I don't have ambitions like that,' she said exasperated. She liked her life as it was – well, not right now, but before. She didn't have the confidence for all this. 'I—'

'Stop. Stop right there. I know what you're about to

75

do. You're about to allow Gav the Tool's words to cock-block your big break. And the answer is no, sorry, no dice. You're going to do this, if nothing else to prove how wrong he was, how after ten years he still couldn't read you properly. And, so help me Tiff, if, when you are riding high as a proper Lord Sugar, you so much as think of going back to him when he comes sniffing – and I guarantee you he will – I shall break your legs.' Shelby drained the last of the latte before adding, 'His too. But that'll be just for kicks.'

She looked at her watch.

'Crap. Gotta go.' She was out of the seat before Tiff could even think. 'You can do this. Love you babes,' she said, planting a kiss on Tiff's head, and was promptly gone. If Tiff hadn't already been in a daze, then Hurricane Shelby would have done the job.

Shelby's words rang in her ears as she walked back towards *Blackie's*. For all her best mate's encouragement – which was heartening even if she still had Gavin all wrong –Tiff didn't know if she had what it would take, because it would take a lot, and right now she hardly had the energy to shower. When she got to the club car park she stopped and took a long hard look at the place. She owned all this. A building and a business. If she wanted it. It could be a future too. *If* she wanted it. But looking up at the sign above the front door, she didn't know whether she could fulfil Blackie's faith in her. Hadn't Gavin said she wasn't a striver? And didn't he know her better than anyone?

But. But but but. The words kept bouncing on her lips. Like Leonards said, Blackie wouldn't have given his club away to just anyone. She *knew* that. He believed she could do something with this place. 'Capable' Leonards had said. She liked being seen as capable. Shelby thought so too. She'd like to remind Gavin that she was capable – not only in his interior design needs. Heading for the doors she wondered whether this was the universe sending her a way to show Gavin he was wrong. About all of it.

She felt a splat on the shoulder of her coat. Bird poo.

That settled it. She had it on very good authority being crapped on by a bird was lucky. Given how the last week had gone, she'd take any good omen she could get.

Smiling, Tiff ran her hand lightly across the door pane. '*Mine*,' she mouthed.

'Y'know, this place will turn to shit.' The low snarl made her jump. She hadn't heard his approach. Spinning around she found herself almost nose to nose with Aaron. He had little perception of personal space, no more than he had for his personal hygiene. Tiff instinctively took a step backwards, but was met by the door. Aaron didn't budge. Ah, it wasn't that he didn't care about personal space; he wanted to intimidate her.

'Blokes won't join a boxing club run by a woman. A woman who doesn't box.' He was repulsive, from his sneer to the gopping nails of his nicotine-stained fingers. Tiff reminded herself she had Blackie's backing. It didn't quite cloak the fact he was bigger and wider.

'You think they'd be more attracted by a bloke who doesn't box? At least they've seen me in the building. They know Blackie liked me.'

Aaron's eyes narrowed. 'Yeah, obviously liked you a whole lot to leave you everything. That how he pegged out, was it? You riding him for the inheritance?'

'Don't be disgusting!' Tiff exclaimed. 'Your stepdad was a lovely man. He knew my grandad.'

Aaron merely shrugged. 'Age doesn't bother gold-diggers, does it?' Tiff resisted suggesting he asked his mother. He moved a step closer, so his mouth was right up against her ear. 'The older the better, right? Then you don't have to keep it up so long.' He sniggered snidely. 'Bet Blackie couldn't even do that.'

Appalled, Tiff turned and scooted through the door, keen to get it closed between them. Was that what people would think? She tried to quell the nausea.

'That business should be mine. I was his son,' Aaron shouted right against the door pane. Spittle splattered on the glass.

'*Step*son and a rubbish one at that,' Tiff muttered. She didn't have a plan if he chose to storm the building, but instead he walked slowly backwards, staring at her. 'You should have been kinder to him while he was around then,' she said louder, so he'd hear.

'Like you did?' he sneered, giving her a filthy leer before turning and swaggering away. Tiff watched him cross the car park like he owned the place. He didn't look back. He'd come to rattle her, and he'd done the job.

Chapter 8

'Afternoon.' Ron stood in the doorway to the office. Tiff froze with her mug of tea halfway to her mouth and looked at the clock. It was still morning. He was having a dig.

'I was at the will reading.'

Ron's brow furrowed. 'That was today?'

'Nine o'clock.' The scowl on his face told her exactly how he felt about not being invited.

'What's the score then?' He needed to know whether he had a job or not. Whilst he was a grumpy bugger, Tiff knew he worked hard. He'd have a job if he wanted it. She tried not to think about how much she was depending on him if she was going to do this. He was her continuity.

'You'd best sit down,' she said. Ron slumped in the corner armchair, an apprehensive look on his face.

'Is it closing?'

'No,' she said, adamantly. Whatever happened, she'd

do everything to keep it open. Blackie's legacy demanded it.

'Being sold?'

'Not if I can help it.' Ron's face perked up. 'See, Blackie left the place to me.'

'You?' he asked, incredulous.

'Me.' There didn't seem much to add. She could desperately start justifying it, but she didn't want to come across as panicking. And she *was* panicking.

'Didn't see that coming.' Tiff didn't take it as a compliment, nor had Ron meant it as such. To be fair she hadn't seen it coming either.

'You and me both.'

'You don't box.'

'No.'

'You don't even follow boxing.'

'No.'

'And you're a w—'

'Yes.' Tiff considered having a feminist debate with him but didn't have the strength. What would be the point?

'What the hell was he thinking?' Ron exploded, expecting her to share his outrage.

She tried to placate him. 'Um, perhaps he was thinking I didn't need to box or follow the sport,' or have a penis she added, but only in her head, 'to be a business manager. Perhaps he thought, having worked with him, I knew enough about the place to keep it going, to progress it, and more importantly give proper consideration to the people who work here.' Tiff gambled Ron's primary concern was his own job.

'Too right. About the staff, I mean.' Neither mentioned that beyond themselves, the sum of the staff came to precisely one, in the form of Vonda the intermittent cleaner. 'He should have told us what he was planning.'

'Well, he liked his surprises,' was all she could think to say.

'This is going to have a major impact on the business. The lads aren't going to like it.' She hadn't really considered that bit, but his prejudgement seemed a tad unfair.

'Apart from Blackie's absence, the clients shouldn't feel any difference, Ron. Blackie's will stipulated that your job should be safeguarded, if you still want it.' She'd hoped to see relief in his face, but he'd moved on from that. 'I'm hoping you do want it, Ron,' she added to be clear.

'Well, I'm sure you do. A club without a trainer isn't much of a club, is it?'

'No, of course not.' He was talking to her like she was an idiot. She wanted to show him she wasn't. Vision. Vision and ambition, that was what impressed people. 'Going forward,' she said, feigning confidence, 'I'll be looking to modernise the club, but it will always be a boxing club at heart, and you're integral to that.'

'Blackie didn't want to modernise it. It works perfectly as it is – provided I'm here to make it work – so what's the point?' Ron was sporting a fine display of outrage. 'Don't mess with things that aren't broken, Tiffanie. Why do women always do that?'

Tiff bit her tongue.

'He left you *everything*?' Ron double-checked, with an air of disbelief and a hint of resentment.

'The building, the land, some capital,' she detailed, feeling uncomfortable. She tried to divert the conversation. 'The ring goes to Mike Fellner as some penance for the past – don't ask, I don't know – so I'll need a new one ASAP. All the sappy pictures with the moody shots and emo texts go to Aaron. For guidance apparently.'

That raised a wry smile from Ron.

'Nice one, Blackie. He always liked a subtle jab to the nuts.'

'So Ron,' said Tiff, making her first managerial move, 'if you're on board then the title of Head Coach is yours and obviously there'll be a salary increment attached.' She tried to sound as professional as possible, until she saw his eyes ker-ching at the money, which caused her to falter a little, 'The exact details of which to be confirmed once I've checked the figures.'

Ron stood up, nodding. His staying was a massive weight off her mind.

'Glad you can see sense, Tiff. You leave running the club to me while you crunch the numbers and things will be fine.' He left the room shaking his head.

Watching him disappear down the stairs and finally having a large gulp of her tepid tea, Tiff couldn't help but feel her first step into her future had lacked any clout or elation.

Tiff's lunch hour mainly involved staring at the office in fear and disbelief. It was all hers, from the walls to the bins. Yet little plan-bubbles were beginning to form. She'd be thinning out the glut of furniture for a start; navigating the office was an obstacle course in itself. The posters on the walls were going, which would expose the fade of the paintwork, adding another thing to the To-do list. Still, with their phrasings of *Dream Big* and to go *Above and Beyond*, she'd happily lose them. They annoyed her. They were Gavin's clearly destructive life-coaching DVDs in paper form.

Getting into it, she wandered down the corridor and stairs, surveying her domain until she found herself standing outside the sparring hall door. It was years since she'd set foot in there. She'd spent hours in there as a teen, watching one Mikey Fellner, but that had stopped when he'd left. Coming to work for Blackie she'd still managed to dodge it; there was nothing urgent enough in the bookkeeping to force her in there.

''Scuse me, love.' A client moved around her and entered the hall. The open doorway blasted Tiff with the squeaks of footwear on the polished floor and also a potent waft of testosterone and sweat. She couldn't think of a space smelling more of bloke. And yet it was a nostalgic odour to her. She'd never minded it back then.

It took her a moment to realise the guy was holding the door for her.

'Oh, thanks,' she said, scurrying through. This was hers now. She needed to know it again.

Brick walls and wooden floor, it wasn't a million miles away from a school gym, with the exception of the massive ring at the far end, with its white ropes keeping the boxers in, and the royal blue pelmet to hide the supports. Ron hung over the ropes barking at the two fighters for being a couple of wimps and not being worth his time if they weren't going to 'put some bloody effort in, ya pair of pansies.' In the rest of the space, boxers trained with skipping ropes, weights and punchbags until it was their turn to vie for Ron's approval. Tiff suspected they'd more chance of winning Miss Universe than winning his praise.

Walking around the perimeter of the room, the sound of her heels drew attention. She didn't feel unwelcome as such, the guys just got on with what they were doing, more out of place and surplus to requirements. She had no role in there. She got half-way around the room, before Ron abruptly acknowledged her.

'Need something?'

Ron's glare forced her to fabricate something. He made her feel she was trespassing. 'Um, yes,' she said, clip-clopping up to the ring. She didn't want to shout, she wanted to sound in control. 'The new ring. I wanted to check the required dimensions.'

'Twenty by twenty. Feet. No point having anything smaller than competition size if this lot are to have any sense of space. RingPro is the best make.' He turned back to his boxers. Tiff wondered whether they needed the best. Best usually meant most expensive. But she didn't have the spuds to question Ron. His glare was pretty ferocious and it would be remiss to doubt him in front of the clientele. Instead she fingered the fabric of the pelmet. 'RingPro. Is that what this is?'

Ron tutted loudly as she distracted him again. 'Are we compromising on quality now?' She cowered at his hostility. Clearly he'd been mulling the news and his mood had turned sour. Sourer.

'You don't need to worry about quality, Ron. We're on the same side here,' she said. She pulled herself up to full height, but it didn't help when he was already three feet off the ground. She took a couple of steps back to create a clear line of sight between them, without the ropes getting in the way. 'I'm not here to cause havoc, Ron.' Her next step back caused her to trip over a discarded kettlebell. Tiff felt her balance going, instinctively twisting, bringing her face to vinyl with a swinging punch bag.

'Hello? Can you hear me?' She opened her eyes to see a relieved face. 'Are you okay?'

Tiff nodded, trying to convince her eyeballs to align.

'It's Jess.' She was looking Tiff over intently. 'You passed out.'

'Umm...?' Tiff knew her, but she couldn't place the face. It was a sweet elfin face, severely framed by cropped red hair. She understood and helped Tiff out.

'Jessica Dent. Akehurst Street.'

Tiff's eyes widened. 'Whoa, didn't you grow up,' she said, now recognising the features of a girl she'd tutored when she was eighteen. Last she'd seen Jessica, she'd sported a dodgy perm.

'I box here. With Amina.' On cue, they were joined by another woman, gorgeous with tight cornrows on her head, who rested her hand gently on her girlfriend's shoulder.

'She okay?'

Tiff nodded vigorously before Jess could answer, embarrassment setting in. She pushed herself up from the floor, keen not to look a complete lemming.

'Sorry. I should've cleared my weights and I didn't see you behind the bag,' Jess said.

Tiff shook her head insisting she hadn't looked where she was going. Taking a look back towards the ring, she saw Ron hadn't budged. He sent her a withering glance and turned back to his fighters.

'Nice seeing you again, Jess,' she said, checking her skirt, hoping she hadn't flashed everyone in keeling over. 'What are you up to now?' Small talk. Yes that worked; inane small talk could cover all sorts of humiliation. Plus she was getting to know the clients. Ron couldn't begrudge her that.

Jess stood up straight with a proud smile. 'I'm a builder now. Took over my dad's business.'

'Oh, that's wonderful, Jess,' she gushed, enthusiastically. 'He must be delighted to hand it on to family.'

'He died.'

'Oh god,' she choked, plunging straight back into a state of mortification. 'I'm so sorry.' She reached out and gave Jess a sympathetic squeeze on the arm. It was rock-solid. The equipment definitely did the business. 'I'll see you around, all right? Stuff to do upstairs.' Flailing, she pointed upwards, then to the door, then felt like a prat. Wobbling back across the gym, wishing again she wasn't in heels, Tiff suspected she'd be hard pressed to make it more obvious she was way out of her depth.

*

Her intention was to hide for the rest of the day. She worked through the admin, but progress was slower than normal, her mind getting distracted constantly. Finally she gave up, deciding to sort out her boxes and bags currently stashed in the storage cupboard next to the office. Shifting them had taken several trips up and down the stairs the morning after Mike's nocturnal visit. She bristled at the thought of him. Seeing him stride in at Leonards' made her want to gnash her teeth. And he'd shot her a cocky look which tempted her to hurl a ledger at him. So much for telling him to stay out of her life.

If she was going to try the hotel tonight, she thought, dragging her cross thoughts away from him, she'd need some clothes and various nick-nacks for her overnight stay. The idea of living out of a bag depressed her. It didn't feel like money well-spent either.

Switching the light on in the storage room she took a proper squizz around. It was large – the club had never lacked space – and Blackie had been tidy. One corner homed a stack of exercise mats and the opposite wall was racked-out with shelves, half-filled with yet more files of outdated paperwork.

Ditching the files would free up more shelf room for… well she wasn't sure yet, but *Storage space is gold-dust, Tiff*. Hearing Gavin's words in her head made her eyes sting. Blinking it away she looked at the mats in the corner. The way they were stacked reminded her of *The Princess and the Pea*. An idea started to germinate.

So it was a bit grim, but there was shelving, space to move about and the door locked. That wasn't much different from a hotel room. In Tiff's mind it was a battle between a window at the Premier Lodge versus no cost here. Not having to pack up again was the clincher, she was sick of that already. The building was hers, and the store cupboard with it. If she was going to buy a flat when she finally found time to start looking for one – *screw you, rental market* – then she shouldn't be spaffing the cash on a crappy hotel room. Seen like that, she could easily cope with temporarily living in a cupboard. A nice lamp and her duvet would make this quite cosy, she convinced herself, conveniently ignoring the strip lighting and the chipped floor tiles. A rug and fairy lights maybe...

'You got a minute?' Ron's gruff voice ripped her away from her planning. He didn't wait for her to respond and she followed him obediently into her office.

'I should take it on,' he said, rounding on her.

'Take what on?'

'The club. Watching you down in the gym I reckon it'd be best for all concerned, yourself included, if I took over the club.'

Tiff's jaw flapped but no words came. Ron went on.

'I can't see how Blackie didn't see it; I'm far better qualified to run it.'

'You're head coach,' she pointed out, finding her tongue. 'As far as the clients can see, you *are* running it.' Additionally, she doubted he had the money to buy her out. If it was the glory he needed, he already had it. There was no need to tie up his finances.

'Yes, but let's be honest, it's only a matter of time before you start making unnecessary changes. You setting foot in the gym was one and look how well that went.'

'I tripped over strewn kit. It was an accident.'

'My point exactly. The gym's always like that. We're all used to it. You're clueless.'

This was grossly unfair, Tiff thought, taking a breath to say so, but Ron shook his head to stop her.

'I'd been thinking about this before all of that anyway. I'll rent the place off you. Blackie wanted this place to stay as it is, or he would have changed it himself. It's what the lads would want too. I'll run it as normal and pay you rent out of the profits.'

Tiff hadn't expected that. Not for a second. She didn't know what to say. Instinctively she wanted to shout *But it's mine!*, but his words had her stumbling. He thought she was *clueless*.

'Think about it, Tiffanie,' she noted she wasn't Tiff anymore, 'you could expand your bookkeeping business, you could keep the days here obviously – that's two bites of the cherry given I'd have to pay you for that too – and then you could spend Blackie's money and the rent on other things; shoes or whatever you women spend money on nowadays.'

Tiff bit her cheek at the reference to Blackie's money. She supposed every penny she ever spent hereon, anywhere, would be seen as Blackie's money.

'And no offence,' he continued, though from experience Tiff knew any sentence beginning with 'no offence' was about to cause exactly that, 'but you can hardly call yourself a poster girl for fitness.' Tiff instantly looked down at herself. So fitness wasn't her thing, but she wasn't massively out of shape. Okay, maybe she *was* puffed scaling the stairs, but she could still *recognise* her sixteen-year-old self in the mirror. They might just not have shared clothes for a while.

'Nobody joins gyms run by chubbies. Just saying.' He said it with a shrug, and his face wasn't twisted in the malicious sneer such a sentence should be accompanied by. It was his honest opinion. Embarrassed, she wanted to exit the room immediately.

'You really don't want me to do this, do you?' she stammered.

'It's not a matter of want. I don't think you *can*. I don't want Blackie's hard work and sacrifice wasted, when I can do the job.'

His words plunged her right in the chest, but not

like a sharp implement, rather something wide, blunt and far more devastating.

'You think about it,' he said, 'but for the sake of getting on I'll expect an answer by Friday.' Tiff could only stare at him speechless. Ron took this as assent. 'And Tiff,' he said, more kindly now, like she was a sad child, 'in the interests of health, safety and corporate image, best stay out of the gym, eh?'

Chapter 9

She desperately needed some fresh air. Some non-Ron air. Speeding down the stairs she hoped he wouldn't spot her – or her chubby form – slinking out of the building in search of somewhere to hide.

Indoors or out, she'd always seek out a sunspot. Gavin once said she was catlike when she did that. It'd made her feel desirably feline.

The sun was shining on the side of the building, where Blackie had banished the smokers, refusing to allow their anonymously donated bench to sit at the front of the building. *What kind of health message would that send?* he'd demanded, before having an 'In memory of those who smoked here' plaque screwed to it.

Dropping onto the seat, Tiff rested her head on the wall behind to stare at the sky. Really this should be simple. Blackie had given her a shot at something. Things were already established in one respect; there was a client base to build on and money coming in.

But every time she thought about the plans she'd nagged Blackie with, the task seemed huge. No wonder he hadn't wanted to touch them with a shitty stick. And maybe Gavin was right about her not being ambitious. She had ideas, but maybe she didn't have the *drive* to see them through.

Was that what Ron was seeing? She'd wanted him onside. Whilst she hadn't expected to inherit any of this, she hadn't considered him having his eyes on it. Although maybe he didn't harbour those ambitions at all – he seemed to think taking it on was his moral duty. He really had no faith in her. That hurt. A lot. Tiff had always given a hundred per cent to her work. She'd assumed Ron had a decent impression of her, when instead it turned out he thought her clumsy, incompetent and fat.

She'd never considered the nature of hurt and how it could lie in layers. She was so hurt by Gavin's decision it took her breath away. She had similar pain from ten years before when Mike walked away. It rested in her now like an old wound; prone to playing up in dank weather. Together the two sat heavily in her heart, making it difficult to engage with her normal self. This latest hurt of Ron's rather changed that. It cast itself on the established layers, churning them up. It made her feel impotent while desperate to escape, rather like those dreams where she ran in terror through immobilising mud. And like those dreams, it was so very lonely.

She closed her eyes to quell their prickling and inflated her cheeks to deflect the tears. Ron's words were unfair. She hadn't done a single thing but he'd already decided she couldn't do it. And aside from the stinging hurt, what had her wanting to curl up in a ball was simply: *what if he was right?*

Since she was a teen, Tiff had worked hard at the things she knew; the numbers and pleasing Gavin. Having precious little self-confidence otherwise, focusing on those things allowed her to curb her self-doubts. Not now though – they all came hurtling back. What *had* Blackie been thinking giving her the club?

She hadn't considered who would take over, she'd simply assumed at some point she'd have to hand over the keys and see if they wanted a bookkeeper who knew the business. Effectively, that was Ron's offer. Her current work was fine; she could take the money and use it for something else. The rent could cover the mortgage for a small place. No more sleeping on lumpy sofas or sweaty PE mats. Or she could buy a bigger house and have a lodger. Maybe Shelby would—

'Having a moment?'

Tiff expelled the air from her puffed cheeks. Mike Fellner stood, hands in pockets, watching her, bemused.

Oh. Bloody. Hell.

'What is the matter with you? Can't you follow simple

instructions like *Do one?*' She'd been pretty clear. And she'd made a concerted job of blanking him at Leonards'.

'What you doing?' he said, imitating a toddler, ignoring her barb. God, he was annoying. Had he always been this annoying? Perhaps she'd overlooked it while being ensnared by his teen good looks. 'My smug battered mug was wondering.'

'I'm thinking,' she said tersely, ignoring his jibe right back. She had too many thoughts churning in her head to spare him any of them. She'd said her piece the other night. While she hadn't been particularly in control of what came out of her mouth, it had been wonderfully cathartic. Her sleep afterwards had been the best in a week.

'Sure,' he nodded, like he saw loonies pulling faces on benches all the time. Keen to look vaguely sane, Tiff rose to sit upright, only her hair got caught on the roughness of the brickwork. She attempted to smooth it down without it looking too obvious. He still wore his well-cut suit from this morning, though he'd lost his tie somewhere, the top two buttons standing open, a glimpse of smooth collarbone peeping out the top.

'You want the ring?' she started. His face clouded at her sharp tone. Her intention was to move him along ASAP. He was, of course, entitled to take it immediately; the pro was she'd finally be shot of him, the con being it'd leave her ringless. In a boxing club. It didn't take a genius to predict how Ron would react to that. He'd firmly place that cock-up at her feet.

Mike scratched the back of his neck.

'I, well, no actually. I wouldn't mind a look at it sometime, a proper look, in daylight,' he gave a small smirk, 'but I was hoping I might leave it a while.'

Tiff was conflicted; the being shot of him wasn't working out, but the relief of having a ring won over. She kept her relief under wraps and her defences staunchly up.

'No room at home?' she snarked.

'Actually, I've already got one at home. Sort of comes with the job,' he justified, although they both knew not every boxer had space to accommodate, amongst life's other essentials, a boxing ring. Unless, of course, he slept at the gym, like she did, which she suspected wasn't the case. 'I need a bit of time to get it dismantled.'

'You're going to use Blackie's then?' She couldn't help but ask. Her fondness for Blackie dictated her interest in where his things went.

'I couldn't sell that ring. It was his,' he said simply. Clearly didn't need the money, Tiff noted, but then the cut of his suit and the way he held himself told her the Mikey Fellner she'd known – constantly skint – was purely a figment of her memories. He'd come a long way from the tired terrace houses of Delaney Row. Now he had a girlfriend worthy of *OK* magazine. Tiff's eyes slid down her own body. Verity could fit twice in this skirt. Ron's words still stung.

'I'm not sure how much longer it'll last, though,' she said. 'It's seen a lot of wear.'

Mike sent her a lopsided smile. 'That'll make two of us then. I don't plan on putting her through too hard a time in the future. We can have our retirement together.'

Tiff considered what she was doing, engaging him in conversation. Just seeing him made her bristle with... with... she wasn't sure, but it wasn't comfortable. But Blackie had always said it took more energy to be angry than not and saddled with her hurt and loneliness already, she resigned herself to giving up the angry. Didn't mean she had to be nice though. Civil would do.

'You're retiring?' She'd determinedly not followed his career, but she hadn't envisaged a time when he wasn't boxing. He was only twenty-seven. Gavin said these were the investment years, where you worked your balls off, so you could retire at fifty. Obviously Mike was on some fast-track.

Mike pointed to his face.

'You might not have noticed, but I took a patent beating recently. It's called a sign of the times.' The bruises had faded somewhat over the weekend, turning to mottled plum and autumnal yellow. The hints of *thug* were gone, now suggesting 'unfortunate' rather than 'he had it coming.'

'What, one fight and you're out?' she challenged.

'It's been a couple now,' he shrugged, as if it really didn't bother him, but she knew it would. He hated losing. 'And I'm getting tired, Tiff.'

His use of her name sent a small twinge through her. He said it like she was the only one to get it; to understand how far he'd come, how much he'd had to fight for, and the toll it had taken. It felt like an honour, only she neither deserved nor wanted it. It felt too friendly. And they definitely weren't *that*. Civil or no, she still wanted to lamp him. She found herself studying a bird poo on the armrest for distraction. So much for being lucky. Now she thought of it, it was Mikey's gran, Nanna Bea, who'd convinced her of that when an enormous seagull had unceremoniously shat on her new leather jacket. A huge-spirited woman, always keen to find the positives, Tiff wondered how the old lady was—

'Congratulations, by the way. Inheriting the club,' he said, changing the subject abruptly.

Tiff's head swung up to look at him. 'Oh god, did you want it too?' Was that what he'd planned for his retirement? Mike recoiled as if slapped.

'No. God no. Why would you think that?' Tiff saw her natural instinct was now to assume the worst. Argh, it was an awful state of mind, she hated it. It – *he* –

brought the worst out in her. She shook her head to get a grip.

'You wouldn't be the first person today to feel they'd be a better bet or were more entitled to the place. I think I'm feeling a bit tired and emotional about it. And shocked.'

'Overnight vigils on office sofas aren't helping you,' he said, quietly. 'Didn't we once... on that sofa—,' he started with an enthusiastic grin.

'Don't,' she cut him off. She wasn't going there. *That* was a scab she wasn't unpicking with him. She knew her face was colouring – she'd remembered it many times when walking into the office. But that he could be so blasé about it really narked her. Tiff felt her temper simmering again and tried to regulate it back down in the name of civility. Soon he'd disappear back out of her life and she could forget all about him. Again.

'Probably best. Blackie would've had my nuts if he knew we were doing more than holding hands.'

'Blackie would've done his nut if he knew you'd found his secret key,' she pointed out sharply, keen to take the conversation elsewhere.

'I told you, he gave me the key, or at least told me where he hid it.'

'Really,' Tiff said, unconvinced.

'Really,' he insisted. 'Wanted me to have somewhere to escape to.' That left a gulf in the air. Everyone local knew how Andy Fellner had treated his wife and son. Some sounds couldn't be masked from neighbours and word carried. While Blackie was unable to save Mike's mother from an early grave, he'd made it his mission to equip the boy. That Mike had turned out to be a naturally gifted boxer, quick on his feet and in his thinking, had been a bonus.

'So, what are you going to do with yourself?' she asked to break the silence. 'Retirement before thirty leaves some years to fill.'

'Not sure yet,' he said, his mouth forming a wide but flat smile. 'I've invested here and there and TV have been asking me to commentate, but nothing really stands out.'

'You sure you aren't wanting my gym?' she said with mock suspicion. She experienced an unexpected thrill at referring to it as her gym. She owned a gym. OMG.

It amused him.

'Not today. Besides, Blackie wanted you to have it. Don't want his spirit harassing me, now do I?' Tiff was under no illusion that he wasn't mocking her for the other night. 'I might not have liked all of his decisions,' he added, 'but I never knew them to be wrong.' Given Ron's response, it was nice to have a crumb of support. 'How's it going?' he asked, nodding towards the wall.

She felt herself sag. Good question and again she wished she could call Gavin. He'd direct her. Was this a conversation she wanted with Mike? She thought about the arrogant arse he'd been at the wake. And the teasing he'd started the other night and seemed intent to continue. Did she want to risk more ridicule from him? But teasing aside, they'd always been honest with each other as teens. She could do with impartiality right now, even if it was from him.

'Lots of choices to be made. Deciding what to do.' Her brow was furrowed. Uninvited, he sat on the bench next to her, Tiff budging along without comment, though clearly unsettled by it. He was too close.

He waited for her to continue, apparently not in any rush. 'I guess it was a surprise?' he prompted. 'Overwhelmed?'

'Definitely. To both questions.' She leaned her head back onto the brick and closed her eyes, the sun warming her face and calming her.

'Who thinks they should have had it?'

'Aaron, the evil stepson.'

'The scrote from this morning?'

'The very same. Stopped by to offer his opinion.'

'Ignore it. He'll be all mouth.' She opened an eye to see if he was sure. Apparently so.

'Ron, the assistant and now head coach. He's worked with Blackie for years.'

'Head for business?'

'Not to my knowledge.'

'Well Blackie didn't think so either, Tiff, or he could've left it to him instead. Which he didn't.'

While Tiff had had the same thought, it was ridiculously uplifting to hear it from someone else. And oddly, *this* someone felt new to her; *this* Mike sounded business-like and experienced. It wasn't a Mike she'd met before. It eased things.

'So, having established your true entitlement to the bequest, let's hear the troubling decisions.'

She sat up properly and faced him. 'In a nutshell; keep the status quo or modernise? Ron's pushing for me to be a silent partner. He'll take over and pay me rent. He wants an answer by Friday.'

'Aggressive,' Mike nodded. 'But do you really think he'll walk if you say no or don't give him an answer by Friday?'

He had a point. She'd been thrown by Ron's bolshiness.

'There are no clubs anywhere near and he's not skilled in much else as far as I know.'

'He's not young either,' Mike pointed out, 'That's on your side too.'

'So there's the easy option,' she concluded. 'Take the money and run. Plus there's the top floor which I could lease separately.'

'What's up there?'

'An insurance firm used to rent it. I've never been up

there. It's been closed since they moved out years ago and Blackie didn't release it, in case the ex got her hands on the income.'

'So it's still rentable?'

'Probably needs some sprucing. In that scenario I'd maybe expand my own business.'

'What's your business?' he asked, his interest heightening.

'Oh, um, bookkeeping,' she mumbled. 'Small clients. Just me.'

He tilted his head to the side. 'You wanted to be in high finance.'

'Yeah well, teen dreams and that,' she brushed it aside, not wanting to bring back the past or her negative feeling towards him. This neutral territory with the new Mike was tenable. 'The thing with the "take the money and run" route is I don't believe the club will sustain itself over time. That's what I'd been telling Blackie; the club should transform into a modern fitness club, with the boxing at its heart.'

'Go on,' he coaxed, sensing her mood pick up.

'There's loads of unutilised space in this building. I'd invest in spinning bikes, rowing machines and treadmills. The upper floors can be divvied up to incorporate studios for movement classes. I'd love some kind of social space too.'

'The thing is,' she continued, 'if the gym wants a long

future, then we need the women. This place is a huge vat of testosterone. We only have two female boxers. There are fitness centres popping up all over and eventually the boxers will go there instead. Not to box obviously, but if they're offered memberships with their partners, they'll go. I could offer both. Let's be honest, boxing is a dwindling sport. Lots of sports *are* now, given kids have so many other distractions. Focusing solely on the boxing club feels like putting all my eggs in one basket. I genuinely believe this place could be so much more.'

She came to an abrupt halt. She'd been getting all passionate about it and Mike was grinning at her.

'*There's* your plan, Tiff. The first didn't get you fired up at all. That was the safe option. Blackie didn't give it to you to play safe.'

She suddenly felt *shy*. Saying it all aloud to him had regenerated the confidence she had, if not in herself, then in her ideas. Moreover, he wasn't mocking her plans. He wasn't telling her not to change things. He believed in her. He took her seriously.

'And you need pole-dancing in the mix.'

'What?' she said, taken aback. Maybe not taking her seriously after all. Bastard. He'd totally had her there. *Nothing* had changed – he was still taking the mick.

'Seriously, it does miracles for the abs,' he said, seeing the appalled look on her face. 'Pole-fitness. That's what it's called. Pole-*fitness*. It's legitimate. There's dedicated clubs for it.'

'Yeah right,' she snapped, unsure whether to laugh in his face or shout at him again. She'd seen adverts for *those* clubs. They weren't affiliated to Sports England.

'Straight up, Tiff, there's proper pole-fitness studios out there. No dodgy stuff. It's bloody hard work. Arms, legs, abs. It all gets toned,' he insisted, then shrugged and added, 'If the husbands and boyfriends get demos at home, that's a bonus. Nothing wrong with that.' He seemed sincere. Maybe she simply couldn't tell if he was taking the piss anymore. It put her on edge. But... she needed to talk about the club.

'You think women would come to do that?'

'I know so. They get fit, lean and flipping confident. Sexier all round. That's priceless. You'd have boxing downstairs and pole-fitness upstairs and everyone will leave confident. They'll barely make it to their cars. There'll be a baby-boom, you'll see.'

'I won't be responsible for overpopulating the town and I hadn't planned for a crèche,' she stated, although the crèche thing might work for daytime classes...

'Future clients, Tiff. Don't knock it.'

'Right. Good thinking,' she said, almost laughing, but not quite. 'Is that what Verity does to keep fit?' His face clouded momentarily, before swiftly reassuming his game face.

'Verity's fitness regime is down to her personal trainer, shopping marathons and parties.'

Tiff garnered there was more to that statement than the simple facts, but it definitely wasn't her place to pry, nor was she overly interested.

His pocket buzzed. Checking the text, he rolled his eyes.

'Speaking of ... I need to go.' Getting up, he asked, 'So you're okay to hold onto the ring for a little while?'

'Sure, no problem.' She didn't confess he was doing her a favour. She'd never liked being beholden to anyone. Rich international sportsmen who'd seen her naked then left her, were definitely on that list. The hurt began to creep back into her head and she was glad this was coming to a close.

'But you'll let me know if you need it gone?' he asked, handing her his phone. The new contact page was headed *Tiff*. Just *Tiff*.

'Of course.' She got up from the bench and followed him towards the car park, typing in her number before handing it back. He hit call, then cancel, linking them.

'Great. I'll give you a shout when I want it.' A smirk leapt onto his face. 'My turn to shout at you.'

'Yeah, about that,' she said, slightly sheepish, 'it was a rough day in a rough week.' The sparkle in his eye and the wave of his hand said it was forgotten already. She guessed he'd suffered worse blows than her venting at him.

They stood for some moments facing each other, not quite knowing the protocol. His pocket buzzed again, but he didn't bother looking at it.

'Good luck with the club, Tiff. Call me if you need to.' He walked away with his hands back in his pockets, resolutely ignoring his phone.

As she watched him disappear across the car park, Tiff still felt some misgivings – he'd walked away from her once and not come back. Memories like that never really went away; their damage was permanent. But he seemed to believe she could do it. Not only that, looking back up at the building, Tiff saw the new Mike had left her with something else too; a new spark of determination.

Chapter 10

The office telephone rang at precisely 9 a.m. Tiff had been up for hours, having spent the night negotiating the new mattress. In contrast to the undulating lumps of the sofa, the mat stack was perfectly level but only fractionally softer than concrete. She'd given up at six, pulled on a *Blackie's Gym* sweatshirt she'd found in a storage box and her trackie bottoms, in an effort to appear more club-corporate. She'd brushed her brown curls up into a tight pony tail, imagining this was what gym staff did. Her supermarket trainers finished the look.

Looking the part, Tiff ran six laps of the empty gym before knocking out a cartwheel at the door. It wasn't competition standard; it had been years and she'd changed shape, but that wasn't the point. She was reminding herself she owned the room. Ron wasn't going to run her off her own property.

She puffed and panted out of the hall, vowing to

make the purchase of a water cooler the first task of the day.

The webpage for cooler suppliers appeared on the screen as the phone rang.

What should she answer? *Blackie's?*

'Pull yourself together, woman,' she imagined Blackie barking and snatched up the receiver.

'Tiffanie Trent,' she said. It seemed the safest option.

'Tiffanie? Your phone's ringing out.'

Gavin.

Gavin! OMG! Tiff was totally thrown. She hadn't heard from him in over a week, and here he was calling the gym. *He* was calling *her*. That was good, right? Her heart picked up its pace. Hearing his voice again, his lovely firm voice, which had steered her for so long, made her want to cry, in a reaching-the-promised-land kind of way. But she needed to play this right. Keen, but cool. Enthused, but not needy.

'Gavin. Hi. I'm fine, thanks,' she gushed, then realised he hadn't actually enquired how she was. Brilliant. 'How was your course?'

'Awesome. Enlightening stuff. Focused my thinking about things.'

Now Tiff's heart started to gallop. Had the focusing brought him to the epiphany of having made a hideous mistake and he couldn't live without her?

'Oh yes?' she asked, trying to manage her anticipation. 'Lots has happened here too—'

'Yes, I see you moved your stuff out,' he cut in. 'Thanks for that. We should probably divvy up the furniture now I'm back. Actually, it's quite serendipitous, as I need to tweak my surroundings with regard to moving things on. Framing my mind properly, you know?'

Hang on. Wasn't serendipity about good luck? Was he saying it was good luck she'd moved out? It left her reeling. He hadn't had a change of heart at all. He wasn't remotely concerned about how she was doing. She dug her nails into her thigh to distract from her hurting heart. *Nothing* had changed.

She couldn't think of a single thing she'd want from the flat ... except...

'I only want the bed, Gavin. The rest is yours.'

It sounded snippy – which she wouldn't normally do with Gavin, nor would it help her quest to win him back – but she needed him off the phone before she started to cry. Also, crucially, she could kill for a decent night's kip. If she could just get some proper sleep she'd be able to deal with him more sensibly. With a bit of rearranging, their bed could fit in the storeroom.

'But—'

'Sorry Gav, I need to go. If you have it sent to the

gym, I'll handle it from there.' It probably came across as officious, but she was trying to keep a grip on a tsunami of begging him to take her back, whilst simultaneously trying to take his focus off the bed; her stomach cramped with the cringe emanating from the last time he'd been in it with her. With a quick damage-limiting 'Bye' she hung up. She hadn't had a chance to tell him about the gym. Which was perhaps just as well, where impact was concerned; he apparently hadn't changed his mind about them, so she was going to have to implement her show-him-your-striving-abilities plan.

Tiff slid out the lower desk drawer at her side and assessed the contents. Blackie had had it stocked with brandy but she'd made some changes. She considered a Pot Noodle but it was too early. Scampi fries it was then.

Snack scoffed, water cooler contract sorted, the morning's can-do attitude had been reinstated. She was doing it. She was making decisions, (okay, decision singular) and actioning them. Not at Blackie's request, not in response to a problem. For herself. Tiff was annoyed at having let Ron cow her so easily. She'd already grown a business before, she made her own decisions there. Somewhere she'd lost sight of that. Maybe Shelby was right, she *could* do this. She could be capable like Leonards said. Or at least give it a go. Mike too had been right; modernising was the plan she believed in.

She found an A4 pad and started a list of all her revamp ideas. She allowed herself anything that popped into her head, no matter how bonkers. Yes, even the whole foods pick'n'mix display. She wanted everything on there. The mad, the bad and the impossible too. Having immersed herself completely in this for the best part of the morning, she found she had a page-worth of ideas, all in varying degrees of rational.

Outside of her bookkeeping life, which, bar filing her annual tax return, equated exclusively to *Arrive – Do the numbers – Leave*, Gavin had always made the decisions. Her role within their partnership dynamic was to make them happen. With his goal in mind, she was deft at planning. But this sort of planning was far broader, open-ended and flying-by-the-seat-of-her-pants-y than she'd experienced. It was thrilling.

Checking no-one was watching, Tiff stood for a couple of star jumps and air-jabs to psych herself up, before dropping back into the chair to start the second phase of The Planning. Turning to a fresh page, she folded the paper into three columns, which she titled *NOW, SOON, ONE DAY*. There were small changes she wanted immediately, like de-cluttering the office and sorting the storeroom-cum-bedroom for when Gavin shipped the bed. But those things were just for her. She added Water Cooler to the *NOW* column and immediately struck it through as complete. She liked a list with something crossed out already. No, not *cheating* – morale-boosting. Encouraging.

SOON covered the transition from boxing club to fitness club. She immediately listed Locker rooms. The Gents needed an overhaul, and the Ladies – a hastily added DIY-job shower in a former cupboard – barely existed. This could never be a unisex gym without decent changing facilities for the women; nice benches, decent sized lockers, brutal showers and proper hair-dryers. Tiff got quite carried away with her fantasy locker room, not least because she was grossed out using the men's showers after hours. And the never-worked-as-long-as-she'd-been-there lift needed fixing. Her club would be for all abilities.

The final column homed her total indulgences. Top of the list; a café-bar space. Gavin always pinpointed the social opportunity when glamourising sales particulars. She'd have hers under the same roof. She wasn't fussed about a juice bar, she wanted a place where people could wind down together after classes. In the daytime, the mums might stop for a skinny latte before the school run. All of this was pie-in-the-sky, but it got her excited. Perhaps it *was* her dream to run this place, after all. Perhaps Blackie saw more than he'd let on.

She halved the *ONE DAY* column, (there wasn't much on it because she wanted everything right NOW) and added a new title to the lower half. *CLASSES*. Boxing went on first, primarily out of respect for Blackie, but also because keeping the regulars was key to her plan. She wanted to draw in their partners, and she wanted to tempt prospective female members with a hive of buff men (okay, buff*ish* – there were as many party-kegs as six-packs downstairs). Business was business and she needed to use all the resources available. Humans included.

She started listing. Pilates, Yoga, Zumba, Spinning, Step, Jazzercize, Aerobics, and more she'd pinched from Google-searching other gyms ... and finally, Pole-*fitness*. She might not get all of them, but she reckoned she could pull a decent programme together. By early afternoon Tiff looked at her page and was chuffed. It was strong, achievable in most places, with scope for her aspirations. Gavin would be impressed.

It had been a great use of her morning, even if it'd been office-bound. Tiff wasn't hiding per se, but she was doing her best to keep out of Ron's way. She felt awkward around him now. It was easier making herself scarce, sorting the office. And besides, sorting the office was right there on her *NOW* list. In ink. Which made it a high priority.

Whilst 'not hiding', she was scoping the car park.

116

Loitering by the windows, she had a panoramic view of the Eastcote Road and vigilantly monitored all the approaching cars. Quite bluntly, she was on the hunt for a woman.

Finally, as Tiff was contemplating a Pot Noodle dinner, a van pulled up and Jess jumped out.

'Just the woman,' she called down through the window. (Nope, not hiding.) Jess looked up at Tiff, surprised, but pleased.

'S'up Tiff?'

'I need you. Upstairs,' she said, then considered it might have sounded slightly flirty. Jess's eyes grew wide and Tiff was glad Amina wasn't there to hear. 'I mean, I'd appreciate your professional advice. Would you mind coming to the office?'

'That old chestnut,' she said, moving off with a wink.

'So what do you think?' Tiff asked having explained the new ownership and her plans.

Jess looked out into the floor space beyond the office. 'The walls are an easy do; they're mostly plasterboard partitions, so we'd pull 'em all down and you'd start with a blank canvas. Flooring depends on the room usage; some'll need to be sprung, but that's no biggie. The extra changing room would need plumbing and tanks put in, but it's all doable.'

Tiff beamed. She'd been dreading Jess saying it was

a nightmare. She followed Jess to the stairs, expecting to head for the gym, but instead Jess's eyes went up the next flight.

'What about upstairs?'

'Not sure yet. I um…I've never been up there.' Tiff felt daft admitting it. The building had been hers for over a day and she'd not ventured beyond the office.

'Really? Never?'

She shrugged. 'Blackie locked it off after the old firm moved out.'

'Any idea what's up there?'

'I believe there's an open plan office, a few small offices, a kitchenette and loos.'

Jess gave her a mischievous look. 'You got the keys?'

'I guess so,' Tiff said, thinking about the bunch Leonards had handed her.

Grabbing it from the desk, Tiff returned to find Jess missing. The upper stairwell was illuminated for the first time in years.

'This floor gives me the creeps,' she muttered, meeting her at the top.

'How, when you haven't been up here?'

'Well, okay, but it's always been dark up here.' Tiff started trying one key after the other. 'It's the stuff of murder programmes.'

'This is where we find Blackie's sordid secrets,' Jess said in a creepy voice. Tiff elbowed her, as a) Blackie was as straight as they came, and b) it wasn't funny – it was flipping spooky up there.

The fifth key struck lucky, and the door swung open. Tiff was reluctant to be the first one in.

'Get in, you wuss,' Jess scoffed, but pushed her in ahead of herself, 'they were insurers, not gangsters. We'd have heard if it was some torture den.' Thankfully she flipped the light switch, and the room became less eerie. 'You weren't expecting me to carry you over the threshold, were you?'

Tiff didn't answer as she was consumed by what she saw.

'Look at that view,' she said, crossing the room and resting her forehead on the glass. Considering there was only one floor's difference this view seemed a world apart. She could see at least three roof gardens, and there, beyond the grey buildings were verdant fields. She took a quick wander along the window line, then stopped. This view; the one in the furthest corner looking out over the smarter part of town where she'd once lived, both with her parents and then with Gavin, the hills in the distance and hint of the sea beyond, was the view she wanted.

'This'll be the new admin office,' she said, squaring off the space with her arms. 'The rest of the narrow end can be a storeroom and staff facilities; we'll update the kitchen and the loos.' She swung around to the long broad side of the open plan office. 'This'll be the social space; café by day, bar at night. Somewhere to chill out after a workout. Can you see it, Jess?'

'Easily.' She turned to see Jess and the big smile plastered on her face. 'The lights'll look a treat too.'

Tiff imagined dusk settling over town and the cars switching their headlights on. Once it was dark, the uglier business buildings would vanish and only the lights from homes dotted on the hills would remain.

'It'd be best from a works point of view if you did it all in one go, Tiff, closing the gym only the once.'

'Absolutely,' she said, only just managing not to bounce with excitement. 'I want it all and I want it now.'

'Makes sense to have Staff changing rooms above the Ladies downstairs, and we'll locate that above the Gents on the ground floor,' Jess suggested, looking about and making calculations. Tiff watched her, thinking she definitely wasn't the teen she'd once known; Jess'd hardly said boo to a goose back then, and here she was being a professional, interpreting and improving her plans. 'That'd give us the most economical plumbing.'

'Economical sounds good,' Tiff nodded along. 'Thank you. I wouldn't have known where to start on this.'

'Nor did I until my dad showed me.' Jess's dad had clearly been more useful than hers, Tiff thought, but conceded her ability with numbers probably came from him. He'd known exactly what he was doing, even if it was morally wrong. 'And the lads know what they're doing. It's more about management, although they know I can turn my hand to any of it now, if we're stuck.'

'Does that make a difference? Do they accept you?' Tiff was thinking about Ron's insistence that the boxers wouldn't like her running the place. She was royally stuffed if they really intended to hold her gender against her.

'I don't give them a choice, Tiff. They've seen me do the same jobs. They know I have the muscles. I can shout as loud as my dad did, with a more scathing vocabulary. *And* I've the benefit of female charm too, when I need it.' Tiff doubted any of the boxers had ever seen an ounce of charm from Ron, so maybe she was one up there. Jess's experience said she simply needed to knuckle down. Thinking about it, all her bookkeeping jobs were in male-orientated businesses. One was a mechanic's, the other a plumber's merchant. Seen like that, she was already working in bloke-heavy environments, and she'd never had an issue. The thought buoyed her. 'Can I quote for the job?' Jess asked, digging her hands into her pockets and rocking back on her heels.

'Jess,' she said, shocked, 'the job is *yours*. I mean, if you want it.'

'Definitely.' She was pleased, but then her face dropped. 'Do you know any other builders? You should get a second quote for comparison.'

Tiff didn't need to know other builders. 'You're hardly going to rip off your own club, Jess, and I figure you'll do a job you'll be proud of. You drive a shiny new van, so you probably aren't constantly being sued.' Jess shrugged, playing it down, but Tiff saw a glint of pride in her eye. 'Besides that, your reputation here would be in the balance, and if you do a decent job, you'll get more work. I'm assuming, of course, I can report to the other members what amazing value for money you are.'

'Worked it all out, haven't you?' Jess said, knowing she'd been done.

'Absolutely,' said Tiff with a grin, 'Plus if you aren't quick about it all, they'll be complaining to you directly. Works for me.'

'Get some ideas down on paper, Tiff and I'll look them over for a ballpark figure.' She paused for a moment then added 'Talk it over with Ron. He might have some ideas too.'

'On it,' Tiff said, meaning she'd already mentioned changes to Ron, but happy to make it sound like he agreed. The last thing she wanted was for the customers to feel there was division between them. She needed everyone onside if this was to go smoothly. 'It's early days yet, so keep it to yourself, OK?' She didn't want Jess discussing things with anyone too soon. *Right timing is in all things the most important factor*, Tiff – Hesiod. She hadn't asked Gavin who Hesiod was exactly, but right now, Tiff was with him on this.

Chapter 11

Tiff and Jess raced down the stairs like a couple of school kids giddy from hatching secret plans. They came to an abrupt halt at the bottom, as they met Ron's petulant face.

'Some of us are working, Tiffanie. I'm not here to take deliveries for you while you're messing around god-knows-where.' Tiff felt more chastened than she ever had at school. 'Jess, give me a hundred burpees. Your fitness is on the wrong side of slipping.' Ron clearly wasn't beyond taking his mood out on the customers too. Jess winced, but didn't complain and with a quick 'See ya', hoofed into the sparring hall. Judging by Ron's expression, Tiff doubted Jess would be moving as jauntily when he was done with her.

Ron thrust Tiff a piece of paper, flicked his head towards a man standing in the doorway, and stormed off, back to the ring. Scanning the docket, she recognised the dispatch signature as Gavin's. Seeing it made her pine for him. His smooth cursive was a thing of beauty.

The bed! The very concept of decent sleep made her slightly light-headed. Tiff'd expected Gavin to take ages sending it over, but the same day? He wasn't kidding about being focused. He must be really keen to expunge her from his life.

'Can we bring it in then?' the delivery chap asked, consulting his watch. He was out the door again before she answered.

Standing in the entrance she examined the foyer space; essentially a largish hallway with doors to the changing room, the sparring hall, and the stairs leading up to the other floors, next to the knackered lift. Blackie hadn't done much with it, except slamming a couple of the inspirational posters up and a notice board with fixtures and the club's press coverage. She'd need a reception desk; something sleek and efficient. Probably someone to sit at it, too.

A kerfuffle brought her attention back to the doorway, where the delivery man and his mate were manhandling the delivery inside.

'No,' Tiff spluttered. 'That's not right.'

'S'wot it says on the docket, love. The guy helped us out with it himself.'

'No, no, no,' she said, panicking. 'It was the bed. The sleigh bed. Not the sofa.'

The men didn't backtrack, but instead kept coming,

manoeuvring the sofa into the foyer, with a steadfast 'It's on the docket.'

'Yes, I understand it's on the docket,' Tiff acknowledged with frustration, studying the crumpled page from her pocket, vowing never to receive anything again without having scrutinised the paperwork. 'But it isn't what we agreed.'

'You'll have to take that up with the sender, love,' said the first guy, the second apparently mute. 'We just deliver.'

'Can't you take it back?'

'S'already paid for. You'll have to book it in as a new job. Number's on the docket.' He clapped his hands together washing his hands of the whole affair. Sensing this was not going smoothly they were intent on a quick exit.

'But you can't just leave it here,' Tiff insisted. She wanted to stamp her foot.

Looking back over his shoulder, the guy appeared confused, 'But it looks good there.' He sprinted after his mate.

Tiff scowled at the sofa, positioned against the wall. Gargantuan monster that it was, it did fit the space perfectly and Tiff begrudgingly had to concede it made the entrance look smarter.

'But it isn't my bed,' she lamented pitifully. 'And I can't bloody sleep on it there.'

She stomped up the stairs, before poking the digits on the desk phone, trying to imagine what the chuff Gavin was playing at. She'd been very clear it was the bed she needed. His hearing had always been very good. He'd never had any difficulty hearing when she'd turned the heating up – his alertness to the turn of the thermostat dial was sensitive to canine levels.

In spite of Gavin constantly having his phone to hand, *Opportunity doesn't make appointments, you have to be ready when it arrives,* Tiff – Tim Fargo, it took twenty rings before he answered. Tiff wondered what Tim bleeding Fargo would have made of *that*.

'Tiffanie,' he said grandiosely, making her suspect he was within earshot of others.

'Gav,' she said carefully, set on sounding composed, 'the *sofa's* just been delivered here.'

'Excellent. All in good nick, I trust. Check it before you accept it, in case they've damaged it. That cost a shed-load, remember. Designer Italian doesn't come cheap, does it?' He was definitely within earshot of others. 'Write any damage on the docket.' Tiff crushed the docket in her fist.

'Gav, it wasn't the sofa I was expecting. It was the *bed*. Remember?' She was trying for soothing rather than seething, but it wasn't quite firming up. The conversation sat at odds with her; being naturally disinclined to contradict him. 'I asked for the bed. You never really liked the bed.'

'No, Tiff. I love that bed. Always have,' he insisted. 'I know you mentioned it, but when it came to shifting it, it was a nightmare. The sofa on the other hand simply slid out, so it seemed a fair exchange. Actually, penny for penny, you're better off.'

Tiff was still mentally scarred from the day the sofa arrived at the flat and all the hooing and haaing that came with getting the vast thing in.

'The bed comes apart Gavin.'

'It's not a flat-pack bed, Tiff; hand-crafted doesn't come boxed like Ikea,' he pointed out, emphasizing *hand-crafted* for his audience.

'No Gav, I distinctly remember it arriving in parts and slotting together. Agreed, it wasn't flat-packed, but it does come apart and would've been easier to deliver than the sodding sofa.' *Stay calm, stay calm*. The lack of sleep and the disappointment were pushing her buttons, the same buttons which had unleashed The Shouty at Mike. She couldn't do that with Gavin; that wasn't how they worked and wouldn't help her end-game. She took a deep calming breath. She could weather this.

'Tiff, I can't see what you're getting worked up about. It's just furniture. Good designer furniture I agree, but only chattel at the end of the day.'

Chattel. God she hated that word. A mean, tight, wanky word estate agents and solicitors bandied between them, like people's loved items were of trivial consequence.

'If it's only chattel to you then can't I have the bed? Please Gav?' she asked, pinching the bridge of her nose. Decent sleep had become her Holy Grail. 'I don't have a bed.'

'Ohh, right, I see your point,' he conceded. *At last*, she thought, raising her eyes to the ceiling in thanks. 'But here's the thing Tiffanie, if I send over the bed, then the delivery men'll need paying again and one of us still has to buy a bed. But if *you* buy a bed, then the delivery will be included and there's less hassle. Not only that, but the bed suits the room at home. You can buy a bed to suit your new room.' She gritted her teeth. She was finding it tough remembering that in a negotiation there was always going to be some compromise. She was used to doing the compromising, and would normally have done so long before now, but something kept egging her on.

She tried another tack. 'The sofa suited the lounge.'

'Hmm, I've always thought it was a bit over-powering, all that black leather and very boxy. I'm looking at making it a softer space now.'

She could have cried. She'd made many Pinterest boards with her dream lounge furniture carefully divided by styles and colourways, but would he ever admit he'd made a mistake in picking it? Hell no.

'What makes you think it suits my place?' she asked. 'I haven't found a place yet.' Perhaps a sympathy bid might make him change his mind.

'Well that's perfect! You can pick your new place with it in mind. Do you need me to send over some details on rentals?' he asked, then lowered his voice, 'I'll forward the best ones before they go on the website.'

'No thanks. I've got my own plans,' she snapped, almost at the end of her rope.

'Sure, sure,' he said, not in the least offended. Estate agents had very thick skin. 'Blackie won't mind you storing the sofa there, will he? The lads can help you lift it.'

That stopped her in her tracks. He hadn't heard.

'Blackie's dead, Gav. Buried last week.' It gave her a pang just saying it. Tiff suspected somewhere inside her she still carried plenty more grief with Blackie's name on, waiting to be addressed when she wasn't struggling to keep her head above water.

'Ah,' groaned Gavin and took a moment to digest the information. He knew how much Blackie meant to her. 'That is regrettable. Look, don't reject the help of friends in times of need, Tiff – I'll look for rentals in a lower price bracket instead. If I hear of any job opportunities I'll tip you off. You hear all sorts when you're showing people bigger properties. You can check your emails at Shelby's, yes?'

Tiff was speechless. She pulled herself up straight, provoked by his... his...god, everything about him peeved her at that moment. She normally adored every bit of him. Except the all-over waxing. 'No need, Gavin. I can pick them up here at the club. It's mine now,' she said primly and with an uncharacteristic cocktail of pride and malice. 'Blackie left it to me.'

Then she flung the receiver back in its cradle, ignoring it as it rang and rang and rang.

Chapter 12

A note was left on her desk early evening Thursday – *WHO ORDERED THIS WATER MACHINE?!* Obviously it had been her. Ron was spouting off.

Jess however stuck her head around the door to tell her it had been well-received.

'It's the least a club should offer,' Tiff said, chuffed it was appreciated by some. As first moves went it was small, but now Gavin knew about the club, she needed things moving. 'Not that everyone sees it that way,' she mumbled.

'He's pissed off with the inheriting thing, isn't he?' Tiff hadn't meant for Jess to hear, but she had. More to the point she knew what Tiff meant, which signified there'd been griping on the shop floor.

'Pissed off with me or with Blackie?' Tiff asked. Was it bad to hope it was the latter? Yes, yes it probably was...

'Both most likely, although he's prepared to forgive Blackie given he's dead and that.'

Tiff sighed. Of course it was easier to blame the living. How fortunate to be dead in this instance.

'Ignore it, Tiff,' encouraged Jess, trying to be upbeat. 'He's just one of life's grouches. If anyone gets lucky he's the guy who grouses "all right for some", rather than be pleased for them.'

'He thinks Blackie should have left it to him.'

'Yeah, he's mentioned that, but nobody's getting into it. So long as they can keep boxing, they're happy.'

'Even without Blackie?' she asked. She could run the place, refurbish and expand, but if it was Blackie they came for then she was stuffed.

'Blackie was new once too,' Jess said, leaning against the doorframe, 'Ron'll do all right. If he wants to.' The knot in her belly tightened at that last part. 'Look at it this way Tiff, Blackie didn't leave him the club, did he? Aside from Ron's sense of entitlement, that speaks volumes. If there's anything a boxer learns then it's there's no such thing as entitlement. You literally fight for a win, you need to dish up the sweat and the tears. That's what everyone'll be looking for; your sweat and tears.'

'Wow. Sweat and tears. That's really encouraging, Jess.'

'Really?' Jess beamed.

'No. I don't particularly relish the idea of people waiting for me to cry.'

133

'No, so that wasn't what I meant,' she started back-tracking.

'It's okay, I get it. Everyone wants to see hard work, effort and results.'

'Yeah, that,' said Jess, wary.

'Ron, on the other hand, *does* want to see me cry,' Tiff said, wryly.

'Probably.'

'And what do you think?' she asked. Jess was one of the few who knew her full plans.

Jess considered it. 'There's always going to be people averse to change. I think your plans are sound. They'll do lots for this place.'

'Thank you.' Positivity. Yay!

'But, you should know Ron's saying you're handing the club over to him.'

Tiff was incensed. He'd given her until the following day to decide. Apparently he'd assumed her answer and presumed he'd be doing the announcements. Had he no sense of business etiquette?

Jess saw she'd lit a firework and mumbled her need for a shower. Tiff hoofed after her down the stairs towards the gym. Flinging the door open, Tiff stormed halfway around the perimeter of the room before she realised Ron wasn't there.

'Anyone seen Ron?'

'Nipped out for a paper.' His devotion to *The Daily*

Mail superseded most things. His evening pilgrimage to collect it meant he could sly a cigarette. Tiff's courage deflated as she stood there thwarted.

Turning dejected back to the door, Tiff noticed Natalie North standing in the corner with her husband Ed. He tucked a lock of hair behind her ear, which gained him a shy smile, before he kissed her on the forehead and moved to the ring. Tiff looked at the floor, feeling she was intruding on a tender moment, whilst also tackling a pang of envy. She missed those moments and the close companionship so badly.

Looking up again, Natalie was perched on a wooden bench, book in hand. Rather than taking yet another walk of shame, Tiff detoured over to her.

She was a small mole of a woman, with a short black bob and round black-rimmed glasses. She was tiny; barely over five foot, which was exacerbated when standing next to six foot three Ed. It could have appeared comical, but instead they seemed to fit, like the yolk in the white of a boiled egg. What seemed incongruous to Natalie's petiteness was the enormous sweatshirts she always wore over leggings. Tiff wasn't a snob, people could wear what they liked and Lord knew she liked to relax in the evenings in sweatpants, but the outsize-top looked more like camouflage than leisurewear, as if Natalie was hiding in it.

Tiff joined her on the low bench.

'What are you reading, Natalie? Anything good?'

It was a self-help book.

'It's the third time I've read this chapter. My eyes scan the words but nothing goes in.'

Tiff felt bad for her. Blackie had never been above a good gossip, in spite of Tiff not wanting to partake. Subsequently she knew the details; Natalie came because she didn't trust her husband after he'd had a one-night stand. Valuing his second chance, Ed had resigned himself to it. He understood Natalie needed to do this. Of course, the other lads took the mick out of him, incessantly. Natalie ignored it. Tiff supposed that was the deal they'd struck; if he came, she came and the lads would dole out the punishment.

Yet Tiff couldn't help wonder what kind of an existence this offered either of them? Childless, they could essentially walk away from one another, but clearly they'd felt they had something worth keeping, even though at this point, tender gestures aside, it didn't look as if trust was back on the list. Briefly Tiff considered the opposing nature of her own relationship; while she and Gavin had had trust, he hadn't wanted to stay with her. Perhaps the Norths couldn't think of a better solution or way of moving on.

'Natalie, would you do me a favour?' Tiff asked. Natalie looked at her surprised.

'I plan to make some changes upstairs and wanted

to get more views on it. Would you mind?' The way Natalie flushed, she knew she'd asked the right question.

'I don't know how I can help,' she said, tentatively. Tiff suspected her confidence had been eviscerated. What good was it doing Natalie, sitting here, blending in with the racked equipment? Surely, in reassuring herself about Ed's transgression, she was actually dwelling on it. Sounded like a vicious circle.

'Honest opinions are all I need.' Tiff kept her voice low, keen no-one should overhear. She didn't want more rumours before she'd given Ron her decision, but to be frank, he'd started it. The gloves were off. 'I need the feedback before I start wasting money. That's all.'

Natalie nodded, pitching her book back in her bag. Tiff didn't get the impression she was going to miss reading it. Following Tiff meekly to the door, Natalie kept looking her husband's way.

'He's being pummelled by Amina,' Tiff said, 'He's not going anywhere.' Natalie nodded, a tinge of shame touching her face.

Tiff outlined the bare bones of her plans as she ascended the stairs. It took her a while to suss Natalie wasn't with her.

'Erm…Natalie?' Tiff peered down over the stairwell banister. The woman was staring up at her, horrified.

'What's the matter?' asked Tiff.

'You want to bring more women here?' Ah. Tiff saw. She hadn't played this right. At all. She scurried back down the stairs, linked her arm through Natalie's and pulled her along to the next floor. Natalie walked like the living dead. Tiff sat her down on the office sofa and quickly made her a cup of tea, pressing it into her hands. She was tempted to drop a shot of Blackie's brandy in it for the shock.

'Natalie, does Ed like coming here?'

'He loves it. He's come since he was little. It's part of who he is.'

'Right,' said Tiff, nodding keenly, 'and you love Ed for who he is, yes?'

Natalie nodded in return, but her eyes were still as huge as saucers.

'With kids having so many other entertainments nowadays, this gym can't sustain itself if I don't do anything new with it.'

'You need new revenue streams,' Natalie said plainly. This made Tiff smile. Natalie got it.

'Exactly. I could use the space in a way that links with the boxing, i.e. fitness, then the club can be under-pinned.' Natalie was at least nodding again.

'I want to build a studio room so there can be classes. I was thinking about Zumba for starters.' This wasn't the moment to mention the pole-fitness.

'My cousin goes to Zumba,' Natalie said, wistfully.

'Says it's brilliant.' Natalie knew she was giving up her own life in her vigil.

'That's what I'm hearing too, and just think Natalie, you could take a class, while Ed trains. You could both be here, and both be busy.' She didn't need to point out Natalie's behaviour was like a prison warden. Both of them knew what she meant. 'I didn't drag you up here to tout for business,' Tiff hastened to add. 'I'm interested in the classes you'd consider.'

Natalie took a moment to think.

'I'd like an aerobics class, maybe Step.' She briefly looked pleased, then the initial worry caught up with her. 'Couldn't you expand the gym, but keep it for men?'

Tiff pulled her mouth to the side in consideration.

'I'm fairly sure that'd be considered sexist, don't you? I mean even the boxing club takes women.' Tiff knew Natalie wasn't bothered by Jess and Amina, but only allowing gay women wouldn't work either. Natalie's mouth flattened in defeat.

'But a bar though ...' she began morosely, as if it was the last straw.

'That's just my icing-on-the-cake dream,' Tiff said, waving it away with her hand, 'but imagine this, Natalie; you and Ed taking a class together, Spinning or something,' Natalie's eyes lit up, 'and once you've showered, you end the evening in the bar for a drink. Together or with friends. People would know you. It wouldn't be like a bar on the street with strangers.'

'People would know Ed and I were together.'

Tiff watched as the scenario played out in Natalie's head, a host of emotions crossing her face. It had to be an improvement on what Tiff imagined was a life stuck in a rut.

'Natalie,' Tiff said gently, 'I think people already know that. You just have to have faith in Ed. Something like this could let you move on.'

Natalie looked at the floor, sorting something in her head.

'I'd change the entrance for starters,' said Natalie, suddenly and with a new-found confidence, 'new customers need to know where to go.' Tiff grinned, seeing Natalie was on board.

'Exactly what I was thinking. Go on,' Tiff encouraged her. And so the conversation continued, with Natalie suggesting the layout for a Reception, including a shop wall for incidentals such as shampoo and deodorant. Definitely deodorant.

It was simple enough, but it was exactly those small touches Tiff wanted the gym to have. The members should feel looked after. She was glad she'd asked Natalie now. Originally it had been a ruse to get the woman out of the hall, giving both Ed and her a break. Now she saw Natalie thought along the same lines.

'Natalie? Where do you work?' Tiff asked as they returned to the sparring hall.

'Iceland,' Natalie replied glumly. 'Checkout.'

'Would you fancy working here?' Tiff asked, experiencing both a surge of panic for trying to employ staff, and also excitement that she was doing The Business. Natalie looked at her shocked, which made Tiff falter.

'I mean, I don't know if you're looking, there's nothing wrong with working at Iceland, or at the checkout, nothing at all, you might be very happy there, of course. You probably are,' Tiff babbled, 'but if not, and you fancied a change, maybe somewhere you know well, then at some point, soon, I'm going to need some help.' Tiff's heart was in her throat.

'But, but,' Natalie was stunned. Tiff saw she might have made a colossal prat of herself. Why would Natalie leave an established job for a business about to undergo major alterations which might not be for the better? Why would anyone walk into that kind of a headache?

'Yes,' Natalie said, quietly. Then, more determined, 'Yes.'

'You would? Why?'

'Because you've asked,' Natalie shrugged, 'because I already live my life here, I might as well get paid for it. Because I desperately need a change. Because I don't like who I currently am and if anywhere can change that it would be a gym.' Natalie looked up at Tiff, a smile forming on her face as she went on, 'Because if I get my groove back, then maybe I'll feel more confident of Ed not doing it again and cut him the slack I know I have to.'

'Would working here make it worse?'

She shrugged again. 'Can't be worse.' Tiff nodded. She got that.

'Don't say anything yet, and don't resign either, but I want you to know I'm excited about this.'

Natalie looked at her quizzically, 'Why did you ask me, Tiffanie? You don't know anything about me or my qualifications.'

Tiff considered this carefully.

'I like your ideas; they match mine.' This made them both laugh. 'Like you say, you're here all the time, so I should put you to some use. But mainly I look at you and see a hard worker, who's put other things aside in an attempt to make something happen.'

Natalie ducked her head. 'It hasn't really worked.'

'So we try something else. You might not be getting quite the desired results, but the effort is there and that's what's important. If we can make you feel strong again, then you'll be exactly what this place is supposed to be about.'

Buoyed by her conversation with Natalie, Tiff knew she had to grab the bull by the horns. She didn't want to put it off any longer. Ron would either be with her or against her, but not addressing the issue wasn't helping. The sooner she could kick things off, the sooner she could show Gavin what she was capable of. She had a plan; three grown-ups of sound mind and Shelby thought it was a goer. So walking back into the hall, she did so like the Queen of Sheba.

Only, Ron wasn't there.

'Been and gone, love,' said one of the older men. 'It's cottage pie night.' Enough said, apparently.

The deflated Queen of Sheba waited to lock up and went to bed.

Chapter 13

It wasn't one of those *Thank god it's Friday* Fridays. More of an *Oh Crap, it's Friday* Fridays. Ron was due his answer. It had only taken the night for her bravado to wane. Lying in the dark, her self-doubts came waltzing out. It was all very well other people saying *go for it, carpe diem, you are so bloody doing this*, but it wasn't them doing it, was it? They weren't the ones setting themselves up for a fall of Niagara proportions.

Her morning routine hoofing around the gym was more of a limp trot. The cartwheel was beyond her. She'd decimated her comfort food supply but lacked the willpower to shop for more. Food had rather lost its appeal in general, which in turn was no good for gymnastics. If it weren't for fear of exposing her accommodation, Tiff would have stayed in bed all day and shut out the world.

Now though, having dragged herself out, Tiff's state of dread had returned. It was Deadline Day, and there could be no more hiding. Having worked at her other clients' offices for the last two days, she'd managed to minimise her interaction with Ron. Loitering in the office, she watched the car park for his arrival. The warning would let her steel herself. Meanwhile, she chanted under her breath *Keep your eye on the prize.* (Okay, so she'd nicked that off one of the stupid posters, but the moment required desperate measures.) Her prize was a six-foot raven-haired estate agent god in a pristine suit.

She heard Ron in the foyer, grumbling to the postie. Bugger. He was in a bad mood already. Tiff told herself to woman up; he was always in a bad mood. She was about to make it worse, so things could only go as badly as expected, or better. Taking a deep breath and totally faking it, she breezed down to the stairs.

'Morning, Ron.'

'Hmph.'

'Got a minute?' she started, trying to keep things light, though her stomach was leaden. Ron didn't look best pleased, but accepted with a begrudging nod.

She led the way up the stairs, feeling the gallows awaited her at the top. *Toughen up*, she chided herself, *being boss doesn't mean being popular*. Having worked for herself all these years, it had never been an issue. But this was different. Livelihoods would depend on her, and she needed to convince them to either trust her plans, or move on.

'You've made some changes then,' he said nodding at the office. It now centred around a lone desk in the middle. It was tidier, smarter and no longer hazardous. Tiff busied herself at the kettle, while he took it all in. His eye was on the desk when she returned with their teas.

'He's not coming back Ron, and I didn't fancy sitting in the corner staring into the wall for the next decade,' she said. She realised instantly she'd shown her hand, that she wasn't going anywhere. Ron caught on immediately.

'You're staying then.' He took the mug without a thank you.

She took the diplomatic approach.

'I thought long and hard about your offer, but at the end of the day, I don't think that's what Blackie wanted.'

'Blackie wanted a boxing club, he wanted kids to have somewhere to come and learn,' he said, defensively.

'I understand that, which is why the boxing club's integral to my plans. It's at the very heart of it and will remain in the hall downstairs.'

Ron didn't say anything, waiting sullenly for her to continue.

'While your offer would, as you say, be easier and less disruptive, I want to be part of this place. I see it being a bigger entity and I honestly believe it's the way forward if the club is to thrive in the long run.'

'It could do that without all the change,' he insisted.

'I don't believe that's true.' He shrugged in a *Think what you like* manner. His sulky teen act irked her.

Tiff pulled out her planning sheet. Half-expecting things might come to this, she'd typed it up. Giving it to him to read, she hoped he might be swayed by the multitude of possibilities.

'Doing all these things is ridiculous.'

'Ron, it's meant as a starting point, a list of ideas, even ones that aren't feasible, to brainstorm the breadth of potential this place offers.'

'A crèche?!' His eyes bugged out of his head as he prodded the sheet. 'That's plain stupid. No-one wants babies crying while they box. They come here to get away from that.'

'It was just an idea, Ron, it's not set in stone, none of these are. Try to see them as opportunities.' His scowl told her he couldn't get past the wailing babies. He sent the page flying back onto the desk. She wished she'd never given it to him. He'd made her feel her ideas were foolish.

Changing tack she went over all the points she'd covered with Natalie, but he didn't nod along in the same thoughtful way. His ears were closed to all argument.

'You should rent out these two floors to something else, and just take the money,' he tried again.

'This isn't about just taking money, Ron. It's about building on what we've got.'

'OK, so rent me the boxing club and you do the gym upstairs. Two separate companies. That'll be safer: when one goes down—' she was pretty sure he meant hers, 'the other can still run.' She saw he wouldn't be persuaded. He was still sure she couldn't do it. It stung and she felt her resolve waning. But the others had been with her; Jess, Shelby and Natalie. Even Mike. It made her hold on.

'That doesn't make sense in terms of economics or brand identity, Ron. It will all be packaged as a whole.' She made the last sentence as firm as she could, so he understood her mind was made up and this was happening.

'It's just change for change's sake,' he insisted, shaking his head, like he despaired of her. It frustrated her that he couldn't see this was the better future-proofing strategy. It pushed her to grasp the nettle; if she was going to lose her coach she'd be better off knowing sooner rather than later.

'I need to know Ron, whether you're on board. I need to know if you can work for me, and within my plans. I need everyone singing off the same hymn sheet.' *Please say you'll stay,* she willed him. He was a stubborn miserable arse, but she needed him.

Ron slowly downed his tea, taking his own good time

and without stopping to answer. Getting up, he looked at her. 'So now we know what *you're* doing and what *you* need. I'll have a think about what *I* need and what *I'm* doing.'

As he made for the door she stood up. 'I need your answer by Monday.'

Three days, she thought. Three days she could wait, and three days should be enough.

Only, in three days she might be without a trainer and in three days the gossip could be out that the staff had no faith in her.

*

'Get you!' Shelby applauded, when Tiff finished her account.

'I know,' Tiff said feeling a weeny bit proud, 'but I was at full bum-clench trying to stop my legs shaking.'

The pub was buzzing, being a Friday night and Shelby had her eyes firmly set on a lanky chap who was milking the quiz machine.

'Adrenaline,' said Shelby, swallowing a third of her Breezer in one swig. 'That's good.'

'Only the atmosphere's even mardier now. Doubt it'll improve if he stays.' It was getting late and while a break from the gym had been great, Tiff was beginning to flag.

'He'll stay. And he'll get used to it.' Tiff wished she had her friend's faith. Shelby did her failsafe prolonged gaze at the trivia-genius, who returned it with a wolfish smile. Shelby immediately started pulling her belongings together, dropping her purse into her tote then checking the box of condoms for ample contents. 'Babe,' she said, resolute.

'S'all right,' Tiff said, not that Shelby had shown any guilt. 'I'm headed off now, anyway.'

'Want us to walk you to the hotel?'

Tiff ducked her head into her own bag, looking for her keys, hiding her blush. She still hadn't told Shelby. 'Stay and have a drink with him. It's only a street away. I'll be fine.' Conveniently the pub was a street away from both gym and hotel, albeit in different directions, so no actual lies there.

The air was crisp as Tiff stepped out. She pulled her coat around her and started off up the street, head down, thinking about the gym. She was gearing up to implementing her plans. She needed something to show Gavin, but so far hadn't quite built up the nerve.

Dirty Doc Martens appeared in front of her feet, bringing her up short. He'd appeared out of nowhere and she swore at herself for not being more vigilant. She took a step backwards, but he moved forwards, effectively corralling her towards a side alley. *Crap*.

'What do you want, Aaron?' She tried to steady her voice.

'You know what I want.'

Tiff hazarded her guess more as a hope; the alternative being too vile to contemplate. 'The gym?' She took a quick squiz down the alley; it ended with bins and a brick wall. The glass shards set into the top glinted menacingly at her. Keen to stay close to the illuminated main road, she let him manoeuvre her to the near wall.

'It should have been mine,' he snarled. It twisted his mouth in an ugly way.

'Yeah, you said that before, but I don't see why?' She didn't want him to think she was scared, but the hammering of her heart wasn't helping.

'I was family.' He breathed it right into her face. Jesus, gross.

'Not much. Blackie and your mum divorced and you weren't his son.'

Aaron pulled up. He knew she was right. Then a lightbulb appeared to switch on.

'He said it would be mine.'

Tiff couldn't hold back her sarcasm. 'Really?'

'He said I could have it.'

'Blackie would never have just said you could have it. It wasn't a random item. He loved that place. It was everything to him. You don't know the first thing about how it works.' She moved to push past him, back to the empty street. He pressed her back.

'He said it was mine.' He ground out each word.

'Strange how no-one else witnessed that, and it wasn't mentioned in the will.'

'The will's wrong.' If he hadn't been in her face, Tiff would have been tempted to sigh at him for being such a prat.

'You didn't mention it at Leonards'.'

'I was in shock. And the grief.' Tiff couldn't imagine Aaron being shocked at much, such was his sense of superiority. 'The will's wrong.'

'Then take it up with Leonards.' It was like reasoning with a child. Only a big one, who smelled of beer and BO.

'That old duffer doesn't know what Blackie said to me.'

'Probably because it's a figment of your imagination.'

'Blackie wanted me to have it.'

'And yet he didn't change his will. I wonder why that was? Oh yeah, because you're making it up.' Tiff knew she shouldn't wind him up, but he was too much of a tosser not to.

His hand slammed into the wall by the side of her face, missing her cheek by a fraction. It stopped any further sass she had brewing. He lowered his face even closer to hers, nose to nose, his rank breath making her do a small sick in her mouth.

'I. Want. The. Business.'

Tiff tried to subtly swallow her fear.

'It's mine,' she said as bravely as she could muster. 'Blackie gave it to *me*.'

'Then *you* can give it to *me*.' He apparently believed she might comply, prior to hell freezing over.

'Not going to happen. Not while I'm still breathing.'

Tiff's chin hurtled upwards as her ponytail was suddenly yanked down her back. She couldn't hold in her yelp.

'Be careful what ideas you put in my head, bitch.' He didn't let go and the pain in her scalp narrowed Tiff's focus on how vulnerable she and her exposed throat were. He was bigger, stronger and clearly a psycho. He definitely had that on his side.

Voices grew nearer and Tiff had never been happier to see a bunch of pissed rugby lads, winding their way up the street.

'Oi oi!' one shouted spotting them. 'Get a room.'

The thought of someone assuming she and Aaron were in the alley for a rummage made her stomach turn, but Tiff recognised her opportunity to escape and grabbed it. She pushed him aside with all her might. He gripped her arm, squeezing hard.

'You don't want me to get nasty. Sign the business over.'

She yanked her arm free, keen to keep within sight

153

of the rugby lads. She'd rather take her chances with their leeriness than risk another moment with Aaron.

'Stay away from me and stay away from my club,' she growled, but it felt more like a plea. And then she walked, as fast as she could, trying to hold her spine straight, her chin up and her tears in.

Chapter 14

'Seriously, you have to get past this,' Shelby scolded, swafting her hand at the open tabs on Tiff's desktop. 'If you're going to do this, Tiff, you need to start buying the stuff and spending the money.'

'But it feels funny,' Tiff wheedled, 'It feels like I'm spending someone else's money.' No doubt Aaron would agree, not that she was willing to give him much thought. She hadn't told anyone about their 'meeting'. Talking about it would give it more validity and she was determined to view it as purely drunken dickhead-ishness.

Ron would agree about the money too. Blackie had always said it was amazing the difference a day could make. Well, two weeks had now passed, and Tiff thought things were still as awkward as hell between them. He'd given her a sullen shrug by way of an agreement to stay, after his three days of thinking.

His staying hadn't been the encouragement it might

have been. She doubted he'd had a change of heart, more a reluctant acceptance. He still didn't think she was capable. It eroded her self-confidence and under-pinned her insecurities. What if he was right? How would she show Gavin what she could do if Ron was right? Those thoughts had stymied her courage, hence Shelby appearing at the gym in bossy mode.

'It's your money. The solicitor said so, yes?'

'Yes,' Tiff nodded sullenly. She'd double-checked with Leonards again. Twice.

'Then start spending.' Shelby gesticulated again at the equipment sites Tiff was resisting. 'You can't have a gym without kit. Skipping ropes are not going to cut it, and to be honest those need updating too.'

Another thing on the shopping list then.

Tiff didn't like shopping. She had once upon a time. She'd loved shopping with her mother, as a child. Davida Trent had always been a sharp-tongued, hard-to-please woman, but when they were shopping, as they did most Saturday afternoons while Tiff's father played golf, a serenity descended on her. She sailed between shops, buying items briskly and with confidence. Tiff had loved seeing her mother so happy, so entranced. She knew she'd be bought something along the way, but that was secondary. She savoured her mother being... well, nice.

Her father's disgrace had brought a swift crushing

end to all of that. The money wasn't there anymore of course, but also with the name of Trent being dirt all over town, her mother had hidden away, brooding in the house, pacing like a caged animal, lashing out when Tiff put a foot wrong. Tiff had begged her mother to move to a different town, but she point blank refused. Her family had lived there for centuries. The shame might have driven her in, she said, but it wouldn't drive her out. Which was all very well, Tiff reflected as she was sent to school and for the groceries, but her mother wasn't the one on the front line.

Shopping, therefore, had become tainted for Tiff. Sticking with online shopping, which saved her the looks, whispers and nudges, Tiff never developed an extravagant taste – in her head it was part of a lifestyle that lead to disaster. Gradually her shopping needs reduced to only a few work dresses immediately swapped for leggings and a jumper at home. Not glamorous, true, but Tiff had thought she and Gavin were beyond all that.

'Buy something. Now. Go on, stick something in the basket and keep going.'

'I'm not doing it online.' Online was not for purchases of this size in Tiff's head.

'Why not?'

'Blackie would have done it by phone, he liked the personal service. If I'm spending this sort of money, I'm at least going to have the benefit of their customer care and expertise.'

'You're feeling out of your depth and want your hand held.'

'Totally.'

'Fair enough.' Shelby nodded and Tiff sighed in relief as she was cut some slack. 'So make the call. Now. Buy something.' Shelby drummed her fingers on her crossed arms.

The desk phone rang. *Saved by the bell*. Picking it up she was met by silence. About to replace the receiver, Shelby stayed her hand.

'The phone in your hand is the first step. Well done.' Dammit. 'Look, we'll do one together,' Shelby said kindly, pulling over a chair. 'What's an easy one? Not too expensive but essential.'

Tiff handed Shelby the spreadsheet shopping list. She'd printed it off for the satisfaction of striking things through and to procrastinate a little while longer. 'You look at that while I make some tea.' She stealthily laid the phone back in its cradle. 'I need fortification.'

'Wuss,' muttered Shelby, perusing the page.

'Easy for you to say.' By the time she made it back, Shelby had already circled twenty aerobic steps and twenty roll-up mats, plus added twenty Pilates balls and a stack of stretch bands.

'How do you know what to get? I've never seen you

in a gym,' Tiff asked, alarmed at how easy Shelby was making it look.

'The library has *Men's Fitness* magazines. All this stuff is in the pictures.'

'*Men's Fitness?*'

'You should see the abs in there. Buff central without being porny. You need a subscription for your new Reception.' Shelby glanced up from the list at Tiff, who was looking a tad peaky. 'Look, this is basic stuff. It'll store easily while everything else arrives. Well, maybe not the balls, but don't inflate them. Order these now and you'll know you can do it. Then you can get onto the big stuff when you're in the swing of it. When did your builder lady say things should be finished?'

'Three weeks.' Saying it aloud made it scarier. In three weeks, she'd be ready to start classes – classes, which other than Aerobics and Step, courtesy of Amina's sister, she didn't actually have yet.

'These are the best prices, right?' Shelby said, scrutinizing the spreadsheet. Shelby was not one for paying full price on anything.

'Yes,' Tiff said, rolling her eyes. She'd spent the last few nights trawling the internet. It kept her mind off Gavin. She hadn't heard from him and she really thought she would have done. His interest in her inheritance was rather crucial to her plan, but on the other hand she supposed it bought her more time; time to get this right so she could wow his socks right off. Meanwhile, keeping busy had forced her heart to move from the incessant pining to a constant dull ache. She didn't know if that was a win. 'I've picked the quality kit, but I did all the price comparisons. Those three things all come from the same place. See their colour coding? Same colour, same supplier, so I'll try for a decent discount.'

Shelby totted up all the light blue items. 'Okie dokie then. That's more stuff then, but like you say you want the best discount. Get to it.' She placed the phone to Tiff's ear and pointed to the list, before settling into her chair with her tea. Twenty minutes later Tiff found herself hanging up, and sweating profusely. Martin the salesman was possibly her new best friend having advised her to start with fifteen mats, balls and steps, based on the space she'd have, whilst convincing her to up the spec on the multigym equipment. She didn't feel savvy to this part of business yet. Her business purchasing to date had stretched as far as a laptop, bag and Post-it notes. 'I think he got the better of me.'

'You're just used to moving numbers around,' Shelby soothed, giving her an impromptu shoulder massage. Tiff felt like one of the boxers sitting in the corner of the ring between bouts. 'You'll get used to this. You didn't spend more money than you'd intended, you just adjusted the order.'

'But the steps...?'

'Tiff, the classes don't exist yet, you can make them as big as you like. You aren't going to fill them straight off anyway, so by the time the classes are getting full, you'll have a cash flow to cover the extras. It was a sound call,' she encouraged, 'And the last thing you want is the multigym being crappy. No-one wants to hurt themselves on substandard kit. That's a lawsuit right there.' Tiff didn't even want to think about *that* scenario. Pep talk done, Shelby sat herself back down and picked up her copy of *heat* magazine.

'Right,' Tiff agreed, but she didn't sound too confident. In fact, she thought she might have a panic attack.

'Breathe, Tiff,' Shelby didn't even look up from her magazine, as if this occurred all the time. 'You're over-analysing the purchase. It can all be returned, nobody's died. Well, except Blackie obvs, but he's in on the plan.'

The phone rang again making her jump. What were the chances it was Martin ringing to say *Congratulations, as our thousandth customer you get your entire order for free*? He didn't, as the line was silent again. She really did not need faulty phone issues on top of everything else.

A confirmation email popped up on her computer screen. Martin wasn't wasting any time. She had mats, bands, steps and a multigym. And she had balls. She was doing it. She could do this.

She clicked another tab; the company for treadmills, rowing machines and spinning bikes.

'Go on, Tiff, fill your boots.' Shelby turned the page on Ryan Gosling. 'You've already done the multigym. That's like the spine of the equipment. Now you need all the other stuff. In for a penny, in for a pound.'

'Don't say that. It's shed loads of pounds,' sniped Tiff, 'and don't think I don't know you're getting off on spending someone else's money.'

'Hey! Unfair. If the evil witch would let me spend her money, she'd have a better salon.'

'And why exactly aren't you there right now? Tiff asked.

'Publicity shoot for the local paper. Suddenly Lorraine can haul her sorry arse into the shop and my services aren't needed for the afternoon. I'm telling you, that woman—'

Tiff shushed her as the call was picked up and she found herself in the hands of equally slick Colin. She'd picked his website based on his being a local independent and his bragging about how competitive his prices were. As well as sorting her a new ring, he tried to convince her he could offer an even better deal if she also took a Pilates reformer machine. Tiff quickly Googled one, thought it looked like some inquisition torture contraption and said she'd save it for the second phase of her acquisitions strategy. Thank god for the hours she'd invested in watching *The Apprentice* with Gavin.

After that, Tiff had to lie down on the sofa. For once she found its lumps, bumps and protesting springs comforting. Shelby massaging her feet didn't help much to quell the anxiety.

'Argh, what am I doing?' she groaned.

'Building a business, babes. You need to speculate to accumulate. That's what Lord Sugar says.' She gave Tiff a calming pat on the shin. 'If you're worried about the money, you should stop paying for the bloody Premiere Lodge and move in at mine while you flat hunt.'

Tiff *still* hadn't told her she was staying at the gym. There was so much to do in the building, and really the stack of gym mats were proving to be a perfectly adequate mattress, if on the severer side of firm. Firm was supposed to be good for the back, wasn't it?

'I've worked out a deal on the accommodation,' Tiff said. Not quite a lie, more a manipulation of the truth. 'Once this place is up and running, I'll have time to find the right place.' That was true, at least. 'And I plan to buy,' she stated, hoping the decisive tone would appease her friend.

The phone rang, which neatly curbed that conversation, as she crawled up on to her chair to grab it. Shelby grabbed her other foot, continuing the massage.

'Tiffanie Trent,' she said.

The line was silent.

'Hello? Blackie's Gym.' As the silence continued through the receiver, Tiff felt a chill descend on her. Perhaps the phone wasn't faulty at all. She'd experienced this before; the echoing void, the malignant connection. She'd put the fear of it behind her when she'd moved in with Gavin, but now it eked its way back into her. Surely not. Not again. She replaced the receiver and stared at it.

'All right, babes?' Shelby asked.

'Mmm,' Tiff said, trying to rouse herself from her concerns. Why would the calls start again? Why here?

A tap at the door was a welcome distraction.

'Tiff, we can start a day earlier,' Jess said, with a nod of hello towards Shelby, not batting an eyelid at the in-office foot massage.

'That's excellent,' she said. *That's scary*, she thought. 'I've just ordered a ton of kit for delivery on the dates you gave me.'

'Right oh. Catch you later.' Jess moved off, whistling.

Shelby took it as her cue to leave too. With a kiss planted firmly on Tiff's cheek she headed for the door. 'Remember as soon as Jess has the walls up and sorted I'll come over and help you clean.'

'I love you, mate. Have I told you that recently?' Tiff said with a wan smile. She knew Shelby's offer was genuine and she'd be there broom in hand – unless of course a hot date came up in the meantime.

'Not enough. And don't get too excited, I'm expecting a free life-time membership.'

'Of course,' Tiff nodded, 'Snot like you'll do anything with it, so that's no loss.'

'Hmm,' Shelby mused in agreement, 'I'll have my own designated seat in the bar then. See ya, babes.'

Looking at her spreadsheet, with the odd sideways glance at the phone, Tiff felt the room was always much emptier and lonelier when Shelby left it.

Chapter 15

There was generally a lull in the sparring hall's activity around mid-afternoon. The lunchtime crowd had moved off and Ron would tidy the hall ahead of the after-school mob. He'd hardly been upstairs in the last few weeks. While she wasn't desperate for his company Tiff knew she ought to make some effort to fix their relationship, so centred herself when she heard the heavy feet on the stairs.

'Good, you're here.'

She looked up with surprise. Gavin. There was a huge sucking sensation in her stomach and she was pretty sure she heard a thud as her jaw hit the desk. It was the first time she'd laid eyes on him since they broke up.

He was still breath-taking. His jaw was chiselled to perfection and he always, ALWAYS, looked razor-sharp in a suit. Estate agents seemed to pride themselves on their suits and Gavin's collection was impressive. She invariably felt funny in her knickers looking at him in a suit. Which was in direct conflict with her heart which was dancing a tango of pain and hurt.

'I came to see if it was true. About the gym.' *Oh. Not to see me then.* But she didn't say it. She wasn't going to start out being needy.

'You thought I was lying?' Tiff swivelled from side to side. She was hoping the effect was of a global mogul, but really she felt like a kid in Daddy's over-sized office chair.

'No, no of course not,' he said carefully, 'not *lying*. Exaggerating, perhaps?' He cocked his head at her to see if he was right. She'd told him once it made him look boyish and irresistible. He'd done it regularly ever since.

He was inferring she'd deliberately overplayed the facts in order to get at him. How petty did he take her to be? Of course, she *had* blurted it out to get exactly a reaction like this, but it was in fact the truth, which clearly exonerated her.

'Nope. No exaggeration,' she said plainly, resisting the urge to fling her arms open and shout 'Behold! My empire.'

'Well then, congratulations,' he said amiably, which surprised her. She hadn't thought he'd take it so well. Gavin wasn't an envious guy as such; he aspired to be successful and admired people with their own businesses, but he liked to see people earning their successes. *Earning success gives it value,* Tiff – Donald Lynn Frost. So she'd expected him to be put out by hers. Had she really dropped the news on him hoping he'd come spinning over in a pique of envy? Had she done it to show him he should have stuck around, as she was worth a bit now?

Totally.

She knew she had. And if that was why he was here, she'd willingly take him back and share it with him. Shelby would kill her obviously, but how could she turn him down? There was that suit, for starters.

'Thank you,' she mumbled, straightening the paraphernalia on the desk trying to look commanding, but really she wanted to stare at him and drink him in. He wandered into the office and sat in the opposite chair. This was it. This was her moment to start impressing him. She wished she'd had a little forewarning; a hairbrush and some mascara wouldn't have gone amiss. She smoothed her unruly curls as subtly as possible, as she sat up straight and tried to channel Karren Brady.

'So what have you got yourself?' He looked around. 'Three storey self-contained office space—' His voice had shifted into estate agent mode.

'Well two storeys are currently office, downstairs is obviously—' she interjected, but he wasn't listening.

'Mixed usage, I'm guessing a total of about three thousand square metres, yes?'

'I'm not—' she hadn't looked at details like that. Jess had done all the measurements.

'The dedicated off-road parking is an asset.'

'Yes, Blackie was always chuffed with the parking.'

'I'm sure you'd rent it out for a decent value Tiff, but honestly that's a huge faff, unless you engage a management agent and then you can kiss goodbye to their cut every month.'

'No, that's not what I'm doing,' she said quickly, for once managing to complete a sentence. But she could see from his gaze and the way he was steepling his fingertips, he was in the zone. His espousing zone.

'Good girl, I knew you'd be smart.' He thought she was smart! 'Selling to developers is definitely the way to go.' He caught himself as a thought hit him, a look of horror crossing his face. 'You weren't thinking of developing it yourself, were you? You know nothing about house development.'

That was a tad harsh, given she'd watched hundreds of Sarah Beeny shows, and made all his design wishes come true in their flat. But Tiff took his point.

'No, I—' she began, but he took it as a starting pistol and set off again.

'There's a raft of decent firms who'd be interested in this plot. I can connect you, but don't leave it too long.

You want the money out as soon as you can before it starts racking up bills and eating into your savings. No doubt a place like this bleeds heat. It's got money-pit written all over it.'

Tiff felt a stab of outrage, as if he'd insulted her first-born. It made her chip in flippantly, 'That's okay, Blackie left me money too.'

'What?' His head recoiled slightly.

She shrugged at him, playing it cool. Was that a tinge of envy? Was it? Now his ears were pricking up.

'He left me funds to sort things,' she said, willing him to be excited for her and then to please get onto the wanting her back part.

'That's fair enough, I suppose. Decent, in fact. Can't leave someone a fiscal drain and expect them to keep running it without some finance. Hopefully it's enough to get you through the interim until you can sell.' He was back on his pre-determined track. 'This is an up-and-coming area, Tiff.' He stopped and had looked vaguely shifty, 'Okay, there's other parts of town which are probably next in line, but I wouldn't wait.'

Clearly he was in full estate agent spiel at this point, because it was going to take more than some new housing to bring this area up. A fitness club though would help bring it to within a sniff of 'up-and-coming'.

'I'm not selling it, Gav,' she said, firmly, but with a

smile. It was time to lay it on the line and watch the admiration, possibly awe, dawn on his face.

'Pardon? But you said you didn't want to develop—'

'I don't.' She cut him off for once, but only to cut to the chase. She was too excited to wait for him to get there. 'Not develop it into houses.'

'Tiff,' he sighed, as if she didn't understand the first thing about, well, anything, 'I seriously doubt you'll get planning to build anything other than houses here. A factory? For what? The industry's gone. Councils need more housing.'

'Not industry. In fact, not changing the use at all. I want to use what I've got.'

'Bookkeeping? You want to extend the business? Three floors worth of people?' Why wasn't he getting it? She wanted the dawning! Okay then, more clues, but it was killing her.

'No, Gavin. This building is a gym.'

'It's a boxing club. And that's one room downstairs.'

'It's more than that actually. This floor is part of the club too. I intend to spread it all the way up to the roof.' *Oh!* thought Tiff, *a roof garden*. Could she do that? The thumping in her heart stepped up a notch and she noticed it had nothing to do with Gavin who was staring at her slack-jawed. She took the opportunity.

'Blackie left me the money to do the place up to be a proper gym – you know, unisex, health and fitness.

I'm having the upstairs gutted out to home the social club, this floor'll have a studio for classes and the body sculpting area, and the boxing club downstairs will get a comprehensive overhaul.' She stopped and, just because she could, cocked her head at him, watching him process it all. She prayed she appeared ambitious and driven and smart and industrious and brave and extremely capable and, bottom-line, desirable.

'But, you've never set foot in a gym,' he babbled. Where was the dawning!?

'I've worked in this one every week for eight years. Blackie and I discussed these ideas for half of them.'

'You never mentioned them to me.' He sounded affronted. She wasn't sure why.

'Actually I started to a couple of times, but you always said, "Let's not talk shop at home".' Oddly enough though, Gavin had always been ready to moan about missed viewings, gazumping and clients getting cold feet on the eve of completion.

'Well, you never made it sound serious,' he said, sounding sulky. Was he pouting? He was taking this so personally. He must really feel they'd had a lack of communication in their relationship.

'Well, it wasn't,' she said gently, letting her mogul persona go, wanting to placate him, 'Not then. It was pie-in-the-sky stuff. I didn't own a gym back then.'

'Boxing club,' he corrected, as if that made it less of

172

a deal. Definitely sulky. 'You should have shared Blackie's plans with me. I feel totally let down, Tiff. Things could have been so different.' Different?

'Gav, I'm sorry,' Tiff said, baffled. 'It really wasn't proper plans – Blackie wasn't up for any of it. I never imagined you'd be so bothered or even interested.' Had she missed the signals that he'd wanted to do something bigger with her, some combined ambition? But owning the gym hadn't even been on the cards. Was this what the separate paths thing had been about? A combined project? Because honestly, they could start this path together right here, right now. She just needed him to say the words.

'You know how many properties I get in this part of town Tiff, and what a pain they are to shift. If I'd had that nugget of info, Blackie's plans for a fitness club, I'd at least have had something to work with. You can't polish a turd, you know, but you can stick sequins on it.' She had a feeling he wasn't quoting Buddha. 'The boxing club was never a draw, but a *fitness* centre...' He looked at her bug-eyed, like she'd missed the most rudimentary of points and ruined his life.

'The boxing club is the cherry on the cake,' she pointed out. He wasn't getting these were *her* ideas, *she* was the ambitious one here, not Blackie. 'It's my USP, my first stream of income and hopefully a source of members to the rest of the club.' Tiff had switched to

The Apprentice mode again, trying to knock him back on track. She knew this wasn't what he'd been used to hearing from her and she'd hoped he'd be blown away. Instead he looked confused.

And then he looked sort of... full of pity.

'Tiff. Sweetheart,' he began slowly. Calling her sweetheart brought a small lump of joy to her throat, but all the other signs were *off*. 'You can't possibly think this is a good idea.'

'I do——' she started, but he cut her off with the slow shaking of his head.

'Sweetheart, I know you have your little business, and it ticks over admirably. It fills your day neatly and you earn enough to cover all the bills we had, but taking on a thing like this, trying to make it something more, that's not realistic, is it? It's just not you.' He got up and moved around to sit on the side of the desk. Reaching out, he gently tipped her face up by her chin so he had her full attention. 'Sometimes, we need to accept our limitations, don't we? We need to see when we reach our ceiling. That's what I was saying at *Lorenzo's*. You're there already. You've reached your limits. You've no need to make mistakes like this.'

'But Gav...' she began, but faltered. She wanted to say she'd already taken it on. And it wasn't a mistake, because she'd planned it; she'd done the numbers. She slept with a calculator by the bed. She'd been over the figures a hundred times, because there were parts that scared the pants off her, but she knew her numbers and it wasn't *that* risky a venture. The money was there, just, to cover what she wanted to do. But she didn't say any of that. Because she couldn't get her mouth to contradict him, not when he was looking at her like that. That small lump of joy in her throat felt like cement now. 'You ... You don't think I'm capable, do you?'

'Oh, Tiff, you are capable of many things,' he gave her a wink that made her stomach wrench, 'but not business of this size. Taking on staff? You've only ever worked by yourself, for yourself.'

Tiff couldn't disagree with that. She hadn't, but she reckoned she *could*. Couldn't she? She believed decency, diligence, listening and respect were key to man-management and she could give all of those a fair go. But he'd said she was *limited*. The word flashed neon before her eyes, accompanied by a mortifying klaxon.

'Is that what you've always thought? That I'm limited?'

'Tiff, there's nothing wrong with knowing your limits,' he said, as if offering her a blessing. That was a yes then. "*Happiness is to know your limits and be happy with them*", Tiff – Romain Rolland. It's when you try to go beyond them, you fall foul. I still have lots of scope before I reach mine – that's why I'm still striving.' He took a breath, clearly not done yet. 'Let me illustrate; you and I, we were like a horse and cart.'

'A team,' Tiff agreed, nodding dumbly, numbed by his words.

'Well, more that I was drawing you along.' He may as well have slapped her.

'You consider me *ballast*?'

'Don't be unfair to yourself Tiff, the cart can be important too. It facilitates things, brings things to market and so on, but the horse is the driving force, isn't it? It can race off on its own and the cart goes nowhere. Unless, of course, the untethered cart rolls downhill – like taking on a business beyond its capabilities – and then it's in all sorts of trouble.'

Tiff could only look at him aghast. She was NOT a bloody cart. She wanted to say so, but the horror of this conversation kept her mute.

'And a *fitness* centre, Tiff? Really?' He gave her a speedy once over, followed by his mouth pulling up to one side in a 'you know' kind of way. Instinctively Tiff pulled the hem of her sweatshirt further down, but her prickling eyes were locked on his. Just as Ron had been giving his honest opinion saying she couldn't do it, so Gavin's eyes said he was being equally sincere. She shrank with the crushing disappointment. He thought so little of her. She'd apparently been some charity load to his beast of burden for the last decade.

Watching his face now, the dawning was all hers; she was never going to impress him. However brilliant her plan, his view of her was set. Whether she owned a building and business or not, he still thought the same of her as he had at *Lorenzo's*. Which, pain aside, begged one question:

'Gavin?' She stacked her hands on the desk to control their shaking. 'You coming here today? Why exactly was that?'

'We lived together for a long time, Tiff,' he said 'and while we've agreed to go our separate ways, I thought it would be heartless not to offer you my expertise and advice when you'd been lumbered with this... this...' he looked around the room searching for the word, 'prehistoric behemoth.'

'You came here to get business off me?' she asked, with a gulp. 'After dumping me?'

'Now Tiff, we agreed. We had different paths, although yours has changed somewhat since, but it need only be a blip and you can settle back to where you were again, only significantly better off. I daresay I should be sending you sales particulars now instead of rentals.'

'You. Came. Here. To. Tout. For. Business,' she reiterated through gritted teeth. Her hands were still stacked, but more gripped than poised.

'I'm a businessman, Tiff. A good salesman always makes the best of an opportunity,' he said defensively.

'The important difference here is you stand to gain from my help. It's win/win for both of us. I don't see why you're getting in a tizzy.'

'You should go now, Gavin,' Tiff said as calmly as possible. Her heart was singing a sorry lament in her chest, and yet the rest of her; her head, her skin and every morsel of sense, forced her to head for the door and stand by it, fists clenched behind her back, glaring at him until he got the hint and left. She stood like that, trembling, until she heard the front doors slam in his wake. Then she hoofed it into her storeroom, and threw herself onto her makeshift bed, cursing its firmness as she landed with a face-smacking thud, and finally let out the hot disappointed tears.

Her heart had just broken all over again. Only this time, rather than a gaping ragged wound, Tiff felt the chasm fill with fire-spitting molten resolution. For once she saw value in one of Aaron's pictures, one that hung in the stairwell: *Know your limitations and then defy them*. She'd show Gavin what she could do. Her bloody cart would be the one which turned into a horseless carriage, and his stupid horse would be put out to pasture, or something. His metaphors were moronic. Why hadn't she seen it before?

She was going to make a success of this place, but not to wow him, simply to show herself the sky was her limit.

Chapter 16

They met in the entrance of the community centre on Adey Street, under the sorry glow of the lone street lamp, looking somewhat awkward.

'Can't believe you're making me do this. We are supposed to be friends,' Shelby griped.

'I'll remind you of that next time you make me lie to a date you've double-booked,' said Tiff, sternly. Since she'd seen Gavin, she'd upped her game and was taking no prisoners. 'This is what friends do. They help out in times of need.'

'But, honestly? There are limits,' Shelb insisted. Natalie watched the exchange silently, eyes wide. She was apparently resigned to their imminent fate. Or else she was too freaked out to speak, having left Ed in the gym. Tiff had simply collected her, not giving her any chance for excuses.

'Get over yourself, Shelb. It's just a Zumba class. One class, to see what it's about, what they do and how it makes you feel.'

'I can tell you all of that for free. Fu—'

'I said I'd pay for us all,' Tiff defended herself, but Shelby was not to be placated.

'It'll be a hot room full of fat women trying to imitate a gorgeous skinny-arsed dancer and failing miserably. There's going to be grunting, sweating and absolutely no co-ordination whatsoever.'

'I thought you said you hadn't been before?'

'Of course I haven't,' Shelby sounded insulted.

'Then how do you know all of this?'

'I saw it on the *Six o'clock Show*. That was enough.'

'Stop whinging. We're going in,' Tiff said, moving towards the door.

'You owe me,' grumbled Shelby, following. 'Like, huge. Big time.'

'Yeah, yeah, whatevs.' Perhaps bringing Shelby was a mistake, or an unnecessary pain. She wasn't expecting miracles from her classes.

Of the many people milling around in the hall, few were fat. There was a wide spectrum of sizes in fact, not the solid mass of plus-sizes Shelby had prophesized. Tiff made this point to her friend who suddenly developed a case of selective hearing. Noticeably Shelby claimed a spot in the back row, next to a man who was more padded than others.

'Would Ed and the lads do this?' she asked Natalie, who answered with a simple snort. Enough said.

The lights dimming made Tiff feel infinitely better, although she wouldn't have said no to a paper bag for her head. This was so not her thing; the exercising in front of other people. Dancing in clubs with Shelby, she'd been known to do that, but this was different. She was going to have to memorize the steps, keep up with the pace, not faint. She'd have to discretely keep checking herself for sweat patches too. In summary, she was feeling self-conscious. The sulky expression on Shelby's face said she wasn't alone. Shelby had at least been smart in picking a spot by one of the large industrial fans, whose very presence Tiff found ominous.

Natalie though was clearly feeling the buzz. She was straight in when Leonie, the instructor, kicked things off from the stage, bouncing on her toes before the music even began. She had an innate sense of rhythm and could pick up the routines quickly. Either she'd had some dance classes in her early years or she was the lovechild of a Salsa king. But what was even clearer to Tiff was Natalie loved being out in an environment like this. Though fiercely concentrating on the instructor and her directions, her face was lit up in a way Tiff hadn't seen before. Unlike at the gym, here she was thriving as she merengued around in circles, or jumped like a warrior in the African routine. Her insane grin got wider and wider with each command Leonie shouted down her headset mike. She wasn't so much sweating as *glowing*.

'You've got to have a class like this,' she gasped at the halftime break, her cheeks like two shiny red apples.

'Aren't you knackered?' asked Tiff. Tiff was puffing, bent over, trying to not die. Natalie'd definitely been working at a different level from both her and Shelby.

'Not yet. I'll be exhausted by the end and I'll feel it tomorrow, but my heart's going like the clappers and the music just takes you along, doesn't it?'

'It can take me along right out of the door,' grouched Shelby, her pink fringe plastered to her forehead. Tiff took a moment to affectionately brush it to the side with her fingertips.

'Shush now, Grumpy, think of the calories we're burning.' That look Gavin had given her, appraising her shape, kept flashing across her memory and spurring her on.

'Right. I'll think of it as clearing way for the bag of chips I'm buying on the way home.'

Their conversation was interrupted by Leonie's shout for everyone to get back in the mix. She scurried into a Beyoncé routine which involved more gyrating than Tiff had done in years. Judging by how some of the women were twerking, Tiff wondered whether she was missing some vertebrae.

Over the course of the rest of the lesson, two things

became obvious to Tiff; firstly, she was incapable of moving her feet and clapping at the same time, or *in* time. Looking around, she seemed to be alone in this impediment and vowed to practise in the solitary confines of her storeroom. Secondly, even when unable to breathe, Shelby could still swear like a trooper.

As Tiff was about to keel over during the warm down, the instructor made the final upward stretches and brought the class to an end. She was feeling spaced from the exertion.

Spaced or not, Tiff still managed to keep to her business agenda. She took a note of the make of Zumba sticks. And the fans. She was going to check all the windows in the studio could open as soon as she got back. She'd given up monitoring her armpits a while back, but then everyone in sleeves was sporting sweat-patches by the end. For the first time she saw the point in those vesty tops, other than purely to smugly show off toned arms.

'So what do we think?' Tiff asked as they hit the cold air outside and groaned their way back down the street. 'Is it a goer?'

'What's the criteria?' asked Shelb, 'Torture, near death, misery?'

'Pretty much. That's what gym activity is, isn't it?' Personally, she'd always resisted the urge until now. But now she'd done it – and looking beyond the fact she could hardly breathe properly, she was drenched in sweat and if her makeup was anything like Shelby's then she looked like a clown – she'd rather enjoyed it. 'Let's be honest Shelb, it was all right. It didn't kill us, and I'm feeling smug for having done it. Smug counts for something, doesn't it?' She hooked an arm through Shelby's, giving her a small cajoling nudge.

'That's the halo effect,' Natalie piped up. 'It's like some lunatic law that time in the gym makes you a better human being.'

'Well, I'm happy to milk the smug factor,' Tiff said. 'I don't have any qualms about that. I'm not picky about anyone's motives, so long as they come.'

'There's your ad campaign, right there,' Shelby said, wryly. '*We don't give a tosh, just bring your dosh.*'

'No,' Tiff said, horrified. 'That's not what I meant. I'm not here to judge anyone for why they're coming. It should be a place people can feel comfortable, at home even. If they're clinically obese and want to shed pounds, or if a husband said something daft about muffin tops, then we can help without making people feel bad. And if they want to come to meet other people, they should be able to do that too, without feeling like they're Billy-no-mates. See?'

'I'd come to be with Ed,' said Natalie, 'which I suppose others might judge too, but I'll be doing my own thing.' Tiff smiled to herself. Even if Natalie didn't take the job, she was willing to use the building to help her and Ed move forward.

'That's great, Nat. So I'll sign you up for a Zumba class then?' she asked, turning them back to the original question.

'Oh yeah, that was a hoot. I haven't laughed so much in ages. I'm going to hurt tomorrow, but right now, I feel great.'

'I feel sweaty,' muttered Shelby, as if she was dirty.

'Aw, poor baby,' cooed Tiff. 'Not used to breaking a sweat painting nails or plucking eyebrows, are you?'

'Girlfriend, I've broken more sweats than you've had hot dinners,' retorted Shelby sassily, 'I just prefer my exercise under the covers and not on my own.'

Having been TMIed for years with Shelby's sexploits, Tiff was tempted to say she'd expect her to be half the size then. Obviously sex didn't burn off as many calories as Shelby thought.

'Well, maybe a body-toning class would be better for you then, Shelby, to dove-tale with your sexercise regime.'

'Maybe I'll stay in the bar and find willing training partners for that regime,' Shelby said.

'I'll take a finder's fee.'

'Pimp.'

'Slut.'

'Now, now girls. Play nicely,' said Natalie, gathering

Tiff and Shelby had been bantering like this for years, but without being quite comfortable with it. Neither girl could understand the other's lifestyle; Shelby's insatiable appetite for different men and Tiff ostensibly being satisfied with one man for so long. Yet secretly Shelby wanted to find The One, and Tiff had once in a blue moon caught herself wondering whether there was more to it than her and Gavin's playbook.

'I think it's definitely worth a go,' decided Tiff, mentally slotting it into the schedule, 'The Zumba.'

'Definitely,' agreed Natalie. 'I'd come and some of the girls from Iceland might.'

'So I'll have to find a teacher. What did we think about Leonie? I've got her card, though she might not be available. Maybe we should try out some others?'

'No!' stated Shelby. Was that panic? 'Leonie was good. If you like that sort of thing,' she quickly qualified. 'She was personable, but strict. She took no crap, but she let you do as much as you could manage. She'd be great.'

Tiff smiled. She'd thought so too, but a second opinion was helpful. Other people supported her plans. She told herself daily that Gavin was wrong about her. From now on she was listening to her allies. Life was already better, felt more positive for it.

'You just don't want to trial another class,' she said.

'True, but purely because I can spot quality when I see it. I don't need to shop around after that class.'

Tiff squeezed Shelby's arm fondly.

'You're so full of it, doll.'

'Ha!' said Shelby. 'I found you, didn't I?' And that was true; Shelby had adopted Tiff in college, finding her sitting alone in the darker corner of the cafeteria and dragging her reluctantly into the light. Tiff would always be grateful for that, even though she saw it for what it really was; the new-to-the-area less-than-svelte loud girl and the scarred local pariah forming an alliance. She'd seen enough teen movies to astutely identify that scenario.

She pulled Shelby closer, pulling her along, ever-thankful to have her on Team Tiff.

Chapter 17

With the chippie himself having caught Shelby's eye, Natalie and Tiff ambled back to the club, Natalie to meet Ed, Tiff supposedly to finish some paperwork. The full car park was pleasing. People clearly didn't only come because of Blackie. That, at least, should keep Ron happy.

Vigilant after her run-in with Aaron, the lone figure in the shadows near the entrance caught Tiff's eye, only the shape didn't match his, nor the usual physique of the gym clientele. It kept turning in circles as if confused. Reaching the door, Tiff saw it was an old woman dressed in a floral dress, green cardy and burgundy velour slippers. She kept looking at the door, deciding to go in, then changing her mind.

'Can I help you?' Tiff asked, gently. The woman looked at her and her face lit up.

'Ah Tiffanie, honey. I'm looking for Michael. His dinna's gettin cold.'

'Nanna Bea?'

'Yes, child,' she said, as if this was obvious. But Tiff hadn't laid eyes on Mike's grandmother since they were dating. Tiff remembered a huge force of a woman, tough as nails but soft underneath and fully able to smother an adult with her enormous bosom. Now Tiff saw a much smaller woman, sunken with age and fragile, her once-dense, black hair wispy and grey. The fierceness in her eyes had waned too, but they still looked as pleased to see Tiff as always. Tiff had scoffed hundreds of dinners at Nanna Bea's table; she'd done the best home-cooking and her door had always been open.

'I tell him to be home for dinna, but he forget. Jeezam, that boy!' Tiff had always loved the lilt of her Jamaican accent. Mike's impressions had been hysterical, particularly when Nanna had clipped him around the ear for his cheek. Andy Fellner had walked out when Mike became big enough to punch back, leaving Nanna to pick up the pieces of a broken daughter whose fragile heart would shortly give out and an angry grandson who wanted to fight the world. Aside from showering him with her love, Nanna's remit to bring him up had also included a keen interest in his manners. 'He only has boxing in his head. And you, fi sure,' she added and laughed, though it wasn't half the deep raucous laugh Tiff recalled. 'He love you so much, Tiffanie. Any fool can see that.' Nanna Bea started for the door.

189

Although determined in her task, the old woman was confused.

'Nanna, how old is Mikey?' she asked softly.

'Why Tiffanie Trent, don't you be teasin' me, girl. You know full well he just turn seventeen; you buy him that digital watch yourself.'

'Right. Sorry Nanna,' Tiff said, contrite. While Nanna's long-term memory was obviously intact, her short-term cognition seemed to have gone west. Tiff now understood at least one of the things Mike was back in the area for. Why hadn't he said? Obviously not while she was shouting at him, but when they'd met after the will reading? She'd have looked in on her. He must have known she'd have looked in on her. Tiff stopped. Of course he wouldn't. They hadn't spoken in years, and Tiff had cut the old lady off without so much as a goodbye, because she'd been angry and ashamed.

Not that Nanna seemed to be holding it against her. It was lovely to see her. Then Tiff remembered she hadn't even asked after her when Mike'd lent an ear to her woes. She felt herself colouring with shame.

'Nanna? Come up to the office while we find that grandson of yours. I'll make some tea.'

Tiff lead her up the stairs and settled her in her chair, keen to make amends.

'Still take sugar, Nanna?'

'Jus a toops, sweetie.' Though she asked for just a little, Nanna meant three spoonfuls. Tiff felt a spark of delight as she remembered.

It was clear Nanna Bea had wandered off from either her own home, or a care home. The slippers and lack of coat suggested no prior planning. But there were many old people's homes around town and short of working through the phone book, she didn't know where to start.

Glancing at her bag she saw her phone sticking out of it and remembered what it now had on it. Mike's number. Bingo.

'Tiff,' he said, like it was a fact. *Doh*. Her number was programmed on his phone too.

'Mike.'

'Well, this brings back memories, hearing your voice down the phone line.'

'Phone lines? Now you're showing your age.' He laughed at that. She envied him his ease in their exchanges. They had her jittery.

'Do you want rid of the ring already?'

'No. Nothing like that. I'm having a blast from the past of my own actually.'

He drew a breath, but didn't say anything, waiting instead for her to elaborate.

'I've got Nanna Bea here in my office.'

'What?!' Now he'd found his tongue.

'She wants you to know you're late for your dinner.'

'Jerk chicken, wid black beans, and plantain, tell him,' Nanna interjected. 'His favourite.'

Tiff's stomach growled at the memories.

'It's jerk chicken, with black beans,' she repeated.

'And plantain,' Nanna prompted with a frown at Tiff for editing. Always particular with her information, was Nanna.

'And plantain,' she amended, earning her a prim nod and smile.

'She's supposed to be safe in the home,' said Mike.

'Well, I think she's been out for a walk,' Tiff said calmly.

'I come to get him,' the old lady insisted.

'Yes, but he's fighting away today Nanna, which is why I've had to telephone him,' Tiff told her, which seemed to placate her.

'I'll get the home to collect her. I'm an hour away. Can she stay with you for a bit?'

'Sure. They'll need to bring a coat and outdoor shoes. She's in her slippers.'

'Oh god,' he said. Tiff instinctively knew he'd put his head in his hand. 'It's dementia, Tiff.'

'I figured it was something like that, but she found the gym and she recognised me immediately. Your long-term memory is excellent, isn't it Nanna?'

'Nuttin wrong wid *my* memory,' Nanna Bea said with

indignation, 'unlike Michael, who's forgettin his own dinna.'

'There you see? She's on top form,' Tiff assured Mike, then to Nanna, 'Mikey's worried about you. But there's no need is there? You're right as rain.'

'Fi sure, honey. You always were a smart girl. I tell him dat.' Nanna flashed her a warm smile. 'Michael love you, Tiffanie. Writes you love letters, but he too shy to send dem.'

'Okaaay,' Mike cut in sharply, 'I'm sorting her collection before she embarrasses me any further.'

Tiff looked at the old lady and at the clock. It was only nine.

'Give me the address. I'll take her.'

'You don't need to do that. I don't want to put you out.'

'Seriously? Nanna Bea's fed me so many fabulous dinners,' Nanna Bea beamed with delight, 'it's the least I can do.'

There was a pause as he thought it through, but Tiff stepped in.

'Let me do this for her. Please Mikey.' She felt slightly more in control of things now, the business, her life; it was time she started making space for others.

He gave her the address.

'Right. Take care then,' she said and things were back to normal; slightly awkward.

'Right,' he said, 'Bye then. And Tiff?'

'Yes?'

'Thank you.'

'My pleasure,' she said, meaning every word.

*

Tiff's skin was tingling in anticipation as she passed back through the care home foyer. She was heading back to trial the new staff showers at the gym. She'd feel pummelled, exhausted and invigorated all at once. The Ladies' changing room was a huge improvement on the men's downstairs, in terms of shower pressure, aesthetics and odour. The men's locker room smelled, there was no two ways about it; testosterone, which wasn't always a bad thing, but predominantly it was feet, socks and sweat. And Lynx, which didn't cloak it but added more cloy to the cocktail. Bad as it was though, Tiff still preferred it to the almost overpowering potpourri scent of the care home, which had her hustling towards the exit as soon as she was sure Nanna was out for the count.

Her mobile rang.

'Hey Nats, what's up?' They'd only been apart for a couple of hours.

'Can you hear me?' Natalie's voice was a rasping whisper.

'Only just,' Tiff said. 'You got a cold?' In spite of the baking heat in the home, she instinctively pulled her coat closer around herself. The absolute worst thing that could happen was her coming down with something. She didn't have the time to be laid out with so much as a sniffle.

'No, I'm just trying not to be heard,' Natalie responded.

'Where are you?'

'I'm in the pub. With the lads.'

'Sounds like it's empty.' There was none of the banter she'd have expected from the lads after their training sessions.

'Oh, no. It's heaving, but I'm in the loos,' Natalie clarified.

'Then why are you whispering, Nats?'

'Oh,' Natalie said, flummoxed and adjusted her volume to normal, 'Right. Yes.'

'What's up, Secret Squirrel?'

'Ron's setting up his own boxing club,' Natalie blurted out.

At first Tiff couldn't get her head around what she'd said.

'What?' Now it was Tiff doing the whispering.

'He's just told the lads. Starting next week, when you shut the hall for the refurb, he'll open his club. He's said it's early days, so it'll be quite sparse, but the equipment will increase as the membership grows and he's said all the lads are welcome, but he said it in a "You're expected" way, and he pointed out there'd be no trainer at yours anymore.'

'Oh. My. God.'

'He's rented an industrial unit over on Dalton Lane, says it'll look like something out of *Fight Club* initially, but the ring's on its way.'

Tiff felt physically sick. 'That snake. He said he was on board. He said he was staying.'

'Only until he could sort his own thing, obviously.'

'If he'd said, I could have been looking for someone else...' Tiff said weakly. She'd slumped onto a chair in the reception area and was eyeing the drinks machine for a gin option. Sweat was beginning to break across her forehead and it wasn't a catch-up dose from the Zumba. This came from a bottle branded Panic & Dismay.

'Yeah right Tiff, because *that* would be in his interest,' Natalie said. 'He doesn't want the competition. He's stitched you up good and proper.'

'Yeah, I get that, thanks Nats,' Tiff snapped.

'Sorry.'

'No, I'm sorry,' Tiff sighed, rubbing her face, 'you didn't have to tip me off. I suppose Ed'll move with Ron.' If Ed moved, maybe Natalie would move too and she'd be without her receptionist-to-be to boot.

'We haven't discussed it yet. I nipped off to call you

straight away, but Ed definitely looks uncomfortable. The younger lads, well, they'll go wherever the action is, especially if you don't have a trainer.'

'I know.' Tiff's head was firmly in her hand.

'I don't suppose you can hold Ron to his contract?'

'Ha!' Tiff laughed ruefully. 'You know Blackie. No contracts. His word was his bond and all that. They probably shook on it.'

'He should stick to his word then,' Natalie said crossly.

'Yeah but his agreement was with Blackie, not me.'

'But he told you he'd stay.'

Tiff exhaled long and hard. 'We only talked about carrying on as things were. It was nothing formal, we didn't shake on it. Oh, bugger,' Tiff admonished herself. 'From now on everyone has a contract. That's if I've any staff left.' She hadn't meant it as a prompt, but she realised Natalie had gone silent. 'Natalie, I don't want to put you in a difficult position. You've been a real friend calling me and I appreciate it. I completely understand if you need to go with Ed.' The thought depressed her though. Natalie had come out of her shell as well as out of the gym. She'd become a friend and Tiff didn't have a multitude of those. The idea of Natalie returning to her old existence was distressing.

'I don't know what Ed's thinking yet,' Natalie said carefully, and Tiff screwed up her face to quell the sting in her eyes, 'but if the receptionist job's still going, then

I'm in. Ron might think it's okay to poach the customers, but I don't. I'm not sitting in a cold unit watching him do so.'

'But what about...' Tiff didn't know how to say it. Your mistrust of your husband? How exactly did one put that?

Natalie sighed. 'Things are better since I stopped hanging around the gym, Tiff. Between Ed and me, I mean. More relaxed. And the thing is, I'm happier doing other things, helping you, rather than sitting there with the lads ribbing us. I think Ed sees me venturing out as him winning my trust. Maybe he has, but at the end of the day, I just have to have faith, don't I? Or else what's the point?'

'Oh, Nats,' Tiff breathed. Talk about a breakthrough. *There* was the silver lining. Only a thin one though, in a whacking great cloud, because Ron was a heinous traitor and her business plan had just fallen on its arse, possibly bringing the entire enterprise crashing cata-strophically to its knees, rendering her penniless, demoralised and still homeless. Having hung up and ditched the phone beside her, she let rip her feelings. 'Bloody bastard, bugger, bum.'

She stood corrected on her sniffle fear. *This* was the absolute worst thing that could happen.

Chapter 18

Tiff wasn't prone to histrionics – plenty of crying recently as it turned out; predominantly pitiful weeping – but not hysteria. But right now, in light of the call and given she was alone in the foyer of a building largely populated with the sedated or geriatric-of-hearing, she desperately wanted to exercise her right to a good old howl. One from the pit of her gut, Munch style.

So much for crowing '*In your face!*' to the nay-sayers. She'd lost the gem in her crown. Now she'd have just any old start-up gym, in a duff part of town. The climb had gone from Ben Nevis to Everest within the space of a phone call from some toilets. In lieu of the howling, which she couldn't bring herself to execute in public, she scrunched her face up and let out a long low screech.

'Tiff?' Mike was standing in the doorway, staring at her. His jeans, T-shirt and leather jacket ensemble coupled with the motorbike helmet in his hand, made him look bad, in a very good way. She shook the thought from her head, hoping he hadn't witnessed her ptero-dactyl impression.

'What are you doing here, Mike?'

'Came to check on her. And to bollock this place about their security.'

'She pegged out as soon as they got her into bed. Otherwise she's fine. Told me to "walk good" as I left,' Tiff smiled, 'Haven't heard that in years.'

Mike looked relieved and sat down in the adjacent seat. Tiff was aware of the closeness of their legs. Slightly rattled, she said 'I was thinking of visiting her soon. Would that be okay?'

A soft look crossed his face.

'She'd like that.' He looked pleased, but then the smile fell. 'Only some days, she might not know you. She forgets and...'

'Mikey. It's okay,' she said, gently. He was getting upset having to explain. He'd always been close to his Nanna and had never made any secret of the fact he adored her, in spite of frequent ear clippings.

'How often do you see her?'

'Now, every couple of weeks. Used to be once a month, since she stopped coming to me a few years ago. I used to send a car for her. Made her feel like royalty.'

A couple of years. Tiff wondered whether Blackie knew. He hadn't mentioned it to her, but then Blackie'd had his own code when it came to tact.

'I think Blackie might have enjoyed seeing you,' she tested. The soft look on Mikey's face dissipated.

'Think I'll disagree with you there. Blackie said his piece to me years ago.' Tiff's confusion must have been easily read. He shook his head. 'S'water under the bridge now, right? I reckon Blackie had his own plans, he just forgot to keep everyone consulted.'

Tiff didn't know what he was talking about, but didn't get to ask him before he changed the subject. 'How's the gym going?'

'I thought it was going well,' she said. Her normal PR face would have curtailed it at 'fine', but she was still feeling floored and it was easier to tell the truth. 'It's bloody scary – buying kit, booking instructors, the refurbishment – but it's happening, and that's bloody exciting too.'

'But?'

'But, I was relying on the boxing, and apparently Ron's setting up his own club. It'll open while I close for the refurb.'

Sitting back in the chair, Mike quickly joined the dots. 'How many members will you lose?'

'No idea,' admitted Tiff, 'I've only just been tipped off. I don't know who comes out of convenience or loyalty to Ron. I'm not Blackie. They certainly don't have any loyalty to me. I get that. All they want is a good trainer, in a decent location and venue.'

'So you're still in with a shot.' She hadn't got to thinking positively yet.

'I suppose. They haven't gone yet, and it'll take time before he's properly up and running. I'll have to find a coach flipping fast. Unfortunately, in the interim, I'll have to rely on the new classes to draw customers. They won't fill immediately. Those things grow by word of mouth.'

'You aren't thinking of backing out, are you?' Mike's tone struck her as challenging. No sympathy there then. Nice.

'No,' Tiff said sulkily, 'aside from being financially committed up to my eyeballs, I want to do this.'

'There you go then.' He laced his fingers together across his stomach. His *taut* stomach, Tiff noticed. How did that work – sitting without a tyre forming? He looked at her expectantly. Apparently this was fairly clear to him; she wanted to do it, so what was her problem?

'Yeah I know, Mikey, but it's a bit of a kick in the teeth when one of your staff is disloyal and the crux of your business plan disappears.'

'Tiff, this is business. If things go tits-up, you revise and adjust. It was never going to be easy and it's a steep learning curve. Plans have glitches; you find the solutions or you squidge the parameters. Everyone has to do that. People will stab you in the back. Don't assume it, but be prepared for it. You've said before Ron wanted the business.' Here was this new Mike again, considered and plain speaking.

'Yes, but he said he was on board.'

'People lie,' he said brusquely, 'To be honest you were being a bit naive thinking he was loyal.'

'All right, Mike, no need to cushion it,' she grumped at him. She knew this, she should have seen it coming. She didn't need him to rub it in.

'But look at it this way, now you can pick your *own* trainer, not one you've inherited.'

'Sure, smart-arse, I'll just call the job centre and ask for a boxing coach. Pretty sure it doesn't work like that. I doubt signing on's your next step.'

'Or,' Mike said, ignoring her petulance with a self-satisfied smile, 'you could ask your smart-arse world boxing champion first-love to see who's available.'

'You'd do that?' Admittedly they were on amicable terms now, but she hadn't expected him to do her any favours.

'Sure,' he said with a shrug. 'I reckon I can find time between polishing my prize belts to make some calls.'

Tiff preferred doing things herself so she didn't owe anyone anything. However, feeling bone-tired and betrayed, she saw she was royally stuffed, which made her choice a pragmatic one.

'That would be really useful, Mikey. Thank you.'

'No problem. I think Blackie's legacy demands it. From a philanthropic view, I should be bringing more people into the sport and from a humanitarian view you look like you could do with a hand.'

Help from Mike Fellner? It sent a little shiver down her. He noticed.

'Cold? In here?' The care-home heating was set to *Stifling*, presumably to accommodate the thinning skin of the clientele. Or to sedate them.

'No, just tired,' she lied, looking down at her trainers and sweatpants. 'I did a Zumba class and it was knackering. Could do with a shower too. The gym showers were just finished. I might test them for quality control.' She was babbling. He did not need to know about her showering, at the club or otherwise.

'I guess you had a wasted trip,' she said, getting up and slinging her bag over her shoulder.

'Nah. There's a guest room here so I'll see her in the morning.' He shrugged his shoulder to indicate his backpack.

'Right. Night then,' she said and headed for the door.

'So, I was thinking,' she heard from behind her, and turned. 'Next time I'm up, we could have dinner. Catch up, you know?'

That was unexpected.

'Won't Verity find that boring?' she asked.

'Verity doesn't come to see Nanna. Nanna rarely

remembers her and Verity says old people freak her out.'

Clearly Verity had been spawned from a tube.

'Then won't Verity find it strange, you having dinner with an old girlfriend?'

She expected him to look sheepish, or wolfish if he did this regularly, but instead his face was open and plain. 'I wasn't going to ask her permission, Tiff. Everyone's allowed to look up old mates, aren't they?'

She had no answer to that, being referred to as an old mate sat strangely with her, so she simply replied, 'Give me a call when you're up and we'll see how my diary's looking.'

Chapter 19

'Bugger.' The staff showers had been magnificent and she'd taken her time, swearing about Ron under the spray, before drying off, donning her PJs and heading to bed. With the space cleared and windows cleaned, the top floor wasn't half as spooky and Tiff had moved all her possessions and matbed into the new storeroom. Crawling into bed though, and hunting around in her bag, she couldn't find her phone. She must have left it on the office desk downstairs when she'd come in. It would be fine, she told herself; she didn't need it. Only she *did* need it, for the alarm. She should race down and get it. But it was warm in the bed and dark in the corridor, and she'd probably wake up on time with the morning traffic. Most likely. Maybe. Hopefully. Argh. She rolled over, trying to sleep but the thought niggled.

So. Annoying.

'All right!' she snapped at herself and stomped bad-tempered from the room, heading right down to the ground floor first to double-check the door to pre-empt any further niggles. The evening had been a mess of emotions as it was, what with Ron's epic backstabbing, and Mike helping her out. She wanted to rip his guts out and string them like bunting around the ring as fair warning to others considering crossing her. Ron's, not Mike's. *Snake.*

When they were dating, Mike had always been dependable like that; always turned up on time, always walked her home from school, went out of his way to help the junior boxers. The thought made her smile. She should have known he'd jump in to help her. Only, when it had come to the crunch, when she'd needed him most, to her shock he hadn't been dependable after all. Remembering wiped the smile back off her face.

Climbing the stairs to the office, she tried not to dwell on it; how she'd waited for him, but he hadn't come. She should've gone to see Nanna Bea, but at that point everything had gone wrong. And then Gav had stepped in. He'd been her hero, given her the support she needed, picked her up from her pool of dissolved self-confidence. (She dismissed the mental image of Gavin hitching her up and pulling her along. She was NOT a bloody cart.)

Deep in these thoughts rounding the office door, it took a moment to register the limp body in the desk chair. The scream was totally justifiable.

'Bloody hell! Calm down,' Mike shouted.

'What are you doing here?!'

'What are you doing in your PJs?'

'I asked you first,' she insisted, crossly. She was wound up enough tonight.

'I was waiting for you.'

'The door's locked downstairs,' she stated. Unless he'd become Houdini, how'd he got in?

'I unlocked it to get in, I thought it best to lock it behind me,' he explained mystified, 'Who knows who might wander in.'

She gave him an arch look, that said *Precisely*.

'Oh.' He got it and scowled at her. 'I knocked.' He dug her phone out of his pocket. 'You forgot your phone at the home and there was something I needed to say, but you weren't in here and you'd said you were going to test the showers and I figured I shouldn't, you know...' the tips of his ears turned darker as he squirmed, which made her lips want to pull upwards, but she resisted. 'So I figured I'd wait here until you came out and I tried the sofa for old time's sake, but Jesus that bastard is lumpy and my back's dodgy – and the desk chair was fine, and you took ages, and I must have dozed off.'

She was trying very hard now not to smile, because run-on sentences were not his thing, but even pulling her mouth in like a cat's bottom didn't hide her amusement. He gave her another cross look. 'There was no need to scream the house down. You spooked the crap out of me.'

'I thought you were dead!' she defended herself. 'That's where I found Blackie,' she pointed out. Mike's back didn't appear troubled when springing out of the chair. Nor was the balding velour sofa beyond his comfort levels after all. He visibly shuddered. The international champion fighter suddenly looked more like a scrawny teen.

'So, now you've succeeded in scaring me, what was it you wanted to say?'

He took a breath, before being distracted again.

'You didn't answer my question.'

'Pardon?' She wasn't sure what he meant.

He pivoted his index finger up and down at her. 'The PJ's? You can't still be holding vigils for Blackie.' His eyebrow was arched in expectation of a good answer.

She pressed her lips together trying to concoct something sufficient, and came up with zilch.

He waited patiently. She'd forgotten he did that. He'd learnt it from Nanna Bea, who had the same dogmatic patient streak when it came to young Mikey explaining his misdemeanours. She'd found it amusing back then to watch him squirm. Now, on the receiving end, not so much.

'It's comfy working in them at night.' She waved her hand vaguely at the desk, wishing it was piled higher with papers. 'Normally, there's no-one here,' she added pointedly, 'so I can wear what I like.'

'And that's how you travel home?' he asked sceptically.

'Mmhh,' she nodded.

'In bed-socks?'

'No, obviously not in bed-socks. Don't be ridiculous. They're just for here.' She wasn't sure she was convincing him of anything.

'Tiff, is there any chance you are, in fact, living here?'

There, he'd come right out and said it. Why did he have to do that? Now he'd put her in a tough position. Either she'd have to admit everything to him, or tell him an outright lie. How rude was that? Her face flushed from a mix of indignation and shame.

'This is a gym, Mikey. Not a house,' she said, stiffly.

'I know that, and I'm sure the council knows that, but I'm worried you don't.'

'Oh my god, you aren't going to dob me in, are you?' she blurted out, shocked. Too late she realised she'd blown it; her outburst was a confession. Shoulders sagging she sat on the edge of the desk.

'It's just a temporary measure. My stuff's in the store-room upstairs. I'm between places, that's all.'

'Are you sure?' He seemed genuinely concerned.

'Of course I'm sure. Who willingly lives in a cupboard?' Her following laugh was more manic than the nonchalant she'd intended.

'The same stuff I fell over in the entrance that night?'

'I wasn't expecting you,' she snarked, 'but then invites don't seem to be important to you, do they?' He ignored it.

'That was weeks ago, Tiff. Weeks.'

'So? I've been busy.'

He gave her a long hard stare, which she attempted to avoid, fiddling with the top desk drawer.

'What's the deal?' Mike prompted.

'I told you, I'm between homes.'

'You're moving house?' Why wouldn't he let this go already?

'Sort of. Not quite.' She gave up. 'I split up with my partner and I moved out.'

It felt grown-up to refer to Gav as her partner. It made a distinction between what she and Mike had had. Ten years justified that, surely? Theirs had been puppy love, whereas what she and Gav had had was a grown-up relationship with bills, negotiations and compromises. Mainly *her* compromises.

'And the storeroom option?' he pushed, not remotely moved by the partner reference, 'As opposed to, say, a new flat, a hotel, your parents' or a friend's place?' There was some of that she definitely wasn't going into.

'Well, that was timing. Blackie died, so there was his funeral to sort and there were no flats I liked, my parents aren't an option and Shelby's place is minuscule, so I

211

stashed things here over that weekend and then Blackie left me the place on the Monday and since then everything's been manic. Like I said, I've been busy.'

'Why aren't your olds an option?' he asked, surprised. Tiff cast her mind back to the swanky town house she'd once lived in, with high steps to the door and shiny black railings, on the best street in Kingsley. Mike had visited many times and it would have been the obvious place to go – had they still owned it. And had she and her mother been on speaking terms. And had her dad not recently got out of prison and thankfully had the good grace to stay well away from Tiff, who held him totally responsible for ruining their lives and wished him and his mistress all the best of misery together.

'They downsized,' she said, tightly. Well, a prison cell and a tiny flat filled with empty brandy bottles and bilious vitriol definitely fitted that description.

'Right,' he nodded. 'And you're living on ... Pot Noodles.' He lifted an empty pot from the desk bin. 'The food of champions.'

Dammit. She always hid the pots in the kitchen bin. Typical she'd slipped this once...

'Who says that's mine?' she asked, tartly.

'Angel,' he said with a short laugh and a *Who do you think you're fooling?* look, 'if there was ever a sign you were unhappy, it was the licked-clean pot of a chicken Pot Noodle.'

'That was a long time ago,' she insisted.

'Some things never change.' He might have had a point on the Pot Noodles, but she got the impression he was referring to her.

'I've changed plenty, thank you.'

'Really?'

'Definitely,' she said, insulted. Nobody wanted to hear they were the same at twenty-six as they were at sixteen. Other than weight, of course and pertness of boobs. She'd garnered years of experience and wisdom since they'd known each other. Years.

'And you always retreated to your PJs when you needed comfort.'

'It's night time. I was going to bed.'

'I bet you a tenner if you hadn't been "testing the showers",' he did that air-quoting thing which made her nostrils flare, 'you'd have changed as soon as you walked back in.' She crossed her arms defensively.

'I'm not sure what you're basing your memories on, Michael. You make it sound like I lived in PJs while we were together. I don't remember things being bad during that time.' He'd left just before her life had completely turned to poo, so what would he know?

'Strange,' he mused, 'I recall a girl who bristled when her parents spoke to each other, knowing things had gone pear-shaped between them, though she tried to cover it. Some guys thought she was ice cold and

213

prideful. Not me though. I knew the girl who relaxed when others weren't looking, who was tempted to lick the plate after Nanna's brown stew, and who liked to curl up under her duvet – in her PJs – hiding from it all.'

Tiff moved to set the kettle boiling. She recognised the scenes he was describing. He was being diplomatic too, not mentioning the tears he'd witnessed. However, in her mind, all that had faded into insignificance when her dad had been arrested. When everything came crashing down – when the town had turned against them – everything that had gone before had become a past chapter. Living in PJs out of school hours had become the norm and the Pot Noodles had been a staple when her mother had retreated to her bed with her brandy.

Contrite, she handed him his tea, which he sipped gratefully, pulling away to look at it and then sipping again.

'You haven't forgotten everything then.'

'Pardon?'

'Dash of milk, two sugars,' he said. 'You remembered how I take my tea.' He had the grace not to look smug about it.

'I'd have thought your athletic regime wouldn't allow two sugars in tea,' she said, glossing over the fact she'd automatically made his tea correctly, after ten years. She just had a thing for numbers, that was all. Nanna Bea had three sugars, Mike two. Numbers were her thing. There was nothing more to it.

'It doesn't,' he said with a mischievous grin, 'This is the best cuppa I've had for years.'

He sat back, relishing it. 'I'm looking forward to this part of retirement; eating what I like, drinking when I like.'

'Planning it?' It was strange talking about retirement. Tiff felt her own working life was only beginning. The bookkeeping had simply been earning a crust and apparently training for owning a gym.

'What, aside from having an immediate nose-job?'

Tiff didn't say anything. Funnily, she'd got used to seeing his less-streamlined face. He tipped his head back at the thought of it all.

'My head doesn't want to stop boxing, but my body's calling the shots,' he said frankly. 'I've got a duff knee and back. My hands are battered. I probably couldn't spell concussion now, and I've taken fewer blows to the head than many. My average punch connect rate was 42% compared to the average 16% from my opponents.' He ran his hand across his hair. Tiff noticed the muscles and sinews on his forearm. He wasn't looking too damaged to her. 'As you saw at the funeral, my untouchability is on the wane. The younger lads are faster on their feet and to the punch. They recover quicker too. Bastards.'

'You've done well though,' she said, sitting in Blackie's chair. *Her* chair. The narrow gap between their knees however, made her self-conscious.

'I have,' he agreed 'taking punches and doling them out offers a comfortable lifestyle if you're any good at it.' The chunk of gold ticking on his wrist, said he was very good at it. 'I don't know, Tiff,' he said facing her again with a look of discomfit, 'I don't think my heart's in it anymore. The spark's gone.'

'Because you've reached the top?'

'Possibly. It's like the fuel's run out.'

He didn't seem nearly as cocky as he'd done at Blackie's wake. This was the Mike she'd known, talking honestly as he had in the hours they'd spent lying on her teen bed discussing their lives.

'But perhaps that's okay, Mikey. You did it. You did it *all*. Maybe it's okay to be done now. You know, Blackie always said you'd go the distance.'

'Not to my face he didn't,' he said with a hint of bitterness. 'I worked bloody hard for him and he barely managed a "well done".'

'How can you say that?' Tiff asked, shocked. 'He doted on you, he trained you harder than anyone else, then or since. He was never quite as committed after you.'

The awkward silence that ensued said they'd have to agree to disagree. Neither of them wanted to push this further.

'So um, why was it you're here? What was it you wanted to say?' Tiff asked, conceding.

Mike appeared to shake himself into the present.

'Well there was the phone, but I also wanted to thank you, for helping Nanna.'

'Seriously Mike? It's *Nanna*. It was a pleasure.'

Tiff looked at him. His face might have been older and battered, but there was that same simplicity and earnestness she'd known back then. And she recognised she didn't look at that face with annoyance anymore.

'Did you want to see the ring while you're here?' she asked.

'Nah, it's late. You're going to bed,' he said standing. 'I'll come another time.' She waited for him to change his mind, but he didn't.

'I'll walk you out.'

'So why'd you split up?' he asked as they set off.

'What?'

'You and your partner. Why did it end?' She looked back at him as she led the way, in case he was teasing her, but aside from saying 'partner' in a grandiose voice, he seemed genuinely intrigued. *Nosy.*

She faced forward again to hide her embarrassment. 'Well, after ten years, he decided our paths had come to a fork.' It sounded better than *His horse didn't want to pull my cart, anymore.* Thinking about Gavin gave her a twinge of sadness; nothing devastating, it just gave her pause.

'A fork?' She was willing to bet his eyebrow was rising.

'A fork,' she reiterated, swiftly. She wasn't inclined to dredge over *that* conversation. It wasn't any of his business either. 'The End.'

He took the hint. 'And so here you are,' he said.

'Here I am.'

'Well, I'll have to help you with the coach now, or you'll never move out and I'll be forever worried you'll shriek at me when I come visiting.' She noted he said *when*, not *if*.

'I should have the locks changed so you *can't* come visiting.'

'That would go against Blackie's offer of refuge.'

Turning slightly, Tiff cocked her head at him.

'What does a smart-arse world boxing champion need a refuge from, Mike?'

'Then or now?'

'I know about then,' she replied, quietly. His dad's belt scars on his back were probably still traceable. They wouldn't have been hidden during his fights either. The entire boxing world must know.

'Now ...? I dunno. It seemed like a cathartic thing to do the first time. Make peace with the spirit, nab a moment of stillness.'

'Do you not get much stillness at home?' Reaching the

front door, it was her turn to fix him with a look. He withstood it for a moment then surrendered with a sigh.

'Verity's pretty loud. She likes loud music, loud phone calls, she shouts. Even when she's not there, the stillness is more a vacuum she's created and will eventually fill again. It isn't calm. My head, my brain, it needs the rest, you know?' He looked somewhat ashamed about it, and Tiff suspected the boxing had taken more toll than he was admitting. 'I was looking for calm.'

'Warn me next time and I'll try to be out,' Tiff said. 'It's the least I can do if you're making calls for me.'

'Yeah, let's see if I need it,' Mike said, stretching. His T-shirt rode up just enough to flash Tiff a slither of firm skin. She gave herself a mental slap. Why was she looking at his body? 'I don't know how long she'll put up with a former champion. Stars aren't so interesting when they're fading.' He appeared resigned.

'Is that really what you think? She's only with you for the glory?' Tiff was appalled, although having seen Verity, she wasn't altogether surprised. She admonished herself – she shouldn't judge.

'Nothing's as rosy as first-love, Tiff,' he said with a wink, and turned for the door.

'Have you reached a fork, then?' she asked carefully. She didn't want to be nosy – *unlike some* – but there might be comfort in others also experiencing life's bloody forks.

'Let's just say I'm due for the slip road and Verity wants more motorway mileage.'

She took the hint and left it.

'You know,' he said turning back to her, almost causing a collision, 'I've mentioned us being first-loves twice tonight, and you haven't flinched.' His eyes shuttled between hers.

'Why would I flinch?' she asked. 'To deny it? I can't – you *were*. Flinch because I found it uncomfortable? I didn't. Not really. It was an important part of my life.' *Until you buggered off*, she thought but she kept quiet. Now didn't seem to be the moment.

Then he leaned in and kissed her chastely on the cheek.

''Night, Tiff. It's been good to talk.'

She didn't move from the spot as he left the building such was her confusion. Everything about this evening had been *friendly*. There was no two ways about it, Tiff had to admit, disturbed by having had him so close and having been enveloped by the cedar scent of his aftershave; they were friends again. She remembered the feeling – the delicious comfort of it – regardless of how long it had been lost. And yet, framing it, was the conflicting knowledge he'd hurt her so very badly once, and she didn't know how to reconcile the two.

Chapter 20

Tiff meticulously described her Ron's-guts-as-bunting plan to Shelby; it was more considered and embellished now. Pitching up first thing on her best friend's doorstep, Tiff was disappointed when Shelby maintained murder would currently be self-defeating; a police investigation would delay the refurb. Instead they'd come to the excruciating conclusion, that feigning ignorance was the smartest plan.

'How am I going to manage that? I want to punch his face in.' Flailing defeated on Shelby's bed, Tiff gave the pillow a thump in lieu of Ron's head.

'I know, babes,' Shelby soothed, paging through her hangers for a salon tunic. 'I feel the same whenever Lorraine walks into the salon. But you can't. If you confront him now, there'll be a big blow out and you'll end up suspending him for breach of contract.'

'No contract, remember?'

'Right, so you'll have to ask him to leave, on the basis

he's stealing your customers. Then what'll you have?' It was muffled as she pulled the tunic over her head.

'Satisfaction?'

'Yup – for about five minutes. Firstly, you'll feel bad, because Blackie promised him his job, and you'll get hung up on the sentiment. Secondly, you'll have even more days without a coach than planned. Thirdly, there'll be gossip.' Tiff blanched. 'Fourthly, Ron'll find some HR angle and get you for unfair dismissal.'

'But we don't have a contract!'

'No, but he's been there for years and there's most likely some rights to twist. You need him to resign.'

Tiff's heart sank. Where was the justice in that? 'So I have to let him stay on, poaching my clients for five more days, AND pay him?'

'Pretty much.'

'Nightmare.'

'Yup, sucks. Spit in his drinks if you have to. That's what I do when Lorraine's here.' Shelby took a quick slurp of her coffee. Tiff regarded hers with suspicion.

'Gross.'

'Take the small pleasures where you can,' Shelby said blithely, chivvying them to the kitchen.

'I'm not making his coffee.' Tiff was adamant.

'Fine, whatever,' Shelby sighed, popping two slices of bread into the toaster. 'Tiff, take the higher ground here. He's gone in five days, yes? You'll be shot of him, with your head held high. You can stand back and watch his game-plan dwindle after the first month and all the scabs crawl back when they hear how amazing your gym is.'

'Not if I've got no coach.' Tiff loved Shelby's faith in her and the gym, but she needed to grouch. If Shelby wouldn't let her shout at Ron, she should at least bear the brunt of the whinging. Fair was fair.

The toaster flung the slices up and out. Shelby caught them mid-air, and gave herself a silent roar of applause for being the Toast-ninja. 'That's where you should be putting your efforts instead, isn't it? Looking for a replacement on the quiet.'

'Well, I can't do that until he's resigned. These coaches are all besties. Someone'll tip him off straight away.'

'Okay, but sort your plan of attack. Know who you're calling the second he's gone. Replacing him within days would be a kick to his spuds, personally and in business terms. He'll suddenly have competition and the lads'll have less incentive to leave.'

'Mikey said he'd make some calls,' Tiff said, picking at the chipped counter top. Having his support felt good. In fact just thinking about Mike felt good. She liked having him back as a friend.

'Mikey who?' Shelby asked, mouth full of toast. The peanut butter and marmalade combo was sticking to the roof of her mouth.

'Fellner. Mikey Fellner.'

'Mikey Fellner? Rings a bell. One of the boxing lads?'

'Um, sort of.' Tiff suddenly wanted to back-peddle, but she was committed. 'Mike "The Assassin" Fellner. Slightly famous. Remember?'

'Er, no.' Shelby could sniff withheld information at a hundred paces. Tiff felt a touch of panic.

'He was at Blackie's funeral. Beaten face, bent nose, on the brink of retirement. Came to the wake.' Tiff was sure she'd mentioned him when debriefing Shelby on what she'd missed. Fleetingly perhaps, but she'd definitely mentioned it. Maybe. Or perhaps she'd skipped that part...

'Whoa whoa,' Shelby's interest went to high alert. Laying the remaining piece of toast on the plate, her eyes narrowed. 'Do you mean Mikey, your boyfriend before Gavin?'

Tiff resisted the need to face-palm herself. 'Mmmhh.'

'The boyfriend you've rarely spoken of and about whom I've had to wheedle information out of you in tiny, stingy morsels during the last decade?'

'Maybe.' If only she'd kept her mouth shut.

'And this boyfriend is, in fact, a known boxer, with a nickname and everything?'

'Sort of,' Tiff hedged, then sighed. She had to stop fibbing to Shelby. Mike probably deserved his dues too. 'Well, yes. He's world famous.'

224

'I *know* he's bloody world famous, Tiffanie,' Shelby said, sounding slightly snarly, 'even I've bloody heard of Mike "The Assassin" Fellner.' Shelby was cross, possibly livid. 'How could you have withheld information like that?'

'I haven't,' Tiff started, 'He was at the funeral. You were there too.'

'No way, don't even try to get out of this. Wake aside – and for the record I'd have remembered the mention of a celeb – you never disclosed mysterious Mikey and Mike "The Assassin" Fellner were one and the same. What kind of friend does that?'

'I don't follow the sport. I didn't know myself,' Tiff tried. She got up and started to pull her coat on. Leaving now would be ideal.

'Oh please!' Shelby said, with an angry huff. She crammed the last bite of toast into her mouth and left the table. Tiff winced as the plate was unceremoniously ditched into the sink.

Tiff hated arguing with Shelby, and she was primed to launch into a plea of cluelessness, but it wasn't quite accurate, was it? True, she hadn't followed his stellar rise to the top. Too hurt, she'd vowed not to give him another thought, because he was doing the same to her. But she hadn't been able to avoid hearing his name now and again. She couldn't unsee the back page of the newspapers she'd passed in the paper-shop. It was more wilful than actual ignorance about who he'd become.

'I... it didn't seem... I didn't know you Shelbs until after...' Tiff tried many ways to explain as the front door was crossly locked behind them. Finally she gave up finding excuses. 'What did it matter? He was gone, he broke my heart, you weren't going to know him, I had moved on. All of those Shelb, but most importantly, you were a fresh start for me. You were my friend. You didn't care about town gossip, or at least you didn't hold it against me. I wanted to move forward, not mope around in the past. Mikey was the past. You see?'

Shelby took her own sweet time chewing it over. Eventually, she sighed, resigned. 'I suppose so.' Tiff gave her own sigh. Hers was relief. 'But you owe me a full and detailed exposé. The full story.'

'Fine, but over copious drinks,' Tiff agreed as they walked, side by side. 'I can't face it this morning, not if you're making me spend the next five days navigating Ron with an Oscar-worthy poker face.'

'Deal. Now tell me what Mike said. About the coaches. This was at the wake, right?'

'Um, so no. I didn't own the club at the wake, did I? He dropped in for a visit.'

'He dropped in for a visit?' Shelby's voice sounded taut. Tiff felt herself falling deeper into trouble. She chose to omit it being a nocturnal visit.

'Yes, he came to see the place, yesterday. Being

nostalgic and that. Blackie left him the ring in his will.'
Tiff tried to sound breezy, ignoring the blurred time-
line. 'So I told him Ron wasn't staying and he said he'd
call his coaching buddies and see if anyone was available.' Ta-dah. Not lying; simply stripping down the
events to relevant bullet points.

'What about him? As coach. If he's retiring soon,
maybe he wants a job.'

Tiff nearly choked. 'Shelb, that'd be like asking
Beyoncé to give me singing lessons.'

'Not worth a shot then?'

'I'd rather get in the ring myself. The embarrassment
of asking, not to mention the offense he'd take, would
be shocking.' Tiff cringed.

'I'll take that as a no. Come up with your own idea
then. Meanwhile, he'd better be discreet.' Shelb sounded
a little huffy. Tiff didn't know whether it was because
she'd been kept in the dark about Mike, or because
plans had already been actioned without her.

'I'm sure he'll be the paragon of discretion, Shelb.
He's an assassin remember. They're pretty cloak and
dagger about things.' Tiff hoped a joke might thaw her
mood.

'Well, you would know,' she replied curtly. 'I wouldn't,
of course, not knowing much about him.'

Tiff took a deep breath, 'I, Tiffanie Trent do hereby
promise, to update you on all details regarding Mike

Fellner, as soon as our ridiculous schedules allow.'

Shelby snorted. She'd need time to cool down. Thankfully, they'd reached the salon and Tiff could run away.

'Gotta go, babes. Mrs Doyle's having her fanny waxed first thing so I need to crack a barrel of wax on to melt and find the biggest pair of paper knickers we have.' Tiff was relieved to be off the hook, but Shelby wasn't done. 'Wednesday, the *Pig & Whistle*, 9 p.m. Bring your info. And you can start with why he was doing nostalgia visits at night.' Tiff gaped. 'Oh come on, Tiff,' Shelby said, unlocking the door and kissing her cheek, 'I'm not dim. You only heard about Ron last night, so how did you see Mikey if it wasn't later last night or before dawn this morning? You can pick which it was and let me know. Laters.'

Tiff didn't get a chance to say bye before the door slammed shut. Her head was already racing regarding what to admit to. If Shelby wanted to give her something other than Ron to think about, she'd succeeded.

Chapter 21

'What's tonight's torture?' Tiff asked, that Wednesday. She was meeting Shelby later and she couldn't decide which she was least looking forward to; exercise or execution. Natalie had compiled a comprehensive, if aggressive, list of classes to trial. They'd attended a karate class the night before, and while she'd enjoyed imagining each chop connecting with Ron's body, the post-class consensus was the martial arts could wait. For now the boxing, fitness and toning would lead.

'You'll like this one,' Nat said, grinning, which told Tiff she probably wouldn't. 'Pole-fitness, over in Westhampton.'

Tiff dropped her head on the desk and groaned.

'Look Tiff, I know what you're thinking, but it's supposedly god's gift to abs and toning.' Tiff knew all this, she'd seen the pictures online after her discussion with Mike, but it didn't mean she actually wanted to *do* it. Swinging and gyrating like a tabletop dancer in front of strangers must be excruciatingly, toe-curlingly embarrassing. Natalie mistook her cringing fear for her being unconversant in the language of Pole.

'Trust me on this Tiff, it's a hen-do favourite, so you could offer that too; a class followed by drinks in the bar before they go to the next activity. Limos will fit through the car park. Hens'll love it.

'And,' Natalie continued, 'I blew our cover. I told the instructor, Sammi, what we're about. She's got Westhampton sewn up, but she's had plenty of interest from Kingsley too.' Natalie saw the look on Tiff's face. 'Tiff, give it a chance. You can always second-phase it, but try it or you'll never know. It'd be another USP.'

Tiff understood her point, but it was Natalie's passion that persuaded her.

'I've arranged to watch the class tonight,' Nat explained, 'to see who goes and what they do, and then she'll do us a private class, so you won't feel stupid in front of strangers.'

'You got the measure of me pretty fast, didn't you?' Tiff said wryly, hoping for an immediate case of gastro, or death even, to get herself out of it.

In spite of looking uber-sweaty, the women finishing the pole class had beatific smiles on their faces and many were laughing. *Really*, no tears at all. They weren't shaped like they'd slinked out of Stringfellows either. Fit yes, but all normal-looking women of all descriptions. To Tiff's alarm, they all wore sports-bra tops and skimpy shorts. *That* wasn't happening; Tiff was safely cloaked in leggings and an oversized sweatshirt which would remain until the last second.

On an impulse, she sidled up to the nearest woman. She was early forties and the photo on her phone case showed her three freckled kids.

'Excuse me, what do you think of the class?'

'Changed my life,' the woman answered not missing a beat.

'Really?'

'Totally. I've got killer abs now and a sex life to die for.' Tiff wondered if she could use that on a poster. 'Joining up?'

'Checking it out. Thinking about bringing it to my gym,' she said. Would she ever get used to saying that?

'Best thing you'll ever do,' the woman said, moving off to join her friends, 'You'll bruise and hurt like hell, but it's worth it.'

Natalie was triumphant. 'See?'

'All right, smuggie,' Tiff said, removing her sweatshirt, 'the proof'll be in the pudding.'

Six silver poles stood from ceiling to floor at the back of the dance studio. Tiff reckoned she'd easily have room for the same amount. Sammi was lovely and welcoming, but a demon teacher. She blatantly ignored any whining about not being able to do it. Thank goodness Natalie had arranged a private lesson, as Tiff's initial efforts were worthy of *You've Been Framed*. She simply couldn't find her inner table-dancer and her sex-minx had apparently been a one-off.

'Right, put this on,' Sammi said, handing her an in-flight eye-mask. 'Wear it and forget about us or the mirrors. Natalie gets one too. Neither of you will see what the other's doing and you can choose never to see me again after tonight, so let yourselves go.'

The difference was immediate. No vision appeared to inhibit her inhibitions. She swung on the pole, feet near its base, trailing her free arm behind her. She'd swung like that as a kid and there wasn't anything stripperish about it. She needed to get the stripper connotations out of her head. *Cirque du Soleil* used these holds and spins all the time.

Lifting their eye-masks for Sammi's demos, Tiff and Natalie were soon pirouetting and trying out the Fireman spin. They were stepping forwards and leaning into turns, hooking feet around the poles and turning while sliding down it. Once Sammi had lambasted them to point their toes and finger tips, Tiff felt almost balletic. By the time Sammi suggested they try an Attitude spin, Tiff ditched the eye-mask altogether.

She'd never thought she had much upper-body strength to speak of, but Sammi dismissed that as an excuse too. She had them doing Back Hooks, spinning backwards down around the pole and Chair spins, descending as if they were sitting, hands gripping the pole high above their heads. These weren't positions she'd ever imagined herself in, yet there she was, spiralling at a controlled pace down towards the floor.

By the end of the lesson Tiff wasn't sure she could stand. The spins had been linked in a short routine with slow squats down the pole and quick slut-drops. Her biceps ached, her legs bemoaned the awakening of muscles she never knew she owned and her heart was belting. It hadn't felt like a fast activity, but her blood was pumping. Sammi took pity on them, leaving them conked out on the floor, while illustrating what an advanced class looked like. Sammi reminded the gaping Tiff of Lara Croft as she performed her mid-air Pilates.

'I need this at the gym,' Tiff whispered pathetically, 'I know I sucked, but I want to do what you can do.' They'd been at it for well over an hour, but given they'd been laughing throughout, the time had flown – much like Tiff felt she had, around the pole.

Sammi joined them on the floor, but sitting pertly rather than flailing.

'You'll need some poles permanently jacked to the ceiling. You have to have faith people will come, as the studio space will be compromised, but it'll be worth it.'

'How would the classes work?' Natalie asked, her

voice slightly wheezy. She'd pulled herself up to slump against her pole, swigging from her water bottle as if her life depended on it.

'I'd suggest a mix. Daytime classes for Pole-fitness and dance-based evening classes. Hen-do bookings start as dance classes, but always end up with the more erotic moves. You keep the distinction though, so people know it's primarily about fitness.'

'And will you teach?' Tiff asked. She liked Sammi, she liked her style. She'd keep hens under control – *and* the boxers, once they got wind of what was afoot upstairs.

Sammi looked at her. 'I'll pop over to see the gym next week. *My* turn to audition *you*. Sound okay?'

'If you can overlook the demolition going on, then it's a date,' she said with a smile, which didn't vanish at the thought of Mike's teasing when he clocked her poles.

'You need to relax, babes.' Tiff wasn't tense, she was exhausted and aching after Pole-fitness, but she knew better than to bail on this date with Shelby. She'd hunt her down Liam Neeson style. 'You need a fling,' Shelby declared and took a swig of her fourth Breezer in the *Pig & Whistle*. ''S'actly what you need. With all the stuff going on at the gym where's the "you time"?' Slurring slightly, she didn't wait for Tiff to answer.

'Honestly Tiff, you need a young virile male to knob

your socks off and send your eyeballs spinning like a slot-machine.' Shelby leaned across the table and waved her finger tellingly at Tiff, 'And don't tell me I'm wrong,' she slurred on, 'I can tell just by looking at a man what he's like in bed. Gav's definitely not on the winner's podium.'

'He was—' Tiff began, but was stopped by the flat of Shelby's hand in her face. She focused on her drink. She was going to need it.

'I said don't bother. I commend your loyalty, Tiff – I don't understand it seeing as he ditched you – but I totes get you don't want the humiliation of admitting you've had ten years of lame sex.'

'Shelby!' Tiff hissed, looking around, 'Not everyone here needs to know the ins and outs of my sex life.' Shelby snorted her drink out of her nose.

'Ins and outs. Good one. But bless you, babes, that's probably all it was, wasn't it?' Tiff couldn't have given an answer even if Shelby had paused for one, mortification locking her jaw. 'Aww, babes, you have so much to catch up. Time, moves and positions. You must be woefully out of touch regarding current sexual repertoires.' Shelby's volume had increased again. Two lads on the next table swung around to look at Tiff, forcing her to give them a sheepish look.

'Honestly Shelb, can we change the subject?' Tiff pleaded.

Shelby sighed deeply. 'All right. But don't dismiss the random fling idea without proper consideration. Sex is a muscle – gotta keep it in training or it'll wither. And don't think I didn't notice you not denying having a sorry sex life…'

Tiff bit her tongue. Whenever Shelby was criticising Gavin it was her instinct to get defensive, to tell Shelby her sex life was perfectly satisfactory, thank you very much, but something about the class this evening, the way she'd felt about her body, well, it made her wonder whether there had been something lacking before. She wasn't sure what exactly, but it did have her wondering.

There had been moments, when she was getting the pole moves – admittedly brief, but still – when she'd felt confident and sensual and strong. *Invincible* perhaps. And she'd loved it. But she wasn't going to share any of that with Shelby, because she'd say it confirmed Gavin hadn't been lighting her fires. If she didn't argue, she could move the subject – and the attention she was getting from other tables – on.

'What's got you riled this evening?' She pointed to the bottle. Shelby was on a mission. 'Let me guess, your lovely boss?'

'That woman is the she-devil,' Shelby started and a relieved Tiff settled in for a monologue. 'She's enrolled me on a Swedish massage course, to draw more customers. Only, the course is early evening – aka my freetime – and I'll have to sprint across town to do it. And don't tell me it's more strings to my bow, because while that's true, it's only so I can fill every breathing hour in her salon. She won't pay me overtime for going and she won't pay me more when I qualify. It's exactly what she did with the colon hydrotherapy.' Tiff automatically clenched when Shelb mentioned that one. She'd yet to take her up on her offer of a free 'bum squirt', as Shelby so delicately described it. 'Honestly, I run that place while she lounges in Spain and keeps me on an assistant's wage.'

'So leave,' Tiff suggested.

'What?'

'You heard. Leave. If I'm not mistaken I've suggested this... oh what, a hundred times.'

'Tiff, haven't you been listening? My days are booked solid, the cow rings randomly to check I'm there – heaven forbid I should nip out for a sarnie – and unless things have changed nobody does recruitment interviews on a Sunday, although Sunday opening was her second idea for increasing business. It's easy making suggestions like that from a sun lounger. Lazy bloody mare.'

Having met Lorraine, Tiff had to agree; the woman was a parasite and mean with it. She'd married some rich wheeler-dealer who'd set her up with a shop as a hobby. Finding Shelby had been her coup.

'She knows she's onto a winner with you, Shelb. Your conscientiousness is your downfall,' Tiff commiserated. It was ridiculous that Shelby's diligence should in fact be her worst enemy.

'Gotta do your best though, don't you? Or else what's the point?' Shelby asked, perplexed.

'Well, you've always done that.'

'Always,' Shelby nodded heavily, the alcohol having increased the weight of gravity around her head. 'At work and in bed.'

The two lads swivelled in their direction again.

'Go on, ask around,' she told them, 'Never had a bad review.'

Tiff tugged her sleeve, drawing her back.

'Have you considered being your own boss, Shelb?'

'Every time the phone rings,' Shelby muttered.

'Strikes me it'd be the best thing. You'll do the best job and it'll be for your own benefit, not someone else's. Plus you'd choose your own hours rather than have them foisted on you.'

Shelby sat staring for a moment, dazed. 'That would be amazing,' she said, then with a slow blink, she snapped out of it. 'But not everyone inherits a business. Even if Lorraine dropped dead of sangria-poisoning this minute,' she crossed her fingers, 'it wouldn't be me who got it.'

'See a bank manager Shelb, ask how much it would

take to set up. See if they'll do you a decent loan. No-one would work harder. You could rent somewhere small, or you could do a mobile service, lose the rent completely.'

'Returning to point number one, Tiff; I can't get out during working *or banking* hours.'

'Shelb, there'll come a point when you have really *really* had enough, and you'll be prepared to do something drastic. Text me then, and I'll call with an excuse for you to leave. In the meantime, you'll have to quit whining about it, because only you can make this happen.'

'That's it? *Quit whining?* That's your sympathetic advice?' Shelb was outraged.

'Yup. No sympathy here,' Tiff said, sitting back in her seat, arms crossed, channelling Mike. And yes, there was also some joy in slinging a touch of the tough-love back at her friend. 'You don't need coddling. You just need to know someone believes you've got this, and is prepared to support you wholeheartedly when you finally pull your finger out.'

Shelby dodged the issue by staggering to the bar for another Breezer. But there was loud sweary muttering. Tiff predicted a long night and they hadn't even got to the bit she'd been summonsed for. She still had the Mike details to dish. She downed her drink in one.

Chapter 22

Ron stomped through the door. Tiff instantly slid herself behind the desk so he couldn't see the bevy of bruises she'd been examining on her legs. The pole had left her inner arms and backs of knees covered in a trail of what Sammi called *pole kisses*. Tiff was trying to remember which of her boxes contained her arnica cream, because she needed to smother herself in it. And she planned to stay seated all day because the slut-drops had apparently broken her quads.

'When's the ring coming down? I need to schedule it into training,' he demanded.

Tiff looked at him blankly. The night before had been very long, as Shelby had forcibly walked her through Mike's boxing Facebook page and fan website, shot after shot of a topless Mike, which Shelby was very impressed by, whilst still unimpressed by Tiff's previous secrecy. Tiff's steaming hangover also had her befuddled; acting like she didn't know about Ron's back-stabbing didn't help either. He assumed she didn't understand what he was asking.

'You can't build around it,' he went on, 'It needs taking down. May as well have it delivered to "The Assassin" while you're about it.'

While partly amused Ron referred to Mike as 'The Assassin' without any irony, Tiff studied his face for any trace of guilt. He looked so calm, supposedly suggesting something helpful. But she saw it for what it was; the longer she didn't have the ring, the better for him. *Double snake*. She plastered a smile on her face.

'Not before the last class tomorrow.'

Ron's cool demeanour faltered and he started to speak. The phone rang and she immediately held up a finger to stop him.

'Hello,' she said, hoping Ron'd go away, but he remained in the doorway glowering. The line was silent again. This was the second that day, and one of many in the last week. She didn't answer with her or the gym's name anymore. Someone was out to harass her. She'd considered calling the police, but they'd only suggest changing the number and as an established business that wouldn't work. Replacing the receiver, she wrote BLOCK on her note pad. She'd call the phone company for help. Whoever it was only rang during working hours. They obviously didn't know she slept there – thank goodness. Silent calls through the night would have terrified her.

Silent calls held a special kind of malice in Tiff's extensive experience. After her father's arrest, she and her mother had been subjected to a wide and imaginative array. There were verbal slights, of course, and the spitting at school. Their bins were regularly upturned or simply went missing. Unwanted cabs were ordered to their house and, when their address soon got blacklisted, meant they could never get one when they actually wanted one. Ditto the numerous takeaways that would arrive all evening that they couldn't pay for to placate the irate delivery drivers. And the house was regularly pelted with eggs, stones or worse. Numerous panes had been broken. These though were physical acts and, whilst upsetting, were more annoying than threatening. The silent calls however, they played with your mind, allowing your imagination to run wild to the soundtrack of the empty line, gradually building the paranoia. Tiff told herself over and again that it was probably adolescent larks, and she was older now, more equipped to handle it. Staring at the phone as she replaced the receiver, she wasn't sure she had herself convinced yet.

'I'm not coming in to break it down at the weekend,' Ron restarted, annoyed.

'I haven't asked you to break it down *at all*, Ron,' Tiff said, sweetly, almost pleased to have the distraction. 'Mikey should be in charge of that. It's his, after all. I'm calling him this afternoon.' She hadn't planned to, but it pleased her having Ron think she and 'The Assassin' were tight buddies. 'I also need to chase the new one,' she added. 'Thanks for the reminder.' He left with a scowl.

Around the fifth ring Tiff decided to hang up. She was hoping for the excuse though she knew it was silly. She'd phoned him before. Not just the nightly hour-long phone calls when they were young – those calls where she'd no idea what they'd spoken so intensely about before they'd conduct the ritual of not hanging up first – but she'd called him recently regarding Nanna Bea. So why was she so nervous? This was business. Still, she wanted to hang up.

'Tiff.'

Damn. She'd been hoping for voicemail. She could muster some semblance of intelligence in a message.

'Yes!' she yelped. 'Mikey! Hi!' Argh, she was sounding somewhere between being caught out and an overenthusiastic cheerleader.

'S'up?' he asked, easily. He was always composed. Why couldn't she do that? Why was she sweating and behaving like a goofy teen around him? It was ten years ago, for goodness sake. Was this a hormonal thing? Shelby would say it was because Tiff wasn't getting any and that a fling – like she'd been suggesting – would get her past it.

'So, um…I was wondering how Nanna was.'

'Well, she's got no recollection of her break for freedom, but she's fine.'

'That's great. Good.' The conversation petered out. Thankfully he stepped in.

'What you been up to?'

'Oh, you know. Busy busy. You?'

'Honestly? I've forgotten what busy looks like. I miss it. Describe it to me.' He sounded wistful, a little morose in fact.

'Aren't you training?'

'For what?'

'Your last fights and stuff.'

'Tiff, if you're going to run a boxing club, you need to have your ear to the ground a little bit. Did you cancel Blackie's subscription to *The Ring*?' Tiff looked at the stack of boxing magazines she'd lobbed in the corner. She planned to have them racked beautifully next to the sodding sofa in reception.

He sounded a tad unimpressed. Tiff knew she could do better than this. She needed to find a little of the Tiff who'd worked the pole last night. *That* Tiff could come across as knowing what she was doing. She wedged the phone between her ear and shoulder, her achey arm already needing the rest. Pathetic. 'No. Of course we get that,' she bluffed. She was fairly sure she'd seen a recent invoice for it.

'Well, maybe check their website sometimes too. I'm officially retired. I announced it yesterday. It even made the evening news.'

'Oh. Right.' She felt well and truly caught out. She'd thought he was still in the planning phase. 'Does one say congratulations or something?'

'Not really, I'm twenty-seven and too old and knackered to do the only thing I'm good at.'

'Ah, you're taking it well then,' she said, leaning back in the chair. 'I'm sorry. I hadn't heard. Job going here if you need it,' she quipped before she could stop herself, then covered her awkwardness with a loud *Ha Ha!* 'Okay, so you need something to fill the new down time,' she raced on, trying to pep him up. 'Only please not golf, because you cannot become one of those.'

She thought she could hear him smile. Good.

'What? You don't think I can rock a Pringle sweater?' he asked affronted.

'Mmm, I'm sure you were born for Argyle diamonds, Mikey,' she said, finally getting into the swing of the call, 'But I can't imagine you in golf shoes, with that frilly flap thing on the front. Not in my wildest dreams.'

'Well, much as being in anyone's wildest dreams currently would be a win, you needn't worry, I'm not about to start swinging the club. I need something that packs more of a punch. Pun intended.'

'You all right, Mikey? Beyond the transition to old age, Zimmer frames and tea dances? You sound sort of world weary.'

He didn't answer immediately, as if making a decision. 'Verity took off.'

'Oh.' Tiff didn't know what to say. He'd mentioned it the other night as a possibility, but she hadn't thought it was an imminent thing. She flailed around for the right words. In the end she went with a generic 'I'm sorry.'

'I love being British,' Mike said, with a terse laugh, 'The Yanks think we're bonkers apologising for something that isn't our fault.'

'I'm not apologising, Mikey,' Tiff said, exasperated, 'I'm extending my sympathy. I am sad that you're sad. You clearly are sad about this,' she pointed out.

'Well, thank you,' he said, chastened. 'I guess I *am* sad,' he was almost explaining it to himself, 'but more for the wasted time, you know? Verity and I had a fun five years, but I think I knew it had an end date, that she'd go.'

'You did?' She hadn't had a clue she and Gavin had an end date. She'd thought it was forever. 'But you lived together.'

'Oh yeah. Vez moved in after six months. Redecorated the entire house. Even did me a man-den.'

'Wagon wheel coffee table?'

'Formula One tyre coffee table. Plus most bloke-toys known to man.'

'She wouldn't have done all of that if she thought it wasn't going anywhere. Some relationships don't work, but people do their best, *hope* for the best while they're in them.'

'Sure they do, but some people assume life stays the same, and when you live off sport that's never going to be the case.'

'I'm sure she knew, Mikey.' Tiff didn't know why she was defending Verity, but she had an insane desire to make him believe the last five years weren't a waste. Like she wanted to believe the last ten years with Gavin hadn't been a total and utter waste, firmly putting her on the back-foot in the dating game and statistically increasing her chances of ending up a childless spinster. God bless Shelby for kindly pointing that bit out. 'Hadn't you discussed what would happen next?'

'Yeah, well maybe that was the nub of it.' He sounded like he was stretching. 'Our ideas of what we should do in my retirement weren't as compatible as we assumed.'

'What did she want?'

'To keep living the celebrity lifestyle. Which we could, to be fair. I don't plan to sell the place in LA and we have friends out there, but while Nanna's still around, I'm not leaving the UK. Verity wants to stay in the spotlight though and I'm rather done with that, you know?'

'Definitely,' Tiff guffawed, 'I'm ridiculously tired of being in *heat* magazine.'

'Come on,' he groaned. 'You know what I'm saying. It's exhausting not being able to go out without reading about it later.'

'Seriously, was it that bad? No offense but you're not a movie-star.'

'Thank god. That must be hell. No, I guess it wasn't *that* bad, but Verity's intent on pushing her modelling career, so it could be more. She's thinking about acting too, so she needs to work the scene and I was the ticket.'

'I'm sure she didn't think of you as a ticket.'

'Okay, I'm being unfair. We met when I'd just reached the big time but I don't think she was only into me for the fame. Or the incredible sex.'

He waited as Tiff got over her coughing fit.

'Of course not.' She'd thought exactly that at Leonards'. The fame thing. Not the sex thing. She remembered telling herself off for exactly those thoughts.

'I was naive,' Mike went on. 'I thought I could convince her to settle down by the time I retired, maybe have some kids. I figured she could do what Victoria did, you know; the clothing line, or some other business. I have the money to set her up if she'd wanted.'

'Who's Victoria?' Tiff asked absently. She wasn't quite keeping up.

'Beckham? They had a place a block over in LA. Nice couple. Decent kids.'

Tiff experienced the strangest feeling of being transported at least a universe further away from him in a matter of moments. She wondered again what she was thinking, ringing him.

'Of course. *Vics*. You should have said.'

He blew a raspberry at her down the phone, making her smile. In spite of their different stratospheres, he was still Mikey.

'So she's not up for the settling down?'

'Nope. That was made crystal clear.' Mike clicked his tongue in resignation. 'Remember the commentating thing, I mentioned?'

'I remember.' Tiff could easily see Mike on the telly, even with his banana nose. He knew stuff, he was charming when he wasn't being an arse, he would defend his opinions.

'Well, they rang my agent and apparently it was more than commentating, actually more co-anchoring a weekly show based in the US and they thought it was a done deal. Verity'd made them all sorts of promises. And I blew up about it.'

'Not your thing?' Surely it was a golden opportunity? Oh god she wished she hadn't said that thing about having a job going. The guy was world-stage material. Where were her bloody filters?

'I might. I mean, I could. Yeah, that would be okay, but aside from not wanting to leave Nanna, I took it badly that she'd been instigating things without me. I hadn't quite got my mind around the retiring yet, and she'd set wheels in motion I wasn't ready for.'

'The fear of change get you, did it, Mikey?'

'Something like that. And a fair dollop of pride mixed in. Anyway, she said she wanted me to stay in the public eye, and I got bull-headed and said I didn't. Then it became a bit tit-for-tat, and she finally said she didn't know if she'd ever want kids, but her modelling couldn't wait. She said perhaps we had different futures to pursue. I said obviously I wasn't enough for her without the glitz, and then she left, so I guess I was right.'

'Blimey.' Tiff was surprised by his brusque summary. He'd distanced himself from it all. She wondered if that was how he dealt with the hurt. 'So I'm guessing you've told them where to put their job.' He must be quite adamant if he'd let it end his relationship, especially when it sounded like an amazing offer.

'Well, I... let's just say my agent tore me a new one and convinced me to consider it. Job starts in the Autumn, they need an answer in two weeks, for pre-schedule planning.'

'Oh.'

'Exactly. So right now, I'm concentrating on not thinking about it.'

Recently befuddled by huge decisions herself, Tiff quite understood.

'So, back to Nanna,' she said, focusing, 'might you be visiting her this weekend?' Having got to the easy bit of the call, Tiff felt comfortable enough to multitask and, pulling the post pile across, started sorting through it, sliding the bill-ish ones aside for braver times.

'Well, my diary is particularly empty currently. What gives?'

'I was wondering whether you'd help with the ring.' Tiff explained about the refurb reaching the hall, not being able to dismantle it by herself and preferring to streak around the car park before asking Ron for assistance, particularly as she fully expected him to give notice the following day. 'Plus it's yours and I'd prefer you broke it rather than me.'

'Don't you want me to take it away?'

'No, I can house it,' she said, slitting an envelope open, 'Unless, of course, you want it.' Someone had written from Nigeria offering to share an inheritance with her. How nice. But given she'd been lucky enough on the inheritance front already Tiff skipped the opportunity in the bin.

'Honestly, until I work out what I'm doing with the house here, I'm in no hurry for it.'

'You're selling?'

'It's pretty big for one, and Verity's taste isn't exactly what I would have chosen.'

'You could redecorate.'

'True, but I can do that somewhere new too, somewhere without the memories.' So he *was* sad about it ending. Tiff wondered whether Gavin had felt the same. She hadn't noticed a 'For sale' sign hanging off their old place.

'Okay, I'm happy to babysit it. I'm not sure when mine's arriving and if I want a boxing club here, I need a ring.'

'That would be helpful.' The new issue of *The Ring* was next in the post pile, and there was Mike's face – a less recent, triumphant shot with no bruises – grinning at her, the headline predicting his retirement. Typical. She could have done with seeing that earlier.

'Yeah, I sort of shot my mouth off to Ron about the replacement, too.' She didn't mind confessing to him. Looking at his printed bonce in front of her, it almost felt face-to-face.

'What did you tell him?'

'Told him I'd ordered the "ring of kings" apparently.'

'The *king of rings*, Tiff. The other is a body part. RingPro?'

'Oh yeah, RingPro, that's right. He was giving me grief about neglecting the boxing in my plans and it's the same make as downstairs, so I guessed it was safe.'

'Good choice,' he mused. 'Way more than you need obviously, but quality.'

'And expensive. I nearly choked when Colin told me the price. Four grand!' She binned a letter offering bookkeeping services, feeling grateful for the saving she could at least make there.

'You could buy a different one. You don't actually need one worthy of Wembley.'

'Too late,' she said glumly.

'Change your mind. Cancel it.'

'Yeah Mike, because, as we know, that's how pride works. Ron would love that.'

'Ah yes, pride. Life might be far more straight-forward without that gene.'

'And cheaper,' she said with a grim laugh.

'Definitely,' he agreed wholeheartedly. 'I'll be at Nanna's Saturday morning, Tiff. I'll come after that. What time do you open?'

'Well technically we don't, because we're closed for refurb, but then you always manage to let yourself in.' So far, neither locked doors, shouty rants or direct requests to stay away had stopped him. He'd never liked being told what to do.

Clamping the phone between her ear and shoulder she wrenched open the final bit of post, a jiffy bag, then, whilst grinning back at his face on the magazine, she said goodbye. Plunging her hand inside, the moistness on her fingers registered simultaneously with the stench hitting her nose. Oh god. Someone was now sending her faeces.

Chapter 23

'Ready to sort you out downstairs,' Jess said, catching Tiff staring into space in the office. She'd been working on autopilot for the last day, since she'd finished manically scrubbing the dogshit off her fingers. Convinced the smell still lingered, she kept surreptitiously sniffing her nails. Meanwhile, she kept obsessing over who was doing this to her.

Her prime candidate was Aaron. It was exactly his nasty style and he had motive. Well, he could get stuffed. She wasn't surrendering her business over some silence and poo.

It couldn't be Ron. He'd been right next to her during one of the calls and if he was going to send her poo, he'd be better off doing it once he'd resigned.

She considered it being the second Mrs Black, still aggrieved about Blackie's money. Instinct told her it wasn't though, not least because the amount of jiffyed poo suggested an enormous dog. Tiff couldn't envisage

Mrs Black owning anything bigger than some tea-cup pooch which pooped mini-pellets.

That assumed, of course, it was just the one person. Tiff shuddered. The thought of numerous people out to intimidate her was too much. It'd land her right back to her teen years, when the phone kept ringing with heavy breathing or silence, and the post also brought dead and disgusting things. She slammed the thought into a mental box called Denial and closed the lid.

The phone company were investigating blocking the nuisance calls, but the withheld number complicated things. In the meantime, they advised simply placing the receiver on the desk in the event and leaving the room, to frustrate the caller and run up their bill. The shitty jiffy bag lay sealed in a zip-lock bag, under police instructions. They'd said they'd look at the labelling, but had been rather vague on the timing. Tiff wasn't holding out much hope; realistically, there were more urgent crimes in town than an envelope of excrement.

Leonards was the only person she'd told. Like her, he thought Aaron was an obvious choice, but without proof he couldn't send a Cease and Desist letter. He'd assured her she'd followed the right procedure, but hadn't dispelled her fears. In his mind she simply locked up and left each night. Knowing otherwise, Tiff felt more insecure than ever living away from Gavin. She'd even considered staying with Shelby, but the thought of confessing it all and the dreaded futon spurred her to stay. Having sunk all the remaining money into the club, staying at the Premiere Lodge was ruled out too, and Tiff simply had to console herself with the knowledge that the poo-poster didn't know she was there at night.

'Tiff? What do you think of it?' Jess prompted. Tiff pulled herself together and focused. Jess was eager for her appraisal of the rooms beyond the office. And rightly so, because she'd nailed it.

The duck-egg blue Tiff had picked, with the black for all the trimmings, made the whole gym look like a Tiffany gift box. At least, that was her aim. She already had large black and white stills from *Breakfast at Tiffany's* to go on the walls of the bar. She saw more aspirational values in those pictures – who wouldn't want to look like Audrey Hepburn or George Peppard? – than any of Aaron's sappy posters. Sending them off in a van to him had been a pleasure.

Diverted from the gloomy thoughts, a huge smile rose on Tiff's face. Fresh paint on the walls had brightened everything, giving it a new lease of life. It showed everyone she meant business. It would show shit-senders she wouldn't be cowed. When it came to following omens, she'd be sticking with the bird poo.

'It looks fabulous,' Tiff said, her eyes on the large space with the windows. The bar was in. Once she had the furniture and a commercial espresso machine, she'd be open for coffee. She added *Barista* to her list. More staff. Eek.

'You're doing an excellent job, Jess. Drinks are on me when you finish.' Jess was a bona fide slave driver and with only one week to go, her team were on schedule. The builder beamed at the praise as she sauntered away, leaving Tiff alone in the office once again.

Beyond the poo paranoia, and her legs being seized up from the Pole-fitness, Tiff had already been feeling tense. It was Friday and Ron hadn't mentioned resigning. She harboured a bad feeling he might simply not show up the following week. Based on recent form, she wouldn't put it past him, but a small part of her wanted him to prove her wrong, to have him do this in a professional manner.

She loitered around the office towards the end of the day, but still nothing. Finally, her bladder got the better of her, so she hobbled to the loos for a speed wee before racing back as quickly as her unhappy leg muscles would allow, only to find a scrawled envelope propped on her desk. Ripping it open, there it was; a solitary line, tendering his resignation.

Fury exploded in Tiff's gut. Amplified by the shitfest of the last twenty-four hours, it welled up inside her with such force, it carried her down the stairs at an astonishing velocity to wrench open the doors to the sparring hall. The guys all stopped at her dramatic entrance, as the doors sprang back on her, whacking her into the room.

She swallowed a swear and straightened herself out. 'Ron here?'

'Gone to the pub.' No-one looked her in the eye. They all knew. She didn't swallow the next swear, but at least said it low as she swung back out of the door with as much dignity as she could manage, dodging a vicious door spring.

Her mobile rang as she stormed inelegantly across the car park.

'Babes.'

'Not now Shelbs. I'm about to murder Ron.'

'Where are you?'

'Heading to the pub where he's about to breathe his last. He just resigned while I was in the loo and buggered off. Wanker. I need to give him a piece of my mind.'

'Oh crap.' The line went dead. Weird.

Stalking down the street towards the *Pig & Whistle*, adrenalin muting the wail of her muscles, Tiff muttered through gritted teeth all the words she wanted to pelt at him. She needed to tell him what she thought of him. She needed to vent her rage at the mystery intimidation, and he was copping that too. It might not be fair, but she was incensed. Tiff felt herself grow taller with each stride, channelling the confidence she'd harnessed in that Pole-fitness lesson, and it carried her forcefully through the pub doors.

She spotted him at the bar and tapped him briskly on the shoulder although she was inclined to punch him in the ear. He turned to look at her and scowled, which topped her anger up nicely.

'That's it? One line? *I'm off?*'

'That's not what I wrote,' he said, gruffly. The bar was half empty and immediately the other patrons started to earwig, but she didn't care.

'May as well have done. *I hereby resign with immediate effect,*' she spat, reading the paltry words aloud to him. 'No "thanks for having me, I've enjoyed my time but fancy a change", no "I'm off to start my own club and poach your clients", no "best wishes for the future"?' Ron's eyes narrowed. 'What?' she carried on, 'you think I didn't know? I've known for days.'

He shrugged. 'You could have kicked me out.' Surly as he was, he still scanned her face, slightly unsure of her. He wasn't used to vehemence from her.

'Blackie promised you a job as long as you wanted. I'm too principled to deny him that wish. But you know nothing about principles.'

Ron's face adopted a stone-like expression.

'Think what you like. You and your ridiculous ideas. I didn't wish you luck, because I don't.'

'No surprises there,' Tiff snarled.

All eyes were on their slanging match. There wasn't much else by way of entertainment in this neighbourhood and Ron was fairly well known. Normally the attention would have been the last thing she wanted, but today she wanted them all to know the snake that he was. It encouraged her.

'Blackie would have been disappointed in you.'

'Not half as disappointed as I am in him. I've given years to that club.'

'And now you're looking to bring it down. I hope you can look yourself in the mirror, I doubt Blackie would've been able to look at you.'

He started moving past her with his pint. 'May the best man win,' he said. Was that a smirk? Yes. Yes, she believed it was. She wanted to slap it right off his face.

'Or woman,' she said, defiantly. He stopped and half-turned towards her.

'What?'

'May the best man *or woman* win,' she stated. 'I could win, and I'm not a man, so in the interests of gender equality, and you being a misogynistic dick, I'm saying "may the best man or woman win".' Tiff had no idea why she was picking now to highlight Ron's sexist tendencies – Lord knew she'd had many other opportunities – but she was livid with him and for once had the inner strength to take on all comers.

261

'Right. See, that's never been a phrase, has it?' he sneered at her, 'There's a reason for that.'

Two things happened then. Firstly, her hand flew up to smack the bottom of his pint, sending his beer all over him. Secondly, she was grabbed from behind by two strong arms which hauled her backwards, out of Ron's reach.

'Enough Babes. He's not worth it,' Shelby soothed. While sending a pint over someone was absolutely Shelby's MO, they both knew it wasn't Tiff's style.

Ron stared at her, beer dripping from the tip of his nose. His gaze narrowed. 'First rule of boxing, Tiffanie; never lose your rag. Clear sign of weakness.' He placed his empty glass on the bar and tucked his *Daily Mail* under his arm. 'They'll all see it soon enough: you aren't cut out for this.' He departed with an arrogant wave. 'Cheerio Tiffanie.'

He didn't give her a backward glance and Tiff felt the fight subside. She wished she'd had some pithy and brilliant cut-down as the final word, though. She was overjoyed to see the back of him, but it still felt like a safety line had been severed. She was more on her own with the club than ever. And yet...

Ron was right; she *had* lost her rag, but it hadn't felt like weakness though. It was strength. She might not have been particularly controlled by the end of it, but Tiff had experienced a side of herself she hadn't properly known since she was a teen, one which had been doggedly trying to resurface over the last few weeks. Finally, euphorically, unleashed, Tiff knew while Ron would never have confidence in her, the only real vote of confidence she truly needed to make this happen was, in fact, her own.

Chapter 24

'I like what you've done with the place,' Mike said, looking around the upper floor.

Tiff glowed. 'Me too.' After her run-in with Ron the night before, she'd got up early and surveyed her building. Her euphoria hadn't waned, the doubts hadn't come crawling back in the night. She viewed the place with a newfound sense of achievement and was ridiculously chuffed about it. 'It'll look even better with the furniture and I plan to add a balcony for the summer, but the structural bits need checking.' It was a clear crisp day, and the view out over the rooftops was as good as this end of town got. Turning, he took in the rest of the space; her office, the staff facilities, the locked door at the end.

'That's my um...' she began.

'Bedroom?'

'Storeroom,' she confirmed with a nod. Why was she blushing at the acknowledgement of a bedroom? He already knew about it. She'd already done the shame part. What was that all about? 'One day it'll be something else. Not sure what yet.'

Mugs of tea in hand, they moved down to peruse the middle floor.

Tiff leaned against the wall watching Mike examine the changes. He moved gracefully, fully at ease in his body, using it in a highly efficient fashion. He might have let his training slip by his own standards, but Tiff couldn't see any detrimental effects. She couldn't help but correlate her view now to the Facebook pics. His back was broad and taut, his arms were muscular and toned. She caught herself leering. When had she become a Mills & Boon novel, savouring a man's muscular arms? Thankfully, he hadn't noticed.

'I've always wanted to do this,' he said, sticking his head inside the Ladies changing rooms.

Tiff laughed. 'Perv.'

'I prefer *opportunist*,' he countered, his easy smile spreading across his face. That smile had always charmed her when they were younger and yet, she might like it even more now with the additional years. The small scar at the edge of his mouth was new to her. She wanted to know how it got there. She liked to think his few wrinkles had come with years of smiling. Her own had definitely come with years of frowning. One of them certainly had Ron's name on it. She gave Mike a quick summary of their run-in.

'The pint was a nice touch,' he said.

'I was wound up and frustrated. I'm glad he's gone, I'm only anxious about having no coach.'

'I'm putting feelers out,' Mike said, sticking his head in the studio door. 'Do you think you'll fill three studios?'

'One's going to have the big machines. The other two, I hope so, with classes. But if not, then that wall pushes back so it becomes one big room. Zumba gets the full space.'

He nodded. 'Good thinking.'

She moved for the stairs so he wouldn't see her face fill with what? Joy? While it was great to have found her self-belief where the gym was concerned, she enjoyed having others reaffirm it. Shelby had total faith in her and told her so regularly. Jess was making it happen without any issues. Natalie gushed delight at each new development, diligently updating the running blog on the gym website Tiff had charged her with setting up. And apparently, Mike's opinion mattered to her too. Allies, she concluded, made taking chances far less scary.

The ground floor was a mess. Jess's men had moved their stuff down so they could start first thing Monday morning. It was also in response to Tiff's faint hysteria over her beautiful new floors upstairs getting damaged by tools or whomping great workmen feet. She'd ignored the rolling of eyes.

The sodding sofa was safely shrouded under a dust sheet and the rest of the foyer was stacked with the ladders and tools. They navigated their way single-file through the obstacles. Given she'd checked out his physique, Tiff sucked her stomach in, in case he was doing the same behind her. She doubted she'd hold up so well in comparison.

The ring stood silhouetted until Tiff turned on the lights. The windowless walls all sported some training-slash-torture instrument. She had neither the plans nor inclination to alter much. Without a coach, she would trust Blackie's expertise on this. As she walked around the edge of the room, she pushed aside the growing worry about the missing coach. She was riding high this morning. Not even pressing thoughts like that were going to spoil her mood.

Mike ran his hand along the base of the ring, as he circled it.

'I spent hours in here,' he murmured.

'Tell me about it,' she said. 'Other girls' boyfriends came to pick them up. We always met here.'

'I was always out on time though,' he said, imitating her pout. It made her laugh.

'I'll give you that,' she said, watching him absorb the ring and the memories it held. 'Didn't you already do your nostalgia thing the night of the funeral?'

'Actually, I didn't. It didn't seem right, me mooching around down here in the dark, while you were convening with the spirit world upstairs, so I left.'

'In that case, do you and the ring need a little time alone?'

He dealt her a sardonic look and didn't comment. She took a moment busying herself tying back the climbing ropes.

'Have you been under?' Mike asked.

'Under the ring?' The raised floor was cloaked with its blue pelmet. 'God no. Years of soaked-through sweat, safely hemmed in by synthetic fabric? It must reek.'

'The flooring is rubber. The sweat doesn't drip through, muppet.'

'You sure? Bloke sweat is pretty toxic.' He didn't rise to her bait. 'Why on earth would I go under the ring? Oh god, it's some boxer's sex-fantasy thing, isn't it?' She did not want the mental image of boxers going at it under there. Vonda had been shy of cleaning under desks, there was no way she'd have ventured under the ring.

'Well, it wasn't until you suggested it,' he smirked, 'now I feel I haven't achieved a thing in my career.' He lifted the fabric and bent to look under it. 'This ring is special, Tiff, unique.'

'It is?'

'Honestly? How don't you know? The underside has the signatures of all sorts of famous boxers. Blackie got his fighters to sign when they left for the bright lights. Many of them were champions. This ring is one big autograph book.'

'Blackie never mentioned it.' Joining him at the corner she could make out some signatures and messages written scrawled by the corner. 'Why do you think he did this?' she asked. 'Was it an incentive for the lads to strive? Was he banking on you all being famous?'

'If he did, then he didn't see me getting so far.' Tiff turned her head to look at him, but he moved away.

Mike flipped one side of fabric up onto the ring floor and disappeared from view.

'You coming in?' Mike's voice sounded muffled, causing Tiff to crouch by Mike's protruding feet. 'Get in here.'

She was slightly reluctant to be crawling around on the ground but in she went, manoeuvring herself alongside him on her back as he illuminated the space with the light on his phone.

'Wow!' Their exclamation was simultaneous. They'd just been able to make out scribbles in the gloom earlier, but the light unveiled a whole canvas of names and messages written in black marker. And right in the centre, taped to the wood, was a jiffy envelope. Immediately, Tiff panicked it might contain more poo, but got a grip; it wasn't addressed to her. The envelope had two words written on it, in Blackie's shaky cursive. *Michael Fellner*. Mike tore it off and she watched as he turned it over, confused.

'Open it, Mikey. It was important to him, whatever it is.'

Mike ripped it open, looked inside, then removed a piece of paper followed by a Sharpie. He scanned the note before reading it aloud. *Because I never got to ask you and I always wished I had. I'm so sorry. You did me so proud. Blackie.*

Tiff looked away as Mike's eyes began to glisten.

'Well, do it then,' she said, when the silence had become too painful. 'Sign it.'

She shuffled onto her side, propping her head up with her hand. She didn't follow the sport, but as the sole witness to this moment in Mike's boxing career, she figured she should appreciate it. After scoping the boards, Mike located a suitable spot and with an enormous smile on his face, scribbled his name. His hand shook just a little as he did so.

With his index finger Mike proceeded to guide her through who was who and what level they'd got to in their careers. Blackie had been far more prolific in his coaching than Tiff had known. Her plan to cocoon herself from it all had clearly been successful.

'You're made for the LA job, Mikey. You're a boxing

Wiki,' Tiff said, truly impressed. Lying like a couple of kids in a den, the relaxed cosiness made it easy being herself with him now.

Mike gave a small laugh. 'I always enjoyed the history and the trivia. And following other people's careers is... *was* research for my fights; if I knew their moves, I'd have all the options in front of me to make the right choices. The LA job though...I don't know.'

'Still not thinking about it?'

'Yep,' he said with a grin, knowing she was chiding him really. 'Still not thinking about not having a coach?' he lobbed right back, well aware she shared his denial tactics.

'Yep.' She poked him in his side. He grabbed her hand with lightning reactions. *Ha!* she thought, *still ticklish then*.

'They've made the terms difficult to ignore,' he conceded. 'They thought my reticence was about the money, so they've upped it and honestly, it sounds like it would be more fun than hard work.'

Tiff knew this was tough for him. It had to be a fantastic deal if he was contemplating still living in the limelight. But she knew what was holding him back.

'Can't you take Nanna with you? They have care homes in the US too.'

'I can't do it to her, Tiff,' he sighed, turning to face her. 'She's confused enough already. She'd know no-one.

Here she has her church mates to look in on her.' He was the only family Nanna had left, and he appeared to have made his decision. He sent a sad smile her way. He loved his Nanna deeply, and she knew watching her deteriorate would be painful for him. She gave his hand a squeeze. He still didn't release it.

Their noses only a few inches apart, Tiff suddenly became uber-aware of their close proximity. The concealed space and shadows under the ring created a far more intimate atmosphere than she'd realised at first and it left her supremely dry-mouthed. He held her gaze and she couldn't drag her eyes away from his face. Seeing it again so close up, brought a mix of emotions rushing back, not least what Shelby called 'rampaging lust'. Clenching everything, she tried to keep it under control. Some things however couldn't be hidden. Encouraged by the dilation of her pupils, Mike slowly rolled the remaining distance until his lips tentatively touched hers.

The small moan that escaped her was like a starting pistol. Within seconds hands were sliding up bodies, in each other's hair, touching faces as if regaining the years they'd missed and confirming this was really happening. Tiff arched into Mike's body as he wrapped his arm around her waist and pulled her in. Her breathing was rapid, her heart was banging in her chest, her blood was hammering in her ears. She couldn't think of having felt like this before. In fact, she couldn't think at all.

It took her some moments to realise the clanging sound hurting her ears wasn't actually her heart, but the gym's fire alarm.

Chapter 25

Her pent-up body froze. 'Noooo,' she whispered against his mouth. The thing was ancient, she was surprised it even worked. Trust it to pick right then to trip.

Reluctantly she withdrew from his embrace, both of them taking a moment on their backs to control their breathing. Thankfully, it wasn't just her panting like a horny teen. Knowing her face was some shade of puce, from surprise, from lust, and from annoyance at that bloody alarm, Tiff clambered clumsily out. Standing, she bent over to dust herself down, but really it was to compose herself.

'Can you make it stop?' Mike asked.

'I'm not a hundred percent sure how—'

Her nose twitched as a scent curled around it. Was that... *smoke?* Looking around, there was nothing on in the gym, let alone alight.

'Can you smell that?'

Mike's head appeared between the struts. He took a long drag of air. His eyes widened.

'Fire?'

Tiff was off in seconds, hurtling out into reception. Smoke was filling the room. Drawing closer to the entrance, Tiff saw it coming from a pile of paper bags on the smouldering doormat. Someone had lit bag after bag, stuffing them through the letterbox. There had to be ten at least, all of them fully aflame. Tiff grabbed for the fire extinguisher as Mike came barrelling out of the gym behind her. He raised his foot above a paper bag.

'Mike, don't! It's—'

He brought his foot down on it, just as the sender had intended.

'What the fuck?' Mike stared at his trainer, now dog-shit brown rather than pristine blue suede. Tiff elbowed him aside and let the extinguisher loose.

'Sorry about your shoes,' she said, when the flames were out and the alarm silenced. They'd wedged the front doors wide open, predominantly to clear the smoke, but essentially attempting to thin the hideous stench of burning dog poo. Mike was staring at his foot, deep in thought. 'It might clean off, Mikey.' She wasn't sure about the soot.

'I'm not worried about the bloody shoes, Tiff,' he snapped. 'What the fuck was that about?'

Quite. Who would do this? Her suspicions rested with Aaron, but would he really do something potentially lethal? Looking at the sprayed debris, there was no proof of ownership. She didn't fancy telling Mike about Aaron's threats. He'd go ballistic. '*Assassin turned Enforcer*' under a banana-nosed mugshot wasn't a story Tiff wanted in the paper.

She tried to make light of it. 'Oh you know, *kids*. They're bored…'

'No Tiff. It's arson. They didn't care if anyone was in here.' His eyes narrowed. 'Why aren't you more freaked out by this?'

'Because we put it out,' she hedged, but he wasn't having it.

'That's not what I mean and you know it.' Mike was angry now. 'You knew what it was, you said not to stamp on them. Why was that? And why aren't you surprised by any of this?'

Tiff looked away. 'I've seen the burning bag thing done before,' she wasn't getting into the details, so moved on, 'and someone's been making prank calls and sending poo-stuffed post recently, so I guess it's them again.'

'You aren't sleeping here anymore.' He said it like a command. While part of her wanted to agree, it also put her back up. He couldn't tell her what to do.

'No-one knows about that. The calls only come in the day. Nights aren't a problem.'

'No.' He put his hands on his hips.

'Yes,' she mirrored him back. 'You are not the boss of me, Mike.' Furious now, he slammed back into the gym, where she heard him swear loudly, before he slammed right back out to her again.

'You're calling the police.'

'I don't really want to. The press will get on it. I have a club to open and I don't want to lead with a story about dog poo.' She didn't want the town laughing at her. Not when she hadn't even had a go yet.

A staring stand-off ensued.

'It's over now,' she said, caving. She wanted to get it cleared and gone. She'd do her major freaking in the privacy of her own room. She'd wanted to show him the gym and for him to be impressed with it. This wasn't in keeping with her plan. But he didn't back down.

'You can either move out, or you call the police and report it. Choice is yours, Tiff.' He wasn't budging. Stubborn git.

'Fine then!' Grumbling, she stamped up the stairs like a sullen teen and plucked the post-it with the crime hotline number off the zip-lock bag which still sat on the furthest corner of her desk. As she dialled, she tried to still her shaking hands, telling herself over and over that she'd survived this before, she'd survive it again.

*

Mike and Tiff exchanged few words as they dismantled the ring, each lost in their thoughts of the morning's events, but in synch with each other and without issue – other than the huge kissy elephant in the room neither of them seemed prepared to address. Soon they had it all dismantled and stacked in the first-floor storeroom. The manual labour appeared to have rubbed off their mutual crossness.

'You doing anything this afternoon?' Mike asked. It felt like an olive branch.

'Nope.' She'd cleared the day for him and the ring. The police had been, arriving promptly to detail and photograph the scene, and take away the zip-locked poo, which they hadn't been as excited by.

'Great. Would it be okay if Tiffanie got in my car?' What was he doing? 'I thought it best to ask, you being the boss of you, and that.' Right, he was taking the mick again. That was a good sign. Ignoring his smirk she grabbed her coat, and walked out, neatly stepping over the remainders of the fire mess and waiting to lock the doors behind him. The letterbox had been secured to Fort Knox levels with layers of Jess's industrial tape.

At his Aston, Mike plucked a black beanie out of the glove compartment and pulled it down on her head. It was enormous and covered her eyes, effectively blind-folding her.

'What are you doing?'

'Shush. It's a surprise.' Tiff wasn't a fan of surprises, and having the scent of him wrapped about her head was disconcerting, although it did reduce the smell from his shoe. She supposed this was his incognito beanie. A less-flash car might have been more useful. 'Can't I just shut my eyes?'

'Nope. Have a little faith,' he said, as they pulled away from the club.

'I look stupid.'

'You look lovely. Gangsta-cute. Only your horsey jammies would improve it.'

'They're unicorns. Unicorns are the ones with the horn.' She heard him snort. Feeling decidedly on the back foot, she was not in the mood for innuendo. 'Oh, grow up!'

'Says she, with the unicorn pyjamas.'

'They were a gift.'

'Thank fuck for that.'

They drove in silence. She wasn't giving him the satisfaction of her badgering for details. It allowed her a moment to consider what had happened. Not the fire thing. She'd locked that away in the Denial box too for another time. She was trying to get a grip on what the bloody hell was going on between them. They'd kissed. A proper knock your socks off kiss, the likes of which she hadn't known for a very long time. Had the alarm not interrupted, who knew where it would have lead,

279

because she'd have surrendered to it without question. But it was Mike. *Mikey Fellner*. Who'd left her. Regardless of how they'd changed and how they were getting on now, her teenage self would've been spitting bricks. Oh, but being touched again had felt soo soo good, grown-up Tiff pointed out. Was that the crux of it though? Skin hunger? That was a thing; she'd seen a documentary on it. Maybe her skin was craving touch. Any touch. Gavin's dumping her might have been so they could follow other paths, but at the back of her head she felt if he'd desired her, then he wouldn't have done it. That meant, in Tiff logic, essentially, he hadn't found her attractive enough. Enough to sleep with her that last night, but not enough to work things out.

That little nugget sat festering in her head. It had been further basted when he came to see her and hadn't immediately seen the error of his ways. So wasn't it possible she was merely rebounding and desperate for connection? Was Mike simply the first guy to come along? What if Mike was just *a* right guy in the right place at the right time?

She felt the car pull up.

'Sit tight. I'll be ten minutes, tops.'

'But Mike—' The door shut before she could finish. She was sitting there like a prize-prune; semi-balaclava'd, who-knew-where. She was going to check as soon as she thought he'd gone. The door opened again.

'No peeking. I'll know.' The door slammed again and the locks clunked down. She assumed it was for her own safety. She settled in and let her mind continue doing its worst.

By this point, it now played out in her head, as if she, in her touch-deprived state, had leapt on him. In which case, what had he been playing at? He had kissed back. She was sure of it. He had not, she could categorically say, been fending her off. He was a world champion boxer. Even with her lips leeched to his face, he could have swatted her away. That part had her flummoxed. As she remembered, he wasn't the lad who would go with any girl. He'd fought hard for her when they'd first met. She'd followed the teen magazines' advice and made him do the chasing. A lot of chasing. And he had always treated her well, valued and cherished her; he'd truly seen her as a prize.

As promised, he was back quickly, ditched something behind them and closed his door. Her CSI skills told her they were parked outside a bakery as her nose detected the comforting scents of hot pastry, which thankfully outweighed the poo smell from his shoes. Her stomach rumbled in response as they set off again.

Where was Mike's head at now, she wondered. He'd just split up with an *OK Magazine*-level prize. That might explain everything. Just as she craved to be touched, why shouldn't he? Most likely, the reality was both of them were rebounding, and unfortunately they'd crossed each other's paths. Her mind lingered on the notion of *unfortunately*, wondering exactly what she meant by it.

Finally, he stopped the car, and whipped off the beanie, making her hair go mad and her eyes blink like crazy adjusting to the light. He'd parked on the brow of a hill. Once she could see again, she could clearly make out the gym down in the distance, a black Lego cube in a sea of grey. It looked less ugly from up there.

'Late lunch,' he said. 'Gotta eat.' He held up a large paper bag from Greggs. No wonder the bakery smells had lingered. Oh man, it was years since she'd had lunch from Greggs.

The warmth from the bag wafted up around her nose. Her mouth was salivating and her stomach groaned again. Perhaps he'd let her steal some. She was prepared to beg.

'Chicken and Mushroom slice and an iced bun, right?' he asked, handing her two smaller bags and a cup of tea. She was glad he had his head back in the carrier; he would have seen the dopey grin on her face, tempered by the worry she might just have fallen in love with him all over again.

She didn't speak for the first three mouthfuls. Ecstasy like that was not to be interrupted, and he seemed to appreciate this, partly as he was experiencing the exact same thing, but also because he was enjoying watching her and her pleasure.

'What?' she finally asked, feeling self-conscious. Strike that; *more* self-conscious. The kiss thing was hanging over them, and neither was touching the subject with a shitty stick.

'I never met a girl who could demolish a pie as quickly, yet neatly, as you. Nobody manages puff pastry without flakes or crumbs, except you.'

'Should I be proud or ashamed?'

'Proud. You're an arbiter of non-wastage. At least in food matters. I can't currently comment on the rest.'

The 'currently' was interesting. Implied future inter-action was interesting.

'Can't beat a Gregg's chicken slice,' she murmured. The view out over her business was a close second though. They both sat on the grass, leaning against the front bumper of the Aston, the sun shining on them. It was lovely up there and she wondered why she'd never been before. It wasn't like she and Gavin had done much with their weekends; he went running while she caught up with the chores and perhaps a soap omnibus.

'Gastronomic alchemy,' he agreed, polishing off the last bite of his Cornish pasty. 'I haven't been allowed these for years.'

'Training rules?'

'Verity rules.' He lowered his eyes and reconsidered. 'Probably training rules; these things are addictive.'

'You could live on Greggs now,' she mused.

'I should buy shares if that's the plan,' he played along.

'Not sure your sports channel would appreciate your five-a-day habit. The camera already adds pounds. You'd fill the screen eventually.'

'What's wrong with that?' His indignation made her giggle. 'My enormous wonky face in your living room.'

'There'd be complaints.' The sunlight cast a golden hue around him. No wonder the TV wanted him; he was total eye candy. Surely, he couldn't not take the job... The thought cast a shadow over her memory of their kiss.

'Or I might get offered the Sumo show too.'

'Greggs might sponsor you,' Tiff pointed out, shamelessly licking the last of the pastry crumbs from her fingertips.

'I could have a triple XL tracksuit and everything. Happy days,' he sighed.

'Do you want some of this bun?' she asked, tentatively. She hoped he'd say no. She couldn't wait to sink her teeth through the thick icing into the soft white bread.

He snorted. 'Don't give me that, Trent. D'you think I know nothing about you? I value my kneecaps. I bought myself an Eccles cake – at least I can claim the dried fruit is healthy.'

284

Relieved, Tiff attacked the bun and while floating through the sugary heaven, she wondered whether she'd have got his Greggs order exactly right, like he'd got hers. They'd spent every Saturday lunchtime in there as teens. She recognised his selection immediately, but she wasn't sure she'd have remembered when faced with the whole counter of choices.

'Where did they come from?' she suddenly asked, noticing his feet. A brand-spanking pair of Adidas Sambas adorned them. Not a speck of soot or poo in sight.

'Sports shop next to Greggs. Otherwise, I would have been out in five. I signed the non-shitty old one for the guy at the till.'

'Wow,' she said in mock awe, 'Two signings in one morning. Mikey Fellner really is famous.' She popped the last morsel of bun in her mouth and savoured it. If she put someone trying to burn down her business to one side, and focused on the view, the food and the company, it was turning out to be a lovely day. She wanted to share the joy. 'I think you've got your answer now Mike, about Blackie rating you.'

'He should have told me when he was alive.' She turned, sensing some bitterness.

'Mikey, you keep coming down on him, but I guess he might just have been angry and hurt.' She absolutely understood not wanting to talk to Mike due to anger and hurt. And yet, here they were. If she could reach this point of reconciliation with him, perhaps Blackie could have too. Panged with regret for them both, it took her a moment to interpret the look on his face as confusion.

'What did Blackie have to be angry about?' he asked, plainly.

'Well, you leaving, for starters and the never contacting him again,' she rolled her eyes to make light of it, but it didn't work. Mike's brow drew further together. 'He sent you off on that training camp,' she expanded, 'and when you didn't come back, he took it really badly. From what I heard, he was a bloody nightmare for a long time after you left.' She didn't add that the exact same went for her.

'I didn't leave.'

'Yes, you did,' she insisted, amazed he would dare deny it. 'You went to train for two weeks in Kent and when they made you a better offer you took it.' He'd ditched Blackie without so much as a backward glance. He'd ditched them both.

Mike was shaking his head, his jaw tight, an appalled look in his eyes.

'That's not how it was. That's not what happened at all, Tiff.'

Chapter 26

Tiff crossed her arms. Granted, it had been many years, and she'd moved on, but it was an intense, upsetting time and she remembered it clearly. Mike sitting beside her, declaring things weren't as she thought, made no sense.

'What do you mean?' she asked.

'I didn't just not come back.' He crossed his own arms to mirror hers. The air between them crackled with defensiveness.

'I distinctly recall you didn't come back.' She had waited. God, how she had waited. No Mike, no call, no message at all.

'No, I didn't come back, that's right, but it wasn't that I couldn't be arsed, or I got a better offer. I fought to come back, but I wasn't given a choice.'

He was adamant. Whatever the story was, Mike definitely felt he hadn't stayed away of his own volition.

'Look, I did go on the training camp. We had that

287

date the night before, remember?' Tiff detected a smirk. Really? Now?

'Of course, I remember. First times are generally memorable,' she snapped.

'I thought I'd died and gone to heaven that night,' he said, the smirk widening to a grin. 'I dreamed about it through the whole camp.'

She looked out over the town which appeared quaint from a distance with the surrounding summer greenery, but had also had her trapped. She'd relived that night for a long time too, but when he hadn't returned, her sleeplessness was from questioning what she'd done wrong. That pain, the blow to her confidence, had been devastating.

'So I was primed to come back,' he continued, his grin giving way to concentration, 'when Nanna calls to say the hosting club wanted me to stay on. It *was* a huge honour, they were right up there at the time, but I didn't give it a second thought. I said no. But she says it's already agreed with school, and she's sorted accommodation with a host family. *Then* she says she's spoken to you, you understood and wished me the all the best.'

'What? No.' That wasn't true. Nanna Bea hadn't seen her and there was no way she would've wished him all the best. Sixteen-year-old Tiff would have kicked-off big time. It hadn't been her selfless period – not as a rule, nor during the stress of what had followed. While she'd been at home waiting for Mike, the police arrived with news of her father's arrest at the bank. All their accounts were frozen. People started coming to the door demanding compensation, which they didn't have and couldn't give. It was awful. And all she could think of was when would he show up, hold her tight and tell her they'd get through this?

'No, I didn't think so either,' Mike said, 'so I rang your house and your mum picked up and said not to call anymore. Honestly, Tiff I didn't know what to think. Your mum was acting weird. I mean, I know she probably wanted someone posher and white for you, but she'd never tried to split us up.'

Tiff felt herself rock. Her mum had seen Tiff beside herself, but never mentioned a call. Sounded exactly like her; her mind had twisted completely when the final blow of Tiff's father's mistress came to light. The Saturday 'golf' games had been a somewhat different ball sport.

'She never said,' Tiff said, stunned. 'She had the number changed soon after because of the other calls…'

'What calls?'

'Malicious ones,' Tiff supplied, but changed the subject quickly. The evil calls had stopped but been replaced by more activity around the house, including those burning bags of shit sliding through the door. And all the while she'd kept asking herself what she'd done wrong with him. 'You could have written?' Mobile phones had been way too expensive for kids back then. If only...

'I did Tiff. You never replied.'

'I never got anything.' If she'd heard it third-hand she might have doubted his story, but seeing his face, she knew it was true. Her mum must have binned it.

'I missed you, Tiff,' he insisted. 'I knew no-one, the training was bloody hard, and the school was awful, but I would've been alright if I could've spoken to you.'

'I didn't know.' She shook her head, 'I just thought...' She couldn't physically say it.

'What? Go on.'

'I thought you'd slept with me and gone,' she whispered, embarrassed. Had they not been sat side by side, he might have missed it on the breeze.

'Aw no,' he said, appalled. He turned to properly face her, holding her knee. 'It wasn't like that at all. I mean yes, technically that's what happened, but it wasn't my intention. I thought of you constantly. I wanted to be around you – not just for... you know,' he twitched his eyebrows, 'You were my best mate. I missed my best friend.'

'I hated you at one point,' she said quietly, ducking her head. 'Hated you. I cut up the photos and ripped the cinema stubs I'd kept. All of it.' The hurt lay between them for some long moments.

'And that other guy?' she heard him ask. She snapped her head up.

'What?'

'I came back. I saw you with some guy.'

'What? When?'

'About ten weeks later. Nanna fell off that stupid stool she had for the high cupboards. Remember it? She toppled trying to reach some tinned ackee. Bruised her hip. Bloody lucky it wasn't worse to be honest, and I travelled up. It was my chance to see you. Your mum answered the door, and she didn't look pleased to see me. She said you were out with your boyfriend. That was probably one of the worst punches I've ever had; sucker punch right to the heart.'

Tiff sat shaking her head. This was unbearable. She hadn't known any of this; her mum had never said. How must it have looked to him?

'And then I saw you,' he added. 'I was walking through the town and there you were in the window seat of that posh restaurant.'

Tiff's heart sank. She remembered that night. She'd not felt like going out, but her mother had forced her near enough, virtually slapped the makeup on her herself. Her mother said Tiff shouldn't let Gavin go; he was a good prospect. While his attention was flattering, Tiff hadn't been thinking about his credentials. At the time she'd mainly agreed to date him to get over Mike's rejection. A retaliation of sorts, which was daft as he wasn't there to see it, or so she'd thought. It was an act of defiance against the town for shunning her too; still going out, being wined and dined was a visual 'screw you'.

She'd desperately needed to feel she was still attractive, that Mike walking away was due to his stupidity, not her flaws. That was what Gavin had offered her, all rolled up in a good-looking, upwardly-mobile package, and it was exactly the rescue she'd needed. When she broke it down like that now though, Tiff experienced a sensation of shame. One day, when everything wasn't so manic and screwed up, she should probably take an objective look at her relationship with Gavin. But not now, because right now things were crazy enough, as Mike was deftly turning the world on its head.

'I stood rain-soaked in the street, watching you. You were laughing.'

She'd been faking. It was a while before she'd twigged Gavin's sense of humour, but sitting there in that window, she'd wanted the world to think she hadn't been defeated.

'All I could think was it hadn't taken you long.'

'It wasn't like that,' she began.

'It's fine, Tiff. It's fine,' he said waving it off. 'It was what I needed, I guess. Focused me on the boxing. On fitting into the new club. It cut the ties I'd been hanging onto, you know?'

Tiff hung her head again. She didn't know what was worse; thinking he'd just left her, or knowing leaving her had been so beneficial.

'Did Blackie know you came back?' she asked suddenly.

'Course,' Mike said, plainly. 'After seeing you, I needed somewhere to think. I let myself in with the key, but he was up there working.'

'He never mentioned it. He was always careful never to mention you around me.'

'Yeah well, we had a bust up that night. He wasn't chuffed to see me back either. Not even for Nanna. Said he'd seen the old girl himself and she was fine. If there'd been a need to come, he'd have called. He said I should get myself back to Kent and focus on my future, and not to let anything get in the way. But the way he said it, his anger at me coming back, felt like he wanted shot of me.

'I said I'd seen you and he went mental, spitting that I couldn't throw talent like mine away on some girl, which hacked me right off, because you weren't just some girl to me. And then he said you'd been seeing some guy before I'd left but he hadn't wanted to say, and now I should know the truth and walk away.'

'I had not!' It exploded out of Tiff. 'I never did. I

didn't meet Gavin until six weeks after.' She'd been a mess at that point, scraping her up-ended bag off a pavement, the other kids laughing, when he stopped his sports car to help her. 'I was completely faithful to you. I never liked girls who two-timed. You know that.' She corrected herself. 'You *knew* that.'

He hung his head slightly. 'It was a pretty rough night, Tiff. I reckon I was prepared to accept anything, because I'd already seen something I'd believed impossible, you know? It pushed me over the edge. I told him he was a bastard for not telling me before. It felt good to lay into someone. And he just took it. He took it all. In the end I told him he wouldn't see me again, save on the telly. I slammed the key on the desk, called him a bastard again for good measure and left. Didn't set foot in town for the next eight years until Nanna moved to the home.'

Tiff's heart was racing. Everything was inside out and upside down.

She got up, needing some space between them. He'd thought she two-timed him, while she'd thought he'd abandoned her. And he still didn't know the half of it. She'd thought Blackie had cut him dead for not coming back; they'd had a silent agreement not to mention him. She'd thought it was down to hurt feelings. Turned out there might have been guilt in there too.

Kicking a stone about, while Mike was lost in his own thoughts, Tiff began to piece things together. She knew why Blackie had lied about her. He must have heard about her dad and immediately been onto Nanna. They knew Mike would have ditched everything to come back. The two of them working together – he hadn't stood a chance.

Ultimately, Tiff could see Blackie's plan had worked. Mike had had a fantastic career, and she'd still managed to salvage something of a life for herself. She couldn't have done it without Blackie; he'd kicked her bum through college and the bookkeeping course. He'd been her first client and set her up with others. Clearly he felt guilty. Suddenly she wondered whether he gave her the gym out of guilt too. She didn't know what she wanted the answer to be.

Tiff decided not to tell Mike the rest, about the trouble her dad had brought. What good would it do? He already felt bad about her thinking he'd just left. He'd feel worse if he knew about the awfulness that followed. He didn't need that. More to the point, she was shrouded enough in the shame of what her dad had done and its impact; businesses folding, pensions wiped out, homes repossessed. She didn't want to chance Mike's judgement or his pity. She was already feeling sick that Nanna and Blackie had regarded her a millstone about to drag him down.

'I never came back, in case I saw you,' Mike said, interrupting her speculations. 'I was in two minds about the funeral. But I needed to pay my respects. I owe most of it to him. I regret calling him those names.'

'He put the key back,' Tiff said.

'What?'

'That first night you came, you said the key was still hidden.'

'Right.'

'Well, in spite of everything you said, he decided to replace it.'

Mike considered it. He got up, neatly tackling the stone off her, before chipping it back to her.

'I see what you mean. Unless he left it for some other kid to have a refuge.'

'I don't know who it would be, Mikey. Blackie never attached himself to anyone like he did with you. You were special to him. I thought your leaving had broken his heart too; that he'd vowed never to make that mistake again. Us both losing you felt like some kind of bond.'

Mike ducked his head and stayed quiet for a while.

'There were times,' he said, quietly, 'when I thought he'd really wanted shot of me; that I wasn't all that and he was happy to pass me on. Those were the low points, and then I'd get so bloody angry, I'd tell myself I'd show him, I was going to rub it in his face what he'd lost and I'd train until I nearly passed out. If he lied to get me to concentrate on the boxing, then he played me perfectly.'

'He knew you were going to be good, Mikey. That's why he pushed you to go.' *That's why he had to get you away from me.*

'You believe that?'

The truth might be horrible, but it was still the truth. 'I do. Completely.'

'And you accept that?'

'Well, the teenage-me thinks it sucks, but looking at what you've accomplished, how can I say he was wrong? He and Nanna took a risk, at huge personal cost, and it paid off for you.' She reckoned if he'd been alive Blackie would be pushing him to take the LA job. Nanna would too, had she had all her faculties. Tiff thought about their kiss. What if she was at risk of becoming a millstone for him again, standing in his way, threatening to sink him?

'The words in his will make more sense now,' Mike said. Tiff saw his nose twitch and his eyes were watery. She took his hand and squeezed it.

He reeled her in towards him.

'No wonder you were so pissy with me, Angel,' he said with a small smile. Likewise, Tiff understood why he'd got off on winding her up, too. 'It's a good job Blackie's dead, as I would've lamped him.' His off-the-cuff remark made her laugh. The image of Blackie in his wizened form and Mike slugging it out in the ring was pretty comical.

'You'd have had to beat me to it,' she added looking up into his eyes. The smile they shared was bittersweet, but the misgivings were gone. Everything was different now. The kiss had been amazing, but in hindsight confusing; it was lust overriding sense. But now, knowing he hadn't meant to hurt her, it felt all the sweeter for not being a betrayal of her teen self. He carefully tucked a breeze-wafting lock of hair behind her ear, a gesture so tender it made her melt. Now they could address what happened that morning. His eyes dropped to her lips, as his face drew slowly closer to hers. She took a low breath and—

The ringtone from his pocket made them both jump. Mike didn't budge for the first couple of rings, watching her until Tiff stepped back. Seeing the moment between them was over, he dug out the phone.

She didn't want to eavesdrop, but she saw the colour drain from his face before she could move away.

'I'm on my way,' he said, ending the call. 'It's Nanna, Tiff. She's gone.' He looked so stricken, she wanted to fling her arms around him, but there wasn't time for that.

'We'll find her, Mikey,' Tiff said, moving for the car door. 'Let's start at the gym, in case she heads there again.'

But Mike wasn't following her. 'No, Tiff. She's *gone*. She died.'

Chapter 27

'How's your boxer?' Shelby asked, setting a second cup of tea in front of Tiff. Breakfast at *Viv's* was beginning to become a therapy venue. So the yellow floral wallpaper was decidedly old fashioned, with the cooking done right behind the chipped counter, but Tiff found its familiarity and aromas deeply comforting.

'He's not my boxer,' Tiff replied, but asked herself why she couldn't stop thinking about him. One lunchtime had tipped ten years of hurt on its head. One conversation had shown her how she felt about herself was unwarranted. And one kiss had her heart healing again.

Thinking about Gavin no longer left her feeling broken. She missed him but she didn't feel at a loss now. Initially she'd felt untethered, adrift without him anchoring her. While she was certainly still floating, homeless and alone, it didn't scare her. She'd find a home eventually and obviously she was still kissable. And what a kiss it had been...

'He's gone to ground,' Tiff conceded. Frustratingly, communication in the last week had been minimal.

Mike had held it together as they drove from the hills but only until he reached Nanna's room. Then he was consumed with grief for the woman who'd raised him, and all Tiff could do was hold him as they waited for the undertaker to come.

After that he'd retreated into himself and she'd let him, because support was all she had to offer and if privacy was what he needed, then that was an easy thing to grant him. While she busied herself at the gym, she sent him texts which all went unanswered save for one to say the funeral would be the day before the club opened. The distance between them though felt a million miles from where they'd been up in the hills.

Meanwhile, Tiff had her own issues. She still had no trainer and given there was no way she'd bug Mike about making calls, she cobbled together an ad for *The Ring*. The police hadn't got any leads on the arsonist, but the calls at least had been blocked, making it easier for Tiff to lock *that* worry away. The club kept her busy, but that was mainly her stressing, as Jess had things covered. In light of Ron's defection, Tiff wound herself up looking for ways to offer some form of sparring space, or perhaps start the fitness classes early upstairs. Hence, Shelby's bringing her to her senses over breakfast at *Viv's*.

'Seriously babes, let's think clearly about this. You're doing the refurb to entice new clients in. *Female* clients. Do you really want their first impression to be builder's bums and swearing? They get that at home. You're looking to offer them a haven.'

'But he'll have the jump on me,' Tiff groaned, despondently working her way through her grilled mushroom fry-up. Shelby was face deep in the Full Workman. Tiff couldn't forget Ron's smug face as he'd left. Natalie estimated half of the adult members would stick with Ron. Tiff knew the rest, and their kids, might follow once they'd had a review or missed their mates.

'Babes, he's *already* got the jump on you,' Shelby said, matter-of-factly. 'And so what? He's only got a boxing club – in a cold industrial unit. You're going to have a boxing club *and* classes, *and* a bar. Once women start pouring in at yours, he won't be able to compete. Can't see him trumping up classes on a concrete floor. And then he'll have to pander to the scabs who defected with him. They're the "grass is greener" types anyway; they wouldn't recognise loyalty if it spanked them. They won't feel an ounce of shame coming back either.

'Key fact about blokes:' Shelby carried on, 'they like their efforts acknowledged. In their jobs, in bed – if they aren't praised for their hard work, they get sulky and dejected. Some guys I've met expect fanfares for the most basic efforts. Honestly, this one guy, he expected applause for going dow—'

'Shelb,' Tiff interrupted, indicating the room with her knife, 'family show.' Shelby looked around. *Viv's* was full of kids.

'Your boxers will be the same,' she recommended, assuming Tiff perceived the main thrust of her example. 'If they can come out after a session, showered and buff, to work their tight T-shirts and buns around a bar to even a grain of appreciation, they'll be happier than Ron's pack who'll just go home.'

God, she hoped Shelby was right. In terms of specialist advice, Shelby did know men – if not in quality, then at least in quantity.

'How about Mike?' Shelby pitched in with what felt like a change of subject, as opposed to digging for gossip.

'How about Mike what?' Having promised to keep Shelby informed, Tiff had overlooked mentioning The Kiss in the emotion of Nanna's death. Given the current radio silence, she was reluctant to put it up for dissection now.

'Still not asking him to be your coach?'

'We did this already, Shelbs. It's totally beneath him plus he's been offered a diamond-deal to front a sports show. In Los Angeles. Which he was born to do. Who'd turn that down? Moreover, who'd ask him to? Not me.'

'Ha! So you *have* been in touch with him and not told me.'

'Of course I've been in touch, Shelby – his nan just died. I knew her when we were kids. Funeral's next Friday.'

'Can't hurt to ask him.'

'Sure. *Mike, how d'you fancy coaching seven-year-olds who can barely shift the punch-bag in the drizzle of Kingsley, for a measly wage OR would you rather an exciting life hob-nobbing with famouses in the sunshine of California, for megabucks?* Hmm,' mused Tiff, fingertip to chin, eyeballs to ceiling, 'dunno which I'd choose.'

'No need to be sarky,' Shelby said, more unimpressed than offended.

Tiff sagged. 'Sorry. Given the responses to the ad, I'm almost considering it. They're dire. But I just can't do it, Shelb. He said he was staying here while Nanna was alive, and now she isn't. He's free to go. The answer's obvious even without asking. Besides, he knows I'm coachless and he hasn't offered.'

'Have you called the press yet?' Shelby asked, prompted by the rustling of the local newspaper at the adjacent table.

'Yeah, so no, because no coach,' Tiff hedged.

Shelby tapped the man next to her, asked to borrow the paper, and found the relevant page. 'Make the call,' she insisted, offering Tiff her own phone and pointing to the number.

'I will,' Tiff said, pained. 'In a bit. Back at the office.'

'Wuss. Stop putting it off.'

'I'm not.' Tiff dug her heels in. 'I'm crazy busy building the club and am, right now, having a rest. You said I needed "me" time. This is it. No press allowed.'

Shelby wasn't buying it. 'I'll do it.' She started to dial.

'No! I can do it,' Tiff grumped. She'd spent years trying to escape the local limelight but memories were long in a small town. Courting publicity in the local rag appealed as much as sticking her face in a fire. She'd hated that paper since it ran daily reports on her dad's trial.

'Babes. Just do it. A pic in the paper is priceless. The studio looks amazing. Women will come running. If nothing else then for a nosy. Then it's down to your instructors to keep them coming.'

Pole-fitness Sammi and Leonie the Zumbist had both confirmed and Fliss had been discovered instructing a Pilates class. Neither Tiff nor Natalie were able to move sensibly the day after. Fliss was thorough and brisk, with an air of drill sergeant about her. If things worked out, Tiff was thinking of some bootcamp classes. There were people out there with a masochistic streak, who wanted to come away feeling like they'd been flogged. Vomiting-point was a positive goal. Nutters. Tiff thought of them as the 'no-pain, no-gainers', but their addictive streaks offered balance-sheet stability, so she wanted them.

Shelby growled at her. Properly growled, like a dog. 'Quit stalling. Make. The. Call!'

Ten minutes and much sweating later, Tiff had a date with a photographer and a journalist the Sunday morning after Jess should finish. The story would be in the paper and on the internet the following day as they reopened. This was a watershed moment. It was all very well her spending the monies, making the plans – now she was committed to opening the doors, putting it all on the line and seeing whether Shelby's stolen faith of '*Build it and they shall come*' was justified. Alternatively, they might just stay away, watch her monumentally fail and laugh in her face. No pressure then.

*

'They're here!!' Natalie came screaming into the office.

'What? Who?' Tiff looked up from the accumulating pile of invoices.

'The mats, balls and steps. They're in reception, need

a signature. Can I do it? Can I?' Natalie was almost panting, then stopped short. 'No, you should do it. It's the first equipment, isn't it? Ceremony and that.'

Tiff laughed. 'We'll do it together. I'll sign, in case there's a problem – there should be Zumba rattles, stretch bands, free weights and the poles too – but you can open everything.' Natalie bounced like it was Christmas.

'The uniforms are in as well,' Tiff said, as Natalie hurtled down the stairs. Tiff had stuck with keeping the gym closed. Standing in reception watching Jess's men gut the changing room with vicious gusto, Tiff admitted Shelby was right. All the arriving boxes added to the mess. 'Would you help me check and store them? You'll get to model the first set.'

Natalie grinned with pleasure. She was a different woman compared to the pasty shell-shocked mole who used to sit in the corner of the gym. This woman stood upright, smiled and was growing a decent batch of confidence.

Together they spent the morning sorting the polo shirts, shorts, skorts, trackie bottoms and zip-necked fleece sweatshirts, making neat duck-egg blue and black stacks on the first-floor storeroom shelves. Then, like delirious teens, they raced to the locker room. Tiff never imagined getting excited about lycra. Shelby would be disgusted. Yet she was pulling on sports-tech fabric with glee. This fabric had magical properties, holding her podgy bits in, leaving no bulges or muffin tops to be pointed out. Tentatively looking in the mirror for the first time in weeks, Tiff was relieved to finally look the part of a gym manager.

Things were moving fast. Natalie had turned out to be a techie queen, revamping the once single-page gym website, setting up an additional Facebook page along with a blossoming Instagram account to track and share all the new developments. Her Twitter game was strong too. With the instructors confirming, Tiff and Natalie had also gone old-school, stapling posters all over the town from surgeries to nurseries, schools to bus stops. They'd left flyers at the station, the library and Shelby's salon. You couldn't move through Kingsley without seeing duck-egg blue rectangles.

Arson attempts aside and overlooking the lack of coach which now had her in a constant bum-clenching sweat, everything was coming together. The refurb was on the home straight. She'd spent all the money Blackie had left her and she'd resigned her other bookkeeping jobs. She was committed up to the hilt, but she felt okay (save for the coach thing – *Lalala, can't hear you, can't hear you…*). Considering it all, Tiff felt totally capable. She didn't need Gavin to tell her she could do it.

*

No amount of lycra-delirium could completely anaes-thetise the aching muscles Tiff was now used to having daily. Natalie hadn't stopped her regime of trialling new disciplines – *Kick-boxing, Tiff?* – but in the last week Tiff had snuck into a couple of Sammi's pole classes. Something about it was a siren's call to her, topping up her confidence, in spite of it hurting like holy hell the next day and the constant bruising on her legs making them look like they were covered in camouflage. She'd added poles to the equipment order immediately after Sammi's taster class, almost singing the credit card details to Martin in her excitement.

Sticking to jobs she could stay sitting for, she called Colin to check on the large equipment delivery, but it rang out. The rest of the day was spent balancing the various budgets and accounting. She felt better with the numbers in place. Sure, the spending looked scary, but she tried to view it as purely numbers, not cash out of the bank. God bless Denial.

It also distracted her from the fact she'd heard little from Mike. She'd finally received some short responses to her texts; Yes, he was bearing up, the funeral details were sorted, no, he didn't really want to talk about it. But that was it.

Tiff began to ponder whether this was him dealing with the grief, or deliberately keeping her at arm's length. Despite now knowing the truth of what happened all those years ago, Tiff couldn't help reminding herself it wouldn't be the first time he'd got close to her, before disappearing out of her life. Last time he was pushed towards reaching his potential and carving a career, this time he was being offered a stellar new one on a plate. What was more, his two weeks to accept the LA offer must almost be up.

Chapter 28

By the final Thursday morning of the refurb, Tiff was walking normally again and not swearing when pulling on a top. Her body was getting accustomed to this exercise malarkey. Feeling brave, she'd dared to ditch her habitual safe trackies for a pair of skorts, which, bruises aside, had her feeling positively girly.

She tried calling Colin again first thing, to no avail. He was impossible to pin down apparently. But they'd agreed the kit would be delivered by Saturday, so she was expecting it anytime now.

'That's it, Tiff. Job done,' Jess popped her head around the door. 'The lads are taking the last of the kit out to the van.' Jess had kept the guys slaving – even when they got leery fixing the poles in place – *No, there'll be no demos in part payment.*

'Amazing. Thank you.' Tiff had been down to admire the ground floor four times already; 'chuffed' didn't cover it. The new *Tiffanie's* sign had been screwed to the front of the building and inside the new reception desk sat primed for business. Looking at it, Tiff remembered Mike pointing out that this, the refurb, was the plan which fired her up, not keeping the status quo. He'd been exactly right. Change had been the way to go and an exciting one at that.

Mike though, was a sore point. She'd attempted to call him on the pretence of re-checking the funeral details, but hung up again feeling pathetic. His not calling her after The Kiss, kept her from seeing it through. He was mourning, of course, but he'd said he'd phone when he dropped her off, and hadn't. Perhaps he'd patched things up with Verity. Maybe, on consideration, he'd decided The Kiss was a mistake.

Thinking of Mike raised a wardrobe issue. On inspection, she'd only one outfit choice suitable for the funeral which wasn't a bundle of creases from living in her suitcase. It would be strange wearing it again. It was the knitted dress she'd worn for Gavin the night they split. Simple, plain, black. Sophisticated not showy. Holding the dress a worry hit her. Racing into the changing room for its long mirror, she dragged off her polo-shirt, dropped her skorts and slipped the dress over her head. Two months ago it had shown her curves, now it had lost its cling factor.

She hoiked it up to have a proper look at herself. Trying the new gym kit on, she'd assumed the sports fabric was holding her in, but maybe not. The reflection showed a body she hadn't seen in years. There was less flab there – not Barbie taut or anything like that, but she was definitely less muffiny. Some muscles had definition, particularly in her arms while her abs had aspirations. Granted her eating was currently rather sporadic and salady for ease, but otherwise it must be down to the classes she'd trialled with Natalie. Her constant stair climbing had probably helped too; overseeing the build across three floors, she'd been up and down like a tart's knickers. She considered her calves. They weren't her worst bit by a long shot now.

The dress was hanging on her. Granted, it was a funeral, not a fashion show, but after the state she'd looked at Blackie's she'd wanted to up her game. She'd even ventured out for a haircut. She was too busy to shop for another dress. A belt was the only solution. Resigned, Tiff took her skinny calves back to her desk.

Mid-afternoon, she tried Colin again, but yet again, it just rang out. Seriously, she understood people needed their holidays, but an answer machine would be more professional. Small businesses couldn't afford to be lax with customer care. She'd picked a local company to keep the money in the community, but was beginning to wish she'd gone with one of the big nationals, who'd at least have had some holiday cover to handle her order.

Putting down the phone it rang immediately, making her jump.

'Tiff. It's Mike.' Oh man, that voice. Her belly tightened and her thighs clenched, then she remembered her disappointment at his not calling. 'Sorry for ghosting you, I was snowed under with the funeral and the house. It's gone on the market.' He was sounding much brighter than she'd expected given the taciturn texts.

'Oh. That was fast.' She half-forgave him instantly.

'Yeah, no point hanging around. It kept my mind off things, you know?' She did. She got it. But a call would've been nice...

And the house going on the market? Surely that meant he'd made his decision.

'Did the gym get finished?' he asked.

'It did. Just now. The building, that is. The lift is being fixed next week and I'm waiting for the kit.'

'Right, did you get the new ring?' It was small talk, which made her want to shout. They had much *much* bigger things to discuss.

'It's due Saturday. Yours is fine in the storeroom until you're ready for it.'

'Great.'

'Not that I have a coach,' she said, gloomily.

'Right, the coach. I didn't come back to you on that. Sorry.'

'S'alright, you've had enough going on,' she conceded. It was her problem after all, not his. 'I put an ad on the website and in *The Ring*, but the responses have been pants.'

'Yeah, you're probably better off with word of mouth for this kind of job.' That was the problem though, his was the only relevant mouth she knew.

'I tried a couple of sports recruitment websites too, but they haven't turned anything up either. So, short of advertising at a televised match, which is ludicrous, I'm out of ideas.'

He might have sensed her growing panic so they had a lame brainstorming attempt, but she could tell he was distracted, and they got no further. To be honest, her attention was elsewhere too and for now it took precedence over the coach anxiety.

Enough was enough. 'How's your job situation looking?' She wanted to know where they stood. His lack of immediate answer was a bad omen.

'The channel's pushing for an answer. I'm supposed to let them know by tomorrow. My agent's almost apoplectic.'

'Well, they want to get you while you're hot.' He didn't respond to that. Had she said the wrong thing? Was it a daunting prospect seeing your stardom fading? She didn't want his confidence to take a hit. 'It's a great opportunity, Mikey.' It was true, she couldn't deny it, much as she might want to; it *was* a great offer.

'You think I should take it?' *No,* she thought. Her reaction was instinctive, but also selfish. The more she'd thought about the revelations on the hill, the more she'd wondered what might have happened had Blackie and Nanna not stepped in. What might they have become? There was something about The Kiss she wanted to investigate, to let blossom. Not as some nostalgic thing, more as a second chance.

However, she was waylaid by the fact he was asking her. His wanting her opinion was both flattering and important; with Nanna and Verity gone, maybe his circle of advisers had disappeared. No doubt his agent was leaning towards the dollar signs. Tiff felt he deserved an unbiased discussion.

'Well,' she began carefully, 'you said it was Nanna Bea keeping you here...'

'It was.' Not anymore though. Point to LA.

'And what do you think she'd have said?' Tiff asked, knowing the answer.

'She'd have said *Praise the Lord!* and had my bag packed before I could blink.' Yup. That was what Tiff thought too. Another point to LA. Tiff had a vision of Nanna shooing her on her way, so as not to hinder Mike's ascension to further glory.

'She always wanted the best for you, Mikey.' Both
Blackie and Nanna had wanted the best for him. Tiff
knew that. They'd made hard decisions in the past for
exactly the same reason. And those decisions had paid
off. Tiff couldn't help but feel they were showing her
the way, much as it might hurt. 'We all want the best
for you.'

But she was so torn. What she wanted wasn't neces-
sarily what he needed, or what was right.

'So you're saying I should go?' Something about his
voice said Mike wasn't just asking for her opinion. *No.*
She pressed her lips shut tight. *Tiff, be fair, be objective...*

She couldn't do it and so took a seat on the fence,
not proud of her cowardice. 'Mikey, that's for you to
decide.'

'I'm just trying to figure out if there's anything...
anything to stay for.'

Me, she wanted to shout. *Ask him. Ask him. Go on.*
The scrawled CV's on the desk in front of her were
pushing her and a small something in her head kept
yelling he'd already been given the lucky break once,
weren't they due one now, not least in compensation
for the past? She wanted to see what The Kiss could
be.

But.

What if it was just a kiss, nothing more nothing less?
She couldn't ask him to pass this up based on a *what*

if. Dropping her head quietly onto the desk and shutting her eyes to crush the threatening tears, Tiff knew the only answer she could, in good conscience, give.

'Not sure I can think of anything to beat LA, Mikey. It sounds amazing.' The words felt like shards.

'Right,' he said, finally with a sigh. 'Tiff, I gotta go. If I get my agent now he can place the call to LA before end of play.'

The following silence was her cue to change her mind. Instead she mentally stepped aside to stand beside Blackie and Nanna, out of his way. She could not, *would not*, be the one to drag him down, to keep him in a small town. Having had her own future fettered by the actions of others, she couldn't do that to him. His prospects weren't hers to shape for her own selfish desires.

Accepting her decision he asked, 'Can I pick you up for the funeral tomorrow? Can we go together?'

'Of course,' she said, but her mind was reeling with the capitulation. She didn't know where they stood. 'Will you be staying?' *Please.* It might sound like a proposition, but that was because it possibly was.

'I don't know, Tiff. I've got things to finalise here, so I'll have to see how things pan out, you know?'

'I guess,' she said, but as they said their goodbyes, she felt she'd already lost him.

Chapter 29

'Bossy as she was, Nanna obviously had no more sway with the man upstairs regarding funeral weather, than Blackie did,' Mike said, looking out of the Pentecostal church hall window. It had been a lovely service, complete with gospel singers and the women of Nanna's congregation were now plying them with wedges of ginger cake. The weather though was true to form; dismal. Cold miserable drizzle wasn't going to overturn Mike's decision.

'Maybe it's their punishment for meddling in the past,' she said, but more to herself.

'They got off lightly then.' Mike's face wore a wan smile. Though tearful, the service had been a true celebration and he seemed to have been released from a great weight. He was dressed in a dark suit again and looking so handsome. Not having a battered face this time helped too. Tiff kept sneaking peeks at him, only to see Mike covertly eyeing her too.

Things were awkward. She'd met him at the club. Her own smile was spontaneous. His though was like he was trying to constrain it. They were at odds from the off. She suggested tea before they went, but he declined. She asked about the traffic, but it'd been fine thank you. Small talk done, they'd sat quietly as he steered the Aston through the streets to the church. The hearse had arrived shortly after and raw emotions had taken over.

Coat in hand, ginger cake in tummies, Tiff saw her time with Mike disappearing far quicker than she was ready for. She'd overheard him telling Nanna's friends he was going back to the States. As they left the wake and sped off in the car, she needed to know whether she'd ever see him again. While all the signs indicated this was over before it had begun, she wanted clear-cut facts. She'd done the not-knowing thing before and she'd done the hoping-for-a-reprieve recently with Gavin. She craved clarity.

After ditching his tie, he got out and opened the car door for her outside the gym. She couldn't let this be it. If she asked him a question and kept walking, he'd have to follow her in, wouldn't he? She'd act like it was a given he'd come in for a bit. It was worth a punt.

'So, when's your flight booked?' she asked. She kept her eyes to the ground but was pleased to hear his footsteps behind her.

'Monday night. Sunday was sold out.' He wasn't wasting any time.

'Got any plans to come back?' she said, unlocking the door and ushering him into the reception. She locked it behind him, but still didn't look up. She didn't trust her face not to crumble. Being so matter-of-fact about it was hard. This was what she'd decided was for the best, but it didn't curb her need to grab his legs and wail *Don't go!* She headed for the stairs and the office. Tea. She'd make tea. It was always the answer.

'None currently,' he said. 'Depends on the schedule. Maybe when the house sells...' There were companies that would box all his stuff and ship it to him. Mike wasn't coming back for that.

'Tiff? What am I doing here?' Turning she saw he'd stopped following her. He looked dejected.

'Would you chuck an eye over the applications I've had?' she tried. It sounded as desperate as it truly was. 'I *am* getting applications, but I'm slightly nervous to interview the ones who took their coaching qualifications in prison. Not that I'm against giving someone a fair chance, but—'

'Tiff. Why am I here?' He wasn't buying it. And she was at a loss.

'I thought... I just thought we could spend some time together before you go.'

'And why is that?' he coaxed. She had nowhere to hide, and felt forced to the truth.

'We kissed,' she stated.

'We kissed,' he agreed.

'What did it mean? Did you feel it was a mistake?'

'Not for a second,' he said calmly. 'I wanted to kiss you since I first saw you in your jammies again.'

'And now? I know you're leaving, and rightly so, but I wondered if—' she broke off, not quite able to say it for fear of being rejected.

'If?'

That lust-over-sense thing won over again. She'd take the heartache for more of what they'd started under the ring. Hearts could heal. She'd learnt that. They weren't as delicate as she'd once thought – if anything, scar-tissue made them stronger. Moments, however, they were lost, she'd come to see that too, and so she wanted hers, however short, with Mike. 'If we could do it again.'

He took a step towards her. She stayed put. He took another and another until they were nose to nose. Her breathing was off kilter.

'I just lied,' he said, his voice low. Tiff's mind reeled through all the possible things he'd said that could have been a lie. Was this a cruel game? 'I wanted to kiss you since you banged your leg in the pub at the wake and were too far in a snit to let on.' Given his proximity and the change in the air, Tiff couldn't help gulping. It roughly translated to *come and get it*.

Under the ring or against the corridor wall, the kissing was the same; heart-thrashing and exhilarating.

'Do you want to go upstairs?' Mike rasped between his kisses around her neck and ear. Decision-making was difficult at this point. The office sofa was nearer but offered approximately the same discomfort of her mattress, so it was much of a muchness. However, the fairy lights of her room would be more forgiving than the strip-lighting of the office when it came to showcasing her body after all this time.

Ascending the stairs, she briefly re-questioned herself on what she was doing. He was leaving. She knew this. He'd love her and leave her, like last time. She knew that too. Only, this time she *knew* he was going; there'd be no mystery. This was a one-night deal. As he nibbled her ear, whispering very naughty things, she knew she wanted this to happen. She deserved to have her moment with Mike, to make up for the past and if Shelby was right, set her up for the future. This would be the best fling she could dream of, and one she'd look back on joyfully when he'd gone. She needed this.

That said, she still felt shy as she led him inside her room.

'Homey,' he said as she switched on the fairy lights.

Yup, that was definitely the maximum illumination she could cope with.

'Behave,' she said, dropping her phone on the archive box bedside table. 'One day I'll have my own place again.'

'Will you invite me over?' he asked, releasing her belt before sliding his hands down her thighs to the hem of her dress and pulling it slowly up over her raised arms and head. They'd reached an accord; he was definitely going, but they needed this too.

'You wouldn't turn up unexpected, with a suntan and daft trans-Atlantic twang? I've got used to your visits,' she said, pulling his shirt up but getting stuck around his shoulders because he was stupidly broad and she was too short. He took over, choosing a more sensible approach of unbuttoning it, affording her a shameless gawp at his chest. Blimey. For a retired guy he would put the cover-shots of *Men's Fitness* to shame. (Yes, okay, she'd succumbed and bought a copy. Then placed a subscription. The reception needed magazines for waiting clients. It was totally legit.)

'Me too,' he said back at her neck, resuming where they'd left off, his hands now gliding over across her skin, sending her eyeballs fluttering within their lids. He stopped and bereft Tiff opened her eyes to find him gazing concerned at the bruises on the soft skin inside her upper arm. She quickly understood his worry, knowing he'd grown up tending his mother's welts.

She kissed his shoulder to reassure him. 'They're from the pole-fitness, Mike.' This clearly satisfied him *and* more; his eyes growing darker again at a rapid speed. He moved his lips to the top of the bruise trail, and began planting tiny kisses on her pole kisses. It was sublime.

They manoeuvred to the bed and sank clumsily down on it. He pulled his face from her.

'Jesus, Tiff. How d'you sleep on this? My kitchen counter has more spring.' She looked back at him appalled. 'What? It's marble. It's bloody hard.'

'Mike, I don't want to know what you've been doing in your kitchen unless it's making food.' God, blokes were idiots sometimes.

'That's not what I meant. I haven't, I mean we didn't... well maybe once... but—'

She slapped her hand over his mouth. His eyes showed a hint of panic, then settled with a look of apology.

'Shutting up now?' He nodded and she dropped her hand. He waited, holding himself above her. He wanted her to make the first move, to say it was okay to carry on.

Trembling, she ran her hand across his chest, appreciating the muscle definition. A new growth of baby hairs made a soft down under her delighted touch, his retirement having ended the waxing. He waited, still, keenly watching her face. Her fingertips reached a nipple and she gave it a tweak for the hell of it. That spurred him into action and they were off again. The kissing, the touching, all of the exploring was as pulse-racing as she'd imagined it would be. She *had* been imagining it. There wasn't much else to do at night in the store-room; she'd reread all the books in her boxes.

As they both kicked off their shoes and he carefully, with precision verging on the painful, peeled off her remaining layers, she began considering how she must look to him now after all this time. In spite of recent changes, she was bigger and definitely softer than when he'd last been so close. Admittedly, that had been fren-zied, racing against time to get the deed done before they got caught. This Mike, by comparison, moved in slow-mo. This Mike worked as if he had all the time in the world, leisurely investigating every inch of her. But Tiff began falling to the struggle in her head; trying to raise the vixen she wanted to be, while the fear of being a disappointment mounted a concerted attack.

'Tiff?' Mike asked gently, drawing away from her belly and rising to look up at her. He brushed an errant twist of hair way from her cheek. 'Tiff, stop. Breathe.' Running his thumb along her collar bone, his eyes darted between hers. 'Relax. It's me. Mikey. Remember?'

'I'm nervous. It's been a while.'

'Don't be nervous, Angel. It's just me.' His hushed tone as he spoke between his kisses to the base of her throat and up to her ear was intoxicating. 'You remember me, don't you? Two thrusts, a grunt and we're done.'

She snapped back, rather less spellbound. Then she saw his smirk spread wide across his face and she slapped his arm. Her hand bounced off the solid muscle.

'Don't joke about it.' Actually, she was glad he was joking; she was anticipating more. Much much more. 'Why am I the only one who's nervous?'

'Well,' he said, trailing the tip of his nose lightly down her side, 'I have the benefit of knowing I've improved over the last decade. I've been practising and getting better at it. You, on the other hand are having to take my word for it, so I understand your apprehension. After all, you've got all dressed down for this, and the expectation could be quite high.' His tongue drew a small delicate circle around her belly button, causing new conflict with her brain relaxing as her body tensed. It felt delicious.

'Then surely you should be nervous too,' she said, releasing herself to it. His calm demeanour, his confidence, reassured her.

'Angel,' he breathed into her skin, 'I've made a career of hiding my nerves and surprising people. Right now, I'm thinking it was all training for this.'

Tiff had lost her appetite for surprises long ago, but

for the next long while Mike showed her exactly what she'd been missing.

Was it wrong, wanting to call Shelby to give her a play by play recount? *Was it?* Not that Tiff's gelatinous limbs were in any state to shift, and Mike's arm across her chest held her firmly in place. *Finally* she knew what all the fuss was about – anything over twice would have been viewed as unnecessarily extravagant in Gavin's book. And those recent classes she'd taken were useful – some of what they'd done took some flexing.

Mike breathed steadily in her hair as she bathed in the afterglow, considering how much more she liked this room now. It really was cosier than she'd given it credit for. Not the bed of course. That was still god-awful, but she'd have better memories of it now. She'd made the right decision. Some ghosts had been exorcised that afternoon, some demons extinguished.

Her mobile started ringing. It was about blooming time Colin got back to her, but honestly, his timing was flipping awful. Reaching across Mike's utter buffness, she cack-handedly tried to grab the phone just as Mike surprised her with an intimate twiddle. She fumbled it before seeing who it was, simultaneously accepting the call and dropping it between the archive box and the bed.

'Hello?' It had hit speaker on the way down. It was

a male voice and lots of background noise. It sounded like he was driving.

'Tiff? Sweetheart. It's Gavin.' Oh crap. Not now. NOT. NOW. She launched herself head down into the gap, scrabbling in the gloom. The fairy lights were not helping now. Mike's hands steadying her confirmed he was wide awake.

'I'm hearing good things about the gym,' Gavin went on.

'Hold up a minute, Gav,' she spluttered, desperate to get her hands on the phone, to get him off speaker and off the line. She didn't have much dating experience, but even *she* knew this – the lying on top of one lover talking to an ex – was bad form.

'Where are you?'

'The gym. Shush a sec, Gav, I can't reach the phone.' Finally, she could see it. She had to shimmy up Mike to reach, boobing him in the face. Emergencies often came with collateral damage.

'Look, I'm returning from a viewing. I'm coming by, sweetheart. I'm taking you to dinner.'

'NO!' she screeched. 'I'm busy.' *Fucking* phone. The tips of her fingers reached the case, and she tried to drag it closer with her nails.

'That's fine. I'll wait for you to finish up. God, it's a bad signal around here.' She snagged the phone and tried to lever herself with her abs up to some kind of upright, smacking her head into the archive box with an *Argh*. 'Line's bad, Tiff, but I'll assume you can hear me. I'll see you in about twenty, sweetheart.'

'Nooo,' she wailed into the phone, finally right way up, but the line had cut out. She desperately tried to return the call, but there was no connection.

And again.

Nothing.

Slowly placing the phone back on the box, bloody bloody thing, Tiff took a deep breath and slid her eyes up Mike's body to meet his. He still had his hands firmly on her hips, but they felt like iron.

'This looks really bad,' she started.

'Not great,' he agreed. His light smile didn't reach his eyes. 'I thought the two of you were over.'

'We are! I haven't heard from him in a month. I've no idea why he's coming.'

'You're having dinner, *sweetheart*.'

She pulled herself off him, shocked. 'That's not fair, Mike. You heard me say no. I didn't get a chance to say I wasn't available.'

Mike pulled himself up to sitting, crossing his arms annoyed.

'I didn't hear you asking *Gav* what he was doing calling you,' he said, 'or is it just me you don't have a problem shouting at?' Tiff couldn't think how to answer that. He was right; while she was stymied when it came to conflict with Gavin, she'd always felt at ease dishing her moods at Mike. She doubted it would sound like a compliment right now though.

'Look, there's nothing going on with him,' she tried to placate him, 'I'll go down when he gets here and tell him I'm busy and I'll talk to him another time.'

'Why would you do that?' Mike asked gruffly.

'What? I can't just leave him out there knocking.' Some things were simply a matter of manners.

'No, why do you need to talk to him another time, if it's over?'

'Mike, I've known him for ten years.'

Mike remained unmoved. 'So?'

Tiff pulled the duvet around herself, the chill in the room now giving her goosebumps. She didn't understand why he was being mardy about this. She'd said there was nothing going on.

'So, we can still talk, if we want to.'

'And *do* you want to?' He was being unfair. She was beginning to get annoyed.

'I'll talk to whoever I like, thank you, Mike.' He stared at her, then swung his legs out of the bed and started searching for his stuff.

'This is ten years ago all over again,' he said. That sent her over the top.

'Don't you dare! There was nothing going on then, as you well know and there is nothing going on now.

I'm not like that, I never was. But I *am* a grown up Mike, and I'll speak to and see whoever I choose, even if it's Gavin.'

'What for? He *dumped* you,' he yelled, genuinely indignant on her behalf.

'Who said he dumped me?' She was naked in a storeroom. Why was she suddenly embarrassed about being the dumpee?

'Look around you, Tiff. If it had been mutual d'you think you'd be living in a cupboard?' Bugger.

'Point taken,' she conceded, but drew herself up, 'But he saved me once too, when my life turned to crap. When you're sitting in the first class lounge Monday night, you Google my dad's name with the word "embezzlement" and see what pops up. Read about his arrest and the horror Mum and I went through; the shame, the abuse, the dropping out of school, and how my high finance dreams became basic bookkeeping. All of which you missed as Blackie and Nanna shielded you from it, because you were the one they could help.

'He gave me support, he made me feel better, he gave me a new home. He gave me security and an escape. So while he may be considered a prat by many, he was salvation to me. And dumped or not, *I* will decide whether I talk to him, especially when you aren't going to be here anyway.'

Mike stood gaping at her. That was exactly the look

she'd expected if he found out what had happened, what he'd missed. So much for not telling him. Tiff knew him well enough to know how upset he'd be. She dropped her shoulders.

'Mikey, *please*. This,' she wiggled a finger between them, 'this has been amazing. Mind-blowing. I'll dream of this.' His appalled expression softened a little, but only to concern. He still didn't know what to say. 'But you're leaving, Mike. *You're* the one who's going. You're off to an exciting new career, living the high-life with your famous mates. I'm left here, building *this* life. You can't say who I can and can't see. I knew Gavin for a long time. He's still someone who knows me, who might give me some support if I need it. God knows my parents won't. So give me a break, okay? There is nothing going on.'

Mike took a breath, then released it. Whatever he'd planned to say was gone. Hands on hips, he hung his head. Looking at Mike now, she didn't see an international champion with a battered nose, but a contrite young man with a battered ego.

'You're right. I'm sorry. You need some stability. You need your mates.' *Mates* might have been over-egging it where Gavin was concerned, but she wasn't splitting hairs right now.

'I'll be back soon,' she said, cloaking her dressing gown around herself, and retrieving her dress from the floor. 'I'm grabbing a shower and I'll meet him at the door to send him away. After that you can gripe at me and I'll make it up to you with all sorts of favours, even some kinky ones,' – she'd hoped for a crack of a smile, but got very little – 'and *then* if you're interested we can go out for dinner and you can stay over. All the nights until Monday, if you like.' Based on this afternoon, she'd take whatever she could get.

She waited. But he remained mute. His forehead was creased, his eyes fixed on her. They weren't angry, just... sad. She moved to place a firm kiss on his lips. He didn't return it. 'Let's make the most of what's left, Mikey.'

'Ask me to stay, Tiff,' it gushed out of him. 'Ask me.'

It would be so easy; to have him in her life, in her bed, in her heart. The words sat there like a bullet on her tongue, but she couldn't pull the trigger. She couldn't spoil his chance. She'd allowed herself a moment of having him, but she couldn't take his future from him. Above all else, she couldn't ignore her deep-seated want for Mike to realise his potential and prosper, even if it was at her own expense, just as Blackie and Nanna had done.

Cupping his cheek, she could only shake her head and whisper 'I can't.'

Not wanting him to see her cry, she raced for the locker room and took the quickest shower ever, all the while trying to stem the tears as she cobbled together a proper speech of why she couldn't ask him, but also properly defining what he meant to her. She should tell him that at least. He deserved to know how she felt. She wished he hadn't been in any doubt last time. She'd tell him straight away before dealing with Gavin.

Only, the words never made it out of her mouth, as she stood in her bedroom doorway, still dripping slightly in her saggy dress, surveying the devastatingly Mike-free space.

Chapter 30

'You look shot, sweetheart,' Gavin said bounding in to reception, pausing only to kiss her cheek, which had her momentarily stunned. It was the closest they'd been since *that* night. Tiff began to cringe at the memory, but then the muscles released. He was here, wasn't he? He couldn't think her too much of an idiot. She was no longer going to feel bad about putting things out there in the privacy of her own bedroom. She'd made an effort and that was what counted. It was a much easier, more charitable stance to take after the joys she'd experienced that afternoon, which somewhat blotted out her earlier, lesser experiences.

'Gav, can I take a rain check on the dinner?' Tiff asked. She didn't think she could cope with more emotion. Being around Gavin required firing on all cylinders. 'It's been a long day. I was at a funeral.' Besides, what had her properly drained now was the dismay at Mike's leaving. She didn't want things left like that. She didn't want him to go away hating her.

'But you need to eat. The table's booked. Speaking of, you've lost a tonne of weight. Well done.' He moved further into the building. 'The grapevine's buzzing about this place. Do me a quick tour.' Without waiting for her, he strode up the stairs. 'Glad I sent you that sofa,' he called behind him, 'Looks great there. But then, it was always your favourite piece.'

Fists clenched, she bleakly followed him through the rooms. All she wanted was to bury herself in her duvet, fall asleep and end the day. Was that too much to ask?

'That part of the roof not stable?' he asked, nodding at the poles in the fitness studio.

'Pole-fitness, Gavin,' she said, sighing. Now she found it disappointing when the poles didn't light up a guy's eyes. 'Google it.'

'Decent office,' he noted on reaching the top floor. It was twice the size of his own and had a view to boot, but she didn't say so. She knew he knew. 'I'm impressed.'

A month ago this was an accolade she was desperate for. She'd thought it would be the ticket back to her old life. And now she had it, Tiff realised she knew it was impressive; she was genuinely proud of it and herself. Having Gavin tell her so wasn't nearly the validation she'd thought it would be.

'Right,' said Gavin, clapping his hands together, 'Food.' He wasn't going to budge on this and falling into her old ways, Tiff resigned herself to going. The sooner she went, the sooner she could be home again.

'New dress?' he asked getting in the car. She looked down at it and wished she wasn't wearing it. Gavin looked as handsome as he'd always done, though Tiff found herself for the first time looking for some flaws; not to diminish his looks, but to soften them.

Wittering about his recent sales figures, Tiff sensed Gavin was slightly on edge. Could the ever-confident Gavin be nervous? She was a little tense about the whole thing herself, primarily because she didn't know what this dinner was about. And there was the Mike thing. She willed herself to sideline thoughts of Mike for now.

Oh for fuck's sake. Tiff realised where Gavin was taking her. For some reason, incomprehensible to Tiff and probably the rest of mankind, he found it appropriate to bring her back to *Lorenzo's*. In whose mind was it tactful to take someone back to where you dumped them? Oh, yes, that would be Gavin's.

He guided her across the cobbles of the old High Street and through the door into the restaurant with a warm hand on the small of her back. It felt strange to be touched by two men in such a short window of time. Not even the wonderful aroma of Italian food could set her on an even keel.

'I got our usual table,' he murmured in her ear. It

was flattering; he wanted other people to see them out together, on display. The first time he'd booked this table it had meant exactly that to her, but this time, knowing Mike had seen them, she couldn't think of anywhere she'd less like to sit. But she couldn't bring herself to ask him to change; she'd have to explain. 'It's still the best place in town.' *After Greggs,* she thought.

Lorenzo himself, a charming older man whose rotundity confirmed his testing everything on the menu personally, pulled her usual seat out for her. Gavin was already parked in his.

'Can *I* have the seat by the radiator tonight?' She needed to change something up. Gavin frowned.

'Really? You always sit there.' She didn't remember it ever being by choice. Rather than backing down, she did the silent waiting thing. She was beginning to get the hang of it now. Gavin looked perturbed, his eyes flitting from the seat to the view of the high-end butchers across the road. 'You prefer the one with the view.' Tiff had never considered dead, hooked game birds a fine view.

'Actually, no, I've just never had the option.' He looked at her askance, not quite sure of her.

'Lorenzo? Do you have another table? This one is a bit chilly,' Gavin said to their host and flashed Tiff an accommodating smile. Well, she could have swung for him then. He'd always taken a chilly table and given her the cooler seat at it even though he knew she got cold. She quietly seethed as Lorenzo led them to a booth-style table with padded banquet seats. She slid in, expecting Gavin to take the opposite side. He slid in next to her. Somewhat confused she covertly edged further around on the shiny maroon leather.

'This is nice,' Gavin said, perusing the new angle on the restaurant. 'Cosier, more private. I like it.' Tiff busied herself in the menu, not sure what to make of things.

Lorenzo appeared with two glasses of Prosecco, his notepad and a smile.

'Gamberetti followed by lasagne with a side of zucchini fritti,' Lorenzo reeled off, like a pleasant joke between them. He was spot on, of course. As Tiff started in on her Prosecco, Gavin gave his staple order and Lorenzo vanished to the kitchen as if transporting the world's most important missive.

'So tell me about the gym, Tiff.' It was the first question he'd asked her about herself. So far, he'd steered off so much as a simple *How've you been?* She opened her mouth to tell him, but he didn't wait. 'Clearly the change is suiting you – you've sorted your hair, you're looking better. You'd become a bit of a pudding when we took our break, hadn't you? A bit of a couch potato.'

It had been a long day. Strike that, it had been a long *sad* day, (with the exception of the sex bit which had been fan-bloody-tastic, but exhausting nonetheless) and suddenly Tiff felt the full weight of it. Why had she agreed to come out?

'Other than critiquing my figure, was there something you wanted, Gavin?' She wiggled to sit on her hands. It seemed safest. Thumping people in public ahead of a planned news story was probably not best business practice.

'I'm just getting there, Tiff,' he said, sipping his drink, oblivious to her simmer, 'I see a shift in you. When we decided to separate, we were clearly on different paths.' *OMG, not this again.* 'You didn't appear to share my ambitions. But look what you pulled out of the bag. You were on my path after all.'

'I was?' What was he saying?

'Maybe you were simply recouping. Stopping at the services, so to speak. A detour perhaps.' He sat back as if beholding her. She leaned forward, trying to understand. She was getting lost in his conference twaddle. 'Either way, look at you, sweetheart. You're back on track. You're the Tiff who set up the bookkeeping business. You have drive again. In hindsight, taking the break was probably the best thing that could have happened to you. You weren't going to do all of this, lounging on the sofa in your saggy leggings watching *Jeremy Kyle*, were you?'

'I have never watched *Jeremy Kyle*,' she said, indignant. No-one had ever *lounged* on the sodding sofa either.

He waved his hand in the air dismissively. 'You know what I'm saying, Tiff. You needed us to take a break.'

Something about this was ringing alarm bells. He was flattering her, acknowledging her achievements. None of that was normal. She wolfed some more Prosecco as she corralled her thoughts.

'Gavin. We split up. You ended it. Here. On our anniversary. Your *closure*, remember?'

'But relationships are more fluid than that, aren't they, Tiff?' He slid his hand over hers. 'We know that, don't we, entrepreneurs like us?'

'Gavin,' Tiff snapped, wanting things clear in her head, 'you keep saying "break". That infers a gap, a space between two things, a temporary entity, as if we could get back together.'

'Exactly Tiff. I knew you'd get it.'

Tiff wondered whether Lorenzo had slipped something in her drink. Something hallucinogenic. Any moment now she expected baby unicorns to come floating past on clouds of tiramisu.

'You want us to get back together?' Her voice had gone pitchy. What was that? A little incredulity, a touch of hyperventilation and a pinch of shock.

'Tiff, it's perfect; we understand each other, we have

ten years of history – you don't just throw that away do you? – and we can hit the ground running. Some couples are destined to be together.'

Tiff's jaw flapped as she tried to work out what to address first. He beat her to it.

'I have the connections and the business acumen; I'll pinpoint the buildings and negotiate the deals, then you can tart them up like you have the gym. We could have a chain across the country.'

'Gavin. Stop. Just stop.' She held her hands up to him in case the words didn't go in and signing was the only way. 'I'm confused. Are you asking me to get back together with you or be your business partner?'

'Well, both. Obviously.'

'What happened to *Never go back*, Gav? Abe Lincoln. Abraham bloody Lincoln!' She downed the rest of the Prosecco and started scoping the room for a refill.

'Life's about adaptability Tiff, *All failure is failure to adapt, all success is successful adaptation* – Max McKeown. This wouldn't be walking backwards, like Abe worried about, it would be something forward-looking. Something new, a fresh start. Partners in business and pleasure. Think of the team we'd be, Tiff.'

Tiff felt her eyes widen, roughly to the size of the ostentatious plates Lorenzo served.

'I've surprised you,' Gavin said gently, as if addressing a scared child, and patting her hand to soothe her. 'I understand that. Perhaps our break has given your confidence a little knock, but sweetheart, I hope you never doubted that I loved you.' He touched her chin for her to look at him, said 'I still love you, Tiff.'

Two months ago, she would have sobbed with joy at this conversation. She'd have taken him back with both arms, and legs, in spite of Shelby coming at her with a swinging bat. And yet…

'Gav. I don't know what to say, to be honest. After everything you said on our anniversary and the time that's passed, you're now saying you didn't mean it.'

'I didn't say I didn't mean it; our break was evidently very useful…' a growl rolled up through her stomach, but she pressed it down with her free hand, '…but life's moved on and now it's clear being together is the obvious path.' He cocked his head at her. 'Surely you *must* feel the same, Tiff.' It really wasn't much of a question. 'Love like ours doesn't just disappear overnight.'

Two months! she wanted to shout in his face. But she didn't, because at the end of the day she *had* loved him, for many many years, and she'd been fully geared up to marrying him, had he asked her, which he hadn't, but still.

'Of course it doesn't,' she hedged weakly, feeling the seat for support as her world rocked. Spurred on by her words though, he leaned over and cradled her face in his hands. Before she knew it he'd drawn her in for a kiss, which made her eyes bug, more in shock than passion.

He started talking again, something about markets and their combined potential, but she was only hearing odd words. He was moving way too fast. She needed her brain to catch up and for him to stop a minute. For that she needed to be brave. 'Gavin. Stop. We need to talk,' she said, firmly. She knew guys understood and dreaded those words, but it was necessary to deploy them in this instance. Desperate times called for desperate measures. Gavin stood up abruptly.

'Definitely. We've got so much to plan and rediscover,' he gave her a wink making her entire stomach knot. 'But first there's this.' He dipped his hand into his suit pocket. 'Perhaps I wasn't precise about the extent of my intentions, but I'm sure this will dispel any doubts and give you all the reassurances you need.' He pulled out a jewellery box, and opened it in her face, like the jaws of a croc. Tiff's dumbfounded gape was somewhat similar. 'Princess-cut emerald, set in white gold, surrounded by diamonds, Tiff. The green matches my eyes.'

He was giving her Forever.

The entire unexpectedness of the moment had her gobsmacked. Gavin, taking his usual lead, lifted her hand and slid the ring, pushed the ring, onto her finger.

'I bought it a size or two smaller, to incentivise you,

but look, you're already nearly there for a perfect fit.' Tiff looked at it stunned, then back to his face, then back to the ring. *OMFG.* But still she had no words. The pressure wasn't helped by numerous heads in the near vicinity turning to watch them.

'The champagne's on ice back at mine.' He bent and cupped her face for another kiss. 'Come on, sweetheart, make it official. What do you say?'

Tiff's mouth opened and closed several times. She shook her head to clear it. Gavin – and the other diners – waited intently for her reply. She wasn't sure what had just happened. She had two further false starts before managing an answer.

'I need the loo.'

She braced herself on the sink and gasping for air, stared in the mirror. Shock glared straight back at her. This was the last thing she was expecting. True, she hadn't known what he'd intended when he'd called, she'd thought perhaps an apology for the last time they met, but definitely not this.

He loved her. He *still* loved her. He'd *always* loved her. That's what he'd said. Out loud. In a public place. And then there was the ring on her finger. Two months ago this was how she'd imagined it in her head, (although perhaps with a ring that didn't cut off her circulation).

Still no words came to her, her tongue had ravelled in knots as it so often did around Gavin. It always had. Either she'd been happy to follow his lead, or she was unwilling to contradict him. Tiff took a harder look at herself, why was that? Why was it she time and again held her tongue or allowed him to steamroller her? She didn't have that problem with Mike.

Tiff turned to rest against the counter top, to think it through without the judgement of her own reflection. She knew. Deep down she knew. She'd always been scared if she rocked the boat, if she hadn't been compliant, Gavin would change his mind about being with her. Looking at her ring, she saw it clearly now. Their 'successful dynamic' was simply her appeasing him, so he wouldn't abandon her, as she'd thought Mike had, like her dad effectively did.

Yet for all of that, he'd left her anyway.

Tiff felt the shame and the grief begin to envelop her, but then she batted it away. Yes he'd left her, but she'd survived it. And this ring, this enormous ring, said she'd survived admirably. She was a prize again, a *trophy* like Shelby had said. It gave her a huge surge of confidence.

She could have it all back; Gavin, her home, her life as she'd known it (obviously not her legs, because Shelby). Like Mike – Mike who was leaving, possibly never to be seen again other than on the telly – had said; she could have some stability. It took her a moment to pinpoint the last time she'd felt stable; her anniversary – just before her bum hit her cold seat by the window.

Tiff looked at the door to the restaurant and back at her face in the mirror. She looked at the ring and what it represented; his leadership, safety, a familiar life.

Why was she even having to consider it? This was a no-brainer.

Taking a deep breath, Tiff strode directly up to the table. She didn't sit. She wanted her full height for this moment.

'Gavin, thank you.' He looked up at her and smiled, triumphant. 'Thank you for believing in me and in my new business, to the point you'd commit to being part of it. And to being with me. That is very, very heart-ening.' She took another breath. 'Regardless of that, the answer is no.'

He opened his mouth to protest. 'No. No, let me explain,' she said, holding up a hand. She was back to sign language, but she thought he was going to need it. 'Firstly, you've only come back when there was some-thing in it for you. You're only wanting *me* back now I'm slimmer. If you thought I was a couch potato, you should have said, instead of all that faff about bloody paths. You could have encouraged and supported me to get fitter, rather than ditching me. But that's fine, as yes, you *did* do me a favour.' Much as she was telling him off, Tiff couldn't help but have a big smile on her face.

'Being by myself showed me I'd stayed with you for so long because it was the safe option. The gym, *my* gym, isn't the safe option; it feels like I'm flying by the seat of my pants, and I'm loving it, so thank you for that; for forcing me to stand on my own two feet again. If we'd been together when I got it, I would have followed your advice to sell. But now I know I can do it, and more to the point, I can do it without you. Which means Gav, sharing it with you would be a choice, not a necessity, and so I choose not to.

'No, no, still going,' she said, as he tried again to cut in, '*Were* I to share it with someone, it'd be someone who supports me, who doesn't make me feel crappy, someone who doesn't think I'm limited. He'd be someone, who even if we were on different paths, would still stick around, because he likes me for me, sweatpants and all, whatever their size. He wouldn't be with me for what he can get and *that* Gavin, is what counts.

'I think I might have been guilty of that when I first went out with you,' she admitted, lowering her head ashamed, 'you offered me safety. I grew to love you and rely on you, but it was the safety which won me, and I'm sorry about that, because that's lousy isn't it? I see it now.' She caught his eye again. 'I hope you'll forgive me for that. But you should know I'm grateful for it too; you *did* make me feel safe. But it was a safety to hide in and it was very dependent, whereas what I need is a security to *fly* from, and if that's with someone else, he'd be there to cheer for me *and* commiserate with me.' It dawned on Tiff she might just know exactly such a person. She might recently have sent exactly such a person away. *Oh bloody hell.*

'I used to worry what I would do without you, Gav, and the answer is simple really – *Anything I want*.' Tiff pulled at the ring as she stepped back, her smile still wide on her face, 'In summary, Gavin, I'm not up for sharing your path; I want to blaze my own trail, and I'll steer it myself as I'm not the bloody cart to anyone's horse. So thanks for the ten years, and thanks for the belief and the offer, and possibly the worst proposal in history, but no thanks. Not in a million years.' With a final concerted yank the ring came off.

Boom, she thought, striding past the nosy diners, out of *Lorenzo's* to find a cab, away from an astounded Gavin with his ring in his hand, feeling like a walking motivational quote. So her love life might be in flaming tatters, but she was capable and she'd rustle up a plan, and in the meantime she had a business and a future. Tiff thanked the heavens for that.

Chapter 31

Lying on her mat plinth she couldn't sleep. She was partially in shock over Gavin's bombshell, but more pressingly she was pretty sure, no fairly certain, actually totally one hundred percent convinced, she'd made an error of epic proportions. She'd honestly believed she was doing the right, decent, honourable thing in sending Mike away. She'd been selfless, so pat on the back for that, but she'd been a monumental fool too. Bummer.

She wasn't a millstone, or a cart, she was as much an opportunity as LA. It had just taken her a while, and perhaps a proposal, to get it. Maybe, had she told him how she felt, they could have devised some alternative plan where they got their second chance and he still got his new career.

Oh pants. She drew the duvet up to her nose. Her mussed sheets still carried the scent of him, of them. She'd left him a message from the cab, to call her, but he hadn't. *He might be asleep,* she told herself. *He might also be packing.* He had his ticket, he'd agreed to the job. He was pretty hacked with her too, she imagined. What if he walked out of her life as calmly as he'd walked back in? She couldn't even begin to quantify how much that would hurt.

She needed an action-plan. She started a list. It calmed her ranting brain. She'd keep calling him. That was a given. And if he didn't take or return her calls, then what? She didn't actually know where he lived. Scouring Rightmove for pictures of a house with a Formula One tyre coffee table, or a boxing ring would not be efficient use of her time. The airport! She'd track him down and do one of those climactic declarations at the gate à la Ross and Rachel. Except it'd have to be at check-in because she didn't have money for the ticket to pass Security.

If he *still* went, she coached herself – in spite of the public humiliation in front of the check-in queue, whose sympathy should surely be with her if she'd given it her best shot – she'd understand. He'd made a commitment and he was a man of his word. It would be a setback obviously, but she'd just have to revise and adjust.

She considered the list. Two action points weren't enough. She could text him, invite him to dinner next time he was over. What was the worst he could do? Laugh in her face? She could overcome that. She'd start with offering him a Greggs lunch and if he declined then at least there'd be an extra pasty for her as consolation.

Physical exhaustion finally winning over, that was as far as she could get; a two-step plan of attack with a contingency. That would have to do for now. She was also supposed to be planning the coming day. In hindsight, even before her new Mike emergency, organising the press visit so close to the equipment delivery might not have been smart, but she'd wanted the place to look pristine for them. She wanted the bikes to be shiny and the treadmills scuff-free. She planned to push the paper for a follow-up story on the hopefully teeming classes. Secretly, in her head, the story led with a picture of herself hanging upside down on a pole, but she knew she'd need a shed-load of practice to reach that point. Perhaps Sammi would do her a couple of fast-track private lessons—

It was more of a plink than a bang from downstairs, but it caught her attention. Her ears were fine-tuned to the building now, she could differentiate the pipes gurgling on all the floors; each had their own timbre according to age and repairs. This sound however, wasn't one she recognised. Listening hard she caught a few nondescript noises, but clearly someone was moving around the building.

Mike.

'Yessss.'

She'd been convinced she'd have to do the running and yet here he was on another of his nocturnal visits. Obviously he'd calmed down. Fighters were like that, she imagined; they needed time to cool off. On the other hand, he could have come to shout at her. For being a fool and not asking him to stay. That was fair enough too. She'd take it.

Sitting up, she quickly tried to sort her hair. She wrenched her bed-socks off too, flicking them out onto the floor. Bed-socks were not sexy. Cute dragons on them did not change that.

Actually, on reflection, this wasn't how she wanted him to find her; lying in bed as if waiting for him. Mike shouldn't think she'd been expecting him – she definitely hadn't and it would swipe at his pride which she could ill afford. Should she pretend to be asleep? No, too cringy. She'd rather meet him halfway or something. That felt like the better choice, a truce. Getting up, Tiff smoothed down her PJs. Serendipitously, they were a newer pair but she made a mental note to invest in something silkier, skimpier.

Approaching the staircase she reached out for the light switch. There was no point breaking their necks. Something stopped her. The sounds from below weren't ascending. She was expecting Mike to jog up the stairs towards her room. These sounds were decidedly shuffling around in the foyer. There was a long hissing sound. What was he doing down there? She took the first flight on her tiptoes. If he was sorting some surprise for her, she didn't want to spoil it. Mike was good at surprises – she blushed at the thought. That hissing sound again; like helium balloons being filled. Moving further down the stairs she endeavoured to be super-stealthy and hear as much as possible.

There was only one person as far as she could make out and an odd thwumping sound reminding her of walking across a bouncy castle as a child. Something regularly interrupted the hissing; something rattling, something metallic. The sounds connected in her brain as the smell of paint hit her nose. Ball bearings in a spray can.

'NO!' she screamed, slamming her hand against the light switch and barrelling down the remaining steps.

Aaron stood slack-jawed on the sodding sofa staring at her. The newly-painted reception was a maelstrom of black scrawl. The slim window at the side of the doorway was smashed.

Initially, she could only formulate a babble of No's. She couldn't believe anyone would do this, wanted her to walk in the next morning to this horror. It was the art of bus shelters, all swear words and knobs. Had it been bored teens, it would've been depressing enough, but it was Aaron; this was personal. This was pure bilious spite. God, it made her angry.

'Put down the paint and get off my sodding sofa, you arsehole.'

'Fuck off,' he snarled, his breath sour with booze.

'Now!' she shouted. He gave her the one-fingered salute, then turned to the wall intent on more. 'No way.' Tiff launched herself at him, grabbed him by the belt and yanked. With a yell he smacked her aside and she fell on her bum. Incensed, she wrenched herself onto her knees and dug her nails into the nearest point of contact, his ankles.

Swearing, Aaron kicked her off his legs and descended from the sofa. 'I gave you enough warnings, you thick bitch,' he raged, 'the calls, the shit, the fire. You should have taken the hint.' Tiff crab-scrambled back a couple of paces as he advanced towards her. She barely registered the pain of the glass shards in her palms as she watched his eyes fix on her, his expression pure, unadulterated loathing. She wasn't sure what he had in mind, until it was too late.

He sprayed her in the face.

The pain was excruciating. Balled over, she tried to paw the paint away from her screaming eyes. She only sensed the kick to her gut as he landed it.

'You took my money, you slag,' Aaron roared.

She wanted to tell him it wasn't his, never had been,

he hadn't deserved it, that Blackie could see the piss weasel he was, but the pressing issue of her vision, topped by being winded, trapped the words inside her. She started to crawl for the stairs, but he landed another kick to her ribs, which made her sob as much with anger as pain. She had to get up. In terms of fight or flight there was only one choice. She had to get away, but navigating a broken window blind was a no-no. The only option was up into the darkness of the floor above, where he'd be equally disadvantaged.

Squeezing her eyes tighter shut, she forced her hands down to the floor. With all her might she yanked at the protective matting the builders had left on the flooring. Admittedly, it wasn't much of a pull; the pain seared across her ribs, but it was enough to topple him and give her time to scramble for the stairs.

Blind or not, Tiff knew this building backwards. Adrenalin-fuelled, she was up the first flight, smacking the light back off as she went, acutely aware of her pain, her laboured breathing and Aaron's thumping footsteps behind her.

She wanted somewhere to lock herself in. Given her current state, she could only think of protecting herself and hoping he'd leave. Both her office and bedroom had phones and could be locked but each were on the top floor now and she doubted she'd make it. The Ladies locker room on the first floor had slide bolts on the cubicles. That was her plan.

Apparently Aaron had played rugby at school. Metres from the locker room she felt his arms wrap around her shins bringing them to a sharp standstill while the rest of her continued with alarming momentum towards the floor. With a screech, she just managed to extend her hands, preventing a full face-plant.

Tiff flipped over, but seconds later he was on her, pummelling with a terrifying fury. Terrified, she hoped he'd be satisfied just to have her pass out rather than die. *I'm not up for dying today*, the delirious thought floated across her mind. *Not today. I want to see this place open.* She stabbed her nails towards her estimate of his eyes, scratching like a wildcat. Aaron shouted, calling her filthy names, then raised himself to backhand her across the face. Concurrent with hearing her nose crunch and feeling the corresponding explosion of pain to her face, Tiff brought her knee up as hard and accurately as she could into his spuds.

The scream was bloodcurdling. Pleasingly, this one hadn't come from her.

As he slow-mo tilted off her into a foetal position, Tiff crawled to the nearest doorway. By her calculations, it was the pole-fitness studio. There were free weights stacked beautifully in the corner for body-toning classes. She could use the 1kgs as missiles, or a larger weight as a gonk. On her feet and stumbling, she remembered the poles in front of her just in time to reach out her hand, connect with the first and swerve around it.

She heard Aaron's heavy breathing at the doorway, his hand whacking the wall to find the light switch. Giving up, he moved towards her. She tried to still her breathing, but she was wheezing, crying and bubbling bloody snot out of her smashed nose, so no luck there.

Sensing his approach, Tiff had to make a decision. She didn't know if she'd reach or find the weights in time and she'd rather he didn't have them to brain her with. He was only a couple of feet away now, tracking her wheezy breathing.

She wasn't willing to run and cower in the corner; she was going down fighting. In a final burst she grabbed high on the pole with both hands and launched her feet at him horizontally. Her ribs shot a thunderbolt of pain across her, rendering her kick not nearly as high as she'd intended. A kick to the face had been her goal. As it was, she had to settle for dealing him a colossal double footed blow to the knackers. Once had been hard enough for him – this second assault to his crown jewels made him faint with pain. Tiff landing on him in an untidy heap sealed the deal and he lay still.

Gasping from the landing and a shit tonne of pain, Tiff thought to escape, but sensed he wasn't moving. She could keep blindly running and pray he didn't follow, or she could ensure he didn't continue the chase and buy some time to call the police, because god knew she wasn't going to stay conscious much longer. She frantically patted the floor in front of her, crawling in the direction of where she knew the stacked equipment to be. Reaching it, she grabbed a couple of the most resistant stretch bands and with the last dregs of adrenalin, her burning eyes scrunched tight, Tiff roughly managed to bind his hands behind him. She could feel the blood dripping from her face, but didn't have time to wipe it and didn't care whether she bled on him. She tied his feet for good measure too, simultaneously stressed and relieved as he began to squirm. She hadn't killed him, then.

She emitted a wracking sob as she hauled herself to her feet and staggered to the staircase. Her mobile phone and her bed upstairs tempted her. The idea of waiting there for the police to arrive, snuggled in her duvet felt like deliverance, but her survival instinct (and ribs) told her to head downwards, letting the walls of the staircase support her, to stay closer to the doorway and use the phone at reception, rather than climbing further into the building.

After several frustrating misdials, Tiff found

Emergency Services were calm and patient as she struggled to align her words. If she could just finish the call, she could curl up on the sodding sofa to wait. Only, Tiff's legs gave out and she slid unconscious down the wall as she tried to recall and convey the address.

Chapter 32

The beeping woke her, but the host of irregular sensations dragged her into consciousness.

'You were out cold when they stretchered you to the ambulance.' Someone was talking to her, jabbering along as though she was listening. Her hand was warm, enveloped in the skin of another. Tiff wasn't inclined to open her eyes because lying there in the toasty soft bed, she'd been having a marvellous sleep. The noises in the room were foreign to her usual wake-up routine. The voice was male for a start and it'd been a while since she'd woken up to one of those. Confused, she decided to have a quick check about before she dozed off again, but found she couldn't.

'Don't try your eyes, Angel. They're bandaged shut,' the voice said. 'I know you're awake. Your swollen nose is flaring.' She knew that voice. Hearing it made her happy, but her face wouldn't smile.

'Mikey, where's my bedroom gone?' Her voice was

slurry. She knew he'd just told her various questionable things, but she couldn't sort them in her head.

'You're having an NHS mini-break, Tiff. Seems you fancied breakfast in bed.' The hold on her hand tightened.

'Hmm, not hungry.'

'Not surprising,' he murmured.

'Maybe sleep now.'

'Go ahead, Angel. You're drugged to the gills.'

She thought to reply, but lost the thread.

Her hand was still enveloped when she woke again.

'Mikey?'

'Right here.'

'Gotta get up.'

'Yeah, but not today.'

'Gym to sort. Kit coming. Press.' Why was speaking so hard? She felt breathless with every word.

'It's Sunday morning, Tiff. You're busy here at the moment.'

Something there caused her to focus. She was missing everything at the gym.

'Noo,' she moaned, her eyes stinging a little as the tears welled. Then they stung a whole lot. 'My eyes!' Once, she'd accidentally rubbed them with chilli-fingers; this was much worse.

'They've bathed them as much as possible to remove

the paint. Now your eyes have to do their own thing.'
She recalled something about paint. Had she had a
decorating accident?

'Can I see?' It was a question she'd never imagined
having to ask.

'We're hoping for a full recovery, Tiff. We have to wait
and see.' He stumbled. 'Oh shit. Sorry, that's not what
I meant. We just have to wait, let your body heal.
Keeping your eyes closed is best. Means they can focus
on – oh shit. Sorry...'

She squeezed his hand to stop him babbling.

Things were beginning to unmuddle in her head;
Aaron holding a spray-can, a fight, tying him up, but
not much more.

'What happened?' she asked, turning towards him,
before being overcome by pain across her entire torso,
howling, then instinctively rolling back, to more pain
and howling.

'Want more drugs?' He sounded worried.

She shook her head. That hurt too. Everywhere hurt
now she'd started to notice.

'The diagnosis says you've three broken ribs, a busted
nose, cut hands, bruising and eye trauma.' Mike
sounded formal as he repeated what he'd been told,
then dropped to a low growl. 'Bastard blinded you, then
kicked and thumped the crap out of you. If the police
hadn't been there, I'd have done the same to him.' Tiff

winced, but even that ached. The drug offer sounded more appealing.

'Did they find him?'

'Yeah, they found him, trussed up like a Christmas turkey. Nice job with the knots. Clearly you've got more skills to show me.'

Tiff sensed some innuendo going on, but she couldn't quite work it out.

'You were out for the count in reception with the phone in your hand. Fuck, you scared me, Tiff.' Her hand was pulled up to meet his unusually stubbly cheek. 'You were white as a sheet, blood streaming out of your nose with black paint across your eyes. You looked like The Joker slumped against the wall. I thought you were...' He couldn't say it. She squeezed his hand again and he nearly crushed hers in response, until she yelped from the cuts. 'The paramedics got you sorted. I said I was your boyfriend so they'd let me come along. Sorry.'

'S'fine.' She rather liked the sound of that.

'They brought him out to the police car. I don't know what you did to him, Angel, but he's walking kinda funny.'

'Blunt-force trauma to the balls.'

'Good girl.' She felt him push some hair away from her face with his fingertips. 'Shitbag.' He was reining in his anger.

Something occurred to her.

'How come you were there?' He'd walked out, hadn't he?

'I wanted to see you.' He made it sound obvious.

'Okay.' That would do for now.

'I'd just pulled up. The lights were all off. I assumed you'd gone out.' He paused and drew a breath. 'Then a car passes, headlights lighting up the club and I see the broken window. So I get out to see if it's kids playing silly buggers, pelting stones. I get to the front door, see all the graffiti and I know the place's been done over. I didn't go in, because I figured it'd be best waiting for the police. Finger prints and that. And then I saw your toes. Sticking out from behind the desk. And I thought the worst.'

She didn't need to see him to know he looked stricken. Mike cleared his throat.

'I sat inside, holding you. There were sounds coming from upstairs; groans and dragging sounds, but I wouldn't shift. You had a pulse, but without knowing the damage, I didn't want to move you. I left the police to investigate.'

Tiff felt spent. She was hungry but also tired and couldn't decide which to go with. And she'd a nagging feeling there was something she needed to tell him...

'Want some food? Soup or something?'

Oh, that sounded good. She started nodding, but the sleep overtook her again.

Tiff was ravenous and her rumbling stomach had woken her. Her hand was free and cold. Her eyes were still bandaged. She wasn't sure what to do now and it made her feel vulnerable. She started frantically feeling about for the button to call the nurse.

'Seriously, Tiff?' said a voice from the other side of the room. 'This whole time you've been living in the gym? Sleeping in a cupboard? You won't believe how pissed off I am with you.'

Ah.

She should have known this was coming. She should have been worried about the wrath of Shelby as opposed to her potential blindness.

In preparation for the onslaught, she attempted to look as pitiful as possible, but had to swear a bit as the head of the bed raised with Shelby plonking herself on the foot-end.

Tiff took a pre-emptive strike. 'I was embarrassed about being single again when I thought he was going to propose. I didn't want to spend evenings dissecting the break up or my failed relationship. I didn't want to be that friend sleeping on the sofa. Blackie left me the gym and there was so much to do and it was easier. Any of those reasons. You can pick one or combine.'

'And you put yourself in danger and nearly got your-self killed,' Shelby added.

366

'That wasn't one of my reasons or one of your choices.'

'What were you thinking, taking him on?' In respect of it being a hospital Shelby was speaking quietly – but in a hissy screech, 'I bet you didn't think for one second what I'd do without you.'

'I'm sorry,' Tiff mollified her. God, it was good to hear her voice. Between Shelby and Mike, she felt safer, supported.

'The nurse said someone left you this thermos of soup,' Shelby said, still in a snit, but pressing a cup into her hand. The warmth of the soup working its way down to her belly was a welcome distraction from her aching ribs and throbbing face. It made her feel fractionally more human. Shelby took the cup off her and stole a big slurp.

'Ugh, mushroom. Gross.' The cup was placed firmly back in her hand. 'The whole place was cordoned off yesterday, Tiff. Like flipping CSI. Nat phoned to tell me. They wouldn't let me in here last night because a) it wasn't visiting hours, b) family only, and when I pointed out I am virtually the sum total of yours they said that c) your boyfriend had already been and you were off your tits on the sleeping drugs. So you've shit-loads of explaining to do. If you've let Gavin waltz back in and take over—'

'Mike. Mikey was here.'

'Mike is your boyfriend? Whoa there, missy. That was one huge omission.'

'He only said it to get in the ambulance and it kind of stuck.'

'Hmm.' Shelby sounded suspicious.

'Shelby, it's customary to bring sympathy with you to hospitals.'

'Not sure sympathy helps anybody. Just makes you dwell on your issues.'

Tiff was about to suggest potential blindness as a sympathy-worthy ailment, but it freaked her out even beginning to think about it and thankfully, the door swung open before she could start to.

Shelby snorted a laugh. 'It's the doctor, Tiff. You should have seen your little face light up. If Mike'd seen it, you'd have been mortified. No sense of cool at all.'

'Yeah, because cool is key when there's a bandage around your face.'

'Lots of people like being blindfolded, Tiff,' Shelby lectured, before adding to the doctor, 'She's had a very limited sex life.'

'I... Um... that's not...' the doctor blustered. He sounded young.

'You look familiar,' Shelby said to him, 'Did we...you know? Last Christmas?'

'Leave him alone, Shelby,' Tiff warned, turning expectantly towards his voice.

'I've come to remove the bandage and examine your eyes.' He sounded relieved, possibly grateful, to change the subject.

Shelby took her hand. She might be stingy with the verbal sympathy, but she knew when Tiff needed her. Tiff starting to shake might have been a clue too.

The doctor worked quickly. Most likely to escape Shelby. First the gauzy bandage was unwound from Tiff's head and then the two pads were removed from her closed eyelids. She liked the cooler air on her skin again but she was reluctant to open her eyes, scared witless of what she would – or wouldn't – see. The doctor explained what they were hoping for, but she didn't take it all in.

'Come on, babes. One at a time if you have to, but you need to do it.'

Tiff felt a tear slip out from one. It didn't hurt as much as before.

'Tears are good, Tiffanie. They'll flush out the detritus and you can gauge the pain levels,' the doctor encouraged her, apparently chuffed to see her crying.

'What if I can't see?' She didn't know where to start in that scenario, the implications of it being overwhelming. Her entire world would change and she'd only just rebuilt this new one.

'Then we'll deal with it,' Shelby answered, as if Tiff had been asking her. Which she hadn't. 'Let's work out the state of play, yeah? Then the doc can do his job.'

She held her breath and tried. Nothing much moved. She hadn't realised how swollen her eyes were until then. Trying again she opened one a fraction. Small steps seemed like a plan. Whacking them both open to nothing but black felt like a nightmare. There was definitely light coming in at the crack. A little more and she could determine colours and basic shapes. Fully open, she could definitely see, but nothing was clear. She didn't give a sound or clue, but her fingers were clenched tight around Shelby's who was clenching pretty tightly back. She opened the other at a faster pace, but the result was the same, perhaps a little worse. It looked as if Vaseline had been thickly smeared across everything. She knew the shapes and the colours, but suspected her brain was filling the gaps. Shelby's face, which she knew so well, was fuzzy. She let out a sob.

'Tell us babes, tell the doc what you can see.'

'Shapes, colours, but it's very blurry. The left eye is worst.'

'The left eye took the most paint,' the doctor explained, 'so that's to be expected. It's early days, but seeing shapes and colour is very encouraging.' He tilted her chin up and towards him. He shined a light in her eyes, making her wince. She did the follow-my-finger thing. He seemed happy with her responses.

'Will it come back totally?' Her mind was loudly filled with a desperate *please, please, please!*

'We'll have to wait and... we'll have to wait. The signs are good though.' He briskly tucked his lightpen back in his breast pocket, promising to return tomorrow. If Tiff wasn't mistaken, she saw the form of Shelby's free hand reach out towards his bottom as he left.

'Fwoar. Doctors. Yum.'

'Were you about to goose him?' Tiff asked, momentarily distracted from her fear.

'You saw that? That's good. I should go and tell him.'

'Shelby, no.' Tiff clung on to her hand. 'You're not jumping my doctor. Not before I'm signed off. Agreed?' Spurred by the doctor's optimism, Tiff decided regaining her sight was a new goal, and it was calming to let the ambition override the worry. Keeping a rein on Shelby was just the first step.

Shelby ungraciously agreed. There was a mutter of 'selfish'.

'I wasn't going to goose him. I just wanted to see under his white coat.'

'What for?'

'Butt fitness.'

'Give me strength.'

'More soup?'

A knock at the door announced another visitor. Tiff deduced it was Natalie; extremely short and in a duck-egg blue fleece. Tiff gave her a brief rundown of her diagnosis.

'What was that – a private kick-boxing class?' she asked, plumping herself down in the chair. 'What were you thinking, you looney?'

'I asked that,' Shelby chipped in.

'He was breaking my club. I didn't really think. It was all a bit fast.' Tiff couldn't explain it further. She remembered her anger in the moment, that someone was destroying what she'd worked for. She remembered the rage and the defensiveness kicking in. She'd do it again. She knew she would. She didn't share that though. Shelby would punch her lights out.

'How bad is it? Have you been in?' she asked Natalie. While her key concern was still her vision, Tiff's mind was now feeling sharper, and ready to think more widely. She prayed Aaron had only got to reception and not started his destruction in the gym.

'It isn't pretty. I guess you interrupted him. Apart from the window, he hadn't broken anything yet. The walls though, they're a mess. Not quite the welcome you want.'

Tiff winced. 'Does it say stuff?' Natalie didn't answer at once. 'Tell me, Nats. My imagination will only do its worst.'

'Okay, so across the full back wall, above the sofa, it says "FAT FUCKING BITCH".'

'Well, he clearly hadn't seen her recently,' Shelby said,

patting Tiff on the leg. 'You're quite the skinny bitch now.'

'"Fat fucking bitch",' Tiff turned the words over in her mouth, 'not quite the slogan I was planning to launch with.'

'Otherwise it's willies and swear words, some misspelled, across the other walls, the sofa, the plants. I think he was going for impact rather than artistry.'

'Right,' Tiff said, nodding. She wasn't sure whether she'd been expecting better or worse, but knowing helped.

'And the press? I guess they have a nice shot of all of that?' Neither of her friends spoke. A morsel of hope rose in her. 'They didn't turn up? Result.'

'No, they came,' Natalie said, glumly. 'They got well excited. Thought it was a much better story.'

'And?' Another silence. 'Dish it.'

'We should come back tomorrow,' Shelby said abruptly, withdrawing her hand. 'You're looking tired, Tiff. Need me to bring anything?'

'The paper, Shelb. I need to know what they wrote.'

'Sure, sure.' Shelby got up to leave. Tiff had the distinct feeling she'd forget the paper.

'Is the building secure now, Nats, and did you let them in to deliver all the equipment?' Tiff asked, settling into the pillows. Now Tiff was thankful Colin had delayed the delivery until the last minute.

Natalie cocked her head. 'Nothing came yesterday. The police left and I swept up the glass while Ed fixed a board over the window, but there was no delivery.'

Tiff felt her mouth dry.

'The police probably turned them away,' Shelby said, matter-of-factly. 'It's a crime scene right? They'll redeliver next week.'

'Oh!' Natalie suddenly said, a thought hitting her, 'I forgot. You might have extra time to get everything sorted.'

'Like how?'

'Ed's mate Steve said Ron was effing and blinding as he's been let down by his supplier. You know, the ring and training kit he'd ordered? Supplier's gone bust. He's lost the money and has them all doing sit ups and burpees until he can sort another plan.'

'Couldn't have happened to a nicer bloke,' Shelby muttered. 'Bastard.'

'So the pressure's off a bit, right Tiff? If you can get things moving this week, the guys might be tempted back sooner.'

Tiff wasn't ready to get excited yet. She wasn't exactly in a state to be hoofing up and down the stairs in the club. And the competition wasn't her prime concern. 'Bring me the paper, read me what they wrote and we'll see what we've got.' Nat was right; this was a much better story than just a gym opening. With violence and almost a family feud, it was perfect gossip fodder and it made her shudder. As soon as they left the room she pulled the blanket up over her head and hid.

Waking, she knew she wasn't alone. She could hear his breathing again. Steady and deep.

'Haven't you got a home to go to?'

'Want me to go?' Mike asked, blithely, not sounding as if he would.

'No. I'm just worried you have houseplants or vegetables that need tending.'

'Yeah, right. Just you.' He poured her a glass of water. 'How's the peepers, Tiff? The nurse says you can see things.'

'Shapes, colours, movement. But everything's blurry.'

'Look at me, Tiff.' He said it so gently, so tenderly it made her want to weep. She'd been keeping them shut so he couldn't see them. She hadn't asked anyone how she looked, because obviously she must look rough as hell. Her nose throbbed like a clown's hooter. Her eyes would only make the general picture worse. But she opened them. Because he wanted her to. Because he'd found her, looked after her and sat by her.

It was night outside, but the room was well lit. It was clearly his face. The wonk in his nose was helpful. Close as he was, she sensed his eyes were roaming her face.

'Well?' she asked, having never felt more naked.

'Still beautiful,' he said, running a fingertip down her cheek. Tiff decided there and then some lies were totally acceptable. 'How about your sight?'

'I think someone's broken your nose at some point,' she said, and watched as the line of his mouth spread. His jaw was definitely more shadowed than normal. His shirt, the top two buttons undone, was the same he'd worn at the funeral.

'Well, you're not getting points for that one.'

'I can see more than when the bandage came off. I think.' She didn't want to say too much in case it tempted fate and this was as good as it got. She pushed the thought aside, determined to stay positive, even though her chest constricted every time her mind considered the possibilities. 'Your turn.'

'What do you mean?'

'What do you see? A proper assessment this time, please.' The doctor hadn't described how her eyes were actually looking. The nurses were consistently vague. She trusted him to tell her the truth.

'Eyewise, you look like a demon, Angel. Beyond the swelling, they're bloodshot to hell.' Her mouth pulled in as she took in the words. 'Doc said that should pass. From where I'm sitting, you still have gorgeous brown eyes though. Rest-of-you-wise, you're one bruised fruit. You look like a rejected plum.'

'Probably best I missed the photoshoot then.'

'They'll do a follow-up when you've opened, Tiff. That's two stories for the price of one. They'll be delighted.'

'I doubt they'll be kind, Mikey.'

He sighed deeply and considered it.

'Paper won't be out until tomorrow, Tiff. I imagine it'll be front page stuff. The journo was waiting out in the hall when I came in earlier. Thought you might be up for telling "your side of the story", as if there is more than one. I sent him packing, little scrote. The questions he was asking weren't about the gym facilities, Tiff. It was your dad's history, and how you'd got enough money to own a gym. Said it was a *human interest* story now. I told him to talk to your lawyer. Thought it might scare him off a bit.'

Tiff had closed her eyes again when her dad got mentioned. She'd hoped the paper would send some junior to the opening, who'd take nice shots of the studio, maybe the staff out the front, then potter off with details of opening times and classes. Instead they'd been handed a juicy story and for once decided to turn investigative. She'd been lucky they hadn't picked up on the arson story. Now though, the paper would relish the chance to put her in the spotlight, for the town to point at and pillory all over again.

'This is where you're supposed to say all publicity is good publicity,' she said bitterly.

'You're partially blind, not deaf. You'd spot that lie a mile off. But hey, you're right, people will know there's a new gym in town.' He didn't sound as peppy as his words.

Depressing as it was, this was another thing she couldn't do anything about. Other things however...

'Mikey,' Tiff said, 'I need a favour.'

'Foot massage?' That stumped her. That sounded amazing, and possibly with a better outcome than her actual request.

'Yes to that, but I also need you to investigate something. I didn't want to ask Natalie because the news might affect her, and I need to know first.'

'Tell me and it's done.'

Tiff briefly summarised how the kit hadn't arrived, and Colin had gone AWOL. It seemed too much of a coincidence that Ron's supplier had let him down.

Mike made the connection instantly. 'How much have you paid him?' Her eyesight must have improved as his wince was quite clear when she told him.

'I'll make some calls, see what I can find out. But *only* on the condition you leave it with me and don't lie there worrying about it. I'll be back tomorrow and I'll tell you then. Until then you have to concentrate on you, OK? They won't let you out to sort things until you're fit.'

'You think I can sort things?'

'Tiff, you just demolished a guy trying to maim you. I'd call that sorting things.' He stood and started pulling on his coat. 'And I know you'll pull things together at the gym. It'll be open in no time. But you need to rest, sort your bones, lose the bruises so you won't look scary on the publicity shots.'

He made her smile. He lifted her hand to his lips and kissed it. Her eyelids were drooping and her mind beginning to drift. Turning for the door, he hesitated, then moved back to kiss her on the forehead.

'I'll see you tomorrow, Angel.' It was the best thing she'd heard all day.

Finally she remembered the thing she wanted to tell him and as she sighed into sleep the words released, in time with both her eyelids and the door closing.

'I love you, Mikey.'

Chapter 33

She'd convinced them to let her out. Not discharged, just outside. The room faced out into a small quad, nothing pretty, simply paving and a weather-worn bench dedicated to *Grandad*. Eye-maimed or not, Tiff could still sniff out a sunspot. Shuffling out there hadn't been pretty either and required both assistance and many swears. Wrapped in her blanket, she managed to find an acceptable position, where she could enjoy the afternoon sun on her face, the warmth easing the ache of her closed eyes. The specialist was happy with her progress; things were gradually less blurry, but her eyes were still sore. Seeing improvement, she'd allowed herself to accept his optimism that she'd make a full recovery. That's what specialists were for, wasn't it? Parking the terror for now freed her mind to tackle all the other things she had to think about.

She was itching to get out and back to the gym. She needed to know the state of play. She had things to fix, calls to make and equipment to locate. Venturing into the fresh air was her first step, but pleasant as it was, she was still frustrated.

'While it's good seeing you up and about, sitting there worrying isn't helping you, Trent.' Mike stepped out from her room and sat beside her. She deigned him a single opened eye, then added the other as he literally was a sight for sore eyes. Clean-shaven now, fresh shirt and jeans, he also brought the scent of his cedar after-shave with him, which was a blessing over the smell of hospital. He'd obviously made it home. No doubt he'd been back to pack and prep. It was Monday. He flew tonight. Her worries about the gym were instantly muted as it dawned on her this was the goodbye visit. 'Don't bother denying it. I've been watching the cogs turning out here, from the window.'

She liked the notion of Mike watching her. She wanted to tell him so. He ought to know. She was going to tell him what their one night meant to her and she wished she could make it more. Only, she couldn't quite work out how to segue into it.

'I got treats.' He held up a sparkly red gift bag and a bunch of red roses. He'd clearly picked the colours for maximum visibility.

'I like treats.'

'I know.' He held up a Greggs bag. 'Three iced buns. Don't spend them all at once.'

'You are officially my Hero of the Day,' she said, the first proper smile in days spreading across her bruised face. 'The cape is optional, but I'd personally prefer it if you refrained from the pants-over-tights.'

'Hmpf,' he said, delving further into the bag, 'I'd look mighty fine in tights and pants. Here, there's more. But these are only if you get desperate. Think of them as medicinal.' Mike waved a Pot Noodle and a bag of scampi fries in her face before dropping them back in the bag. *Oh this man.* 'Maybe I should leave those two with the nurse.' She slammed her hand down on the bag so he couldn't move it. He laughed. She'd have been prepared to wrestle them off him, ribs or not.

'Iced buns and misery food, Mike. I'll assume the news is bad.'

Sighing, he stretched his legs out in front of him and slung an arm around her.

'It's not all bad news.'

'Really?' Thank chuff for that. 'What's the good news?'

'Everyone sends their love.'

Not wanting to appear ungrateful, Tiff stifled her desire to wail into his shirt.

'Brilliant,' she mumbled. It was the best she could do. 'The bad stuff then.'

He hesitated. Which she took to be a piteous omen. 'Bad or worse bad first?'

'When you put it like that Mike...'

'Honestly Tiff, shouldn't you wait until you're out? Either can wait. You need to focus on the recovering.'

'Mike, you might as well hit me with it, because it's doing my nut in sitting here thinking about it, not knowing what I'm really thinking about.'

'That makes no sense.'

'It does. You know what I mean. Tell me where it's at and my brain can start processing and planning.'

'Okay, but I'm going to tell you fast, like tearing off a plaster.'

'Bring it.'

'Colin went bust. The kit's with the receivers. The money's gone.' Tiff took several starts at a sentence, but gave up each. Her gym was half empty; no spinners, no treadmills, no rowing machines, and she didn't have the money to replace them. She felt like someone had taken a crowbar to her kneecaps and gone to town. Mute, she twitched her fingers desperately at the bag, until Mike understood and fished out the scampi fries. Shovelling a couple into her mouth like pills, she told herself she could get through this. She'd suspected this was a likelihood, so it was more devastating disappointment than shock.

Still, it took some calming breathing before she managed to squeak 'Was that the bad or the worse bad?'

He see-sawed his head from side to side, weighing it up. 'Depends. There's this too,' he said reaching back into his bag of treats and retrieving something which definitely wasn't a treat. He let the newspaper unfurl like a theatre curtain in front of her. She could make out a familiar building in the picture, the *Tiffanie's* sign spray-painted to read *fanie's* and the headline which screamed FRAUDULENT BANK-MANAGER'S DAUGHTER BEATEN, but she hadn't the sight or strength to read on.

Mike read it and made her weep.

The nearby birdsong was muffled by Mike's arms around her. Tiff's face was securely buried in his armpit. If he hadn't before, then Mike knew all the tawdry details of her dad's crimes now, which brought her an extra layer of shame and dismay.

'It'll be chip paper tomorrow, Tiff. I promise. The press are bastards, but the readers will forget.'

'No, they won't, Mike,' she insisted. 'It happened ten years ago, and they still remember. The paper runs a story like that – with a headline which could suggest *I'm* the fraudulent one – because it serves their sales to remember. I can't fight this. I could build the world's best club – one with a ring for a start—'

'You can have mine, Tiff,' he cut in which gained him a snotty thank you sniff and pat on the arm as she went on.

'— but if they think I'm dodgy, no-one will join.

Aaron, the paper, Ron, they've already won and I haven't even opened the doors.'

Mike handed her another couple of scampi fries which she horsed, before bursting into another round of tears.

'Tiff? Angel, please?' He sounded so sad. God, she was embarrassing herself. He'd have to change that shirt too before he flew. Snot stains in First Class was probably not a thing.

She couldn't tell him how she felt now. How would that sound? *Mike, I know my life is a shitshow, but I love you. I'm so in love with you I can't see straight, well I can't see at all really, but you get the picture. And I know I'm damaged, and homeless, and my business is flailing, but I'm head over heels for you. Interested in that?* The truth of it pushed out more sobs. She'd come back from the business set-back, she knew she would, even if on a smaller scale, but it would take time. As a couple though, time was something they were out of.

'I can replace the kit,' Mike consoled her, speaking into her hair. 'Call it a loan, or repay me in kind, I'm easy either way, but use it to show the haters and the nay-sayers what you can do.'

Just when she thought he couldn't be more amazing, he offered her this. It sliced away a layer of her resolve. She pulled away and looked him straight in his gorgeous face.

'Mikey, you don't need to lend me the money, but I'll hang onto the ring if I can. Thank you. I'll make it work with what there is; I'll hope the classes take off, and build from there, and add new kit as I can afford it. But there's something I need to say and that's that I'd be very happy to repay your generosity *in kind*, anytime you're back. Consider yourself on a promise.' His eyes widened and his mouth opened to speak, but she placed a hand over it. 'I know you're going, and rightly so because you will kill it on the telly and you deserve great things, but you need to know that letting you go is so hard. So so hard. Because somewhere after bitching at you in the pub and shouting at you in the stairwell, I've managed to fall in love with you. Again. And,' Tiff felt a new tear trickle down her cheek, 'in spite of you leaving soon, I wanted you to know that, because when you left the other night, I thought you might hate me, and *that* was the very worst bad thing.'

Mike's fingertip followed the tear's trail down her mottled skin, but his face remained illegible to her. He didn't appear able to look her in the eye, which to be fair was still gruesome.

'Do you know why I walked out?'

'I wouldn't ask you to stay, Gavin arriving, me getting shouty, the hating me thing? Any of those would be fair.'

'I was jealous,' he said and swallowed as he properly

considered his answer, 'And scared. I suddenly couldn't see how I'd stand a chance with you, when you and he had ten years of history. That's a lot to contend with and I didn't fancy my odds, so I ran. I'm not proud of it; it's not usually my style. Only, it seemed to me you deserve someone who has a fix on what they're doing, what they're offering and that isn't me, Tiff. Not right now. I might be shit at the TV work, and I'll be sacked and back to square one, probably several steps back in fact and having to go on *I'm A Celebrity*.'

'I'll shoot you first,' she snuffled.

'Deal. I don't fancy scoffing kangaroo bollocks,' he said, kissing her on the head. 'But my point is, I have the fame, the house, the cash, but I don't have firm plans and you deserve security. I figure the man who loves you should offer you something reliable, Tiff.'

Tiff looked up abruptly. What had he said? Rewind, REWIND!

'You love me?'

'God, woman, *yes*. So much it hurts. That's why I came back Friday night. I wanted to put my hat in the ring, tell you I'm up for the fight.'

'There is no fight, Mike.'

'Oh,' Mike's face fell with disappointment, and then creased with crossness. 'Where is he then? What kind of a bloke doesn't show up at the hospital?'

'Mike, didn't I just blab I'm in love with *you?* Gavin

isn't of interest to me. I believe I said that on Friday,' she added tersely, 'He knows we're done.'

'Oh. Oh!' This time his face glowed.

'But Mike there's something you need to know about us. *This*,' she waggled a finger between them, 'isn't a nostalgia-fest for me. I'm not in love with the teen Mikey. And you aren't competing with ten years of someone else. *This* is new to me. I'm in love with the you who came back; older, smarter, wiser, differently handsome you.' His wonky nose twitched. 'The Mike who gives me straight advice, who brings me my phone in the middle of the night, who sits by my hospital bedside. That Mike.

'That's the same Mike who doesn't know what he wants to do with his retirement,' Tiff continued and his brow creased. 'No, don't look embarrassed Mike, it's okay not to be sure, to try and also to fail, but I want to be there with *that* Mike. I want to support you and be your cheerleader. And if you're across the ocean doing it, we'll work something out; there's flights, there's skype. Your future might not be reliable, but *you* are.'

His eyes were glistening. 'Why d'you tell me to go?'

'Because I want you to have the best in life, Mike. The opportunity is too good to pass up and when you asked my advice I almost bit your hand off to stay, but it felt selfish. I asked myself what Nanna and Blackie would have done. And they'd already done it. They showed me the way.'

'You were being *selfless*?' He looked sort of appalled.

'Well...yes. It felt like the right thing to do; helping you reach your potential, and while it broke my heart, it filled it with the most bittersweet, rewarding pleasure too, knowing I could help make it happen. Isn't that what Blackie said in his will? Saying things you regret in the pursuit of a goal you don't?' She gazed at him doe-eyed, sending him all her love.

'You're an idiot,' he said plainly.

'What?'

'Tiff, I'm twenty-seven, not seventeen,' he said with a smile, 'Nanna stopped making decisions for me soon after I left, and provided I have all the information in front of me, I've been able to make fairly decent choices for myself. All in all, I think I've done alright.'

'You have,' she agreed.

'So had you shown me your hand, not got all noble on me, I would've had *all* my choices to consider.'

He was right, completely on the money; she'd narrowed his choices. She administered a mental face-palm. What did it matter, though? His flight still left in a few hours.

'Can you commute?' she asked, looking for solutions. 'Is that possible?' *Heat* magazine showed celebs jet-setting all over.

'Nah, commuting's not really an option.'

'No, I guess not,' she agreed, forlorn. 'When you come back to visit, *if* you do, will you come and see me? Please?' For all the second chances which did work out, being a numbers girl, Tiff knew statistically there had to be those that didn't. Theirs was just one of the impossible ones.

He tipped her chin up to look her right in the eyes. Her eyes were definitely improving, there was no mistaking his intensity. 'Tiff, I turned the job down Saturday morning. Seeing you on the floor in the club, I knew I wasn't going anywhere.'

'But you're flying tonight,' she said.

'Tiff, I'm not flying anywhere tonight. I've agreed to commentate at fights for them, but that's all. I'm not leaving.'

'You're not?'

'Well, not unless you're with me. If you want to ditch all of this, escape Kingsley, then I'm with you. We can go to LA, or we can try somewhere else. Didn't we have a list once?' She was prepared to bet he'd already been to or done most of it. 'And if you want to stay here and take on the haters, I'm going to be right here with you too. If you'll have me.'

She tried to fling her arms up around his neck, but nearly fainted with her ribs' response, and after the howl managed a 'Yes, yes of course, I'll have you.'

Regardless of scampi fries breath, there was kissing. Copious kissing. A couple of pursed-lipped patients drew their curtains to safeguard themselves from the snogging. Finally Tiff pulled away, partly for air, but also for something else.

'Um, reality check; you did just pass up a sun-drenched life in Los Angeles, to be here with me? That actually happened, right?' She didn't quite believe this wasn't a drug-induced dream.

'That actually happened,' he confirmed, with both a nod and a smile so it had to be true. 'Why would I need a City of Angels, when I've got mine right here?'

Her face was filled with 'Awwww', then she snorted a laugh. 'That was so cheesy.'

'I thought it was cute. Clearly, I'll have to work on my lines. But I have a spot of unemployment on my horizon, so I'll have time enough to practice on you.' He gave her another kiss and she knew she was already looking forward to hearing them. Only...

'Mike, can I ask you something else. Something serious?'

'Anything, Angel.'

'Mikey.' She took his hands in hers and cleared her throat, because it had gone claggy with all the emosh. 'Michael, Mike "The Assassin" Fellner, sniper to my heart, slayer of my fears, would you do me the stupendous honour of being my coach?'

Chapter 34

'Seriously?' Tiff couldn't help rolling her eyes as Mike pressed his key-fob and the lights flashed on a black Range Rover. He couldn't see them roll – she was wearing sunglasses. She said it was due to the gloriously sunny day, they both knew it was to hide her black eyes. The whites of them were now pink, but her vision had almost fully returned, for which she gave eternal thanks every morning.

'What?'

'Blacked-out windows? What are you, a pimp?'

'Verity kept getting cleavage-shot by the paps. This was a necessity.'

'Of course. There's nothing more discreet to pass the paps in, than a blacked-out black Range Rover. Nothing about this car says "*Chase me, I'm someone worth hedging a snap on*".'

'Look, Miss Picky,' he said, calmly depositing her bag in the rear seat, 'Getting you down into the seat of the

Aston seemed cruel. But next time you land in here, I'll bring that. Then the paps can snap you scowling.' He opened the passenger door with a gracious smile and helped her and her aching ribs slide in. Hopping into his own side Mike added, 'Or I'll stick you on the back of the Harley. The helmets will keep things incognito and muffle your complaints.'

Tiff didn't say anything as she was swept away in the thought of sitting behind him on the bike, arms around his waist. Mike wore a rather wistful look on his face too.

After six days in the hospital Tiff had finally convinced them to let her out.

'Where first? Hotel or the gym?' he asked, pulling out of the hospital car park. Mike had gone ahead and booked her into the posh country pile on the greener outskirts of town where he'd been staying, having quickly ditched the hour's commute to her hospital bed. That was a decision she didn't mind someone else making for her – she couldn't face sleeping in the gym again. Her body was already feeling lured by the thought of some nights in a plush hotel room with a spa bath, but her head won out.

'Gym please. I need to see it.'

He looked at her sideways, but didn't ask. She didn't know whether she needed to see the damage for herself, or whether she was going to face the demons of the attack. His warm hand on hers told her she could handle both.

'The offer still stands, Tiff,' he said.

'Which one?' She lifted her sunglasses and gave him a wink, which didn't quite come off due to the remaining swelling.

'Smut,' he said with a prudey look, but his eyes lit up a notch. 'Leaving Kingsley. If you want. A fresh start, away from any bad feeling and memories.'

Tiff watched the streets of her home town pass by, as she formulated her answer.

'There've been times when that would have been music to my ears Mikey, but now…? I have a club – with staff – one I've worked hard for, and while I haven't seen the state it's in, and even though it isn't open yet, I have hopes for it. I've made big changes and want to see them through. So let people point, and let them laugh or sneer. I can't change them, but I won't let them run me off my own property.' Oh god, she was turning into her mother.

'I get that, Angel. Succeeding will be the best "screw you" to the haters. Only, I seem to remember you once shouting at my smug battered mug in a stairwell about my having been fortunate enough to escape some shithole. I want you to have the same opportunity. You can lease the club, we can go wherever we like. We can stay in bed for a few years, make up for lost time.'

Talk about an offer.

'Are you welching out of being my coach?' she asked, trying to arch an eyebrow, but failing because of the swelling thing again and because she wasn't Mike. 'You accepted. I double-checked. I'm pretty sure your word is your bond.'

'No, I'm not backing out, Tiff,' he huffed. 'I want to be your coach. I want to put something back into the sport and further Blackie's legacy. It's ideal. But I got my chance at my dream. I want you to have yours.'

Tiff caressed his cheek. She loved his battered mug. 'You're here Mike, so I'd say, I'm good.' He took her hand and kissed her palm. 'Thank you, but I'm not running. I want to build the club and then we'll see what happens. We'll make it up as we go along.'

'Roll with the punches?'

'I'm off punches at this week,' she said, squirming slightly in her seat, 'I'm going with "playing it by ear", revising and adjusting and if, or when, we've had enough, we can go, no running required.'

Having lived in the gym for six weeks, it was strange to have been away for six days. Tiff felt she'd been away from her child. Rounding the final corner before the building appeared, she braced herself for the worst.

But it didn't come. There were no boarded-up

windows, no police tape. The *Tiffanie's* sign was missing, but that was all the change she could see.

'Sign's coming back tomorrow,' Mike said, getting out to open her door.

Walking towards the reception she couldn't see the sprawl of graffiti. If she hadn't been there that night, if she hadn't seen it in the papers, she would now have thought she'd imagined it.

'Where's it all gone, Mikey?' she asked, pushing her sunglasses up on her head and looking around the room. Save for the sodding sofa missing its cushions, there was no sign there'd been anything amiss. The panic that she *might* have imagined it, or her eyes couldn't see properly after all, gave her a lump in her throat.

'A lot of hard graft by your friends, Tiff,' Mike answered from where he stood, leaning against the wall, hands in pockets. He was giving her space, but watching her intently. 'You okay? Being here, I mean.'

Tiff nodded slowly. 'I remember all of it, but walking in here and not seeing the damage – that's disconcerting. Makes me think it didn't happen. That I've gone a bit doolally.'

Mike moved to wrap his arms around her waist from behind her and rest his chin on her shoulder. He slid one hand carefully up to rest on her ribs.

'This tells you it happened, Tiff. There wasn't any

point leaving it. Nobody wanted to upset you. The papers got the pictures. The police have no doubt got a stack. You'll see it all in court.' That made her shudder. There was all of that to go through yet. Incredibly, Aaron was professing his innocence, insisting *she* attacked him and faked the vandalism. The spray paint on his fingers, a second can in his pocket and B&Q CCTV footage said otherwise. 'The plan was to get things fixed. They knew what you wanted it to look like.'

'No, you're right,' Tiff agreed, with a nod, 'Who's "they"?'

There was a tramping sound on the stairs followed by voices Tiff knew well.

'Is that you Mike, with that lazy mare who left us with all the donkey-work while she lounged in bed?' Shelby and Natalie. Tiff was landed with a huge double hug, until she couldn't stifle her groan and they backed off with apologies.

'You two did all of this?' Tiff asked.

'Well, there was Jess and Amina too, and we did a lot of press-ganging and delegating,' Natalie admitted, without an ounce of shame. 'And I guess we were seen with rollers and paint too. That spray stuff takes loads of coats to cover. The sofa cushions should be back Friday; thankfully they were black already, so it shouldn't show, once the paint residue has been removed.' Natalie always liked a clear summary. She was definitely an organised woman when given a chance. Iceland should have spotted her as management material, but hey, their loss...

'I was in charge of the tea supply, keeping Jess's men satisfied,' said Shelby proudly. Tiff dreaded to think what that entailed.

'I love you guys,' Tiff sniffed. It was overwhelming; being back, seeing everything they'd done, and them being here.

'Right,' said Natalie, seeing Tiff's wobble, 'Who's for a cup of tea?'

Mike looked at Tiff for direction.

'Actually, Nat,' Tiff said, getting a grip, 'I only want a quick look around, to get the lay of the land. Then I need to lie down for a bit. I'm staying at Crabthorne Hall.'

'So we've heard,' Shelby said, salaciously. Tiff chose to ignore it. The hotel was local, and she wanted to stay close.

'I'll be in tomorrow though to...well, I was going to say get things moving, but honestly you've got us miles ahead of where I thought we'd be.'

'There's lots of membership interest, Tiff. That thing about there being no bad publicity might just be true.' Tiff's pleasure was quickly curtailed as Natalie's smile turned to concern. 'The equipment still hasn't shown up though,' she said. 'I keep waiting in for the delivery.'

'It isn't coming. The supplier's gone bust,' Tiff told them as succinctly as possible. Thinking about it made her want to cry. So denial and minimal thought was the strategy she'd picked.

Nat's eyes grew the size of saucers.

'It's okay, Nat. It's all under control,' Tiff tried to smooth it over. 'The gym will open with what we have, I'll order new kit. I'll sort it.' She concentrated on her voice as she said it, trying hard to sound more confident than she felt. Mike gave her a reassuring squeeze on the shoulder. 'We have a ring, we have a coach,' she looked up at him with adoration and a heap of grati-tude, 'we have a multigym, studios with kit and staffed classes. People can come and we'll build as we go.'

'So we don't need to worry...?' Natalie asked tenta-tively.

'Your job is super-safe, Nat. I'll let myself go before I set you loose. I promise.' Tiff held her gaze until Natalie nodded and relaxed.

She started in the sparring hall. Mike let her go by herself. It still smelled of lingering sweat, but also fresh paint and varnish. Flipping on the lights, she saw the ring back in centre stage. It looked magnificent. As intended, the refurb made the room look sleek and up to date. Tiff walked a clear straight line directly across the hall to the ring and laid her hand flat on it, as the heart of the gym. This place was hers. It had given her a home when she needed it, it was her future too and she would fight tooth and nail to protect it. No-one was going to take it from her. It felt like a pledge.

'Ahem.' Engrossed, she hadn't heard the footsteps behind her. She turned to see a familiar, if unwelcome, figure loitering halfway across the floor.

'Can I help you, Ron?' she asked. Mike stepped into the room and leaned against the far wall, arms crossed. He had her back.

'Tiff.' He gave her a curt nod. 'Heard about the accident.' She cocked her head at him. Perhaps this was his attempt at small-talk.

'It wasn't much of an accident, Ron. It was an attack. Broken ribs, broken nose, eye trauma and extensive bruising.'

'Yes, right. Well, good to see you're on the mend.' He nodded at her body. She looked a bruised mess and her sleep was filled with nightmares and flashbacks. Not that she wanted to discuss it with Ron, and judging by his awkwardness nor did he. 'The gym's looking all right,' he said, pained to say it.

'Well, it's taken some work and some repairs.' They stood in silence for a moment. Tiff broke it. She had things to do; *Mike* hopefully. Inane chat with Ron wasn't on the list. 'Is that why you came, to admire the changes?

Go ahead, then let yourself out.' She was out of manners where he was concerned.

'Actually, there's something I came to discuss.' He cleared his throat. 'My plans fell through. With my club. The supplier went bust.'

'I know. Mine too.'

'Oh. Right. Bastard. Well, I'd rented my unit on a short-term lease to start with, and the landlord's got cold feet due to the glitch in the cashflow.'

'That's unfortunate.' She was trying to be civil, but honestly she wanted to drag him by his hairy ear and hurl him out of the door. She saw his expression pull together.

'So I've become aware most of my lads plan to come here, and on that basis, I'm not going to have much of a club, am I?' Tiff waited for him to reach his point, which made him more irate. 'Look, I'm not going to have a gym or a job. I won't have a business.'

Finally Tiff bit.

'Ron, you call them your lads, but you pinched them from here. Aside from them being a disloyal bunch who you shouldn't count on, I can't see how you think this warrants you any sympathy. You stabbed me in the back. You set up a competing club and took the clients with you. You didn't give a stuff what happened to me.'

'I made you an offer to rent this club and you turned

it down,' he said indignantly. Apparently she had brought his actions on herself.

'I considered your offer and decided it was best for the whole business to follow my own plan, which still made room for you.'

'Well, the lads would have had nowhere to train while you did all of your alterations,' he huffed.

'Yeah right, like *that* was your motivation. It was only two weeks, although admittedly it's become three. You could have gone on holiday in that time. But that's not what this is about, is it?'

'What's that supposed to mean?'

'What are you here for Ron?' She was going to make him spit it out.

'You need a coach.' He pulled himself up to his tallest, which wasn't very, and puffed out his chest. Tiff wondered whether he had brought any humble pie with him at all.

'Actually Ron, I have a coach.' She gave Mike a super-cheesy grin. Ron looked behind him, then back at her, more layers of mardiness setting on his face as he came to understand.

'Well, an assistant coach then. He can't do all the sessions.'

'Mike can pick his own assistant.'

'I know these lads. I know this club and the job.' His face was puce now, little bits of spit flying from his mouth as he argued.

'I'm sorry,' said Tiff, needing clarification, 'are you asking for your job back?'

'I figure you owe it to me.' Ah, not asking, *demanding*.

'Really? How's that?' she choked. He was serious.

'Years of service to Blackie.'

'None to me.' Good god, she thought, he must have thought he could walk in, accuse her of damaging his business and walk back out reinstated. He must think her desperate or stupid, and as far as Tiff believed, she was neither.

'I have no clients now. I can't keep my business afloat.'

'That was the risk you took, Ron. That's the risk I'm taking now. That's business, I believe and what was it you said to me? Oh yeah, *may the best man win*.' Tiff leaned back against the ring, resting her outstretched arms along the edge. 'Ron, to not waste your time, I'm going to be completely straight with you; I'm not re-employing you. I want staff who are trustworthy and reliable. You're neither. I *can* wish you good luck with your club though; everyone needs some luck with a new venture, and for what it's worth, I think having two boxing clubs in town would be good; we can spar against each other. But Ron, there's no role for you here.'

Ron looked like he was about to explode.

'I might owe you some thanks however, Ron. You made me think I wasn't capable of running this place, that my ideas were ridiculous. Seeing you here now, I guess I proved you wrong, which gives me no end of confidence. And as thanks for that, I'm going to do you a good turn – although you might not think so at first. You hate change as much as I did. You think it's safer. But it isn't. Change is healthy and exciting and can bring you so much more happiness than you ever thought. So if you like, consider me *not* taking you back a favour.' She sincerely doubted he ever would. 'I gift you the joy of change, Ron.' Though her sentiments were sincere, she couldn't resist returning the smirk he'd given her in the pub.

Ron on the other hand virtually had steam coming out of his ears. He turned to Mike, expecting him to talk some sense into her, but he simply shrugged and said 'She's the boss.'

Ron stormed out without another word.

She stayed where she was, eyes shut, focusing on her breathing, centring herself as Fliss had taught her to do in the Pilates class, then growled loudly 'What an arse,' which made her feel so much better.

'Man, you were badass.' Mike was looking at her moony-eyed. 'I'm going to need a minute before I can walk...'

Chapter 35

Wishing she really was badass, Tiff headed for the upper floors trying not to relate the space to the attack, but it was difficult. She remembered being chased up the stairs, her eyes screaming in pain, she remembered stumbling through the studio trying to breathe through blood.

She felt Mike's hand take hers and was grateful for it. The daylight, as it streamed through the studio into the corridor, made all the difference to her being able to walk the hallway again. She paused by the poles, running her hand down the nearest.

'Want to demo your skills for me?' Mike whispered into her ear. He felt her shudder. 'Ah, god, sorry. Too soon?'

She turned to give him a small smile. 'That was a tremble at you being close, muppet.' His pupils dilated at that, and he pulled her by the hand away towards the top floor. The tour was obviously on a time-line.

Her bedroom door was closed. Given they all knew it was where she'd been sleeping, she supposed someone had shut it for privacy. Letting the door swing open it looked exactly as she'd left it; the duvet cast aside on the mat bed, her bed-socks curled up in little balls where she'd hastily deposited them. Only her bag had been touched, where Mike had collected her some clothes. It was far too late to get embarrassed about him rooting through her smalls.

Tiff had no desire to spend significant time in there again. The sooner she cleared her things out the better, and the sooner it could be returned to some practical use. Cogs now turning, she considered the room again. She tilted her head as she looked at the right-hand wall that was adjacent to the cleaner's store. That wall could go and it'd be a bigger, more useful space. The cleaning kit could shift elsewhere.

'Shelby!' she yelled down the corridor. They waited a while and then, preceded by an unfamiliar *ding*, the lift doors parted majestically, revealing an unimpressed Shelby.

'You rang, ma'am? It was Nat, not me, who offered you a cuppa.'

'Small change of plan, babes.'

*

Natalie had been right; people weren't put off by the bad publicity. Two weeks after officially opening, it was still early days but they were coming. Tiff got a thrill with every new member to join, ecstatic when the initial classes started hitting their quotas.

Once word got around that 'The Assassin' was the new trainer, there'd been a surge of signups to the boxing club and most of the old group had miraculously reappeared. To Tiff's delight, Amina had asked if she could train to be Mike's assistant coach. Amina took no prisoners in the ring. She was totally into equality; she'd aim to whoop anyone, regardless of age, gender or orientation. She was going to be a great asset.

Eyes recovered and improving on the physical front, Tiff was relishing having a thriving shiny hive of activity around her. Much as she loved her numbers, this definitely beat doing the books. Ribs allowing, she always took the stairs up and down with a skip in her step, and she always broke into a grin as she passed *Shelby's*.

What had once been a clandestine bedroom and the adjacent cleaning cupboard now housed a serene treatment suite, tastefully decorated and offering the latest therapies. It was one of her ideas that Tiff was most proud of. It was a USP and a heartfelt thank you wrapped up in one.

Shelby had stood so still when she'd outlined her idea, Tiff wasn't even sure she was breathing. Mike had squeezed Tiff's hand in encouragement. He didn't think it was beyond bonkers. Shelby stepped into the room and took a good look around, giving little away, appearing very business-like.

'What did you have in mind?' Shelby asked.

'What, other than customers having treatments?'

'No, I got that bit, but what's the deal? Would I be staff? I don't mind being staff,' she qualified, lest Tiff thought her ungrateful. 'I just want to know from the start.'

Tiff looked at her long and hard.

'Shelby, I love you, but the thought of you being staff is a living nightmare. I was more thinking of you being your own boss. How about you get the first six months rent-free while we both set up and bring the customer base in. You'll be as much a part of that effort as the rest of us. Thereafter we agree a rent and the rest is yours. You can call it *Shelby's at Tiffanie's*, or whatever you want if you need the distinction, but it'd be your business to run and own.'

'Do I have to wear lycra?'

'God no. You can stick with a beautician uniform. House colours might be nice though.'

'How about reversed – black with blue trim?'

'Done.'

'And I get first dibs on any future gyms you open?' Shelby demanded, as if this was a full-blown negotiation and she was Alan Sugar's love-child. Tiff gaped at Shelby envisaging more gyms. 'Oh come on babe, go big or go home right? Global domination or damnation...?' Tiff was still stunned. 'Jesus, am I the only one around here with any imagination?'

'Shelby. Do you want it?'

Shelby took Tiff's hand, and the three of them stood there looking at a cupboard like overawed kindergartners.

'It's a dream come true, Tiff,' she said squeezing her hand. 'I love you too, babes.'

The 'Closed' sign now hung askew on its hook, the proprietress having granted herself a later start for two mornings a week. It was great having your best friends working under the same roof, but Tiff found Shelby's later morning helpful when it came to getting admin done. She had some rather important paperwork to handle now. She had her nose in it as she walked into a wall of muscle in the empty bar.

'I was just looking for you,' she said.

'I was just looking for *you*,' Mike replied, gently sweeping her off her feet and sitting in one of the seats, Tiff on his lap. The smell of new leather wafted up around them. 'I'm *always* looking for you.' That earned him a kiss. Aside from the full complement of kit, the only thing not fully operational was the bar, as the licence was still pending. In the meantime, the space had opened as a café. In the earlier hours of the day, the quieter hours, it made a useful venue for Mike and Tiff to curl up in a chair for some mutual lip exercise. Like just then.

'I've got these to show you.' She waved some estate agent particulars in front of his face. They were looking for somewhere, together, close by.

'*My* thing is way more serious,' he said. That didn't bode well.

'What is it?'

'Well,' he said gravely, 'I'm not sure if you realise, but now you've got a wonky nose—'

'I do NOT have a wonky nose,' Tiff said, outraged. She swatted him with the particulars.

'Sorry, now you've got a mildly kinky nose,' Mike conceded, clamping his arms tighter around her waist, 'they fit together better when we kiss. How lucky is that?' He kissed her nose for good measure.

'So very lucky,' she said.

'I like it.'

'Not so fussed myself.' Three weeks on from the attack, Tiff still wasn't used to seeing the new shape of her nose.

'We could have them reconstructed at the same time. His 'n' hers nose jobs.'

'How very *heat* magazine.'

'If we got them done in LA, stayed at the house, we could sell the spread to *OK*.' He nuzzled her neck. It made her quite swoony. God, she was lucky to have him. They didn't stop until Shelby slapped Mike on the head, en route to her salon.

'Sucking face isn't good for custom, you know. Grosses people out.' She didn't wait for an answer.

'Was that it? The kisses?' Tiff asked, 'Was that your thing to out-serious my thing?'

'Those were pretty serious kisses,' he said, 'but I came bearing business gossip.'

'Spill.'

'My old club in Kent is for sale. The building's smaller, but the setup is quite similar. The old coach is retiring, the assistant is ready to move up.'

She looked at him and waited. He was almost bouncing with the information, so the wait was short.

'I know this place only just opened, and there'd be some travelling needed for the refurb, but I thought you could do the same there as you've done here. The next link in your chain.'

Tiff looked around. She loved this place. There were still things to finish – she still wanted that balcony for starters. She'd assumed she'd have some time to settle in, adapt to this change, but then, what was Gavin's quote regarding *opportunity*? Nope. She couldn't remember, but she had the gist.

Only, there was the tricky issue of her having used all the monies.

'I'll lend you the dosh,' Mike went on. 'You don't need to go to the bank.'

He knew her well enough to understand her aversion to banks. But now she needed to tell him she didn't want his loan.

She took a deep breath. 'Mike, you've been coaching for a couple of weeks now, and I think we need to revise and adjust.' Confusion crossed his face. He slowly nodded for her to go on. 'I don't want you to be my coach anymore.'

She watched him pull away and the hurt ride across his face. 'Right.' He tried to sound like he understood, but he really didn't.

'Or rather, I don't want you to *only* be my coach anymore. Don't make it a loan. Make it an *investment*. Be my partner, Mike. In this gym and the Kent gym if we can get it, and any future clubs.' Now she held her breath and waited.

That smile she loved, the one that did funny things to her, resurfaced on his gorgeous wonky face.

'*That* sounds like a plan,' he said.

Tiff smiled a very smug smile.

'What?' he asked.

'I totally out-serioused you.' He made to tickle her, then when she squealed 'Ribs!' diverted to a deep kiss.

'If we're going to be partners,' she said sternly, 'we need to be straight with each other. Totally straight.'

He tucked her hair over her shoulder and nibbled her neck.

'Totally. Always.'

'Good,' she said, kissing him gently to seal the deal. 'Tell me where that bloody key is hidden.' He threw back his head and laughed, then dug around in his pocket, almost spilling her onto the floor, before holding up a solely-stocked key ring.

'It's been here since that night after Blackie's funeral. I ... well I didn't want anyone else to find it.'

'What, after ten years, you thought someone was going to chance on it?'

He nodded slowly, eyes fixed on hers. 'Can't be too careful. Plus it meant I could see you.'

'*Pff!* You didn't even *like* me after Blackie's funeral.' Rubbing the key between her fingertips she remembered how snarky they'd been towards each other, and her shouting at him. Then she pushed it into his palm and closed his fingers around it. It was *his* key, to the gym and to her.

Mike gave her a heart-melting smile, one that made it unimaginable that they could ever have been anything but meant for each other. 'Angel,' he said, pulling her closer, 'even when you're shouty you're impossible not to like.' He kissed her neck bringing on the swoony all over again, before whispering, 'And seeing you in your PJs I was already wondering whether I could take you for breakfast.'

Tiff raised her hand to his cheek and kissed him. 'Not unless it was breakfast at Greggs.'

A Q&A with Pernille Hughes

What was your inspiration for *Sweatpants at Tiffanie's*?

This was one of those instances where the title came first. I'd been writing short fiction for a couple of years and had decided to give a full length romantic novel a go. But where do you start? I'd noticed that some books used puns on film or song titles and, loving a pun, I was bouncing that around in my head. A trailer for *Breakfast at Tiffany's*, a film I love, appeared on the telly. I made a pun on that, which was Sweatpants at Tiffanie's and thought, 'What would that story be about?' after which lots of notes were scribbled about who Tiffanie might be and what conflict she has to face in her sweatpants. They are very different stories of course, but both Tiff and Holly Golightly in the film have to take a hard look at how they are living their lives.

Have you always wanted to be a writer?

I've made up stories since I was little, playing them out with pictures crayoned on scraps of paper when really little, or chatting through the dialogue to myself, when on walks on holiday. (Nooo, not a nutter...) At ten I won a junior story competition in a magazine and decided writing was The Thing. I wanted to be a journalist all through secondary school until my English/Careers teacher said it wasn't for me. I believed her and it crushed me. It nixed all my plans and I flailed for the next years, not knowing what to do with myself. I did various jobs that were in the creative industries, but always from the business side of things, secretly wishing I was part of the creative teams. It took me until I was at home, surrounded by babies and feeling my brain shrinking, to pick up a pen and try my words again. (Admittedly, I've never stopped making up conversations in my head – but mainly it's that thing where I go over what I should have said in a public situation, but didn't want to make a fuss or cause a scene. That's not just me, is it?)

How do you find time to write? And where do you write when you do?

I write when my kids are in school and I've cleared all the chores, which I try to stack at the beginning of the week. Some days are waaay more productive than others and school holidays are a disaster where the words are concerned. That said, I can write while we travel, if driving. I'll sit writing either long hand or on a little *Alphasmart* word processor thing (no power cables or internet needed, which is also good for my distraction issue. Twitter is my nemesis.). Long boring roads are best for letting the mind wander.

I don't have a study or writing room. I'll write wherever the sun is in the house, moving from dining room to lounge sofa depending where the sunspot is. I'm like Tiff in my joy of a sunspot. I get cold easily and crave the warmth.

What would you like readers to take away from *Sweatpants At Tiffanie's*?

That they, and they alone, can decide what they are capable of. I put my writing away for a decade because someone told me it wasn't for me. It took me that long to decide that No, *I* get to decide that. It takes Tiff a while to see it too, but she gets there in the end to huge personal gain and satisfaction.

(That and not to tether your cart to a horse that spouts lofty quotes at you.)

Who are your favourite authors and have they influenced your writing in any way?

Any writer who gives me Happily Ever After is a favourite - I'm absolutely not one for an ambiguous or sad ending. Other than my amazing fellow Romance writers, I'm a fan of Young Adult authors such as David Levithan, John Green, Meg Cabot, Maureen Johnson, Maggie Stiefvater and Rainbow Rowell, as the plots are fast and pacey, straight into the action while the dialogue is sassy, fresh and funny. I love dialogue and try to bring that humour and sass to my writing.

If you could run away to a paradise island, what or who would you take with you and why?

My husband and kids because we have a laugh, a stash of board games for the evenings, a cardigan in case I get cold playing the board games, unlimited supply of chocolate, an Aperol spritz for food and hydration, my kindle because life without books is no life at all. And Sunscreen.

Acknowledgements

I had it in my head that I would carefully write down who helped me, as they helped me, so that in the event of *Sweatpants* ever being published, I would have the list instantly to hand and not risk forgetting anyone. And then there is real life. So if I've forgotten anyone, I apologise profusely, but you were a star!

Going back to beginning, I need to thank my olds, Lisa and Bjørn Knappe for buying me all the books and feeding my love of reading. And for letting me loose when on holiday, to walk about talking to myself making up stories.

There are some women who have been key to my journey and need thanking, in historical order;

(Actually, NO thanks to my careers/English teacher, who said professional writing wasn't for me and stalled me for ten years because I believed her.)

Big thanks to Tina Iacovelli who those ten years later pointed out that my reoccurring stress dream was a sign to get my bum on the seat and my fingers on the keyboard.

Huge thanks to Christina Walker, previously of the *Sunday Times* Travel section, who bought my first *Confessions of a Tourist*, which was a massive boost, and then to Belinda Jones for picking my story to go into the first *Sunlounger* anthology and again in the second. It helped me focus where I should be writing and gain some self-belief. To Emma Beswetherick for your advice and also to Jo Unwin, for connecting me with my fabulous agent.

Ah, my fabulous agent Federica Leonardis, who *got* me, my characters and what I was trying to do from the word go, who kicks my butt when I am being a whiney wuss, and who praises me to a point of blushing when I get it right. Thank you for your editing wisdom, making this a better book, for being my wingman when we are both being introverts and for having my back when I need it. Thank you, thank you Lovely! All the spooky coincidences tells me this was fate. ALL the unicorns to you.

Huge thanks also to the gorgeous Charlotte Ledger, who picked *Sweatpants* up and loved it and was willing to take punt on something a little different. You made my dream come true. And to the HarperImpulse team, especially Claire Fenby (a wheelie bin?! Really?!) for handling my lemming Facebook questions, and Helen

Williams and Genevieve Friar who waded through my typos and weird phrasing. And of course Holly Macdonald for the super cute cover art. You all rock.

To you, lovely reader – thank you. If you enjoyed it, fabulous! I'm beyond delighted (please please leave me a review). If not, no hard feelings, try the next one you might prefer it. xx

There may be writers who can sit alone in their garret, coughing up the words in solitude. I'm not that writer and there are more lovelies to be thanked for their long-time and daily support in pulling this story together.

Firstly to Suki Yamashita, my lovely critique partner, who has been my writing buddy since 2011. You see my words at their ugliest and you still manage to be compli-mentary, for which my ego is eternally grateful. Your kindness, generosity, encouragement and support has been vital and I am so grateful for it.

To my divine beta readers; Charlotte Knappe (did you find the dragons?), Elizabeth Dunn and Gillian Evans, who read the first draft and gave gold-dust feed-back. You are my dream team.

To a third gorgeous Charlotte, Charlotte Vicary for your synopsis eye.

To the ladies of the Autumn '17 Book Camp; Cesca Major, Cathy Bramley, Alex Brown, Holly Martin, Jo Quinn, Sarah Bennett and Brooke Winters, for your stories, experience and advice to a newbie. And to Basia Martin for feeding us. Cheers lovelies!

To Annette Stevens of Pole Attack, Aylesbury for the brilliant pole dancing 'research'. I loved it in spite of you breaking my quads. And to the lovely Beth Lee for organising it all off the back of a fizzy night and a throw-away comment, and the First Avenue ladies who made our road trip such a blast.

To my Pilates coven – Sarah Rowntree, Mel Jamieson, Georgy Hales, and Gill Cotterell who have followed this journey and been the best weekly cheer-squad.

To my wonderful friends and wider family who have taken the time to ask how it's going and woo-hooed each step. Special mentions to Nina, Izzy, Ailsa and Rosie for bringing fizz, and Beth again because fizz is our theme...

To my kids, Clan Hughes, who have had to put up with my distraction because I had too many brain tabs open and was beyond concocting so much as a shopping list. (You must have been delighted when Mormor said she'd cook for deadline week and you got proper food.) Thank you for your patience. There are kisses here for all of you. (What?? What's with the unimpressed faces...? You were expecting cash???)

And to Ian who laughs with me, for giving me the time and support to give this a go and to see if I could make it happen. All my love as always x

HELP US SHARE THE LOVE!

If you love this wonderful book as much as we do then please share your reviews online.

Leaving reviews makes a huge difference and helps our books reach even more readers.

So get reviewing and sharing, we want to hear what you think!

Love, HarperImpulse x

Please leave your reviews online!

amazon.co.uk   kobo   goodreads   Lovereading   iBooks

And on social!

f/HarperImpulse   🐦 @harperimpulse
📷@HarperImpulse

LOVE BOOKS?

So do we! And we love nothing more than chatting about our books with you lovely readers.

If you'd like to find out about our latest titles, as well as exclusive competitions, author interviews, offers and lots more, join us on our Facebook page! Why not leave a note on our wall to tell us what you thought of this book or what you'd like to see us publish more of?

f/HarperImpulse

You can also tweet us 🐦@harperimpulse and see exclusively behind the scenes on our Instagram page www.instagram.com/harperimpulse

To be the first to know about upcoming books and events, sign up to our newsletter at: www.harperimpulseromance.com